ARIZONA CARESS

The silvery moonglow cast the entire scene in a surrealistic light and Chance blinked, not quite believing what was before him. It was definitely Rori who stood there, but not the Rori he knew. The Rori who stood before him was female . . . a flesh-and-blood female. He blinked again, trying to form a coherent thought between what he thought he knew and what he was actually seeing. Rori . . . a girl . . . Why had she pretended to be a boy all this time, and why hadn't he noticed before?

No wonder he thought her so soft. She was soft. No wonder he'd thought her thin. She was thin for a boy, but perfect, he realized now, in a feminine way . . .

Books by Bobbi Smith

DREAM WARRIOR

PIRATE'S PROMISE

TEXAS SPLENDOR

CAPTURE MY HEART

DESERT HEART

THE GUNFIGHTER

CAPTIVE PRIDE

THE VIKING

ARIZONA CARESS

Published by Kensington Publishing Corporation

ARIZONA CARESS

BOBBI SMITH

ZEBRA BOOKS
KENSINGTON PUBLISHING CORP.
http://www.kensingtonbooks.com

ZEBRA BOOKS are published by

Kensington Publishing Corp.
119 West 40th Street
New York, NY 10018

All Kensington titles, imprints, and distributed lines are available at special quantity discounts for bulk purchases for sales promotion, premiums, fund-raising, educational, or institutional use.

Special book excerpts or customized printings can also be created to fit specific needs. For details, write or phone the office of the Kensington Special Sales Manager: Attn. Special Sales Department. Kensington Publishing Corp., 119 West 40th Street, New York, NY 10018. Phone: 1-800-221-2647.

Zebra and the Z logo Reg. U.S. Pat. & TM Off.

ISBN-13: 978-1-4201-1444-7
ISBN-10: 1-4201-1444-1

First Printing: August 1989

10 9 8 7 6 5 4 3 2

Printed in the United States of America

Prologue

Arizona Territory, 1856

It was near sundown when Burr Prescott, a bearded, buckskin-clad man of slight stature, reined his mount in and paused at the edge of the clearing a short distance from the small cabin. Camouflaged by the heavy shadows of early evening, he blended perfectly with his surroundings, and at the moment, he was glad of it. Though everything appeared peaceful at the homestead, his instincts were screaming a silent warning.

Almost without thought, the tracker reached down and pulled his rifle from its sheath. Clutching it in readiness, he let his piercing blue-eyed gaze sweep the scene before him. This was his son's home. There should have been some sign of life . . . some sign of Jack, his lovely Pima wife, Atallie, or their three-year-old daughter, Aurora. It was time for the evening meal, but there was no indication that anyone was about. All was quiet . . . too quiet.

Burr missed nothing as he studied the house, the seemingly deserted stable and its empty paddock. It was the last that troubled him most, for he knew Jack took great pride in his stock of horses, and they were nowhere to be seen. A deep-seated worry was born, mingling with the menacing sense of foreboding that was disturbing him.

Burr knew he could hesitate no longer. Years of living in the untamed wilderness had taught him to anticipate the unexpected, so he was alert and ready as he urged his horse forward with only the slightest pressure of his heels.

The fact that nothing happened immediately after he'd showed himself stretched Burr's nerves to the limit. He had hoped his instincts had been wrong and his caution had been for nothing. He had hoped that Jack or Atallie would rush from the house to welcome him, but it didn't happen. The silence of the moment was overwhelming. Only the clip-clop sound of his horse's hooves on the rocky ground broke the unearthly stillness.

Burr was a brave man, not generally given to fear, but the cold knot of dread that was forming in the pit of his gut left him shaking. Something had happened to his son and his family . . . something terrible.

Burr brought his horse to a stop before the cabin as he eyed the door that was standing slightly ajar. Gun still in hand, he dropped soundlessly to the ground and ventured cautiously forward. He had just reached the partially open portal and was about to push it wide when a shot rang out, exploding into the wood just inches from his head. Realizing instantly that the shot had come from within, Burr dove to his right, hit the ground, and rolled away from the house.

"Come on! Just try to come in again, you dirty, murderin' bastards! Next time I won't miss!" came the strangled shout from within that Burr only barely recognized as his son's voice.

Hearing the pain and agony in his tone, Burr scrambled to his feet and rushed forward, calling out, "Jack! Jack, boy, it's me, your pa!"

The horror of the scene that greeted him as he burst into the house would stay with Burr for the rest of his life. The one-room cabin was in a shambles. The furniture was overturned and broken, the lamps were smashed, and all the foodstuffs had been thrown on the floor. He looked about in pained disbelief until he spotted his son, bloodied and battered, sitting propped up against the far wall with little Aurora cowering at his side.

"Jack! Good God, son, what happened?" Burr demanded as he charged forward.

"Pa . . ." Jack's voice was weak now, his earlier fierceness fading rapidly. He tried to say more, but the effort was too costly.

"Easy, boy . . ." Burr murmured as he knelt beside him and quickly examined his wounds. One fast look at the gunshot wound in his chest told him all he needed to know. His son was dying, and there was nothing he could do for him. "Let me get you up on the bed."

"No, Pa . . . there's no time," he told him desperately.

"What do you mean?"

"They might come back . . ."

"Who?"

"There were three of them. They said they hated Indians and anybody who loved them. They . . . Don't let them come back, Pa," Jack gasped in fear.

"They won't be back, son. I'm here and I'll take care of you now." Burr tried to comfort him.

"Atallie and I sent Aurora to hide so she'd be safe, and then we tried to fight them off . . . I managed to shoot one of them, before they got me. I winged him in the head, but I don't know what happened after that . . . I must have passed out . . ." he mourned in abject misery.

"Atallie . . ." Burr realized then that he hadn't seen her yet. "Where is she?"

"There, Pa . . ." Jack said brokenly. Keeping one arm

wrapped protectively around his small, frightened daughter, he gestured across the cabin.

Burr looked up and in that moment saw the full horror of the devastation the attackers had wreaked. There, lying dead on the floor, her body partially hidden from view by the overturned furniture, was the beautiful, vibrant Atallie. He could tell at a glance the terrible things that had been done to her, and his stomach churned. Her death had not been quick or easy.

"Come on, Jack," Burr urged as he looked away from the grisly scene, "let me see if I can get the bullet out . . ."

"No, Pa, it's no use . . ." he whispered huskily, the last of his strength failing him. "I know . . ."

"You know nothin'!" Burr argued, trying to fire his spirit.

"Pa . . ." There was desperation in his tone as he sought to gain his father's promise. "Pa, take Aurora . . ."

"Jack, you're gonna be fine, and you'll be able to take care of her yourself." Tears stung the tracker's eyes, but he fought them back. This couldn't be happening! This beaten, dying man couldn't be his fine, strong, handsome son. Jack had been his life, and now . . .

"Pa, promise me . . . please promise me!" Jack's green eyes glowed fervently for a moment as they met his father's. He grabbed Burr's forearm with a strength born of desperation.

"Of course I'll take her, son," Burr managed with difficulty, "but . . ."

"Good . . ." The light that had shone so brilliantly in Jack's gaze faded to dullness as his grip suddenly slackened, and he let go of his father's arm. He had accomplished what he'd hoped and prayed he would be able to do. He had hung on long enough to see that Aurora would be safe. Now he could stop fighting to hold on to his life and welcome the pain-free darkness. He could surrender to it, accept it, embrace it. He could be with Atallie . . . his love.

"Jack, Aurora will be fine," Burr was saying in an attempt to assure him that everything would be all right. He reached for his granddaughter, who was crying softly as she huddled close to her father. "She's . . ."

As he lifted the raven-haired child up, he saw Jack's arm drop lifelessly away from her. Searing pain tore through him as he realized it was over. His son was dead! Atallie was dead!

What kind of monstrous white man could have done this?! In a rage against the heavens, Burr vowed silently that he would have his vengeance. Somehow, someway, he would find the men who had killed them, and he would personally see them dead by the most terrible means possible.

"Grampa?" The dreadful expression on her grandfather's face sent a shaft of fear through Aurora, and when he didn't respond to her immediately, she began to cry harder. She was too young to really comprehend all that had happened, but she could sense it was something terrible.

Her frightened tears touched Burr as nothing else could have. The vicious hatred that had filled him shattered as he gazed down at the tiny, tear-streaked face. Her forest green eyes so like her father's were wide and questioning. Desolate, he clasped her to him, holding her tightly to his heart as he stroked the silken tumble of her ebony hair. He would never forget his need for vengeance, but he would also never forget that Aurora had been entrusted to him.

As Burr enfolded her in his warm, secure embrace, Aurora sighed raggedly and quieted immediately. In the way of innocents, she instinctively knew that her grampa would take care of everything.

Chapter 1

Boston, 1871

Chance Broderick stood at the window in the parlor of his family's Boston home, his stance relaxed, his back to his mother as she related her tale of woe. Agatha Broderick, who was seated on the love seat behind him in the sumptuous sitting room, paused in what she was saying and glowered at her oldest offspring in annoyance. Society matron that she was, she was not accustomed to being ignored in such a manner, not even by Chance, who, since his father's death ten years prior, had been head of the family. True, he was twenty-eight and had been his own man for some time now, but that did not excuse his behavior.

"Chancellor Broderick!" Her tone was full of censure.

Recognizing that imperious command from his childhood, Chance faced his mother. Leaning negligently against the window frame, he crossed his arms across the broad width of his chest and met her brown-eyed gaze across the room. A small smile played about his firm, chiseled lips, but he knew better than to give in to the urge to grin. It would never do when dealing with his mother.

As Agatha studied her dark-haired son, she wasn't sure whether to laugh or rage. For all that Chance was presenting the appearance of complete obedience to her order, she knew better. Chance was just like his indomitable father in more than just his good looks—his classically handsome features and beautiful dark eyes—Chance was subservient to no one. Still, she took advantage of the fact that she'd finally managed to capture his undivided attention. Agatha turned the full force of her disapproving glare upon him as she began again.

"I will not allow you to dismiss this so lightly!" she dictated. "I assure you this is serious! It might even be a matter of life and death—your brother's!"

"I hardly think that Doug's in any real danger, Mother. You know how he is," Chance answered easily. *Some things would never change,* he realized with dry humor. Ever since he could remember, his brother, Douglas, made it a practice to get into trouble, and it was always up to Chance to get him out of it. Even now that Doug was twenty-three, the pattern seemed not to have altered one bit.

"But, Chance, you've been away for months. You haven't even read his last letter," his mother insisted, distressed by his continued disregard of what she'd told him. Her tone was less demanding and more beseeching. It was difficult for her to plead for anything, but her concern for her youngest child was very real.

"And just what was in Doug's last letter that's upset you so?" Chance asked as he let his gaze drift out the window to the view of the city and harbor beyond. He loved the sea. In fact, he had just returned that morning from an eight-month voyage captaining one of Broderick Shipping's best clippers, but there was something about being home this time that felt right to him. When he'd ridden up to the house an hour earlier, Chance had been convinced that he never wanted to ship out again.

"I'll get it for you. It's on the desk in the study . . ."

Agatha was just getting to her feet to retrieve the all-important letter when the sound of voices in the front hall interrupted them.

"Bailey! I just heard that Chance is back! Is he here?"

"Yes, Mr. Chancellor has only just arrived and is in the parlor with his mother, Miss Sutcliffe, but I . . ." Bailey, the elderly, gray-haired servant who'd been with the Brodericks for better than forty years, had been about to detain her until he could make the proper announcement of her unexpected visit, but the bold, young Bethany Sutcliffe was not about to be denied.

"I know the way. Thank you, Bailey." The blond-haired beauty brushed right past the astonished butler and into the parlor. She had been on her way to go shopping when she caught sight of Chance's ship in the harbor. Excitement had coursed through her. He was back! At last! She'd immediately ordered her driver to bring her directly to the Broderick estate. She had wanted Chance and his money for as long as she could remember, and she was determined one way or the other to get him to the altar now that he had finally returned from his trip.

Chance and Agatha both looked up in irritation as Bethany swept into the room unannounced, and Chance stifled a groan of exasperation. Leave it to Bethany to be the first one to find out he was home.

"Chance, darling." Bethany's blue-eyed gaze was hungry upon him as she crossed the room. "It's so wonderful to see you. I'm so glad you're home!"

As he watched her coming toward him Chance had the feeling that she was a hungry predator on the prowl and that he was her prey. Not that he minded altogether, for Bethany was a gorgeous woman with her lush, shapely figure, golden hair, and perfect features. There had been several times in the past when they'd enjoyed each other to the fullest. It was just that he knew her for what she was, and he was not in the mood to play games with her at the moment.

"Bethany, it's good to see you, too," Chance greeted her warmly.

"Hello, Mrs. Broderick." Bethany spoke to the other woman, but did not take her eyes off Chance. She'd missed him while he was gone, and she wanted him now with a burning passion. She had been with other men during the months he'd been away, but they all faded into obscurity now that he was back. All Bethany wanted to do was to drag Chance off to her bed and make wild love to him. Instead, because of Agatha's presence, she had to restrain herself.

"It's nice of you to drop by," Agatha responded politely, although she was slightly annoyed by the interruption. She had to tell Chance about Douglas!

"I'm sorry for arriving so unexpectedly." Bethany kept her expression suitably contrite as she faked her apology for her brazen behavior. "But once I knew that Chance was back, I just had to come by and say hello."

"You're always welcome here, my dear," Agatha assured her graciously. "You know that." The Sutcliffe family was well established in town, and she had no objection to a match between Chance and Bethany, should things turn out that way.

"Has your mother told you about the ball tonight?" Bethany asked, eager that he should attend the party at the Richardsons'. She already had an escort for the evening, but she knew it would be a simple matter to get rid of him and attach herself to Chance.

"I'm afraid I haven't had the opportunity yet," Agatha answered, aggravated. Though she had been planning to attend the fashionable soirée before Chance had arrived, now all she cared about was convincing him to go to Douglas's aid.

"You are going, aren't you?" Bethany cornered her.

"I had planned on it," she confessed, "but . . ."

"Then everything's perfect! I'm sure everyone will be thrilled when they find out Chance is back," she gushed with pseudo-sweetness. Excited that things were working out so well. Mentally, she rubbed her hands together as she imagined what a success the night would be. The new gown she'd had made just for the ball made her look her absolute best.

Chance stifled a sigh. The last thing he felt like doing was going out on the social circuit.

"I'll save you a dance," Bethany promised aggressively, wondering why he wasn't responding to her as openly as she'd hoped he would and then realizing that it was probably because his mother was there with them. Tonight, she vowed to herself . . . tonight . . .

Her blue eyes met his dark ones, telling him without words all she wanted him to know. Feeling cramped by Agatha, she made her excuses. "I really do have to rush off, but I'll look forward to being with you tonight . . ." Her double entendre was clear to Chance, but luckily Agatha missed it.

"It was nice of you to come by, Bethany." Agatha was glad that the young woman was finally leaving so that she and Chance could resume their discussion.

Chance gallantly escorted Bethany to the door, rather pleased that she was leaving so soon. But before he could open it for her, she brazenly linked her arms around his neck and pulled him down for a hot kiss. Never one to deny himself a pleasurable endeavor, he kissed her back. It had, after all, been a long time since he'd been with a woman. The cloud of her heavy perfume surrounded him and with it came the memory of the heated nights they'd spent together. A spark of physical response flared within him, and the evening ahead suddenly seemed somehow less tedious to him.

"I'll be counting the hours,"Bethany responded

breathlessly, and then gracefully exited with one last look of open longing cast his way.

Having just closed the door, Chance was walking slowly back toward the parlor, musing on the promise of the night to come, when Agatha stepped out into the hall.

"Bethany's gone?"

"Yes."

"Good."

"Good?" Her answer surprised him, and he arched one dark brow in question.

"Yes, good. She's a wonderful girl, and I'd certainly have no objections should you decide to marry her at some time in the future, but right now there's no time for you to involve yourself with a woman. You have to see about Douglas."

Chance groaned inwardly. For a moment, he'd forgotten all about his errant brother. "Ah, yes, Douglas."

"Yes, Douglas." Agatha gave him a strained look as she moved past him and disappeared into the study, leaving him to follow.

"Once you read his letter, you'll understand why I'm so concerned about him," she was saying as he entered the room. "Here, read it for yourself." She picked up the single sheet of paper and held it out to him. "It came almost two months ago, and I haven't heard from him since . . ."

Chance took the letter from his mother. He had not expected to find anything really upsetting in the short note, but as he read through it, a troubled frown furrowed his brow.

Mother—

I am in a dangerous situation here in the territory. I've struck a rich vein of gold in my mine, but there are people out here who would kill to get their hands on it. I am desperate for help from someone I know I can trust implicitly. Has Chance returned from his voyage yet? Send him to me as soon as he returns. I'm enclosing a map that shows the location of the mine. Tell him to guard it with his life. When Chance gets to Phoenix, have him look up an old tracker named Burr. He knows the mountains where the mine is located and can bring him to me. Tell Chance to talk to no one but Burr in town as my life depends upon it.

Your loving son,
Douglas

When Chance looked up again, his dark eyes were clouded with worry.

"Now do you understand why I've been so upset?" she pressed, glad to see that he was finally beginning to grasp the seriousness of the situation.

"Where's the map?"

"I've kept it locked in the drawer . . ." Agatha unlocked the center desk drawer and withdrew the vitally important sketch of the mountainous region east of Phoenix. "God only knows what's happened to him since he sent it." She handed him the map and then asked anxiously, "You are going to go, aren't you?"

Chance's expression grew decidedly grim as he read the letter a second time. "Yes, I'm going and, from the sound of things, the sooner the better."

Relief flooded through Agatha at his announcement. "Thank heaven. How soon can you be ready?"

"I've got to see to the ship and finalize those business affairs before I leave," he said thoughtfully, trying to calculate just how much time it would take to get everything in order. "If the negotiations go smoothly . . . two days."

"Good. It's been so long, and I've been so frightened for Douglas."

Chance gave his mother a quick smile, wanting to reassure her and cover his own doubts. "I wouldn't worry too much. You should know by now that Doug has always had a way of making things sound more exciting than they really are. I'm sure when I get to Phoenix, I'll find out he's just fine. You'll see."

"I hope so, Chancellor, I hope so," Agatha said softly. She wanted to believe his assurances with all her heart, but she felt perhaps this time her youngest son had gotten himself into something far more complicated and far more dangerous than any of them could imagine.

Chance's concern for his brother was foremost in his thoughts. The ominous tone of Doug's letter troubled him, and though he tried to pretend that he was in the best of spirits for his mother's sake, he was preoccupied and worried. Bethany was the farthest thing from his mind as they arrived at the Richardsons'.

They were late, and the music and dancing had already started when they entered the stately three-story mansion. After escorting Agatha to join her lady friends, Chance got a bourbon from the bar in the study and then returned to the ballroom. The welcome he received from his many friends was warm and cordial, and he slowly circled the room, renewing old acquaintances.

"Chance, how are you? It's good to have you back." Rodney Allenton, a longtime friend, was pleased to see that he'd returned. Though he was the same age as Chance, Rod's thinning blond hair, slim build, and glasses gave him a studious appearance and made him seem several years older.

"It's good to be back, Rod," he told him as they shook hands. "I missed Boston and everyone . . ."

Chance let his gaze drift around the room as they

talked and caught sight of Bethany and another young woman across the room. The deep rose-colored gown she wore set off her striking blond beauty. His mother's earlier comment about a possible marriage to Bethany drifted through his thoughts, and Chance acknowledged vaguely to himself that a man could do far worse.

Still, despite the fact that his mother had been prodding him for some time now to marry and start a family, Chance had no real interest in marriage. He had loved many women, but he had never been *in love* with any of them. His relationships with females had always been ones of mutual benefit and enjoyment with no commitment, and he'd liked it that way.

Rod noticed his distraction and, following the direction of his gaze, remarked knowingly, "Ah, the lovely Bethany . . . She's been seeing Peter Stanhope regularly for several months now, you know."

"Are they engaged yet?" Chance inquired easily, wondering if she'd come to him earlier that day while being promised to another man. Knowing Bethany, he certainly wouldn't have put it past her.

"Not yet, but I understand Stanhope's quite serious about her . . . just like every other man in the room," Rod drawled, knowing that many had tried to win Bethany, but none had succeeded. As he was watching Bethany, he saw her glance their way, say something to her friend, and start across the dance floor in their direction.

"Chance, darling, I'm so glad you finally got here," Bethany said as she sought him out. "I do believe this dance was ours?"

Chance fought to keep from smiling as he handed Rod his glass. "If you'll excuse me, Rod?"

Rod watched with ill-concealed astonishment as Chance guided Bethany out onto the dance floor, and he wondered why Chance always seemed to end up with the most beautiful women. *It couldn't be because of his good looks and fantastic fortune,* Rod thought cynically, but with a smile.

Bethany was ecstatic as Chance waltzed her around the crowded room. She felt as if all eyes were upon them, and she gloried in it. She knew they made the ideal couple, and now all she had to do was to convince Chance of it. She couldn't believe that everything was going so perfectly! The night, her dress, the music, Chance . . . she could hardly wait to get him outside in the garden so she could show him just how much she had missed him.

Chance was glad that he'd found Bethany at a moment when she hadn't been surrounded by a dozen or so ardent suitors, for he'd wanted to have his dance with her and be done with it. He was in no mood for romance tonight. He just wanted to make his appearance with his mother and then get back home to take care of business. Though he recognized that Bethany moved in perfect rhythm with his expert lead, he didn't care, and when the music ended, he was all too glad to escort her from the floor.

"Would you like to rejoin Regina?" Chance asked, nodding to where Bethany's friend still stood by the refreshment table.

After the heaven of being in his arms, the last thing Bethany wanted to do was to go back to her girlfriend.

"Actually, I'm a little warm, and I wondered if you'd come outside with me for a while?" Bethany gazed up at him. She didn't care if Peter Stanhope was waiting for her. She didn't care about anything but being alone with Chance. Clinging to his arm, she made certain to press the side of her bosom against him as he escorted her through the French doors and out into the black velvet night.

Alone with Chance beneath the stars, Bethany was determined to use the moment to her fullest advantage. She wanted him badly.

"I've missed you, Chance, more than you'll ever know," she confessed when they paused near the center of the flowering garden.

Chance was preoccupied with worries about Doug, but alone here with Bethany in the moonlight he could appreciate her loveliness. She did look ravishing tonight, he admitted to himself. Her hair was drawn up away from her face, emphasizing the finely boned structure of her lovely features. Her gown complemented the flawlessness of her fair complexion, and its off-the-shoulder style set off the gracefulness of her neck and shoulders, while showcasing the sensuous swell of her ample breasts above the low-cut décolletage. The only jewelry Bethany had worn was a necklace—a large, single diamond on a fine gold chain that nestled provocatively in the sweetness of her enticing cleavage.

"You look lovely tonight."

"I'm glad," she said huskily. "I wanted to look beautiful . . . for you."

Chance read the invitation in her tone and in her eyes and didn't hesitate a moment longer to take her in his arms and kiss her. When Bethany melted against him, meeting him willingly in that heated exchange, he pulled her closer and deepened the kiss.

"It's been a long time," he said, drawing briefly away to look down at her.

"Too long." Bethany looped her arms about his neck and drew him back to her, kissing him hungrily, holding nothing back and letting him know by her undisguised desire that she wanted him.

Chance understood her unspoken invitation, and he forgot about his brother for a minute as he took her up on it, caressing the fullness of her curves. A gasp of excitement escaped her at the passion his touch ignited. He was everything she'd ever wanted, and soon he would be hers! Bethany hadn't wanted to end the embrace, but the sound of another couple drawing near forced them apart.

Chance wondered why he felt slightly relieved to have been interrupted. He supposed it was because he knew there was no time for him to become involved right now.

"We'd better go back inside," Chance said after the other couple had moved away.

"I know you're right, it wouldn't do to be out here too long, but . . ."

The look she gave him was so enticing that he couldn't resist one last kiss. The embrace was a torrid one, and when they finally returned to the party, Bethany's cheeks were still flushed with desire.

"There you are!" Peter declared a bit hostilely as he approached her and Chance. "I've been looking everywhere for you."

"Chance and I just stepped outside for a few minutes," Bethany told him mildly. "You two know each other, don't you?"

"We've met," he replied tersely.

"Peter, it's good to see you again. If you'll both excuse me now? I see some other friends I haven't had the opportunity to speak with yet."

Bethany was a little put out that he was leaving her so quickly, but there was little she could do about it. "Of course," she said graciously, giving him her best smile, "and again, thank you for the dance."

As the music began again, Peter claimed her for the dance, and she was forced to pretend to be having a good time while she surreptitiously watched Chance from a distance. The evening seemed to drag on, and to her disappointment she found no opportunity to be with Chance again. Much later she finally managed a few moments away from Peter, and Regina seemed to appear at her side from out of nowhere.

"Did you hear the news?"

"What news?" Bethany asked, more than a little bored. Regina was one to carry tales, and she was certain that whatever it was she had to say would not be important to her.

"About Chance . . ."

"What about Chance?" She turned on her, anxious to learn what it was she had heard.

"He's leaving the day after tomorrow for Arizona."

"Leaving? For Arizona?!" She was dumbstruck. "But why?"

"I don't know all the details, but Mrs. Broderick told my mother earlier this evening that Douglas is out in Arizona and needs Chance's help."

"I don't believe it! He just got back!" Bethany was filled with outrage over the thought of him leaving again. "I've got to talk to him . . ."

"The last time I saw him he was headed toward the study, but I don't know if he's still there. His mother said that they were leaving the ball early tonight."

"Thanks, Regina . . ." Bethany rushed off, giving no thought at all to Peter. Only Chance mattered to her. She found him in the study as Regina had said, and luckily he was alone.

"Chance . . . I just heard the most dreadful news . . ." She stepped inside the room and shut the door behind her.

Chance looked up in surprise at the unexpected interruption, and he asked quickly, "What is it, Bethany? What's wrong?"

"I just heard that you were going to leave again. Is it true?"

"I'm afraid so," he answered. "I'll be leaving for Phoenix in the Arizona Territory shortly."

"I can't believe you didn't tell me yourself! After all we've meant to each other . . . after what we shared in the garden earlier?"

Chance's expression hardened. "My brother needs me, Bethany."

"Damn your brother!" Her temper exploded. She was not used to being frustrated. She was used to getting her own way. "Don't you know how long I've waited for you to come home?"

"There are no promises between us, Bethany, and I hardly think you cooled your heels while I was gone."

"I had to do something to keep from going crazy while I was waiting for you," she quickly defended herself. "Besides, that doesn't matter now that you're here. I need you, Chance, just as much as your brother does. Stay with me . . ." She was ready to offer him anything to keep him with her, but the door opened behind her, ending the opportunity.

"Chance? Oh, sorry . . ." It was Rod who came into the room.

"It's all right, Rod. What is it?"

"Your mother was looking for you. She said to tell you that she's ready to leave."

Chance started to follow Rod from the room, but Bethany stopped him.

"Chance?"

"I have to go, Bethany." He said no more, but strode straight from the room.

Bethany remained behind, fuming. She was glad that Rod shut the door behind them because, as soon as it closed, she picked up a glass paperweight off the desk and threw it across the room with all her might. It didn't shatter, but it really didn't matter. Bethany felt better for just having thrown it.

Damn Chance Broderick and his sense of family honor! *So his brother was more important to him than she was, was he?* she thought in fury. Well, just as soon as he got back, she was going to change all that!

Chapter 2

Burr left his place at the bar and cautiously made his way toward the man sitting at the table in the back of McKinnie's Saloon. It was unusual for anyone to be asking about him, and he wondered just what it was the stranger wanted. His expression guarded, he approached the dark-haired man.

Burr considered himself a good judge of character, and he quickly sized up the newcomer. He figured the man to be in his late twenties and used to an active outdoor life, for he was tan and ruggedly fit. Burr knew he was not from the territory, though, for he was dressed as a gentleman and his tailored clothing was too stylishly cut to be from out here.

"I understand you've been looking for me," Burr challenged without hostility.

"If your name's Burr, I have been," Chance replied, eyeing the buckskin-clad man who'd come to stand before him.

"It is," he replied curtly.

Burr was slightly built with gray-streaked shaggy hair. An untamed, grizzled beard framed a face with a tanned, leathery complexion that Chance knew had come from years of living in the elements. The hard, blue-eyed gaze that openly returned his probing stare reflected a keen intelligence.

"Then I'd like to talk with you a few minutes if you've got the time. My name's Chance Broderick." Chance came to his feet and extended his hand in friendship to the one man his brother considered trustworthy. "Please sit down. Would you like a drink?"

"A beer," Burr said as he shook his hand and then sat down as Chance called for the barkeep to bring the drink. He studied him openly and wondered if there was any connection between him and the young Broderick he knew up in the mountains. As dangerous as the times were, though, he said nothing about the possible connection for the time being. "You're from back East." It was a statement more than a question.

"Yes, I'm from Boston," Chance replied as he paid for the tankard of beer the bartender brought to the table.

Burr took a long, deep draft from the mug then glanced up at Chance again, a measuring, almost dangerous look in his eyes. There was a hard edge to his voice when he finally asked, "So, why are you looking for me? What do you want?"

"I want your help." His answer was simple as he leaned forward, resting his forearms on the table.

"What kind of help?"

"I understand you're the best tracker in the territory." Chance watched the other man carefully as he spoke.

"Some say so," Burr spoke without pride or conceit.

"I need to hire you to take me to my brother."

"Who's your brother?"

"Doug . . . Doug Broderick."

At the mention of Doug's name, Burr's eyes narrowed, and he drew back slightly, sitting back in his chair to take another drink. "I've heard the name," he said stiffly, not giving away anything yet.

Since the word had gotten out that young Broderick

had struck a rich vein up in the mountains, many had tried to locate his mine just so they could kill him and take the gold. This one's approach—claiming to be a relation—was far more clever than anything the others had done, but Burr was not about to fall for it.

"Then you can help me." Chance felt relieved to at last be getting close to his brother.

"I didn't say that," Burr told him flatly.

"You mean you won't?" Chance was confused. "I'll make it worth your while. I'm willing to pay five hundred dollars if you'll take me to him. I'll give you half up front and the other half when we get to Doug."

"If you're from back East, how is it you know about me?"

Chance realized the tracker's motive then and relaxed. "Doug wrote the family about you. He said you were the only one I should talk to here in town—that he couldn't trust anyone else. I have his letter with me if that will help convince you that I'm really his brother . . ." He withdrew the missive from his shirt pocket and handed it to Burr.

Burr read the letter carefully and thought it looked authentic enough, but he still harbored some doubts. He just didn't take chances when lives were at stake. In low tones, he asked, "Says here, he sent a map."

Without another word, Chance pulled out the carefully folded map and gave it to him. He waited in silence as the older man studied it.

Burr recognized right away that the map was accurate, and his suspicions died. This man was Broderick's brother.

Glancing back up at Chance, Burr wondered what to do. Lord knows, he and Rori could use the money. But since he'd made it a practice to keep her away from whites, safe from the hurt and harm that might befall her at their hands, he was hesitant to hook up with this man for the extended length of time it would take to guide him through the mountains to his brother's mine.

Burr knew he could leave Rori behind at their small cabin, but he didn't like the thought of her living alone for that long. She was older now, eighteen, and he knew firsthand what terrible things might happen to her if he wasn't there to protect her . . .

Reluctant as he was to have Rori around this good-looking white man, the fact that she had never shown any interest in men convinced Burr to take the job. The money Broderick was offering to pay was substantial enough to make their lives comfortable for some time to come.

"Put this away someplace safe," Burr told Chance as he folded the map and handed it back to him. "You told anybody what you're doing?"

"No. You're the only one."

"Good." He looked at him with renewed respect. He always admired a man who could keep his mouth shut.

"So do you believe me now?" Chance still didn't know where he stood with the man.

"I'll take you to him," Burr answered, draining the last of his beer and setting the mug down heavily on the table. "We'll leave at sunup."

"I'll be ready."

Rori and her dog, Big Jake, sat on the edge of the rough-hewn sidewalk outside the saloon. She was impatiently waiting for her grampa to emerge. Clad in a loose-fitting outfit of buckskin shirt, pants, and moccasins, her long, ebony hair pulled into two feather-decorated braids and her battered, floppy, wide-brimmed hat worn low over her face, she looked much like a twelve-or-thirteen-year-old, half-breed boy.

The fact was, everyone in town, thought she was a boy,

and neither she nor her grampa had ever seen the need to set them straight. They didn't particularly like the townspeople, and they knew the feeling was mutual.

"You oughtta get out of town, you filthy half-breed!" Fred, a good-sized white boy of about thirteen, taunted hatefully from where he stood across the street with two friends the same age.

Rori bristled at the remarks, but said nothing. Her grampa had taught her long ago not to react to such insults and slurs, explaining that the people saying them were just ignorant. He'd warned her early on that things were not going to be easy for her because her mother had been a Pima Indian and her father white. The supposedly "civilized" white folks didn't approve of such marriages, no matter how much love and devotion was shared.

Burr had also prepared her to handle just about any situation that might develop, and so, as the gang of youths moved threateningly across the street toward her, she let her hand fall to her waistband where her knife rested easily in its sheath. Rori knew she would do nothing to provoke them. She would remain quiet and hope they would lose interest in her.

"Red nigger!!" another one named Dorcas hollered in a hate-filled voice.

Big Jake, a huge, golden, thick-chested, short-coated mongrel, tensed as he recognized the threat in his tone. The way the group was coming at them made him definitely uneasy, and he growled low in his throat.

"Easy, Big Jake," Rori murmured, refusing to be baited into a fight.

The monster of a dog quieted instantly, but the tension did not leave his body. He remained as he was, sitting close beside her, his ears cocked forward, alert against danger and ready to defend her no matter what the odds. Rori had rescued him from death when he'd broken his hind leg as a pup, and his first owner, an old prospector with no time to waste on an injured dog, had been about to shoot him. She'd nursed him back to health, even though his back leg would never be completely normal again, and he had been her devoted companion ever since. Big Jake would do anything to protect her.

"Whatsa matter, Injun? Ya 'fraid?" Dorcas called out, trying to humiliate the breed into a fight.

"I heard half-breeds ain't nothing but lily-livered, thievin' bastards. Looks like I heard right, huh, Fred?"

"Sure does, Sammy. Just look at him," the one named Fred sneered. "He ain't even gonna stand up for himself! All he's got is that sorry excuse for a dog to protect him!"

Derisive laughter erupted from the others.

"Maybe that dog's the half-breed's daddy!" Sammy mocked. "I heard them Injun women spread their legs for anything!"

Rori could stand just about any kind of teasing, but the last remark sent pain searing through her. From what little she could remember, she knew her mother had been a warm, loving woman, and this cruel ridicule hurt too badly to ignore. Rori wanted to scream at them that they were wrong, that they didn't know what they were saying. She could feel the heat of their hatred, a vibrant, almost living thing. It was almost without conscious thought that she came to her feet.

Feeling safe because of their number, the jeering boys had been hoping the half-breed would react. They were spoiling for a fight, and when Rori moved, they were ready. The boys had been carrying small rocks, and they took vicious aim, hurling them with all their might.

Burr had taught Rori never to show any emotional weakness, yet she couldn't prevent the small cry that escaped her as one of the stones glanced off her cheek drawing blood. Big Jake exploded into action at the attack, launching himself ferociously at their assailants and knocking two of them to the ground with remarkable ease, his powerful jaws clamping down on the forearm of a youth who tried to hit him. At the boy's wild scream of terror, the other two surged to help him, beating on Big Jake with all their might to force him to let go.

"NO!" Rori shrieked in mindless fury. No matter what Grampa said, she couldn't let them hurt Jake. She couldn't! Without another thought to the overwhelming odds or her own safety, she entered the fraças.

When she joined the struggle, Dorcas and Sammy forgot about the dog and turned on her. Big Jake kept his restraining hold on Fred as Rori took on her two bigger assailants. Burr had long ago taught her how to fight and survive, and she utilized that knowledge and ability now. Moving with great speed and agility, she practically danced around her opponents as they tried to get a hand on her. Her hat flew off as she moved quickly and precisely, kicking out at the two bullies with brutal accuracy. Her aim was true, and Sammy fell to the ground holding himself in breathless agony as he rolled around in the dust of the street. She felt a thrill of revenge over having laid him low, but it was short-lived as Dorcas charged, tackling her from behind and knocking her to the ground.

"Hold on to the red bastard, Dorcas!!" Sammy snarled in a red haze of hate. "I'm going to kill the son of a bitch!!" He struggled to his feet and staggered toward where the half-breed was fighting off Dorcas with remarkable ease.

Rori heard Sammy's declaration and knew she had to get free of the other boy if she was to have a chance. With all the strength she had, she pushed against him and threw herself sideways. Dorcas was taken by surprise by her move, and Rori scrambled free only to have

Sammy grab her. She tried to kick out at him again, but this time he was up to her trick and avoided what would have been an even more punishing blow. As she fought to break loose, Dorcas moved in . . .

Chance finished his drink. "I'll see you at sunup then in front of the hotel."

Burr nodded and then leaned forward to speak to him in a more quiet tone of voice. "Just remember what I said about that piece of paper you got there." He gestured toward the pocket where Chance had put the map. "Keep that with you all the time. Don't let go of it for nothing if you want your brother to stay alive."

Chance knew the tracker meant it, and he gave an answering nod as he touched his pocket to make sure it was still there. "I'll be careful."

As Chance started from the saloon to go to his hotel and Burr settled in alone to order another drink, neither of them noticed the two scurrilous-looking men at the bar and how they watched Chance leave with more than a passing interest.

The first thing Chance saw when he stepped outside into the fading sunlight was two good-sized white boys beating up on a smaller Indian youth right in the middle of the street. There was another white involved in the fight, but a big yellow dog had him by the arm and was holding him pinned to the ground. Though the Indian was a scrappy fighter, he was still outnumbered. It was easy to see that he was getting the worst of it, too, for blood ran down his cheek from an ugly-looking gash just beneath his eye. When one white boy knocked him down and held him while the other threatened to kill him, Chance knew he had to break it up.

"Hold on there, fellas." He stepped into the middle of the fight and, deftly brushing the white youths aside, hauled the still-struggling Indian up by the seat of his pants.

"What the hell you think you're doin'? Let go of me!!" Rori yelled angrily, trying to break free of his humiliating grip. She continued to struggle as she reviled him with just about every vulgar name Burr had ever muttered in her presence.

Chance ignored the boy's filthy language as he shifted his hold to grasp him firmly around the waist. It took some doing, but he finally managed to pin the battling heathen's arms to his sides and then haul him forcibly back against his hip. It occurred to Chance that, for all the boy's wiry strength and street-fighting ability, he felt amazingly small and fragile-boned. With reluctant respect he wondered how anyone so slight of form could possibly have hoped to beat off those two good-sized thugs.

Rori grew even more furious as she realized the feebleness of her efforts against his superior brute strength. Embarrassment, coupled with some other strange emotion she'd never experienced before, flooded through her. If this damned interfering idiot hadn't trapped her in an iron embrace, she would have had her revenge against those other bastards! Now, as it was, she vowed to make this jackass pay for what he had done to her.

"Yeah! Let 'em go, mister! We ain't done with him yet!!" Sammy choked, furious at being interrupted.

"Done with me?!" Rori cried in outrage, firmly convinced that she could have beaten them both easily if she'd had the time. She gave a violent lurch of her body, trying to twist away from her captor's iron grip, but her effort was to no avail.

"Shut up and hold still!" Chance muttered threateningly under his breath as he gave the young ingrate a bone-silencing squeeze. To the others, he ordered in his most deadly tone, "You're done with him, boys. Now get out of here."

"You ain't got no right buttin' in this way!" Dorcas argued angrily. "This ain't none of your business!"

"I'm making it my business," he returned coolly, keeping a firm hold on Rori.

"Why?"

"I didn't like the odds. Two on one . . . or was it three?" Chance glanced over to where the big mongrel had released Fred's arm but was still standing guard over him.

Big Jake caught Chance's look and, without wavering in his duty, cocked his head to return the regard. The animal made no sound, understanding implicitly just by the man's stance and actions that he was no threat to his mistress.

"So what? He ain't nothing but a dirty half-breed! They shouldn't even let his kind in town!!" Sammy countered heatedly.

The last slur brought a steely glint to Chance's eyes. "You'd better clear out *now,* before I decide to turn my little savage here loose on you again and then join in myself to even out the odds."

Sammy and Dorcas were frustrated and angry, but common sense told them not to cross this man any further.

"Come on, Fred," they muttered as they glared malevolently at the meddlesome stranger. Then, ignoring the amused looks of the few townspeople who'd gathered to watch, they stalked off.

Fred wanted to race after his friends, but with the dog hovering over him, he hesitated to move.

"Go on," Chance ordered. "Get out of here!"

Without another moment's hesitation, Fred got cautiously to his feet. Once he was sure the dog was not going to bother him anymore, he chased after Sammy and Dorcas, the ache in his bruised but unbloodied arm forgotten in his relief at being free.

Rori listened to Chance's words and, if it was possible, grew even more livid. *"His little savage!?"* Just who in the hell did this man think he was? What right did he have to "rescue" her when she hadn't even needed it?! She hadn't needed any help!

And Big Jake—his betrayal infuriated her most of all! He hadn't hesitated to go to her defense when the three boys had attacked her, but he'd sat there like a lump while this stranger manhandled her! What was the matter with him! Why hadn't he chewed the man's leg off so she could have finished taking care of the other three?!

Rori fought even harder to get loose then, for she wanted to chase after her attackers, but the fool intruder still held her immobile. Anger surged through Rori at the helplessness she felt at being pinioned against his side this way. Why couldn't she be the boy he thought she was? Then she would have the strength to break his hold!

Rori was seething as she waited for the moment when her self-appointed savior would finally decide to release her, and the moment didn't come an instant too soon as far as she was concerned. The second Chance let her go, she spun away from his hated touch. Snatching her knife from its sheath, she turned on him with all the viciousness of a cornered mountain cat. Her green eyes glowed wildly with rage as she faced her would-be defender. The thought of attacking him was very appealing until she looked up at him and found herself staring up at the most handsome man she'd ever seen.

Rori blinked in surprise as her heart thudded madly and then skipped a beat. Her interfering idiot was tall . . . towering over her. His face was beautiful—there was no other way for her to describe it, with his dark hair, dark eyes, straight nose, and firm line of his mouth . . . and oh, that mouth! There was something about the slightly mocking slant of his lips that held her spellbound and left her filled, momentarily, with a strange longing she'd never felt before.

Rori could feel heat rushing to her face, and she jerked her gaze lower, tracing downward over the broad width of his chest and shoulders to the flat plane of his stomach. His hips were slim, his legs long and lean, and she knew from being held against him that he was solid, rock-hard muscle. Yet, even as she reluctantly acknowledged to herself that this white man was wonderful to look upon, just the fact that he could affect her so left her even more furious.

The last thing Chance had expected was to be attacked by the boy he'd just saved. He stared down at the young Indian's dirty, bloodied face, and he was stunned by the fierce hatred he saw reflected in the emerald-eyed gaze. Chance didn't know which surprised him more—the color of his eyes or the violent emotion, but he didn't have time to think about it as Rori moved at him, threatening him with the wicked-looking blade.

His years at sea had taught him much about fighting, and Chance knew how to defend himself against a knife attack. Trouble was, the boy was so young he didn't want to hurt him. After all, he'd only gotten involved in this whole mess to keep him from getting beaten in the first place. Surely, the youth couldn't be serious . . .

"Look, just give me the knife. There's no reason . . ." Chance reached out to take the weapon from him, but the boy moved away.

"You ever try to lay your hands on me again, you white bastard, and you'll be dead!!" Rori exploded.

The boy's viciousness angered Chance. "Why you . . ."

When he would have challenged the boy, he made another slashing motion at him, and Chance was forced to jump back.

"Or better yet, maybe I won't kill you," she continued, smiling ferally as she eyed his lower anatomy. "Maybe I'll just carve you up a little . . ."

Burr burst out of the saloon, having just heard the talk in the bar about some little Indian roughing it up with some white boys out in the street. He had expected to find her skirmishing with some of the local youths who always liked to taunt her whenever they got the chance. He hadn't expected to find her with her knife drawn, facing down Chance.

Rori's expression was as angry as Burr had ever seen it, and he wondered what had caused her to react to Broderick this way. Her cheek was bruised and bloodied, and he wondered if he'd misjudged the man he'd just agreed to guide through the mountains. Had Broderick been the one to hit Rori?

"Rori!! What the hell's goin' on out here?!" he demanded.

At the sound of her grampa shouting her name, Rori glanced up, and that single moment of distraction was all Chance needed.

Chance struck out, knocking the weapon away with a powerful, numbing blow. Following through before the fierce, young, would-be warrior had time to recover, he made a grab for the boy, catching him by the shoulders before he could make a dive for the knife.

"You vicious, bloodthirsty little monster! I ought to beat you, right here, right now!!" Chance prided himself on being fairly cool-headed about things, but when the boy had lunged at him intending to do him great bodily harm, he'd become enraged. The thought of throttling the ungrateful hell-raiser held great appeal.

The moment Chance struck out at Rori in anger, Big Jake gave a snarling bark and lunged, teeth bared, intending to give Chance a deadly mauling.

"Big Jake!! No!!" The old tracker came charging forward.

Only Burr's shout saved Chance as the dog froze at his command. Chance looked from the dog, who was crouching menacingly within striking distance, his hackles raised, to Burr, who was pushing his way through the gawking bystanders, and wondered why the animal had obeyed him.

"Broderick!! Wait!!"

"What for?! Give me one good reason why I shouldn't teach this wild animal some manners!" Chance challenged, glaring down at Rori. "Instead of being thankful when I helped him out of trouble, he pulled a knife on me."

"Didn't ask you for no help!!" Rori interrupted defiantly as she met his furious gaze without fear.

Burr picked up on the fact that Chance had not discovered the truth of Rori's gender, and he wanted to keep it that way. He chose his next words carefully as he answered, "There's a damn good reason, Broderick. Rori's my grandchild."

Chapter 3

Chance was stunned, and he glanced over at Burr incredulously. "Your grandson?" He released Rori immediately, and those who'd gathered around lost interest and wandered off.

"Rori's mine," Burr told him, seeming to ignore her anger. In truth, because it was unusual for her to react so strongly to anyone, Burr was very much aware of her mood and troubled by it.

"You know this low-down, no-good . . . ?!" Rori erupted in fury as she swung around to face her grampa. How could it be that he knew the other man? Was this the man he'd gone into the saloon to meet? A sickening feeling filled her as she realized the name Burr had shouted—Broderick—was the same as that of the man who, they'd been told, was looking for him.

"Yes, Rori, this is Chance Broderick from Boston. He's the man who's been askin' around town about hiring me to take him up in the mountains."

"It's no wonder he needs a guide!" she scoffed, giving him a scathing look that told Chance exactly what she thought of him, which wasn't much. "I'm surprised he's managed to find his way here or to even stay alive this long."

"I'm sure you believe there'd be quite a lot less of

me by now if you'd had your way." Chance chuckled tolerantly over the boy's unfailing hostility.

"You're damn right! If Grampa hadn't distracted me like he did . . ."

"Rori!" Burr was growing annoyed with her challenging attitude. "Broderick here is Doug's brother."

Rori was surprised by this news, for she liked Doug. Whenever they neared his diggings, they always stopped to visit him and the Indian woman, Nilakla, who was working the mine with him. Oddly enough, Rori found herself mentally comparing Chance to his brother, and she was startled to find that she thought him better-looking than the fair-haired Doug. Some emotion she could not define jolted through her, and she frowned and looked away, filled with uneasiness at the sensation.

"Well, he sure ain't nothing like Doug. Doug has sense enough to know when to mind his own business!!"

"From the looks of your face, Rori, Broderick was justified in doing what he did. You look like you got the worst end of it," Burr told her.

"Aw, that happened before he even got here. Those jackasses threw a rock at me. But I had 'em, and I was doing just fine till he came along . . ." she defended herself, suddenly becoming aware of the throbbing in her cheek.

"I always learn from my mistakes." Chance, tired of the boy's harangue, drawled sarcastically, his gaze slightly mocking as it met Rori's. "The next time it looks like you're in need of my help, I'll restrain myself."

"There ain't gonna be a next time, mister!" Rori snapped, her pride hurting as badly as her cheek. Her expression was resentful as she glowered up at him, hating him.

Chance didn't notice the flash of emotion in her eyes, but Burr did, and he felt a chill shudder through his soul. Though he was sure that Rori wasn't aware of it, the look she'd just given Broderick was the same one that had always shone in her mother Atallie's gaze whenever she had looked at Jack. It was a look of yearning that came straight from the heart, and Burr panicked at the memories that assailed him. He couldn't let her come to care for this white man. She'd only be hurt!

"I hope there won't be a next time. You're looking pretty worse for the wear right now," Chance taunted Rori. "I'd hate to see what you'd look like if you actually lost a fight."

"You won't live long enough to see the day," she shot back, furiously snatching up the knife he'd knocked from her hand. Her eyes were glittering as she considered first Chance and then the sharp blade.

"Oh, I don't know." He read Rori's murderous thoughts easily and grinned. "If we're both going to be traveling with Burr, we're going to be around each other a lot."

"You've agreed to take this greenhorn up in the mountains?" She turned to her grampa.

Chance replied before Burr had the opportunity. "He has."

She was so mad, she was fuming. "You aren't gonna last a day, let alone the three weeks it takes to get to the mine, white man. The Superstitions are the ruggedest, meanest mountains in the territory."

"And you've been through them?" Chance asked, his expression mocking.

"A hundred times!" Rori told him with a proud lift of her chin.

Burr's fear for Rori was growing as he watched her react to Broderick. Judging from the way they were striking sparks off each other, he was afraid that she was feeling something for him. Before their untimely deaths, Atallie had often told the story of how she'd fallen in love with Jack at first sight. Burr worried now that the same thing was happening to Rori, for he'd never seen her act this way before, not with anyone.

Though Chance was Doug's brother, Burr didn't know him well enough to be sure of him. If Rori fell in love with Broderick, he felt certain that she ultimately would be hurt, and he couldn't risk it. He had vowed long ago to protect her from white men, and his earlier resolve to keep Rori away from the handsome Broderick reasserted itself.

Though the money would have helped out, Burr knew that for Rori's sake and for his own peace of mind he couldn't take the job. He had to end his association with Broderick right then and there, before things went any further.

"Broderick, this isn't going to work," Burr announced with finality. "I'm calling the deal off."

Chance couldn't believe what he was hearing. "What do you mean you're calling it off?" They'd agreed on everything, and now the old man was backing out? Why in the world would he be changing his mind now?

"You heard me," Burr answered firmly. "I've changed my mind."

"You gave me your word!" Chance insisted, confused and wondering what had happened.

Burr felt bad, but not bad enough to agree to go through with it. "I'm taking it back."

"Then your word isn't worth a damn cent!"

Burr's eyes were cold as he regarded him. The insult pained him, but he knew he couldn't make the trip. "I'll find someone else to take you."

"I don't want anybody else! You know damn well that you were the only one Doug trusted."

"I'll get you somebody trustworthy."

"We had a deal, Burr. What is it, the money? You don't think five hundred dollars is enough to make the trip worth your while?"

"Five hundred dollars?" Rori gasped, amazed by the sudden change in her grampa and by the revelation that this Easterner had been willing to pay so much.

"Isn't that enough? You want more? How much? Name your price and I'll pay it," Chance demanded heatedly. He was not accustomed to being denied.

"Forget it, Broderick. Like I said, I'll find you somebody else to guide you." Burr turned his back on the stunned young man and started to walk away. "Whoever I get, I'll send 'em over to you at your hotel."

"My brother trusted you, Burr. Are you telling me he was wrong?"

Burr didn't say another word as he stalked off to where their horses were tied and mounted up, leaving Rori and Big Jake to hurry after him.

Chance was totally frustrated as he stood in the middle of the street watching them go. Burr hadn't struck him as the kind of man who'd lie to him, but he didn't know what had happened to change the tracker's mind. The fact that he was now this close to Doug and yet had no one to take him to him left Chance angrier than ever. Aggravated and annoyed, he strode back into the saloon and ordered a double whiskey. Downing the potent liquor at the bar, he wondered what to do next.

Hal, a big man with a drooping, sinister-looking mustache and dark hair that had a white streak in it from a losing confrontation with a bullet years before, gave his companion Tom a knowing look as they ambled slowly from the saloon where they'd been drinking for most of the day. Excitement shone in his pale, blue-eyed gaze. The plan he'd conceived was perfect, and he was eager to get Tom outside so he could tell him about it.

"He's the one," he told Tom gleefully as he mentally

rubbed his hands together. "Didn't you hear him and the old man talkin' earlier?"

"You're sure about that?" Tom, a thin, average-looking man with less than average courage, had his doubts.

"Hell yes, I'm sure! That old tracker warned him to keep that map safe. It's got to be the one, and all we got to do is get it away from him."

"I ain't killin' nobody unless I'm gonna get somethin' out of it. You know I don't like killin'."

Hal gave him a look full of scorn, for he thought his reluctance to murder in cold blood a weakness. Personally, he had always enjoyed killing people, especially when he got to do it slowly. It gave him a great feeling of power. If his plan was going to work, though, he'd have to kill this Broderick quickly and silently. He didn't want anyone finding out right away. They had to have time to get out of town.

"I got it all figgered out already!" Hal hissed in a low, agitated voice. "We'll follow him back to his hotel and watch him until he goes up to his room. Then, when it gets dark, we'll get him!"

"But how? What are you gonna do? You can't shoot him," Tom worried. "You do, and half the town will be down on us!"

"I ain't gonna shoot him, fool," he told him angrily. "I'll use a knife on him. That's nice and quick and quiet."

"What if he fights back? He's a good-sized man. What if we get caught?"

Hal exploded in annoyance. "Look, you want out, then get out now! Me, I intend to get that map and find me a gold mine . . . a rich gold mine!!!"

Though he was not big on murder, Tom definitely had a taste for money, liquor, and women. "You're sure about the gold?"

"Have I ever led you wrong? We been together for fifteen years, and you're still always afraid. Hell, I don't know why I don't dump you and find somebody who doesn't question me every step of the way!"

"I ain't questionin' you, Hal." Tom was quick to make amends, for he needed Hal. "I jes' don't like the thought of gettin' hung, that's all. I cheated the hangman once, and I don't intend to give him another chance."

"You cheated the hangman 'cause I broke you outta jail. Don't worry, neither one of us is ever going back."

They fell silent as they moved to an inconspicuous place from which to watch. They would wait there until they saw Broderick leave the saloon, and then they would follow him, making sure that they weren't seen. Once they found out what room he was staying in, Hal was set to sneak in, murder him, and steal the treasure map. It was going to work perfectly—he was sure of it.

Rori looked at her grampa in open confusion as they sat around the fire at their campsite later that evening. "You mean he was serious when he said he'd offered you five hundred dollars just to take him up to Doug's mine?"

"Yep," Burr answered, but did not elaborate.

"And you turned him down?" she prodded.

"You were there. You heard me."

"How come?"

"I don't have to explain myself to you, missy," Burr cut her off coldly, not wanting to discuss it. Broderick's accusation that he was not a man of his word troubled him, but there were times when a man had to do what he had to do, no matter what the cost to his pride.

"But Grampa, it don't make sense . . . your backin' out this way!"

"Makes perfect sense to me," he replied curtly. "I didn't want to do it."

"Well, who are you gonna get to take him?"

"I'll think of somebody," Burr said sharply. "Now that's enough about Broderick. I don't want to talk about him anymore."

Burr's evasive, stubborn ways left Rori frustrated. Knowing him as she did, though, she realized there was no point in trying to get anything else out of him. When Burr quit talking, he quit talking, and even a pack of wild horses wouldn't be able to drag anything else out of him.

Rori thought of the white man's insult to Burr's honor then and grew angry. She knew her grampa to be an honorable man, and it puzzled her that he would let Broderick get by with what he said. Still, since Burr had agreed to take him and then backed out, it did appear that he had gone back on his word.

Rori glanced over to where Burr sat by the fire. He looked inexplicably tired and old tonight, and she wondered if it was because of the deal with Broderick. She didn't understand what his motives were in refusing to take him, but she knew now what she had to do. Burr had always taught her that a person's honor was the most important thing in his life. *If you had your honor,* he always said, *you could look a man in the eye without fear.* Their family honor had been insulted, and the only way she could put things to rights was to go to Chance Broderick and tell him that she would take him up to Doug's mine herself.

It wasn't all that long a trip, Rori reasoned. She knew the Superstitions as well as any man. They could leave in the morning and, with any luck, make it to the diggings in a little less than three weeks.

A small smile quirked her lips as Rori thought of how he would react when she went to him, and she found herself growing excited at the thought. Broderick had been so damned arrogant and hateful! It would serve him right to be on the trail with her for two weeks. So he thought he was as good as she was, did he? Well, she'd show him. She'd run him into the ground and enjoy every minute of it! Not only would she get the satisfaction of watching him make an ass out of himself, she'd also get to prove to him just how good she really was. The challenge of it sent a thrill through her, and she wondered distractedly why it mattered so much.

Rori glanced at her grampa again and hoped he wouldn't object. The thought gave her pause, but her reasoning was so logical that she couldn't see where he'd have any objection. Broderick needed a guide. Grampa wouldn't do it, so she would.

She wasn't going to tell him, though, until after the plans were made, that way he couldn't argue with her too much. Confident that it would all work out just fine, Rori sat back to wait until she could get the opportunity to sneak off without his knowing.

After downing two more drinks at the saloon in an effort to cool his anger, Chance had left the bar and returned to his hotel room to wait for word from Burr. As the hours had slowly passed, his frustration had grown. He was used to being in command of all aspects of his life, and the fact that the old tracker had left him hanging aggravated him. The temptation to hire another guide was great, for Chance was anxious to get to Doug, but his brother's warning not to trust anyone but Burr put him off. He knew he'd have to wait, however impatiently, until he heard from the old tracker again. Leaving his room only long enough to eat dinner, he headed back, hoping to hear from him sometime that evening.

It was well after dark when Chance returned to his room. It had been light when he'd gone out, and it hadn't occurred to him to leave a lamp burning. The heavily shadowed darkness did not threaten him as he opened the door and started in.

Hal and Tom had followed Chance discreetly when he left the saloon, and then they had kept watch outside the hotel until they'd seen him leave to go eat. Knowing that his room was empty and that they'd have the opportunity to steal the map without violence, Tom had convinced Hal that they should break in and go through Chance's belongings while he was away. Their search had turned up nothing so they had hidden in the room to await his return. Hal was eager for the kill, and when Chance started unknowingly through the door, he was ready and waiting with his knife drawn.

Rori had waited until Burr was asleep and then had crept off to town with Big Jake. Keeping a low profile as she always did, she made it through night-shrouded Phoenix without incident. She instructed Jake to wait outside the hotel for her and went on in. As she entered the lobby, Virgil Keeps, the owner, tried to stop her.

"We don't let your kind in here," Virgil thundered with menace.

Rori bristled at his ugliness, but faced him without fear. "I ain't here to cause no trouble, and I ain't plannin' on stayin'."

"Then get out," the man sneered.

"I came to see Broderick. What room's he in?"

"I told you to get, and I meant it, Indian. Get out before I throw you out!"

"Broderick's expectin' me. I got a message for him from Burr, and he'll be plenty mad if he finds out you didn't let me see him." She told the lie baldly, justifying it by telling herself that Chance *was* expecting to hear from Burr.

Since Broderick had told him before that he was expecting someone, Virgil figured the boy was telling the truth. He relented reluctantly. "All right. Go on. He just went on up. If you don't catch him, his room's the last door on the left."

Rori nodded and started up the stairs. She caught sight of Chance when she reached the top and called out to him just as he began to step inside his room.

"Broderick! I need to talk to you!"

Chance was already halfway through the door when he heard her, and he turned to look back just as Hal lunged with the knife. Rori's call saved Chance from instant death as Hal's thrust took him only in the upper arm. He gave a strangled cry as the force of the attack sent him reeling into his room.

"Tom! Quick! Get the damn door closed!!" Hal ordered as he launched himself at Chance determined to kill him.

Tom charged forward from where he'd been hiding to slam the door shut, but Rori was already there. Though the room was dark, there was enough light from the hall for her to see Chance and the other armed man struggling on the floor. She rushed into the room to help and, as she did, saw Tom running toward her. Rori reacted instinctively, drawing her own knife and throwing it at him.

"Hal, I'm hurt!" Tom cried as the blade sank deeply into his shoulder. He yanked the knife out and threw it aside in agony.

Hal was furious. His plan had been going so well and now . . . He could hear the sound of voices and the thunder of running footsteps as those downstairs were alerted to the trouble. They had been so close! If only his first attempt had killed the bastard everything would have gone as planned! Snarling in outrage, he hit Chance as hard as he could, hoping to stun him long enough for them to make their getaway. Hal jumped to his feet and was starting to run for the window when Rori attacked.

"You ain't gettin' away, you bastard!!" Rori yelled, grabbing Hal around the neck from the back.

Hal was surprised by the assault, but the boy was so light he threw him off with little trouble. As Rori crashed into the wall, he helped Tom out onto the porch roof. The force of the blow knocked her light-headed for a minute, but she was soon back on her feet racing toward the window. She reached it just in time to see that the two men had jumped down to the alleyway and were making their escape on the horses they'd left tied there. Rori was torn between chasing after them and going back to see how Broderick was. She hesitated, looking back to where Chance was struggling to get up, and at that moment Virgil and several other men burst into the room, their guns drawn.

"Hold it right there, you little red-skinned bastard!!" Virgil shouted, taking aim at her with deadly intent. "See to Broderick, and one of you light the lamp," he directed the others without looking away from Rori.

Rori's eyes widened as she stared at the advancing white man. Surely they didn't think she was the one who'd attacked Broderick . . .

"So you had a message for him, did you!? I knew you were a murdering little savage!" Virgil started toward her, the gun pointed directly at her chest.

Fear seared Rori's soul as she stared down the barrel of the weapon. She fought to keep her expression stoic, but the depth of her sudden terror was mirrored in her gaze.

"Keeps, you're wrong! It wasn't the boy . . ." Chance managed, holding his wounded arm as he struggled to his feet with the help of the other men.

"What are you talking about?"

His pain-filled gaze met Rori's, and, despite his relatively calm expression, he could read the fear that gripped him. Chance hurried to explain. "There were two of them! They were waiting for me in the room. They jumped me when I came in . . ."

"Two of 'em?" Virgil sounded doubtful as he glanced back at him.

"You don't really think he's strong enough to do this to me, do you?" Chance scorned, gesturing toward his injured arm.

"Could have if he took you by surprise," he insisted, not willing to let it go yet. He was looking forward to lynching the damned half-breed troublemaker.

"He came upstairs *after* me, Keeps," he replied angrily. "The two who did it were waiting in the room, and when they heard you coming, they went out the window. Maybe you can catch them outside . . ."

"What did they look like?" one of the other men asked, knowing that what Chance had said was the truth.

"I'm not sure. It was dark, and the one who stabbed me took me from behind. All I know is that he was a big man, had dark hair and a mustache," he offered. "The other one . . . ?" Chance looked to Rori for help.

"Not big, not small. He's got a knife wound in his shoulder," she added with a proud lift of her chin as she bent down to pick up her knife. With pretended casualness, she wiped the bloody blade on the bedsheet and then slid it back into its sheath at her waist.

"We'd better go see if we can find 'em." Virgil grudgingly lowered his gun as he turned to go. "We'll send the doc for you."

When they'd gone from the room to begin the search, Chance shoved the door shut behind them and turned to face Rori.

Chapter 4

Rori remained rooted where she was on the far side of the bed near the window. When Chance turned to look at her, their gazes locked across the width of the room, and she suddenly knew a strange sense of intense isolation. It seemed to Rori that they were the only two people left in the world. The thought made her uncomfortable, and she frowned.

Chance studied the boy from where he stood, staring at his bruised face as if actually seeing him for the first time. Rori was every bit Indian from his black braids to his moccasined feet, and he looked suitably fierce, especially with his battered cheek. Chance knew from his own personal experience that there was nothing the least bit soft about the youth, but something about his slight build and brilliant green eyes made him seem almost vulnerable right now.

It pained Chance considerably to admit that the stubborn, argumentative boy had put up one hell of a fight, and that his unexpected but timely arrival had saved him from certain death. If it hadn't been for Rori . . . .

"Rori . . . thank you," he said earnestly.

The rough velvet of Chance's deep voice sent unexpected chills down Rori's spine. Staring at him in the golden glow of the lamplight, realizing how totally mesmerizing he was, she felt her heart hammer wildly in her breast. Her throat had gone dry and her hands were cold. Rori wondered dazedly if she had hurt her head when she was thrown against the wall, but what she was feeling was not painful, at least not that way. A tiny, niggling voice in the back of her thoughts warned her that this was something else . . . something different . . . something special, and a surge of unexplained panic welled up inside her.

"I told you it was a miracle you'd managed to stay alive this long!" Rori spoke up, being deliberately sarcastic to break the tension that had been building within her. "Who was your nursemaid before I came along?"

"Amazingly enough, until I ran into you, I was managing to take care of myself pretty well," Chance remarked dryly as he stripped off his shirt. Though the cut on his arm wasn't serious, it was still bleeding heavily. Grabbing up one of the towels off the washstand, he single-handedly tried to fashion a tourniquet around his upper arm to slow it down.

Rori had to fight to keep herself from gawking. It wasn't that she'd never seen a man without his shirt on before. She had seen Burr that way many times, but there was something about the sight of Chance naked to the waist that made her breath catch in her throat. His shoulders were wide; his chest, solid, ridged with firm muscle and covered with a light furring of dark hair that narrowed to a vee at the waistband of his pants.

Nervously, Rori jerked her gaze upward. It was then that she noticed the strained look on his handsome, rugged features and knew he was in pain. Oddly, she found herself aching to rush to him so she could be the one to tend his arm, rather than the doctor the other men had gone to summon. She wanted to tell him how glad she was that she'd been there to save him from being killed. She wanted to tell him . . .

The thoughts and feelings that were roiling within her were so powerful and so totally alien to Rori that they frightened her. The only person she cared about was Burr, she told herself adamantly. He loved her and she loved him. Grampa and Big Jake were all she needed to be happy in life! She didn't care about Chance! The truth was she couldn't stand him! He was arrogant and hateful!

Still, worried that his injury might be worse than she'd first thought, she couldn't stop herself from asking, "You all right?"

"I will be once I get this tied. It's just a flesh wound. It's bleeding pretty bad, but I've had worse," he commented as he sat down on the bed, struggling to get a knot in the cloth and not having much success.

Chance's last statement, made so calmly, so offhandedly, sent a chill through her. *He'd been hurt before* . . . Again, Rori wondered at this sudden concern she had for him. What did she care if he'd been shot or stabbed or beaten?!!

"No doubt, from the way you fight!" she taunted, forcing herself to remember·that she hated him.

Chance was growing very tired of constantly trading insults with the boy. Earlier that afternoon he'd found his unreasonable hostility mildly amusing, but right now he had no interest in matching barbs with him.

"Look, I don't know why you showed up here tonight in the first place, and right now, I don't care," he told the boy wearily. "Just help me with this thing before I bleed to death, will you? I can't seem to get it tight enough just using one hand."

Again, Rori swallowed nervously. *Help him? Actually touch him?* She didn't speak; she couldn't actually. Knowing there was absolutely no way she could refuse, Rori moved slowly toward Chance. She sat down on the bed beside him, and the sinking of the mattress brought her hip in full contact with his. The touch of his muscle-hardened thigh against her softer one was electric for Rori, and she shifted uncomfortably away from him, keeping her eyes downcast. She couldn't risk letting him see the confusion she was sure was showing clearly in her eyes.

Chance noticed her discomfort and gave a ragged, exasperated sigh. "Rori, I know how you feel about me, but do you think we could just call a truce until the doctor shows up?"

No, you don't know how I feel about you, Chance Broderick! I don't even know how I feel about you! Rori thought wildly.

"I guess so," she finally said tightly, fighting to keep her hands from shaking as she reached out to him. Struggling not to betray her inner turmoil, she brushed his hand aside and efficiently corrected his clumsy knot before tightening the cloth around his arm. He had lost a lot of blood, but the makeshift tourniquet would help. She moved to the washstand then and got another towel to press to the bloody gash. "Press tight on that. Between the two of 'em, that should do it for now."

"Good. Thanks." He took the cloth, then leaned back against the headboard and closed his eyes. "Damn," he groaned, "I don't know why in the hell I even bothered to come out here. Doug's desperate for help, but I can't get anybody to take me to him, and every time I turn around, somebody's trying to kill me . . . first you and then those two thugs . . ."

"Why d'ya think they were after you? I mean they were waitin' right here in your room for you. Did you know them?"

"No," he answered, opening his eyes to look around the room. "But they had to be after the map. Just look at the mess they made."

For the first time, Rori glanced at her surroundings and realized that everything was in disarray. "Map? What map?"

"Didn't Burr tell you?"

"No. He wouldn't talk about it."

"Well, Doug sent me a hand-drawn map of his mine."

"Did they get it?"

"No, your grampa gave me some good advice. He told me to be careful with it, so I kept it safe," Chance said with relief, touching the pocket where the map was stowed. "Not that it does me a hell of a lot of good. Without Burr to take me up there, I'm at a standstill." Chance closed his eyes again as a wave of weariness washed over him. The day had been one long disaster. "I should have stayed in Boston. At least if I was there I could have Bethany, and a long, hot night in her arms sounds real good right now."

Rori felt her cheeks heat up at the image his words evoked. Chance in bed with some mysterious woman named Bethany . . . She moved away from the bedside, keeping her back to him, just in case he looked at her. She didn't want him to see her blush. "Who's Bethany?" She had to ask.

"One very beautiful, very sexy, very sophisticated lady," Chance said without emotion.

His words stung for some reason, and Rori lashed out at him without thought, her voice full of scorn. "I was thinkin' that was the kind of company you keep." She gestured toward his arm. "It's just pretty clear that you don't hang around with any of the rough boys."

Chance opened one eye to peer at Rori. "I thought we'd agreed to a truce." When the boy fell silent, he went on, sounding irritated and exhausted, "Look, Rori, why did you come here tonight? What do you want?"

"I came to see you about going up in the mountains."

"Burr's changed his mind?" Chance's expression

brightened, and there was a note of hope in his voice. "He's going to take me?"

"No."

"Then he's found somebody who will?"

"Well, not really."

"Damn it!" he roared, his frustration getting the best of him. "Doesn't he realize how important it is that I get to Doug? I've got to get up to that mine!"

"I know, and that's why I'm gonna take you," Rori announced.

"You?" Chance stared at Rori in utter disbelief. He might put on a tough act, but he was just a kid. Chance figured Rori couldn't be more than fourteen or so. How the hell was he going to get him there?

"Yes, me!" she countered sharply.

"And what makes you think Burr's going to let you be my guide, if he won't go himself?"

"I don't know what his reasons are for not taking you, and I don't care. I make my own decisions, and I've decided to do it," Rori told him staunchly. She thought of his earlier remark regarding Burr's honor and knew she had to redeem it.

Chance regarded him skeptically. "Your grampa had decided to take me to the mine, too, but he backed out on his word. How do I know you won't do the same?"

Rori's eyes flashed green fire as she glared at him, and she wondered how she could ever have thought him attractive. She was so angry over his disparaging comment, she was shaking.

"Don't worry, white man, you have my word on it, and I never go back on a promise. Never."

Chance gave him a skeptical look and was about to say more when the doctor knocked and, without further preamble, came bustling into the room.

"I'm Dr. Wallace. Virgil sent me up . . ." he announced and then strode purposefully to the bed. He was a short man whose well-rounded shape gave testimony to his love for food. "He said there'd been trouble up here, and I can see right off he was serious." Glancing at Rori, he asked, "You want the breed here?"

"The boy can stay."

Setting his bag on the bed, the doctor opened it and took out a half-full bottle of whiskey. "Here." He held it out to Chance with a smile. "Best medicine around."

"My kind of tonic," Chance agreed. He took the liquor and drank deeply as the doctor examined his arm. The whiskey burned all the way to his stomach, but at this point Chance didn't care. His arm was throbbing, and any comfort he could get would be welcome. "Thanks."

Dr. Wallace took the bottle back, and before Chance knew what he was doing, he poured the rest of the potent brew over his raw and bleeding arm. Chance went pale as the shock of the alcohol hit him. His jaw clenched in agony as he battled down the pain.

"That should do it," the doctor pronounced proudly as he got some salve and bandages out of his bag and began to wrap up the arm. "You should be as good as new in no time."

"Right," Chance drawled when he was finally able to draw a breath.

"That'll be a dollar, six bits."

Getting up off the bed, Chance pulled some money out of his pocket and paid the man, sending him off happily into the night. As he closed the door behind him, Chance flexed his arm experimentally, wincing slightly at the sharp pain the simple movement evoked.

"I plan on leavin' in the morning, unless you think you won't be up to it," Rori chided.

"I'll be ready, if and when you show up," Chance threw out the challenge.

"The five-hundred-dollar offer still stand?" At his nod, she started for the door. "I'll be here at sunup."

"You think it's safe to build a fire?" Tom asked anxiously as he leaned weakly against one of the massive boulders that surrounded their campsite.

"There ain't nobody comin' after us. We got away clean," Hal replied, throwing a few more sticks on the small blaze. "Besides, I gotta take a look at your shoulder. How's it doin'?"

"It's stopped bleedin', but it still hurts like hell. Damn Indian bastard! Where'd he come from, anyway?"

"I don't know, but I'm gonna find out, and when I do, I'm gonna hunt him down and kill him," Hal swore. "He ruined everything for us. We had that Broderick fella. I'da had his throat cut in another minute!"

"And we'da had the map! Instead, we got nothin'."

"It ain't over yet," he said fiercely. "Nobody knows it was us. You just lay low out here until your shoulder's better, and then we'll go after him again."

"What if he leaves?"

"I'll ride back into town tomorrow and see what I can find out. Maybe we'll get another chance at him."

"And a chance at that breed! This time, though, it's gonna be me doin' the killin'. I got a score to settle with him."

Hal was surprised by the fierceness in his voice, for he'd never known Tom to get enthused about killing anybody. The change pleased him, though, and he knew they were going to enjoy tracking down and murdering the little bastard. After all, the only good Indian was a dead Indian as far as he was concerned.

* * *

"Where the hell have you been?!" Burr demanded as he came upon Rori and Jake a short distance away from their camp. Burr reined in angrily beside her, his expression thunderous. He'd been worrying himself sick about her ever since he'd wakened a short time before to find she was gone. Thinking something terrible had happened, he'd saddled up as quickly as he could and had gone looking for her.

"I had business to take care of in town," Rori answered simply. She had never deliberately gone against his wishes before, but this had been something that she'd had to do, something she'd been driven to do.

"Let's get back to camp," he said sternly, giving her a hand and swinging her up behind him for the ride back.

In silence, they rode back to the low-burning campfire with Big Jake tagging easily along. Burr didn't speak again until they were settled in before the fire.

"Just what was so important that you had to go into town at night without telling me?" he challenged, his earlier concern having turned to full-blooded fury.

Rori gave a stubborn lift of her chin as she faced him. "I went to see Chance Broderick."

"You what?!" *Rori had gone to Broderick?!* Burr's anger plummeted to despair as he believed his worst fears had been confirmed. He had been right! She had been attracted to him! But now it was too late . . .

He had never dreamed Rori would be so brazen as to go to him, but then Rori had never shown any interest in a man before. It was his fault, all his fault, he mourned. He should have taught her about men. He should have told her so many things, and now . . .

"I went to see Broderick, and I told him that since you wouldn't take him to Doug, I would," Rori finished, a hint of the steely resolve that had fired her decision in her tone.

As quickly as the despair had hit Burr, it was gone. But his relief was short-lived when he realized what she'd actually agreed to do. The very situation he'd hoped to avoid was coming to pass. *Could things possibly get any worse?*

"You told him that you'd take him to his brother?" Burr repeated dumbly.

"Yes, I did."

"Even though you knew I'd already refused to do it?" he demanded.

"That's why I *had* to. Grampa, you know I've never gone against you before," Rori started, but he cut her off viciously.

"Then why are you doing it now?!"

"You always told me a man's word was his most important possession," she came back at him. "Are you telling me now that that was a lie?"

Rori's painful logic silenced Burr for a moment. Everything she'd said was true. *Damn, but she was a sharp one—just like her father,* he thought. *Stubborn like Jack was, too. Whenever Jack had been convinced he was right about something, nobody could change his mind.*

Burr wasn't sure if he was pleased to discover these traits in his granddaughter. The fierce determination Jack had shown had been a driving force, a motivating factor, but in Rori, a woman . . .

Burr realized then, with some chagrin, that he had no one to blame but himself for the way Rori had turned out. He'd raised her the only way he knew how, the same way he'd raised her father. He'd taught her to think clearly, judge fairly, and act according to her conscience. She was without guile—completely honest. She was a stranger to society's ways of manipulation and deceit, and it was no wonder that she'd reacted as she had.

"You know damn good and well that a man's word is his bond," he growled, caught in a web of his own making.

"Then you won't stand in the way of me takin' Broderick? I know you have your reasons for not wantin' to go, and I know you aren't gonna tell me what they are. But there's no reason why I can't take him, is there? I mean, the money, think of all the money he's offerin', and I know the mountains as good as anybody," she finished confidently.

"Rori, you just can't go gallivantin' off into the mountains alone with the man."

"Why not?" she asked innocently, her eyes wide with surprise.

"Because you're a girl, damn it!"

Rori's green-eyed gaze hardened. "What's that got to do with anything? You know I'm as good a tracker as any man, 'cept you! You always tell me that! You know I can ride and shoot and throw a knife straighter than just about anybody! Why just tonight, in Broderick's hotel room . . ."

"What about tonight in his hotel room?!"

Rori quickly explained about the ambush and the ensuing fight. "I did real good, Grampa. I got the one guy right in the shoulder," she finished, sounding quite pleased with herself. "I guess I showed Broderick. *I* was the one who rescued *him*. Now if I can just keep him from gettin' himself killed on the way up to Doug's mine . . ."

Rori smiled widely as she thought of how much she was going to enjoy showing the arrogant Broderick just how good she really was while they were making the trip. It had been hard enough for him to accept the fact that she'd saved him in the fight, and he thought she was a boy. If he ever found out she was a girl, she'd definitely have the last laugh.

At the nonchalant attitude, Burr was seized by fear. She could have just as easily been killed tonight! "Do you realize how close you came to getting seriously hurt?"

"Well, I'm fine," she dismissed, stubbornly resisting his attempts to frighten her.

"Right now you are, but what if the two men who got away decide to try to get the map again? God only knows if Broderick can handle a gun or not. You don't know if he'd be able to help you in a situation like that. You got lucky tonight, Rori, and I know you're good, but you aren't that good. Do you really think you could fight off the two of them single-handedly if they decide to come after Broderick again?" he argued, knowing that there was no way he could let her do this alone. He had to protect her. "I'm coming with you."

Chapter 5

The sky had grown light in the east. Standing in the window of his hotel room, Chance was watching for Rori in the street below. The aching soreness in his arm had prevented him from seeking any rest, so he'd used those long, dark, sleepless hours of the night to prepare for the journey. Now, Chance was dressed and his things were packed, but still there was no sign of him.

Long minutes passed, and as the day grew brighter, Chance scowled and turned away from the window. It occurred to him that Rori just might not show up after all, and he swore angrily under his breath at the thought. *Nothing had gone right so far. Why did he think things necessarily had to get easier?*

Not that Chance really believed things were going to get easier. For even though Rori had helped him last night, he still had no proof that the boy was good enough to lead him to Doug. *Hell,* he thought, *the kid might drag him up into the mountains and then get them good and lost!* That happy thought left Chance edgier than ever, and he paced his room like a caged animal.

A sound in the street drew him back to the window, and he looked out to see Rori riding slowly up the street on a big black-and-white pinto and leading a packhorse, his monster of a dog trailing lazily behind. Aggravated at the boy's seemingly casual attitude, Chance threw his saddlebags over his shoulder, grabbed up his rifle and bedroll with his good arm, and went down to meet him.

Rori glanced up at Chance's window as she reined in in front of the hotel. The room was dark, and she saw no sign of him. She wondered if he was even up and moving yet. The thought of the greenhorn Easterner still lying in bed after having been so anxious to get an early start left her chuckling.

Burr had insisted that they pack extra supplies just in case Doug needed anything, and it had taken her longer than she'd planned to get ready. She felt it was important to her to impress Broderick by keeping her word, and she was worried about being a few minutes late in meeting him.

When he wasn't out in front, champing at the bit to get going, Rori relaxed. Smiling in self-derision at her overblown concern with Broderick, she slipped easily from her mount. Big Jake came bounding up to her as she dropped lightly to the ground, and she bent to give him an affectionate pat on the head.

"You're a good boy, Jakie," she told him as he gazed up at her, with his big, brown saucer eyes filled with adoration. "You wait here for Grampa while I hurry inside and . . ."

"You just now worrying about hurrying?" Chance demanded, as he stalked out of the hotel to find her petting the dog.

"I . . . uh . . ." Rori jerked her head up to look at him and almost did a double take. The voice was the same, but . . . She stared openly. It was Chance Broderick all right, but he sure didn't look like any greenhorn. He was wearing a black Stetson pulled low across his brow, a navy-blue shirt that fit perfectly across his wide shoulders, dark, slim-fitting pants that clung to his heavily muscled thighs like a second skin, and boots. Though his clothes were new, they were perfectly suited for the kind of traveling they had to do through the mountains. Chance carried his Winchester rifle as if he knew what to do with it, and the holstered sidearm that rode low on his hip looked altogether too natural on him. Rori suddenly wondered if she might have underestimated the man.

Chance had been prepared to chide the youth unmercifully about his lateness, but he paused when he caught sight of the boy's discolored, battered cheek, feeling a moment of sympathy for him. His own arm was hurting pretty badly, so he knew Rori's face had to be just as painful.

Rori didn't know why he'd hesitated, but she was glad he had. Determined not to let him see the confusion she was feeling about him, she quickly took the offensive.

"It's good to see that you're up and about," she taunted as she gestured toward his injured arm. "I was wonderin' if you'd be movin' this morning."

"I'm moving, but I was beginning to wonder if you were," Chance countered sourly, sorry now that he'd even considered being nice to the boy. He realized with some irritation that there would be just no getting along with Rori. He was aggravating, headstrong, and obnoxious, and this was going to make the next few weeks seem long and tedious. Still, Chance told himself resignedly, Rori was the only hope he had to get to Doug.

"I'm here, ain't I?" Rori bristled.

"You're also late," Chance bit out tersely as he stepped coldly past the boy to where his own horse was tied up and waiting for him. "You had me wondering if you were going to show up at all," Chance remarked as he made short work of sliding his rifle into its scabbard and tying his bedroll to the back of his saddle.

"I told you I was takin' you!" His implied insult sent her temper soaring.

As she was speaking, Burr rode into view leading his packhorse, and Chance was surprised to see him.

"What's Burr doing here?" he asked Rori.

"He's goin' with us," she informed him crossly.

Relief, pure and sweet, swept through Chance, and he thanked God that he wasn't going to be stuck out in the wilderness with a young kid who was still wet behind the ears. He greeted the old man warmly when he drew to a halt near them.

"Burr, it's good to see you. Rori here tells me you've decided to go along."

"I'm riding with you," he affirmed.

"Good. I was worried about making the trip with just the boy. I didn't know that I could trust him, but now that you're coming with us . . ."

Chance continued to talk with Burr, unaware that Rori was glaring at him murderously from behind. *So he was worried about making the trip with her, was he?!* she seethed. *And he didn't think he could trust her?!* What did she have to do to prove herself to him?! She'd already shown him that she could fight just as good as he could! She'd saved his life!! Her expression was disgusted as she gathered up the reins to the two horses and swung up onto her horse Patch's back.

"Look, if you're ready, we gotta leave now. It's gonna be hotter than hell by afternoon." Her tone was nasty. "Big Jake, let's go!" Rori called her dog as she yanked a little too roughly on the reins. Big Jake ran to follow her as she turned her horse and headed out of town to the east, leaving her grampa and Chance behind.

"Rori's right, it's best to travel early." Burr watched her ride away. Having seen the look in her eyes when she started off, he knew exactly how angry she was, and the thought pleased him. His worries about her being attracted to Chance were fading. The longer she stayed mad at him, the better. If she was furious, then she would probably avoid Chance as much as possible during the trip, and that was exactly what Burr wanted—to keep these two apart.

"He's gone," Hal announced angrily as he came charging into their hidden campsite where Tom awaited him late that afternoon.

"What d'ya mean he's gone?!" Tom sat up abruptly, though the effort cost him.

"From what I could find out without askin' too many questions and makin' people suspicious, he rode out early this morning with the old man and the kid."

"Where were they goin'?"

"Nobody could say for sure, but they were headin' east."

"East? The only mountains to the east are the Superstitions . . ."

"And if we don't catch up with 'em before they get there, we ain't ever gonna find 'em! How soon can you ride?"

Tom moved his shoulder experimentally, and though

the pain was excruciating, his need for revenge was greater. "You're sure the Indian's with him?"

"Yep."

"Then I'll be ready when you are," he said firmly.

Hal smiled wolfishly at Tom's determination. "Good, I was hopin' you'd be feelin' up to it. I picked up all the supplies we'd need while I was in town. We'll leave at dawn."

Rori had ridden ahead of Burr and Chance all day, setting a strenuous pace as she led the way across the barren, boulder-strewn land. She'd found enormous satisfaction in forcing Chance to keep up. Easterner that he was, she'd hoped he would falter as the long hours in the saddle passed so she could show him that she was better on horseback. But, to her disappointment, he'd kept up, voicing no complaints as he rode side by side with Burr a short distance behind her.

It became obvious to Rori that Chance knew horses, for he neither pushed nor coddled his strong, sure-footed mount. Instead, he had handled the gleaming, black-coated gelding with a practiced, expert hand. This discovery grated on her, too, although she wasn't quite sure why.

Numerous times during the long hot ride, she thought of Chance's remark to Burr that morning and silently cursed herself for having ever agreed to take him. The man was an arrogant ass, and he deserved to be stuck in town. She couldn't imagine now why his opinion of her or Burr had ever mattered to her. As she neared their intended campsite, Rori slowed her horse and waited for them to catch up.

Chance had expected the trek to the mine to be hard, and he wasn't disappointed. As a boy he'd often questioned his mother's insistence that he learn to ride, but now he felt extremely grateful to her for her persistence in forcing him to master the art. Still, he was used to captaining a ship, not sitting a horse, and parts of his anatomy were definitely suffering the consequences.

Burr noticed the way Chance's posture in the saddle had changed as the day had passed, and he felt a grudging respect for him begin to grow. They had followed Rori's almost breakneck lead since setting out, and he hadn't uttered one word of complaint.

"We won't always be traveling this fast," Burr told him, his green eyes, which were so like Rori's, showing his concern for Chance's plight.

"Some days we'll be going faster?" Chance grinned.

"No. We won't be going any faster than this. I just wanted to get a quick start while the traveling was good. Rori told me about the trouble you had in town, and I didn't want to take any chances that we might be followed. But just in case you are wondering, the trail does get rougher and steeper up ahead . . . where there is a trail."

Chance bit back a groan of exhaustion, refusing to show either of them just how tired he really was. If a young boy like Rori could make this trip, then so could he. As sharp-tongued and obnoxious as the boy was, Chance wasn't about to set himself up for any humiliation. He would keep pace no matter what.

As they rode up to join Rori, who was sitting easily on his pinto, Chance wondered if the boy ever got tired. They'd been traveling for almost twelve hours with only a few short stops for water and food, and yet he looked as if he could go on for another twelve.

"You still want to stop here tonight?" Rori asked Burr as they reined in beside her. "We've still got some daylight left. We could go on."

"It's a good place." Burr understood why she'd ridden ahead of them all day, being mad at Broderick and all, but he wasn't about to let the horses suffer because of her temper. "The horses need rest."

Rori shrugged and led the way through a maze of massive rocks to a small clearing beside a small creek. They each took care of bedding down their own horse. Then Burr built a small fire while Rori saw to the food, a meal of dried beef and beans, and Chance refilled their canteens.

The cool, splashing water spelled relief for Chance, and he decided to wash up before eating. Setting the canteens down, he tossed his hat aside and stripped off his shirt. He got his soap from his belongings and washed as thoroughly as he could, taking care not to get the bandage on his knife wound wet. His arm had stiffened up on him during the long ride, and he massaged it gingerly now as he stood up to stretch.

Rori was busy preparing the meal when she accidentally looked up to see Chance kneeling beside the water, naked to the waist. Against her will, she found herself staring at him, hungrily devouring the sight of him—the hard, lean line of his jaw in profile, the way his dark hair curled slightly at the nape of his neck, and the obvious strength of his back and shoulders. Her gaze hesitated on his bandaged arm, and, remembering how bad it was, she gave him reluctant credit for having kept up with her all day. No matter what he was showing them, Rori knew Chance had to be exhausted, and, though she wouldn't consciously admit it, an inkling of respect for him was born in the heart of her at that moment.

Chance sensed that someone was watching him, and he glanced up to see Rori staring at him. Judging from the way the boy was looking at him, he wondered if he'd ever seen anyone bathe before, or even bathed himself for that matter.

"Want to join me?" he called to Rori, holding the soap out in offering.

The fact that he'd caught her watching him embarrassed her. "Nope. Don't see the need," she responded quickly.

"I didn't think you did," Chance said under his breath as he picked up his things and trudged back to the fire.

They settled down to eat the meal as darkness began to fall across the land.

"How long do you think it will be before we get to Doug?" Chance asked as he finished off the last of his food.

"Dependin' on the weather, if it stays dry, maybe another three weeks," Burr responded.

"Where is this place anyway?"

"See that range off in the distance?" The old tracker pointed toward the craggy mountains that shone blood-red in the reflection of the setting sun. At Chance's answering nod, he went on. "You're going right into the heart of them."

"Are they as treacherous as they look?" he asked as he studied the distant, menacing peaks.

"Worse," Rori piped in, enjoying the thought of worrying him. "There ain't much water, and what there is, is usually bad. There ain't no trails either, in or out. There's been some Apache trouble, too. They believe the mountains are the home of their gods, and they don't take to anybody ridin' in there uninvited. Me and Grampa always make it through, though," she bragged. "We know them mountains real good."

"If they're that dangerous, how is it that you've managed to travel safely through there so often? Are you Apache?"

"No, I ain't Apache!" Rori denied heatedly, her eyes sparking emerald fire at his suggestion. Everyone with half a brain knew the Apache were wild, vicious killers. "My mother was a Pima," she told him proudly. "They're a gentle, peaceful tribe! They ain't nothing like the damned Apache! Why, an Apache'd just as soon kill you as look at you."

At Rori's description of the hated nomad tribe, Chance couldn't help but smile, for it seemed to him that the boy was describing himself during their first encounter.

Rori thought he was laughing at her Indian blood, and she bristled, glaring at him across the campfire. "What are you thinkin's so funny?"

"You have to admit that you fit the description of an Apache yesterday."

"I was riled," she told him, her eyes narrowing dangerously. "Pimas may be peaceable, but they can be just as deadly as the Apache when they're riled. You should remember that."

"I will," Chance said smoothly, wondering why their every conversation ended in confrontation. Lord knows, he didn't want to spend the entire trip at odds with the boy. He had enough on his mind just worrying about Doug.

"Rori . . ." Burr scolded, and she sat back, scowling at them both. He then went on to answer Chance's question. "We manage to get through there because we're cautious, because we know the land and respect it, and because we know our enemies and steer clear of them."

"That sounds like pretty good advice just for living," he commented.

"I've been living by those rules for fifteen years now, and we're still alive." Burr's gaze was warm upon Rori as he was lost in a momentary haze of remembrance. Everything he'd said was true, except for one thing. There were enemies he hadn't tried to avoid—Jack and Atallie's murderers. In the beginning, he'd searched tirelessly for them until he'd realized how hard it was on Rori, and he'd forced himself to quit. He'd regretted that throughout the years. The memory of their brutality was still with him, and though he hadn't found them yet, he knew that someday he would.

"If traveling up there is so hazardous, how did Doug ever manage to find a mine?" Chance was truly curious. His brother had always been the adventurous sort, but, though he would try anything once, he was not the kind who could get himself out of trouble once he was in it. His presence here now was proof enough of that.

"Nilakla took him," Rori answered.

"Nilakla?"

"She's his woman," she elaborated matter-of-factly. "She'd heard the talk among her people of the untold riches hidden in the Superstitions and left everything behind to take Doug up there."

"This Nilakla must love my brother very much."

"She does. She's a Pima like my mother, and Pima women love deeply and only once. They're totally devoted to their men and their families!" Rori was thinking of her own mother and suddenly realized how sentimental she was sounding. She gave herself a mental shake.

Chance was not surprised to discover that an Indian maiden had fallen under the spell of Doug's blond good looks and flattery. Doug had always been a womanizer, and now it looked as though he'd used his charming ways to find the wealth he'd always been searching for.

Thinking of what Rori had just told him about Pima women, he wondered why the boy, young as he was, was living with his grandfather and not with his parents.

"Does your mother know Nilakla?"

Rori stiffened perceptibly at his innocently put question. "No," she answered curtly. "My mother's dead. My father, too."

"I'm sorry."

"Why are you sorry? Aren't you like all the others?

The only good Indian is a dead Indian?" She came to her feet.

Chance felt a twinge of pity for this youngster who'd lost so much. He looked up and met the boy's accusing gaze levelly. "No. I'm not like all the others."

Rori saw the sympathy that was reflected in his eyes for a moment, and she reacted stormily to it. She didn't want any kindness from Chance Broderick! She didn't want anything from him! She hated him!

"Well, you've yet to prove it by me, mister!" And with that she stalked off into the concealing darkness, her dog at her heels.

Burr watched Rori go and understood her need to get away. He waited awhile before he broached the subject to Chance.

"My son and his wife were murdered when Rori was three."

"How? Why?"

"Jack and Atallie had a small homestead off in the wilderness. Some whites decided that an Indian lover and his squaw didn't deserve to live. Rori was such a little thing . . . but sometimes I think the child remembers."

"He was there?"

"Through the whole ordeal. I managed to get there before Jack, my son, died. I promised him I'd raise Rori."

"Did you catch the ones who did it?"

"No," he said slowly. "They were long gone by the time I showed up. I had some leads, but with Rori being so young, I had to give it up. Someday, though, I'll find them. They won't be able to escape me forever." He vowed the last with a fierceness that left no doubt about his dedication to locating the villains.

Both men fell silent, Burr thinking of the past and Chance thinking of Rori. It was easy for Chance to understand the boy's hostility toward him now that he knew his background. Despite Burr's best effort to be both mother and father to Rori and ease the pain of his terrible loss, there had been no way he could shelter his grandson completely from the bigoted hatred in the world. Rori's fight with the white boys in town was proof of that, and so the boy had grown up angry and defensive, always expecting the worst out of whites and never being disappointed.

Chance knew, despite Rori's rough edges, that Burr had done a good job raising him, for there was a definite sense of love, honor, and caring between them. Perhaps time would change things and eventually the boy would be fully accepted into society. Human nature being what it was, he doubted it would happen any time soon.

Chance shrugged back into his shirt and then bedded down by the light of the dwindling fire. As he lay quietly, staring into the flickering, dying flames, Chance found himself hoping that he'd get the opportunity over the next week or so to show Rori that not all white men were evil.

Burr stretched out in his bedroll, feeling good about their first day on the trail. It was plain that Broderick had no idea Rori was a girl, and that eased his mind considerably. The pretense only had to hold up for another three weeks, and then his worries would be over. Since Doug and Nilakla both knew the truth about Rori, there was no way he could keep it from coming out when they got to the diggings. Satisfied that things weren't as bad as he'd initially thought, Burr closed his eyes and promptly fell asleep.

Hidden by the night, Rori stood on the far side of the creek, staring back toward the camp. Her emotions were in turmoil as her gaze followed Chance's every move. She watched in silence as he favored his sore arm while drawing on his shirt, and she felt disappointed somehow when he buttoned it up.

There was no denying to herself that she thought him the most handsome man she'd ever seen. He *was* attractive. But it troubled Rori that she was letting him distract her so much. So what if he was good-looking? Burr had always told her that it was the inside of a man that counted, not the outside.

Rori knew what Chance was really like, had known since that first moment when he'd butted into her business. He was overbearing and insulting and . . . and . . . she couldn't stand him! She just didn't understand why she let him bother her so much, when she hated him. Usually when she had no use for someone, she simply ignored them and stayed out of their way—live and let live. Yet with Chance, she felt almost driven to prove her worth to him, and she didn't know why.

Rori shivered as a slight cooling breeze stirred the night. She rubbed her arms to ward off the chill that threatened and started back to camp. When she reached the site both men were already asleep. Safely alone and unobserved, she quietly moved near Chance and studied him close up, committing to memory every detail of the rugged planes and angles of his face. Unguarded in sleep, he looked strong and manly, yet somehow boyish, and she was filled with a longing to reach out and touch him. Her common sense dictated that she was crazy to even think of such a thing, and after long moments of staring down at him, she moved silently to her own bedroll.

As Rori drifted off to a troubled sleep, Big Jake curled by her side, her last conscious thought was of the white man and what he was going to say when he finally discovered she was a girl.

Chapter 6

The first glimmer of the new day found Rori up and moving. Her idea of bathing was a quick splash of cold creek water on her face, and that done, she jammed her hat on her head and hurried off to tend the horses. Big Jake stayed close by her side as she worked, and she talked to him endlessly in the loving tone she reserved only for him.

"What d'ya think, big guy?" she was asking as she fed her pinto. "Shall we run him ragged again today and see what he's really made of?"

The dog cocked his head, his expression almost comically serious, as if he thought there was some great significance to her conversation.

Rori gave a light laugh as she continued her chore. "Tenderfoot that he is, I'll just bet he'll be achin' from one end to the other when he gets up." Big Jake gave a strange, throaty whine, but she didn't pay any attention. "It'll sure be interesting to see if he's even walkin' today."

"*He's* walking." Though he wasn't exactly in the best of shape, Chance wasn't about to let on, and his tone was droll as he interrupted Rori's vengeful reverie. "And he's feeling fine, thank you." He bent to scratch the lolling hound behind the ears and was rewarded with a wet lick on the hand and a welcoming wag of his tail. "Good boy, Big Jake."

Rori felt the heat rise to her face, and she shot her pet an angry glare for being so friendly with Chance. He noticed Rori's embarrassment and chuckled.

"If you think a long day in the saddle is going to wear me down, you're wrong. I've been riding since I was young. They do have horses back East, you know, in case Burr never told you."

"I know what they got back East! They got a heap of interferin', eavesdroppin' jackasses! That's what they got!"

"You still angry about my interrupting your fight the other day?" Chance asked, trying to make peace with the boy.

"I ain't angry about nuthin'," Rori sulked, turning away from him. "I just plain don't like you."

"Well, that's honest enough on your part," he responded with good humor.

"I'm always honest. I believe in sayin' what I think."

"So I've learned," he drawled. "Well, listen, Burr's got a fire going, so I'll make some coffee and then we can head out. I'll be ready when you are." Chance gave Big Jake one last pat on the head and walked away.

Rori waited until he was out of earshot and then turned on her dog. "Traitor! How could you let him pet you? And how could you lick him?!" she hissed. "Don't you know he's a white man?!"

Big Jake gave a whimper at her harsh tone and lowered himself slowly to the ground, resting his massive head on his front paws as he gazed up at his mistress with a hurt look in his eyes.

"I just don't know what's gotten into you, Jakie." She stood in a threatening posture, her hands on her hips, but she softened her voice a bit as she saw his distressed expression. "You're usually such a good judge of character . . ." Puzzled, she turned back to her work.

Less than a half hour later, they were on their way again. Rori led off, and though she kept up a goodly pace across the rocky, parched land, she did not try to match her speed of the previous day. Burr had seen the two of them talking that morning, but since there had been no change in her attitude toward Broderick, he hadn't worried. Chance had mounted up and ridden out, determined to find some way to win Rori over. But as he rode along behind the boy, he could see the stiff unyielding set of his shoulders, and he knew it wasn't going to be easy.

It was late afternoon when they finally drew near the Superstitions. The mountain range rose abruptly from the cactus-studded desert in craggy, desolate splendor. There was nothing really beautiful about the arid, volcanic peaks. There were no sparkling, snow-fed streams or full-bodied pines to soften their jagged presence. They were as harsh and unforgiving as the land surrounding them.

Rori fell back from her distant lead so they could stay together as they started down the rocky valley that led to the interior.

"You want to stop for the night at the watering hole?" she asked Burr.

"We'd better. As little rain as there's been, it wouldn't do to count on there being water farther on and coming up dry."

Rori nodded in agreement and kneed her mount to action again. They headed straight up the middle of the canyon for the only watering hole around. The afternoon shadows were already lengthening as they reached the small pool and set up camp.

Rori was down by the water's edge letting her horse drink his fill when she caught sight of a jackrabbit a short distance away. The thought of a hot meal appealed to her, so she went to get her rifle after unsaddling and hobbling Patch.

"I'm going to catch us some dinner, Grampa," she told Burr, who was building a fire. "There's some good-sized rabbits around."

"Hope your aim is steady tonight," he teased. "It seems to me that the last time you went out to hunt us up some dinner, we ended up eating hardtack."

She gave him a dirty look that was tinged with humor. "How was I supposed to know that there was a damned coyote around who was faster than I was *and* hungrier? There wasn't much of the rabbit left by the time I showed up, and what there was, the ornery, selfish creature took with him."

"Well, I hope you have better luck this time."

Chance had been listening to their conversation and asked, "Mind if I go along?"

Rori almost threw her hands up in frustration. Why in the world would he want to go along? Just because he'd proven to her that he could ride didn't mean he could shoot. The last thing she needed was a rank amateur hunting with her.

"I hunt alone," she declared. "C'mon, Jakie."

Chance watched Rori stalk off with something akin to amusement. The boy was as prickly as one of the damned cactus that surrounded them.

"Jakie?" Rori had gone some distance before she realized that her faithful companion was not following her. Looking back, she saw the disloyal mutt sitting halfway between Chance and her.

"C'mon, dog!" she ordered, but her traitorous, four-legged friend totally ignored her. Getting up, Big Jake trotted off after Chance, who was heading away from camp in the opposite direction, his rifle in hand.

Rori scowled blackly as she watched Big Jake go after

Chance, and she felt the sting of tears in her eyes at the thought that he had chosen the white man over her. Determination filled her as she fought down the hurt of his desertion. Since Broderick was so sure he could hunt, she'd just go on out by herself and show him who the best shot was around here. She'd bag the biggest rabbit and enjoy watching him eat crow all night. Her course of action decided she moved off into the desert in search of her prey.

Chance moved with a quiet, cautious tread through the low-growing brush. The dry, sandy Arizona countryside was a far cry from the lush greenery of his New England home state, but he figured that hunting a rabbit was hunting a rabbit. It couldn't be any more difficult than it was at home.

The thought that Big Jake had come with him pleased Chance, and he wondered if the dog had any hunter in him at all. As they traveled far afield, it became evident to Chance that the mutt was not exactly of the setter variety. Though he stayed quietly by his side, he did not run ahead to flush any of the furry, fast-footed animals out so he could get a clear shot at them.

Finally it happened. A well-fed hare darted forth from the underbrush and paused motionlessly about fifteen feet ahead of them. Chance could almost taste his dinner . . . roasted rabbit. He moved with the utmost of care, slowly bringing his rifle to bear upon the unsuspecting, soon-to-be meal.

It was almost as if it had been planned, and it definitely left Chance wondering. He had the rabbit dead in his sights, and an instant before he squeezed the trigger, Big Jake barked and charged at the animal. Alerted to their presence, the hare fled to safety in a bramble bush as Jake dashed toward it. Chance's shot missed, whizzing by harmlessly.

Chance's expression was one of disbelief when he

turned to look down at the dog as he came strolling leisurely back to him. "Why in the hell did you do that?" he demanded.

Jake, however, was unthreatened by Chance's annoyed tone, and he sat down easily beside him, wagging his tail. The expression on his face was ridiculously innocent, yet Chance sensed that there was nothing innocent about this animal. He was smart, much too smart. Chance could see it in his eyes. He seemed almost human.

"That was dinner you just scared off, you ornery mutt!" He couldn't resist the temptation to reach down, and pet him.

A shot sounded in the distance, and Big Jake cocked his head as if considering the source. After a moment's pause, he gave a little bark and jumped to his feet. He circled Chance excitedly a couple of times before racing off back toward their camp.

Chance shook his head incredulously, wondering if the dog had deliberately sabotaged his shot. Dismissing the idea as preposterous, he took one last look around in hopes of spotting another rabbit. The area was completely deserted now, so he gave up. Annoyed and empty-handed, he followed after Jake.

Rori had heard Chance's shot and cursed her own lack of quarry. She'd been searching nonstop since she'd left camp, and she couldn't find another rabbit to save her soul. Frustrated and fearing that she was going to be the one swallowing her pride at dinner, Rori refused to return just yet. Instead, she continued on, tense and ready to match what she believed was Chance's triumph.

The hare came out of nowhere, but alert as she was, Rori did not miss the opportunity. With perfect aim, she drew a bead on the racing critter and fired, killing it instantly. She almost shouted in excitement. Though a competition hadn't been declared, Rori knew she'd take great satisfaction in having Chance see just how good she was with a gun. Grabbing up the rabbit, she started back proudly.

Big Jake was waiting for her, and he raced to her side as she came into view, barking a happy welcome.

"Get away. Go on," she told him as she kept on walking and tried not to look too pleased about his warm greeting. "You think I'm supposed to be glad to see you?"

Jake gave such a pitiful whine that she couldn't help but smile. He knew she could never stay mad at him for long. "Well, I didn't need you anyway. See." Rori held up her rabbit for his inspection. "We ain't gonna starve tonight."

"Congratulations on your luck," Chance said as she entered the encampment carrying her prize.

"There wasn't no luck involved. It was just plain, good shootin'," Rori bragged and then asked, "Where's yours? I heard you shoot."

"Mine's probably sitting out there in the brush somewhere having a real good laugh."

"So you missed?" The news delighted her.

"Thanks to Big Jake, I did."

"Jakie? What did he do?" Rori was surprised by this, and she looked from Chance to the carefree mongrel in puzzlement.

"Well, after being quiet during the entire hunt, the first time I got a chance to shoot, he decided to bark."

"And the rabbit got away?" she asked, trying to keep from laughing at her dog's duplicity. Had Jakie known it was important to her to outshoot Chance? Had he gone with him deliberately? She glanced at her pet and saw how eagerly he was waiting for her praise.

"And the rabbit got away," he confirmed.

"That's a shame." Rori fought to keep her delight at his failure from showing. "You know, it's kinda strange, though, 'cause it ain't like Jakie to make a bunch of noise when he's out huntin' with me," she remarked as she hunkered down and started cleaning the rabbit.

"Well, from now on then, he can stay with you," Chance told Rori.

Rori gave a derisive snort as she continued to prepare the rabbit for cooking. "Big Jake belongs with me, but I doubt it was his fault you missed your shot."

"Maybe, maybe not," he responded tightly, trying to ignore Rori's insult. "I was thinking that you might have deliberately trained him that way."

His remark caused her to laugh out loud. "I've taught him a lot of things, but I never taught him to do that. He's a smart dog, though. He probably figured out all by himself that you wouldn't be able to shoot the thing, so he tried to catch it by himself."

The night before Chance had thought to befriend the boy, but now he was having a rapid change of heart. Rori's sharp tongue and abrasive ways were wearing thin his good intentions. Right now, all he wanted to do was to turn the mean-spirited youth over his knee and paddle him. Since kindness wasn't making an impression on him, maybe a good beating would shut him up.

Chance let the thought pass by, though, for Rori was probably expecting him to react that way. The boy had accused him of being just like other whites, and if he reacted to his dislike with anger or violence, he would only be reinforcing the already low opinion he had of them.

Burr's call interrupted their testy exchange, and they both looked up to see the old man heading their way.

"What is it, Grampa?"

"I thought I'd scout around a bit before it gets too dark," Burr informed them. "It gets a mite more treacherous up ahead a ways, and I just want to make sure nothing's changed since we came through here last." He had heard from some of the prospectors in town that there had been some small earthquakes in the area, and he wanted to be certain that their way was clear, for it was a long, tedious, and dangerous trip to the next overnight stop.

When he'd gone, Rori ignored Chance and turned her full attention back to skinning the rabbit. Chance decided to take the time to wash up, and he unself-consciously stripped down to the waist again and began scrubbing off the day's trail dirt. The bandage on his arm was in need of changing, so when he'd finished washing, he got the medical supplies he needed from his saddlebags and approached Rori.

"I could use your help, if you can spare me a few minutes. I've got to change the dressing."

Rori swallowed with some difficulty. She'd been trying her darnedest not to watch Chance as he bathed, but she'd found it impossible to keep her eyes off him. From beneath lowered lids, she'd observed his every move, watching as he stripped away the binding and then scrubbed himself with the soap. Rori found that she wished she was the one doing the scrubbing. The sight of his nearly naked male form left her filled with a curious yet very disturbing aching deep within her.

Now, here he was, wanting her help in wrapping his arm again. There was no way she could refuse, although that was exactly what she wanted to do. Rori didn't want to touch him again as she remembered far too clearly how overpowering being near him had been and how the touch of his rock-hard thigh had felt like a brand against hers. The strangeness of her feelings distressed her. She didn't know what they meant or how to handle them.

Having finished cleaning the rabbit, Rori could see no way to avoid the intimacy the act would require. She was careful to keep the panic that welled up inside her under control as he came to stand beside her.

Squinting against the sun, she looked up at him. He appeared to be some massive, God-like creature as he towered over her, silhouetted by the sun, and to her annoyance, her pulse quickened.

"I gotta finish up here first," Rori told him abruptly, nervously. Trying to stall him as long as she could, she stood up and put the meat on the roast before walking down to the watering hole.

Chance followed. When Rori knelt to wash her hands, he sat down right next to her, and she almost groaned out loud in frustration.

"All right," she said tersely, "I'm ready now."

"Good." He handed her the supplies.

Turning toward him, still on her knees, Rori tried to remain clinically detached. *All I'm doing is putting a bandage on his arm, for heaven's sake!* Rori told herself. *There's no reason why I should let it bother me this way, no reason at all!*

The wound was an ugly slash, but it appeared to be healing nicely. Hurrying so she could get the whole ordeal over with, she applied the salve with less than a gentle touch, and Chance flinched.

"If you had an Indian name, it'd probably be Iron-claw!" he snapped. He knew he should have expected less than compassionate care from Rori, but he never thought the boy would try to break the wound open again.

"Sorry," she muttered resentfully. She hadn't meant to deliberately hurt him. She just wanted to get done!

With a lighter touch, she continued to put the medicine on.

His skin felt hot beneath her fingers, and a current of unnerving emotion shot through her. An inner warmth heated her, and Rori paused in her efforts. Lifting her gaze from his arm for a moment, she stared at his profile. What was there about this man that he could stir these feelings within her? Why did just touching him cause her pulse to quicken and her breath to catch in her throat?

Chance had been bracing himself for another painful, "helpful" assault on his arm, and when Rori stopped for a minute, he was puzzled. He turned his head to look at the boy, wondering what it was that had caused him to pause.

Even with the protection of her floppy-brimmed hat, his gaze managed to collide with Rori's, and the emotion he saw reflected there took him completely by surprise. For just an instant, it looked as if the youth was actually sorry that he'd hurt him. The discovery pleased Chance, and he hoped that he might be making some progress with him.

"Something wrong?" he asked casually.

"No." Rori jerked her head down, tearing her gaze away from his and forcing herself to concentrate on the matter at hand.

"Look, if the sight of this little knife cut bothers you, I can wait for Burr to help me," Chance teased.

Rori, however, thought he was mocking her. "Hell, this little scratch you're so worried about don't bother me none!" she countered. "It's so small, I was just wonderin' why you been favorin' it so much. My cheek was cut worse than this . . ."

Chance lifted a hand to brush Rori's hat back so he could get a better look at his face. He frowned as he studied the marred cheek. The cut where the rock had hit the boy was beginning to heal, but his cheek was still slightly swollen and a colorful combination of reddish purple, black, and blue. Chance knew it had to hurt, and it amazed him that Rori hadn't once complained.

"It still is worse than this," he said, glancing down at his own arm. "Why don't you clean it up and put some of that salve on it? Here, I can do it for you."

Before Rori could respond, he tore off a small piece of bandage cloth, wet it, and quickly lathered the soap into it. He turned to wash her cheek, but she pulled away from him.

"I don't need no tendin'. My cheek's just fine," she snarled.

"Like hell it is!" Chance grabbed the obstinate boy by the chin and forced him to look at him.

"No! Get your hands off me!"

"Hold still!" he commanded.

"I don't want you doin' nothin' for me, white man!"

"For once will you just shut up?!" He tightened his grip on Rori's chin. Then trying not to hurt him, Chance cautiously began to wash Rori's face. He scrubbed the damaged cheek with gentle strokes until he was satisfied that it was clean.

Rori had half a notion to physically fight to get away, but she knew it would be stupid to do so. Besides, there was a part of her that thought it was rather nice having Chance take care of her this way. She had almost lulled herself into enjoying his ministrations when he put the washcloth away and started to apply the salve. As his fingers touched her cheek, a thrill of excitement ten times stronger than anything she'd ever felt before surged through Rori. Her eyes flew open, and she stared at him in profound confusion.

Chance was completely unaware of the havoc he was wreaking on Rori's tender senses. When his eyes widened in surprise, he assumed that the medicine had hurt him in some way.

"See. I told you it needed doctoring. It hurts, doesn't it?"

Rori was relieved that he had no idea what the real problem was, but the smugness in his voice irritated her.

"Damn right it does! But I ain't one to carry on about such things!" She yanked away and pulled her hat back down low. "Now, leave me alone and let me do your arm."

Chance gave an indifferent shrug as he turned away to look out across the water.

Rori finished putting the medicine on the wound and then took up the bandages and began to wrap his arm. To do it right, she had to lean toward Chance, and suddenly she felt the heat of his body emanating from him. The headiness of his fresh, clean, manly scent surrounded her, and when her hands began to tremble, she rushed to complete the task.

"There. You're done," Rori said brusquely, getting hurriedly to her feet, desperate to get away. "I got to see to the meat."

As she moved back toward the cookfire, she silently cursed her bewildering reaction to him. Rori couldn't figure out what it was about Chance that always managed to upset her so. All she knew was that he unnerved her, and that made her angry.

Chapter 7

"Yep, it's just what I thought," Burr groused as they rode deeper into the narrow valley several days later.

"What is, Grampa?" Rori was curious, for he'd had little to say for the past few days.

"Abe and some of the other prospectors in town told me that there have been some tremors up here. Looks like they were right." He pointed farther ahead.

Where the way had been relatively clear several months ago on their last trip through, today massive boulders lay in a barricading jumble.

"It's going to be a mite tougher than I thought."

That was an understatement if Chance had ever heard one. "Just a mite?"

Burr knew the Easterner could handle his horse under normal riding conditions, but he was unsure of just how good he really was. "Maybe we should head out and circle around."

"How much longer will it take?" Chance worried. His concern for Doug had grown, and he was more anxious than ever to reach him.

"Another week, maybe two."

Chance was troubled by the news, and Rori saw it in his expression.

"We can still get through," Rori declared with bold

confidence. "Unless you're afraid to try," she added, giving him a speculative look.

"Rori, I don't know . . ." Burr was surprised by her challenge.

But Chance was more than willing to take the risk if it meant getting to Doug that much sooner. "It's all right, Burr. I'm willing to try it."

"You may be willing to try, but you also might end up dead," the old man pointed out. "This ain't any Sunday afternoon outing."

"I know that."

The old tracker was still doubtful. "I don't know . . ."

"I can handle it, Burr. Let's ride."

They moved onward, their attention focused unwaveringly ahead. The going was difficult, but not impossible as they picked their way carefully through the maze. By midafternoon, though, they'd reached what appeared to be an impasse.

Rori eyed the blocked passage before them. "What d'ya think? Can we get around it or maybe over it?" She studied the treacherous slant of the jumbled rock and soil of the valley's steep sides.

"I'll try goin' up this way. If I make it, I might be able to find some way through," Burr told them. With great caution he urged his sturdy mount up the incline. Even as good a horseman as he was, he found the going nearly impossible. Yet, after several attempts, he finally made it to a slight plateau.

"I'm going to ride on and see if there's a way through. I'll be back."

When Burr had disappeared from sight, Rori nudged the pinto closer to Chance's mount and handed him the reins to the packhorse.

"I'll try the other side while he's gone," Rori announced.

"Wait until Burr gets back."

Her eyes were glittering as she turned on him. "In case you forgot, Broderick, I'm the one who agreed to take you through here, not Burr." Rori had been harboring her anger toward him since the night before, and his lack of faith in her abilities was all that she'd needed to set her off.

"That's true enough, but Burr's a man full grown, and he knows the area."

"And I don't?" She was really furious now. "What's the matter? Don't you think I can do it?"

Chance gave Rori a strained look as he stated in exasperation, "I have no doubt that you can do anything you set your mind to. I just don't know why you'd want to take the risk before Burr gets back."

"I need to take the risk, because it's gettin' late, and the nearest water is an hour's hard ride on the other side."

"Then I'll go with you."

Rori snorted, laughing. "What good would you be? Even if you'd make it to the top, you wouldn't know what the hell to look for. Just stay here and keep a hold on them packhorses. If there's one thing we can't afford to lose it's them."

Chance knew the boy was right. "Then take it slow and be careful," he warned.

She shot him a mocking look, feeling better now that she'd made her point. "I'm always careful, Broderick. Big Jake, you stay here," she told her faithful pet as he sat watching her expectantly. He looked decidedly crestfallen at her order, but lay down in the dust as he was told.

As well as she knew Patch, Rori felt the sure-footed animal could make it. Putting her knees to his sides, she guided him up the opposite slope. The loose terrain slipped and crumbled dangerously beneath her, but she held fast, pushing her mount on with a steady hand and excellent judgment. Twice, just as they neared the top, the pinto stumbled, but quickly managed to right itself. Finally, in a burst of power, he lunged for solid ground.

Chance had been watching Rori's progress, and up until that moment, had believed that the boy was going to make it to the top safely. He was wrong.

In that last fateful charge, the pinto missed his mark and completely lost his footing. The ground broke beneath them, and they fell together heavily. Rori lost her seat as he went down. She careened down the rocky hillside and came to a rest and lay still about halfway up from the bottom.

The horse, neighing in terror, skidded backward, groping wildly to get a foothold on something. When he finally managed to stop himself, he stood immobile, shuddering in the aftermath of the close call with death.

Chance tossed the packhorses' reins into a bush, and then, giving no thought to his own safety, he dug his heels into his horse's flanks and fought his way up the incline with Big Jake at his side. It was a struggle, but he finally managed to rein in beside the fallen boy. Cursing Rori for his bullheaded foolhardiness, Chance vaulted to the ground and hurried to kneel next to him. Big Jake was already there ahead of him, whining worriedly and gently nudging the motionless Rori with his nose, but getting no response.

"Rori . . ."

The boy was unconscious, and Chance was worried that he might have broken something during the fall. Gingerly, he began to check his arms and legs with a light, exploring touch.

Chance had always thought of Rori as a tough little devil, for he looked tough, talked tough, and acted tough. He was shocked when his touch revealed, not the solid muscle and sinew he'd expected on the young boy, but a soft suppleness. Chance had no time to ponder the discovery, though, for Rori stirred and gave a low groan as he came around.

Rori had banged her head when she'd fallen and had lost consciousness. When she started to come around, it seemed every inch of her ached from the rough, wild tumble down the hillside. She groaned and lay still with her eyes closed, trying to figure out just how badly she'd hurt herself.

"Rori?"

At the sound of Chance's deep, velvety voice, so laced with worry and so close by, her eyes flew open. She was startled to find him looming over her, his expression dark with concern. Rori stared up at him for a moment, mesmerized, her eyes wide and filled with wonder as she marveled how it was he came to be so handsome.

"Rori . . . are you all right?" Chance saw Rori's dazed expression and feared that he'd suffered a head injury. When the boy didn't immediately respond, he sharpened his tone. "Rori?"

His impatient calling of her name finally broke through the strange haze that had enveloped her, and it was then that she realized he had his hands on her. Panic struck quickly.

"What the hell do you think you're doin'?" she demanded vehemently. "Didn't I tell you never to put your hands on me?!" She jerked almost violently away from his touch, scrambled free, and stood up.

"I was worried that you might have broken something."

"The only thing around here that's gonna be broken is your nose if you don't keep it out of my business!" she fumed irrationally, frightened as she realized just how close he'd come to finding out the truth.

Chance smiled as he sat back on his haunches to stare up at the irate boy. Obviously, Rori was fine. "Next time I think you're dead, I'll just leave you for the buzzards."

"You do that! They're better company! Where the hell is Patch?!"

Chance merely pointed behind her.

"Come on, Jakie!" she fumed. She turned her back on him and limped off to see to her horse, massaging her aching rear end as she went.

Chance laughed as he watched the boy stalk off with the dog trailing behind. "You know, it's no wonder that part of your anatomy is aching!"

"What's that supposed to mean?" she demanded, stopping rigidly in her tracks, momentarily fearful that he did know about her.

"Only that I thought you were tougher than that, but you're not. You're soft."

To Rori's horror, tears stung her eyes. Damn right, she was soft! She was a girl, damn it! Her fury immediately overcame the pain she felt at his jibe, and she knew a desperate need to kill. At that moment, if she'd had the strength to strangle him with her bare hands, she would have done it.

"I ain't soft, white man," she said through gritted teeth, despite the anger that left her shaking. "Don't ever believe it, 'cause there ain't nothin' soft about me."

Rori trudged on across the uneven ground toward her frightened mount. Drawing a ragged breath, she cursed herself for having failed after coming so close. The humiliation stung her deeply, adding fuel to the raging fire of her fury.

Rori reached Patch to find that he was shaken and scratched up a little bit, but otherwise uninjured. Her rebellious nature urged her to jump on the horse and make the attempt again, but her common sense and love for the animal held her back.

Taking up his reins, she started to lead him down the incline. To Rori's dismay, she discovered that Chance had already made his way down to the valley floor and was sitting there nonchalantly watching her descent. It irked her to see him looking so smug, and she longed for the opportunity to really show him up.

"Rori! Chance!"

At the sound of Burr's distant call, they both looked up to see him waving to them from the far side of the valley.

Burr had been about to tell them that he'd found a way through when he saw Rori walking her horse down the opposite slope. Even from this distance he could see that she was limping, and he realized that she'd been foolish enough to try to make it through on the other side.

"Rori! What happened? Are you all right?"

"I'm fine, Grampa, and so is Patch."

He accepted her answer for the moment, but was determined to find out all that had happened later. "There's a way through over here! It ain't easy, but it'll do," he shouted. "Come on up, but be careful!"

"We're on our way," Chance called back, and then turned to Rori who'd just reached the bottom of the hill, "You want to ride double with me? Your horse looks a little gimp."

Rori saw the way Patch was favoring his front leg, and she squatted down to check it. There appeared to be no real serious damage, but she could not deny that he was hurting. Rori knew she'd only be aggravating his injury if she tried to ride him right now, and since the packhorses were loaded too heavily to take on her additional weight, she had no choice in the matter. She was stuck riding with Broderick.

"He's sore," Rori finally admitted in disgust.

"Let's go then. Your grampa's waiting." Chance held out his hand to the boy, intending to help him up in front of him, but Rori stood immobile, staring at his proffered hand.

"If I'm ridin' with you, I ain't sittin' in front of you, Broderick. I'll sit behind you where I can keep an eye on you."

Chance just gave a rueful shake of his head as he extended his hand to her again. She grabbed it this time and swung lightly up on the back of his horse, grabbing the rim of the saddle to keep her seat.

"Put your arms around me," he ordered. "There's no way you're going to be able to stay on going up that hill if you don't."

Rori balked at the idea of touching Chance, but she knew he was right. Grudgingly, she linked her arms about his waist and held on as they started up the incline leading Patch and the other horses. Rori knew she could not afford to lean against him, so she held herself stiffly away from him.

Still, the feel of Chance's waist beneath her hands stirred strange feelings in Rori. The heat of him, coupled with the clean, manly scent that belonged only to him, sent her beleaguered senses soaring. Her breath caught in her throat as her heartbeat quickened, and she wondered for the first time in her life what it would be like to be held in a man's arms.

The thought was so shocking to her that she immediately dismissed it. *I hate this man!* she reminded herself forcefully. Yet even as she denied any attraction, she was haunted by images of his face, so filled with worry when he'd bent over her earlier after the accident. Her thoughts were spinning crazily as she tried to come to grips with what was happening. It seemed unfair that Chance could wreak such emotional havoc within her when he hadn't even guessed she was a girl!

Rori held on to that last thought, allowing it to

nurture her anger with Chance. She didn't know why she should feel anything for a man who was so stupid he couldn't tell a girl from a boy even up close! Satisfied that he was a complete idiot, she smiled to herself, pleased with her conclusion.

Chance was very much aware of how Rori was holding himself so far away from him, and it amused him. It would have been much more comfortable for the boy had he realized, but then there was nothing comfortable about Rori. It was clear that the boy didn't like physical contact, and Chance had really been surprised when he'd agreed to ride with him. Originally, he'd thought Rori would turn him down and walk up the far side instead. Chance wasn't quite sure why, but he was glad that Rori had accepted his offer.

Burr was not at all pleased to see the two of them riding together, but until he got to the bottom to what was going on, he knew he had to hold his tongue. He watched their approach, noting the way Rori held herself away from Chance. He kept his expression guarded, revealing nothing of his concern. He was greatly relieved when Rori quickly dismounted the minute they reached him on the narrow plateau.

"What happened to Patch?" Burr asked her casually as she came to him.

"I tried to go up the other side while you were gone, and we didn't make it to the top. His leg's not sprained, just sore, but I didn't think I should ride him through this."

Burr nodded. "He might have gone completely lame if you'd tried it."

"That's what we thought," Chance added.

"I'll ride the rest of the way with you, Grampa."

"All right, c'mon."

She climbed up behind Burr and held on to him

tightly. There was no fear in hanging on to her grampa, for he was solid and safe. The fear came from touching Chance, from the bewildering sensations that charged through her whenever he was near. It was a great relief to be away from him.

They headed on through the difficult passage, moving slowly because of the danger involved. They knew from Rori's fall just how deadly their trek could be. Burr took extra precaution as he led the way through the rock-jumbled labyrinth. The going was tricky and dangerous, but they finally made it through to the other side. Burr was concerned about Patch, and as soon as they were clear of the slide area, he stopped.

"Why're we stopping?" Chance asked.

"I want to rest Patch. Ain't no sense in running him ragged tonight, only to have him pull up completely lame tomorrow," Burr told him as they dismounted. "If we go easy on the water, we'll have enough to last until we reach the watering hole."

Rori knew Burr was right, but the fact that it was her fault the horse was hurt in the first place only served to heighten her humiliation. She realized now that it had been a reckless attempt on her part, and it didn't sit well with her. She'd always prided herself on being as good as any man, on being logical and careful in her decisions, yet today she'd fallen far short of that mark. She hadn't thought of the possible consequences if she'd failed . . . that she or Patch might have been killed in the fall. She'd only thought of the glory of showing up Chance.

The realization of her true motivation troubled Rori deeply, and she was abnormally quiet as she took care of her chores in setting up the camp. When everything was done, she wandered off a slight distance to be by herself for a while and think things through.

Burr saw her go and decided that this would be the

perfect time to talk with her alone. Telling Chance he'd be right back, he went off after her.

"Rori . . ." he called her name as he came up behind her.

Rori was startled to find that her grampa had followed her. "What is it, Grampa?"

"That's what I was about to ask you."

"What do you mean?" She tried to act innocent, but she knew Burr was far too perceptive for her own good.

"I mean, what really happened this afternoon?"

"I told you . . ."

"I know what you told me. Now I want the whole story. I want the truth. What's between you and Broderick?"

"Nothin'!" Rori answered quickly. "I hate the man, and it's perfectly obvious how he feels about me."

"Is it?"

She gave him a puzzled look as she answered, "You know it is! He thinks I'm a boy and an obnoxious one at that! You heard what he said in town. He was glad you'd changed your mind and were comin' along 'cause he didn't trust me! Do you believe it? After I saved his life, he still didn't think I was capable of takin' him through the mountains to his brother!"

Burr was watching her intently as she told him what she was feeling. Her color had heightened and her eyes were sparkling, and he felt his concern for her grow. She might not understand what it was she was feeling, but he did.

"So you've been trying to prove to him ever since that he was wrong," he concluded for her.

"You always taught me that I was as good as any man!" Rori retorted stubbornly.

"You are," Burr chided gently.

"I know that, Grampa, but he doesn't!" She glanced resentfully back toward the campsite.

"Does it really matter what he thinks, Rori?" Burr's perceptive gaze was steady upon her as he asked the question.

"It aggravates me, that's all," Rori defended stubbornly, but, in truth, she wanted to blurt out that, for some strange reason, it really did matter to her what Chance thought.

"Well, it'll all be over soon. In another few weeks, we'll be at the mine and after that you'll never have to see Broderick again."

"You're right," she agreed, wondering at the sudden shaft of pain that twisted her heart as she imagined never seeing him again. Why was it that her emotions had been in a constant state of flux ever since she'd met him? One minute she hated him beyond reason, and the next she found herself aching at the prospect of being parted from him. It defied explanation and left her perplexed and more than a little bewildered.

"Now let's just forget all this foolishness with Broderick. The only important thing is that we get him to Doug as fast as possible. I haven't seen any sign that we're being followed, but there's still the possibility that the men who ambushed Chance in town might come after us."

Rori frowned, thinking of the danger of a surprise attack in this rugged section of the country. "I'll keep watch, too, Grampa."

"Good." Burr studied her for a moment, taking in the clear, soft duskiness of her complexion, her wide, expressive green eyes with their gently arched brows and the sweet curve of her mouth. Rori was beautiful, and he wondered how it was that Chance had never seen through her disguise. Still, he was glad the younger man was blind to what was right before him. The last thing he needed was for the truth to come out too soon. Once they reached Doug and Nilakla, it wouldn't matter anymore.

Guilt assailed Burr just then—guilt over having hidden her femininity from the "civilized world." Yet, he dismissed it just as quickly as it came. What he had done, he had done because he loved her and for no other reason. Rori was happy, and he wanted her to stay that way. Her happiness was the only thing that was important to him.

"Coming back to camp now?" Burr asked her.

"In a little while. I think I'll just take a walk. Jakie?" she called out, looking around for her dog. To her aggravation, she finally spotted him settled in comfortably with Chance by the campfire.

"I'll be damned." Burr shook his head in amazement.

"Big Jake!" Rori commanded in irritation, and she watched in disgust as the big dog got to his feet and loped away from Chance.

"I've never seen that dog take to anybody the way he's taken to Chance," her grandfather remarked.

"Me, either, the stupid mutt," Rori muttered scathingly as he stopped at her side and looked up at her expectantly. She'd always thought Jake a good judge of character, but she was beginning to have her doubts. Giving the hound a dirty look, Rori moved stiffly off into the enveloping darkness. Jake looked to Burr for a moment in bewilderment as if trying to figure out what he'd done wrong, then gave a playful bark and chased after her.

Chapter 8

Chance had been enjoying the serenity of sitting quietly before the brightly burning fire with Big Jake when Rori had summoned him away. He watched the dog trot obediently off into the night to join his master, feeling slightly disappointed at the loss of his companionship. Chance didn't know why Jake had taken such an interest in him, but he was pleased. Since he'd taken to a life at sea, he'd had no time for pets, but he'd always loved animals, and dogs in particular.

When Jake had disappeared from sight and he was alone once again, Chance let his thoughts drift to Doug and his real reason for being there in the middle of the desert in the first place. In Boston, he'd been concerned about his brother, but not completely convinced that his situation was as desperate as he'd claimed. Now that he'd seen the land and had had a run-in with the kind of men Doug had been worried about, he believed the danger was very real.

The delay caused by the rockslide wasn't as bad as it could have been, but it had slowed them down. Chance only hoped that he wasn't too late to help Doug. His brother had gotten himself embroiled in difficult situations before, but nothing that even came close to this. As the sound of approaching footsteps interrupted his thoughts, he glanced up to see Burr returning.

"You look worried. Something troubling you?" the old tracker asked, seeing Chance's intense expression.

"Just Doug. I was worrying about not getting to him in time . . ."

"Doug'll be all right," Burr reassured him, "and we'll make it up to the mine in good time just as long as we don't get any nasty surprises."

"You mean this slide wasn't bad enough?"

"The land doesn't worry me. I know the land. It's people I don't trust." He looked out across the desert as he sat down opposite Chance.

"Like the two who attacked me in town?"

Burr nodded. "If they weren't hurt too bad, they might be after us now."

"Have you seen anything?"

"Not yet, but that doesn't mean they aren't out there. As bold as they were in ambushing you in your hotel room like they did, they won't quit too easily."

"I was afraid of that."

"Can you handle that sidearm you're packing?" He gave Chance a measuring look.

"I can shoot," he answered flatly, with no enthusiasm.

"I'm not asking you if you can shoot, boy," Burr snapped. "Any damned idiot can draw a gun and shoot. I'm asking you if you can kill a man."

Chance regarded him levelly, his expression a bit haunted as he remembered years past. "I fought in the war. I kill when I have to."

Burr grunted his approval as he gazed out across the dark surrounding countryside. "Let's just hope you don't have to this trip."

"Do you think it's likely?"

"Greed can turn men into animals—dangerous animals."

"You sound like you're speaking from experience."

Burr's eyes narrowed as he answered, "I've dealt with

my share of vipers. Some crawl on their bellies and some don't."

His elusive remark left Chance even more intrigued. "How is it that you came to the territory, Burr? Sometimes, listening to you talk, I get the feeling you haven't always lived here."

His expression immediately became guarded. "I've been here for as long as I care to remember" was his quixotic answer. "This is Rori's and my home. We're happy here, and I don't intend that we'll ever leave."

Chance felt as if he'd come up against a stone wall, so he let it drop for the moment. "How is Rori? He took a pretty rough tumble in the pass this afternoon."

"Rori's tough." Burr tried to dismiss his concern as nonchalantly as possible.

"That I know," Chance said ruefully as he remembered their earlier exchange. "I still don't see how he walked away from it."

"When you live out here in the wilds, you can't afford to stay down. If you ain't dying, you get up and move. Your survival depends on it."

"I'm beginning to see that," Chance agreed as he studied the desolate, night-shrouded desert. "Yet, even though the desert can be deadly, it does have a mysterious beauty about it. But I don't understand why a man who has everything would give it all up to come out here and search for gold."

"Maybe gold isn't the only thing a man's searching for when he comes to the territory," Burr offered solemnly.

Chance looked thoughtful. "It's just that it makes no sense for Doug to do this, though. Our family's wealthy, he's had the best schooling, he's easygoing and popular with the women. What else could he be looking for?" He thought of all the girls back in Boston who'd made a play for Doug, only to be discarded as he tired of them, and he grinned, feeling rather proud of his brother's amorous achievements. From what he'd seen, Doug's reputation as a playboy had been well earned.

Burr's shrug was eloquent. "Some men need more than money and women."

Chance pondered the old man's statement and quickly concluded it was true. He was living proof that success and riches did not automatically ensure contentment. Despite the fact that he'd parlayed the family business to even greater success and that he could have just about any woman in Boston he wanted, he'd taken to the seas, captaining one of his own ships.

The parallel between his own actions and Doug's generally unorthodox behavior surprised him a bit, and Chance found himself wondering if Doug got involved in all these adventures because he was trouble-prone or because he was searching for something more, something that couldn't be bought with the family's name and money?

"You're right." Chance gave a soft laugh. "Doug refused to go along with any of it. We considered him wild as a boy, always trying something new and different, always getting into trouble and needing to be rescued . . ."

"Doesn't sound like the Doug I know. The Doug I know works that mine tirelessly from dawn till dusk."

"Maybe he's finally found his happiness. Maybe this land has been the making of him."

"It's made many a man," Burr told him reflectively, "but it's broke more."

"I can see how it could. There's nothing easy or forgiving about this desert. It's a far cry from Boston and our family business, that's for sure."

"What business is that?"

"We're in shipping," Chance offered.

Burr gave him a look of respect at the news. "You a master?"

"I captain my own vessel, yes," he replied.

"No wonder you aren't used to being in the saddle all day." He chuckled. "Quite a change from riding the current, isn't it?"

Chance grinned widely. "Quite, but I'm growing used to it."

"You got other family back East? Doug's never said much." Burr's reason for asking was his own, and he waited tensely for his reply.

"Just our mother. Our father died years ago."

"No wives and kids?"

"No. Doug never seemed to settle for long with any one woman, and I'm away so much . . . Although I have to tell you, lately the idea's beginning to hold more appeal. It's a lonely life being a ship's captain."

"You got anyone in mind?"

Chance thought of Bethany and remembered their last encounter at the party. "Possibly. There's a beautiful, blue-eyed blonde named Bethany back in Boston . . ."

Rori stood deep in the shadows, listening to all that was being said. She hadn't meant to eavesdrop, but when the conversation had turned to Chance's family, she'd found herself avidly anticipating his every word. She wanted to know everything about him there was to know.

The news that the Brodericks were rich intimidated Rori. Then, when Chance mentioned that he was considering marriage to the gorgeous Bethany, her heart constricted painfully. Certainly, judging from the things Chance had said to her that night in the hotel room, they'd already been lovers. Did this blond, blue-eyed woman hold his heart, too?

Jealousy was a new emotion for Rori, and it struck her with an awful ferocity as she pictured Chance with the other woman. In the image Rori conjured up, Bethany was a vision of perfection, much like the ladies she had seen dressed up for a dance when she and Burr had been in town a few months before. At the time she had wondered why women would want to gussy themselves up that way, and she'd asked her grampa about it. He'd told her that the women usually dressed that way to please men, that men liked to see women looking "feminine." It hadn't bothered her then, but it did now.

Rori glanced down at herself in the darkness, as if seeing her worn buckskins and moccasins for the first time. With a trembling hand, she reached up to touch the brim of her raggedy hat and then her feather-decorated braids. There was nothing feminine about her . . . nothing.

Not that she cared one wit about trying to attract Chance! Rori denied hotly to herself. But even as she swore she didn't care about him, a small ache in her heart told her that she was lying. Admit it or not, she did feel something for this tall, handsome man who simply by touching her could send excitement tingling through her.

Was this love? The thought jarred her to the depths of her soul, and as quickly as the thought came, she put it from her. She did not love Chance Broderick! There was nothing lovable about him! He was a hateful, arrogant man, and she wanted nothing, absolutely nothing to do with him! After they reached Doug's mine in another few weeks, she would never see him again, and that would be a relief.

Big Jake's soft, low whine brought her back to the present, and Rori glanced down at her two-timing friend she'd been purposefully ignoring. "I don't like you, Jakie," she scolded.

Jake cocked his head and gave a weak wag of his tail as he stared up at her, trying to make sense out of her strange mood.

"Don't give me that innocent look." Rori glared at her pet. "You're my dog, not his."

Again, Jake wagged his tail.

"You're supposed to stay with me, not go lie by the fire with Broderick!" she told him. As she spoke, Rori felt her anger return and grow, and she was glad. Anger she could deal with. Anger she could understand and control. It was those other strange emotions that threatened to overwhelm her and filled her with uncertainty. They stole her confidence and left her floundering before their painful power, and she was glad that, for the moment, their hold upon her had faded.

Wearily, Rori tilted her head back and stared up at the star-spangled, moonlit heavens. Sometimes, just staring up into the vastness of the desert sky helped her to realize how really unimportant her daily troubles were in the scheme of things. Tonight, however, there was no soothing peace to fill her with contentment. Tonight, continuing thoughts of Chance bombarded her— Chance holding her tight against his side after the fight in town, Chance lying wounded on the bed in his hotel room, Chance bending over her, worrying about her after she'd fallen, and a hot flush of desire swept through her.

Rori almost screamed her frustration to the darkness. There had to be some way to push him from her thoughts—some way to escape these unnamed feelings that threatened to consume her! She drew a deep steadying breath and gritted her teeth against the heat that throbbed through her. She wouldn't feel these things for him! She wouldn't!

Regaining a somewhat shaky control, Rori started off at a brisk walk, heading even farther away from camp. Jake remained where he was and barked softly, questioningly, wondering at her wisdom in wandering off into the night.

"Look, either you're with me or you're not! I need to walk. Now, if you're comin', come on." Rori didn't wait to see what he'd do, she just kept on going.

Big Jake looked toward the camp and the men only once, then bounded into the night after her.

The night was quiet and cloudless. Unobstructed, the stars and moon cast their pale glow over the desert mountains and illuminated the small, hidden oasis with a silvery light.

The Indian woman who sat quietly alone in the clearing was exquisitely lovely. She wore the garments traditional to her tribe, a cotton skirt and blouse, but despite their looseness, they could not disguise the lithe curves of her body or the firmness of her breasts. Her waist-length black hair was unbound now as she combed out the heavy mass, and it fell about her in a satiny, protective veil.

Doug stood on a craggy precipice almost directly above Nilakla, his dark brown gaze focused on her and her alone. Nilakla was so beautiful . . . He could feel the heat stirring in his loins as he watched her, and his breathing grew tight in his chest. He longed to take her in his arms and kiss her, to run his hands through the silken, raven cascade of her hair. Lord knows, he wanted her, but . . .

Doug's conscience stabbed at him, momentarily stifling his burning desire for the woman who'd given him everything and asked nothing in return. Nilakla loved him completely, without reservation. It was that freely given devotion that troubled him now, for as each day passed and the prospect of Chance's arrival grew nearer, Doug knew his time with her was coming to an end.

When Chance showed up and they brought the gold out, Doug fully intended to return to Boston. He had made it on his own now, and having accomplished that, he wanted to resume his life there.

Yet, even as Doug planned to go back, a great sense of remorse filled him. He cared deeply for Nilakla, and he knew it would not be easy to be parted from her. She was laughter and gentleness and goodness. His life would be emptier without her, but there was no way he could take her back with him. She was an Indian, and she would never be able to find happiness in the unforgiving strictures of Boston society.

As if sensing his presence, Nilakla looked up from where she was sitting. She saw Douglas then, her blond lover, standing high above her on one of the craggy peaks watching her. Once again she was taken aback by how much she loved him. He was so tall, so masculine, and so handsome. Her black eyes met his brown ones fully and without guile, and though she couldn't read his expression at this distance, she could tell just by his tense stance that he wanted her.

"You want me, Douglas?" she asked, her voice husky with emotion as she held out a hand toward him in invitation.

At that moment, all thoughts of leaving her vanished from Doug's mind. He wasted no time in descending from the mountainous heights, moving straight to her to take her in his arms.

"Yes, Nilakla, I want you," Doug murmured, his lips seeking out the sweetness of her throat as his hands began an impatient exploration of her enticing curves. There was something about being close to her that drove him to distraction. In saner moments, whenever he thought of their abandoned lovemaking, he could never pinpoint just what it was that drove him to possess her with such passionate need—the womanly scent of her, the satiny feeling of her skin beneath his questing touch, the wantonness of her response to him . . . He only knew that he desired her more than he'd ever desired another woman. "I always want you . . ."

"And I, you, my Douglas . . . my love," Nilakla whispered the bittersweet confession. She knew he wanted her body. She knew he needed that much from her, but her heart ached because she also knew it could never be more than that.

Doug was waiting only for his brother to come to him, and when he did, Nilakla knew her love would go away and never return. She longed to cry out to Doug to stay with her forever, to be her love, her husband, but she realized that love is only worth having when it's freely given. She could not force him to stay with her, and she certainly would not plead with him. She would only make the last of their time together as wonderful as she could, giving him all she had to give and treasuring each moment.

Nilakla felt his body harden against hers, and eager to know him fully, she slipped her hands up to unbutton his shirt. She would tolerate no barriers between them when they were making love. She wanted his hot, driving body deep within hers, for it was only then that she felt Doug was completely hers. Doug was her only love, and Nilakla knew that when he left her she would never love again.

They discarded his clothing as quickly as they could and dropped to the ground together wrapped in each other's arms, famished for a taste of each other, naked flesh pressed to naked flesh. In silent desperation, Nilakla reached down and took him to her, guiding him into her soft, welcoming heat. She wanted to clasp him to her heart and hold him captive for all eternity within the circle of her arms. She loved him, and she couldn't bear to think of what she would do when she had to live without him.

Their mating was fierce with loving splendor. Nilakla

held nothing back, and Doug couldn't resist the openness and fullness of her passion. Their bodies one, they soared to the heights of physical pleasure, peaking as perfection was attained.

It was later, as they lay still bound together in love's embrace that Nilakla spoke. "I love you, Douglas," she told him, gazing up at him. As always, his blond good looks enthralled her, and with a single finger, she traced the hard planes and angles of his face. How handsome he was, and how different from her! They contrasted so greatly, but in that contrast, they also complemented. Where her hair was black as night, his was as bright as the day. Where his chest was hard and muscular, she was soft and lushly curved. Where his hips were narrow and powerfully, drivingly built, her hips were wide and perfectly made to accept him. She ran her finger across Doug's lips in a soft caress, thinking of how wonderfully he kissed and how much pleasure he could give her with his lips and tongue.

"You hold my heart, Douglas," Nilakla said.

His passion spent, her words reminded him again of her devotion in the face of his determination to leave her. The moment between them that had been so perfect a minute before suddenly left him feeling uncomfortable. He wondered whether it was fair to continue loving her this way, when he knew that some time soon he would have to go. Guilt stung him, and he disengaged himself from her embrace.

"Douglas?" she asked, clinging to him a little longer than she should have.

"I have to keep watch tonight," he said awkwardly as he moved away from her intoxicating warmth and began to dress.

Chilled by the abrupt end to what she'd hoped would be a long night of lovemaking, Nilakla said nothing. She only pushed herself to a sitting position as she watched him dress.

"I'll be late coming to bed." Doug spoke without meeting her gaze again. He found he was almost afraid to look at her, afraid that if he laid eyes upon her supple, golden flesh he wouldn't be able to stop himself from using her for his own pleasure again and again, all night long.

His words were like a knife to her heart, and Nilakla bit her lip to stop the pain that threatened. Already, he was distancing himself from her, already he wanted to be away from her. Her declarations of love and devotion meant nothing to him. Instead of binding him to her, she had pushed him that much farther away.

"I will be here waiting for you," Nilakla answered simply enough, hiding the agony of her heart.

Doug did not answer, but walked away into the darkness without looking back. She waited until he was gone and then slowly got to her feet. Nilakla stood quietly for a moment, her slender form sculpted by the pale moonlight, and then began to dress.

She struggled to find peace, but silent tears traced silvery trails down her cheeks. There was no point in trying to tell Douglas of the wonderful gift she had to give him . . . of the child she carried deep within her. She would not beg for his love. He must stay with her because it was his choice to do so, not because of some unexpected consequence of their passion. Nilakla held the secret locked in her heart and mourned the end that was near.

Chancellor Broderick . . . Douglas's brother . . . just the thought of him filled Nilakla with hatred. He represented the threat of Douglas's past and future to her, and she knew she would despise him when she finally met him. She dreaded his coming.

A sob caught in Nilakla's throat, and her tears began

to flow more freely as she imagined Doug leaving to go back East with his brother. The reality of her sorrow weighing heavily upon her, she turned wearily to her solitary bed.

Doug had walked a long distance from the mine, for he'd needed time to sort out his thoughts about Chance, the gold, and his future. Chance was everything Doug had always wanted to be, though few knew it as he had been careful to cultivate a devil-may-care attitude so no one would ever suspect. For as long as Doug could remember, Chance had been the logical one, the controlled one who thought every problem through carefully and then invariably picked the right choice. Doug knew he could never be as good as his brother, for Chance had always been successful in whatever he'd tried to do. His single-mindedness and hard-edged business sense had helped him develop Broderick Shipping from the moderately successful company it had been at the time of their father's death into the fantastically successful venture it was now, and Doug admired Chance for it.

There was no envy or jealousy in Doug's admiration of Chance. He loved his brother, idolized him really. Every time Doug had gotten himself into trouble chasing after one daring dream or another Chance had been there to save him, and this had only served to increase Doug's affection. This time, even though Doug had sent for him, things were going to be different when he arrived. Despite the fact that it had annoyed Doug to have to call on Chance for help, he wasn't calling because he was in a bad situation and needed rescuing as it had been in the past. Instead, he had called on his brother because he was the only person in the world he could trust to help him with the gold . . . the gold he had found and mined on his own.

Doug thought of Nilakla then and realized that he really hadn't done it alone. She had been the one who'd led him here, and she had been at his side ever since.

For a moment, Doug's heart warmed as he dwelled on her devoted support, and then he remembered Chance and Boston and all that his life had been before. He wanted to go back. He wanted to let everyone know that he'd managed to become successful in his own right. It was important to him. Yet, even as he told himself that he had to go back, he wondered why the thought of leaving Arizona and Nilakla left him feeling so torn and troubled.

Chapter 9

Rori was furious! Wouldn't anything ever go right in her life again?! The day had started off well enough, though she'd gotten little enough sleep the night before. They had loaded the packhorses and had been out on the trail just after sunup. Then, within the first half hour's ride, Patch had begun to limp. By the time they'd reached the watering hole, there was no hiding the fact that he needed more time to rest his sore leg.

Burr had had nothing much to say. He had merely dismounted and started to set up camp once again. Chance, however, had looked distressed over the thought of losing another day of traveling time in his quest to reach Doug, and though he didn't say anything, Rori felt the sting of his disapproval.

The guilt she felt irritated her, and her mood turned vile. Rori knew she wanted to be free of Chance. She wanted to deliver him to Doug and then get away from him. Yet, here they were stuck at the watering hole for another entire day, while she tried to nurse her horse back to health.

Rori led the limping steed to the water's edge and she knelt beside him to dampen her cloth in the pool. Though the water wasn't as cold as she would have liked, Rori knew she'd have to make do. Pressing the cool, sodden cloth to Patch's injured limb, she hoped the simple but effective remedy would render him trail-ready by morning. After a few minutes the motion of changing the compress became mechanical to her, and Rori found her gaze drifting to where Chance and her grampa stood talking.

"Is there anything that needs to be done? Anything I can help you with?" Chance asked the older man. It was only noon, and the day stretched ahead of them, long and empty. He was worried about Doug and tense over the delay, and he thought that if he kept busy the time might pass faster.

"Nope. There isn't anything to do right now but wait. I'm going to circle out and scout around a little bit, but it won't take me long. Just settle in and relax. Take advantage of it now, 'cause once we start back on the trail again, we'll be moving fast to make up for lost time," Burr told him as he mounted up and rode slowly from the camp.

Pleased that they would be trying to travel even faster once the horse was healed, Chance resigned himself to a day of idleness. He watched until Burr had disappeared from view and then moved off to get his saddle-bags. The day was turning into a scorcher, and since he hadn't had the opportunity to wash up the night before and hadn't really had a bath since they'd left town, the watering hole was beginning to look mighty inviting to him right now. He had time on his hands, so why not?

"How's the leg doing?" he asked as he came down to the bank beside Rori. He hadn't really paid much attention to the boy that morning except to notice how quickly he seemed to have recovered from his fall the day before.

"Patch'll be all right," Rori answered curtly. The last thing she wanted to do was engage Chance in conversation. She just wanted him to do whatever it was he'd come down here to do and leave her alone.

"Need any help?" he offered.

"Nope," she answered curtly, hoping to chase him away. "This is a one-man job, and I'm doin' it."

Chance fought back a smile at the boy's hostile attitude. Some things never changed. "Well, if you change your mind, I'll be right here," he declared as he dropped his saddlebags and began to unbutton his shirt.

"I ain't gonna change my mind," she declared stubbornly, trying to ignore him, wishing him gone. But when he started to strip off his shirt, she could ignore him no longer. Her eyes rounded, and she had to force her gaze away. *Damn him!* she silently cursed him. *He was going to wash up, right now . . . right here in front of her! Didn't that man ever get tired if bein' so damned clean?!*

She tried to think of something obnoxious to say to drive Chance away, but nothing came to mind. Instead, Rori found her gaze drawn back to him, and she watched him from beneath lowered lashes as he slipped his sweat-stained shirt from his broad shoulders. At the sight of the powerful width of his hair-roughened chest, she swallowed nervously and averted her gaze. He was too beautiful . . . too handsome . . . Patch whickered and stirred uncomfortably, and Rori realized with some embarrassment that she'd unconsciously tightened her grip on his leg.

"So Patch thinks you should have been named Iron-claw, too, does he?" Chance couldn't resist teasing the boy.

"You didn't seem to suffer none from my doctorin'," Rori shot back in agitation as she flushed under his jibe. She was glad that she had the horse between them so he couldn't see her.

Chance flexed his arm that still bore the bandage, and he was pleased to find that he suffered no pain at the movement. There was only a slight stiffness to remind him of the attack. He took off the bandage so he could inspect the healing injury. "You're right. Let's just hope you do as good a job on him as you did on me."

"You don't need to worry on that account. I'll do a better job on Patch. I like him," she declared.

Chance only chuckled in amusement at her barbed comment, and it irked her immensely. She hated it when he got the better of her in any of their exchanges, and it took nearly all of her considerable willpower not to continue their verbal sparring. Busying herself with the animal, she pretended to ignore him, when in truth she was tense and very much aware of his presence. Although she was trying to act normal, Patch picked up on her agitation and shifted restlessly beneath her healing hands.

"Sorry, boy. Easy now. We'll make this better just as fast as we can," she soothed, moving down the bank to soak the cloth again. She made sure to keep her back to Chance, for she wanted him to believe that she was totally indifferent to him.

Chance, however, was blissfully unaware of Rori's discomfort. He had his mind set on taking a bath and, after their initial exchange, had easily dismissed the ornery boy from his thoughts. The Lord only knew how soon they'd reach another watering hole out here in the desert, and since he had the time, he wanted to take advantage of it. Stripping off the rest of his clothes, he entered the water and dove quickly into its shallow depths.

Rori was in shock as she stared blankly at the spot where he'd disappeared beneath the surface. *The damned fool idiot was actually taking a bath and with no clothes on!* She'd caught just a glimpse of his nude body before he'd vanished into the cloudy water, and she was stunned. What was she supposed to do?

As much as she gave the appearance of being a boy, she was actually very much the innocent in things of this nature. Confusion filled her. She longed to stay where she was and watch Chance emerge from the water. He was a sleek, glorious male animal. Her curiosity about him was rampant, but her fear of him was greater, overpowering her other emotions. Knowing she had to get away quickly before he surfaced, she snatched up her cloth and rushed back to Patch. Rori knelt strategically beside the pinto so that her back was to the water.

The pool was barely waist-deep, but it was cool and refreshing. Exhilarated, Chance gave a deep, relaxed laugh as he gained his footing and stood up. The water swirled about his lean hips and buttocks, covering the most intimate parts of his body, but leaving much revealed—the muscle-corded width of his chest and powerful arms, the intriguing coarse, dark hair that furred his chest and trailed lower in an ever-narrowing "V," the hard, flat planes of his belly . . .

Rori heard him surface, but forced herself not to look up from her work. She wanted to appear as if she was busily tending her injured mount, not as if she was trying to avoid looking at him as he stood totally naked somewhere behind her.

Chance soaked in the cooling water for a few minutes longer, paying no attention to the busy youth at all. Only when he remembered that he'd forgotten to bring his soap in with him did he call out to Rori.

"Toss me the soap, will you, Rori? It's there among my things somewhere."

Rori stiffened, but did not stop her labors on the horse. "I'm busy," she snapped. "Get it yourself."

As soon as the words were out of her mouth, she knew she'd made a mistake. Surely, it would be better to hand him the soap while he was half submerged than to risk having him parading around her completely nude. When she heard him start moving in the water, grumbling about ungrateful wretches, she quickly rushed to do his bidding.

"Never mind! Wait a minute," she called out in what she hoped sounded like an exasperated, resentful tone and not a panicked one. Standing up, she threw her cloth at him without really looking. "Here! Wet this for me, and I'll get your soap."

Chance caught the cloth easily and soaked it for her as she dug through his saddlebags. Finally, the soap in hand, she took a deep breath and stood up, turning to look his way. Relief filled her when she discovered that he was standing in water deep enough to keep his more vital male parts hidden from her view. For the briefest of moments, she allowed her gaze to cling hungrily to him, studying the beauty of his male body. A liquid, honeyed warmth began to seep through her as she vividly remembered his hands upon her yesterday and how wonderful it had felt to be touched by him.

"Rori? The soap?" Chance's tone was impatient as he waited for the boy to throw him the soap.

Jarred back to reality, Rori threw the soap in his direction before abruptly turning away to head back toward Patch.

"Thanks," came Chance's reply, then he added, "Rori? Didn't you forget something?"

When Rori glanced back in aggravation, only her lightning fast reflexes saved her from taking the wet cloth square in the face. She snared it in midair, but was still soaked by the spray.

"Thanks," she snarled, wiping the water from her face.

"You're welcome." Chance chuckled as he began to wash. "Care to join me? You look like you could use a good scrubbing."

Rori shot him a venomous look. "Washin' so much ain't healthy."

"Says who?" he challenged in good humor.

"Says me," she replied stubbornly as she tried not to stare at him. He looked so unbelievably handsome when he was smiling and laughing. Rori deliberately turned her attention back to Patch's leg. "You know, I ain't never seen a man so concerned with keepin' himself all washed up as you. I'm beginnin' to think you're like those prissy misses I see in town."

At that, Chance gave a roar of laughter as he finished bathing. "I've been accused of chasing skirts in my time, but I never thought I'd be accused of wearing one."

"Might suit you," Rori returned arbitrarily.

"You're wrong there, Rori," Chance remarked. "I've always desired women, but I've never desired to be one."

She heard him moving out of the water, and she swore she wasn't going to look up at him, swore she wasn't going to pay him any mind at all. But suddenly he was there, striding from the water before her, magnificent and wonderful and very, very masculine.

Rori swallowed as her throat went dry. Had she somehow always known that he was this beautiful? Had she somehow intuitively realized that he was this wonderful and that was why she'd been responding to him as she had?

Chance appeared perfect in every way to her, and Rori wanted to imprint this vision of him on her memory. He was deeply tanned everywhere but on the narrow band of paleness about his flanks, and wet as he was, his golden skin glistened in the sunlight. His body was sculpted of rock-hard muscle from the width of his broad shoulders to his lean, hard hips and long, powerful legs. As her gaze dropped, she could no longer avoid seeing the part of him which made him male . . . very male, and though she was embarrassed, Rori was unable to stop staring at him. *So this was what men prided themselves on* . . . she mused as he turned slightly away from her.

Chance got his towel from his saddlebags and started to briskly dry himself. Noticing the unusual expression on the boy's face, he wondered at it.

"You got a problem, boy?" Chance demanded, turning to face Rori.

Horrified at being caught staring at him, she stumbled for something to say. "Nope. I ain't got no problem. Looks to me like you have, though."

"Oh?" His eyes narrowed.

"Yep, looks to me like I was right. Maybe a skirt would suit you better," she continued, digging herself in deeper as she gestured toward his maleness. "Jake's is bigger than yours . . . unless maybe yours shrunk 'cause you been washin' it so much . . ."

Chance prided himself on being relatively even-tempered, but something about the boy's attitude infuriated him. Completely unmindful of his nakedness, he went off like a rocket, snaring the youth by the back of his shirt and hauling him down to the water's edge.

"What the hell do you think you're doin', you no-good rotten bastard?" Rori demanded, struggling to be free.

"I'm tired of listening to you, and I was thinking that if I wash your mouth out with soap, maybe it'll shrink!!"

Chance snarled, and he grinned ferally when he saw Rori go pale in his grasp.

"Get your hands off of me, Broderick!" Rori was frightened, and she resorted to her old line of defense.

"What's the matter, boy? You afraid of a little soap and water?" Chance gave Rori a mean shake as he glared down at him.

"I ain't afraid of nothin'! Just let me go!"

"You're right. I really should let you go, shouldn't I?" He picked the boy up by both the seat of his pants and the scruff of his neck and tossed him bodily into the deepest section of the pool. When Rori came up for air, sputtering in indignation and frustrated fury, he laughed, grabbed up the soap, and tossed it in his general direction. "There's the soap. See what shrinks on you."

Without another word, Chance turned and walked back to where his clothing waited for him. He dressed nonchalantly, pointedly ignoring the outraged boy struggling in the water behind him.

Rori was livid as she sat miserably in the center of the watering hole, drenched to the skin. Her bottom was bruised along with her pride. *Damn him!! How dare he do this to her!!? How dare he manhandle her this way!!??* In fury, she pounded at the water's surface and only succeeded, if it was possible, in getting herself more wet. Her green-eyed glare shot daggers at Chance as he stood with his back turned toward her, coolly donning his clothing. Had she had her knife on her at that moment Rori would have gleefully thrown it at him.

Yet, even as her anger flared, Rori was stunned to find that a different kind of ache was swelling within her heart and that she was crying. She tried desperately to control the tears, but to no avail. They coursed freely down her cheeks, and for the first time, she was glad that she was soaked to the skin, for it helped to camouflage her tears.

When Chance walked away without even looking back, a muted sob tore from her throat, and Rori finally gave in to total misery. Why did Chance have the power to make her feel this way . . . so confused and ultimately helpless? She wanted to call him back to her . . . to strangle him for what he had done to her. Yet, at the same time, she wanted to be wrapped in his arms and held close to his chest.

Rori was visibly reminded of her pseudo-male identity as her hat bobbed limply by in the slow current of the water. She fished it out and studied it in disgust. She'd worn the hat for years and had never thought of it one way or the other. Now, however, she thought it the ugliest thing she'd ever seen. Glancing down at herself, Rori realized that the rest of her clothes were just as bad as the hat. Suddenly, she was aggravated that it mattered to her. She hated Chance, and with good reason, too!

Getting slowly to her feet, Rori stood in the middle of the pond, dripping wet and looking quite forlorn. As the water stilled about her, she looked down at her reflection and stared at the bedraggled, boyish image that stared back. Her dark hair was plastered to her head, and water trickled endlessly from the ends of her braids. She fingered one long braid, wondering how her hair would look hanging freely about her shoulders. Her eyes were wide and reasonably pretty, she thought, but her cheek still bore the mark of the fight she'd had in town, and she could pass no judgment on her own beauty. Wistfully, she wondered if she could ever look as beautiful as those ladies in town.

Rori sniffed loudly as she fought to bring her runaway emotions under control, and it was then that she discovered just how much she smelled like a very dead, very wet steer. Grimacing in distaste, she wondered in humiliation if Chance had always noticed that about her. The discovery left her self-conscious for the first time in her life.

Rori spotted his soap lying on the bottom. She bent down to retrieve it and caught a whiff of its clean, fresh scent. She recognized it immediately as the fragrance she particularly associated with Chance. The thought antagonized her, and more than a little disgruntled, she started to slosh from the pond.

"Rori?" Burr was watching her intently as he sat on his horse on the far side of the pond, his forearms folded across the saddle horn. He'd been observing her for a moment and had seen the strange wistfulness in her expression. It troubled him . . . a lot. It wasn't like Rori to go jumping into a pond with her clothes on.

Burr's presence surprised her, and she looked up, startled, quickly trying to smile as if pleased to see him. "What?"

"What, is right! What the hell happened here?!"

"Nothin'," she responded sullenly, wondering just how much he'd seen and heard.

"You don't look like nothing happened."

"I'm wet, is all," she told him as she trudged out of the water, her footsteps squishing. "I got a little hot takin' care of Patch and decided to cool off. With Broderick around, you know I can't go takin' off my clothes."

"Oh," Burr said, and then asked casually, "And just where is Broderick?"

"How am I supposed to know?" Rori argued testily. "I ain't his keeper!"

"Just thought you might have some idea where he is, that's all."

"Why? Did you find something out on the trail? Is there something I should know about?"

"No. Looks clear up ahead, and there's no one coming behind us. There's nothing to worry about." He added 'yet' in his thoughts as he watched her and worried about what had really taken place here.

Rori nodded and moved on up the bank to where her horse waited patiently for her. She dropped to her knees beside him and once again wrapped the compress around his leg as Burr rode away.

Burr found Chance comfortably ensconced in camp. It was obvious that he'd been in the water, too, and again Burr grew concerned over exactly what had transpired while he'd been away.

"Couldn't pass up the chance of a bath, eh?" Burr asked as he rode in, carefully watching the Easterner for some sign that he'd learned the truth about Rori.

"It was hot, and I needed a little cooling off," he replied easily.

The phrase he chose was so close to what Rori had said that Burr froze. He eyed Chance suspiciously, wondering if there was another meaning to his words, if the two of them had decided together what story to use.

"Besides," Chance went on in open candor, "I didn't know how soon I'd get the opportunity again." He wasn't in the least concerned about his run-in with Rori. The boy had gotten a little too big for his breeches and had needed a setdown. He'd given it to him. That was the end of that. It had nothing to do with Burr or anything else, and he could see no reason to bring it up.

"Not for a while, that's for sure," Burr replied, relieved. "There's only a few small streams ahead, and you never know if they'll be running or not."

"How's it look out on the trail? Think we'll be able to ride out in the morning?"

"I haven't had a good look at Patch yet, but if Rori keeps that compress on him all day, we'll be fine."

They both glanced back to where Rori sat beside the horse working on his leg. Chance thought by the slump of his shoulders that the boy looked sufficiently crestfallen, and he was pleased. Burr thought by the slump of her shoulders that she looked deeply troubled, and he was worried. Neither said a word.

"I'm not going to even think about it," Rori spoke out loud to no one in particular. "I don't care how I look or how I smell . . ." As she said it, the heavy odor of sodden leather assailed her, and she frowned. "It doesn't matter. Nobody cares. It just doesn't matter," Rori repeated to herself. But even as she said it, her gaze focused on the soap she still had in her possession, and she wondered if there might be time later, after everyone had gone on to sleep, to use it . . .

Chapter 10

The idea was haunting her. Like a siren song, the cool, sweet depths of the pool beckoned her near, calling to her to strip away her boyish garb and bathe in its waters. Rori tossed uncomfortably in her bedroll for what seemed like the hundredth time. She knew it would serve no real purpose to do it. She knew she should quit thinking about it, but still the thought enticed her, intriguing her, driving her to distraction.

Wrapped in her blanket against the chill of the desert night, waiting and hoping for sleep to take her, Rori tried to imagine what she would look like if she did give in to the temptation to wash up. In her mind's eye, she pictured herself with her hair unbound wearing white women's clothing. She wondered if Chance would find her attractive *then*.

The fantasy appealed to some secret part of her, and

the desire to bathe became even more powerful. Rori knew she'd be taking a chance, but she considered the possibility of her being discovered remote. Both Burr and Chance had been sound asleep for hours. She'd never even be missed.

Her impulsive decision made, Rori threw off her blanket and searched through her belongings for the soap she'd hidden and a clean change of clothing. She hadn't felt guilty about keeping the soap. After all, Chance had never asked for it back, so why shouldn't she keep it? Knowing him, he probably had more with him anyway.

Clutching her things to her breast, she rearranged her bedding to make it look like she was still there and then started to silently steal away. Big Jake, however, had other ideas. He'd been sleeping close by, and when he saw her starting to leave, he lifted his massive head and gave a low whimper, as if questioning her wisdom in going out into the night wilderness alone.

Rori almost panicked. The last thing she needed was for Chance, or Burr for that matter, to wake up and find out what she was doing. Putting a finger to her lips, she gave Jakie the understood, unspoken signal for silence. Obedient to her every wish, he immediately went quiet, though he continued to watch her as she began to move off again. Worried about her, Jakie rose to his feet in one smooth, stealthy movement, intending to go with her and protect her.

Rori had suspected that he would try to follow, and she turned back again, this time giving him the hand signal to lie back down and stay. She made sure to keep her expression stern, for she didn't want him thinking she was playing a game with him. When she was confident that he was going to obey her and stay where he was, Rori finally made it the rest of the way out of camp.

Her escape made, Rori moved far enough along the

bank so she couldn't be seen in the red-gold glow cast
by their low-burning campfire. When she was confident
that she'd picked the most protected place to bathe, she
sat down, set her things aside, and began to undress.
She kicked off her moccasins, pulled her buckskin shirt
over her head, and then stood to shed her pants.

Rori paused, both nervous and excited. A slight
breeze caressed her bare, slender limbs, and she shivered, whether from anticipation or the chill of the wind,
she wasn't sure. She wrapped her arms about herself for
a moment, and then, with a small gurgle of delight, she
ran down the bank and slipped into the pool, the soap
clutched like a treasure in her hand.

The night air had been so cool that the water felt
warm to Rori. She walked out into the depths of the
pond, savoring the soothing, swirling touch of the water.
At the deepest point, Rori dove beneath the surface and
then came quickly up for a breath. Her braids hung forward over her shoulders, trickling water down over her
breasts in a sensuous cascade, and the sensation was so
unusual that it stirred to life new fires of awareness
within her. Suddenly, Rori felt very conscious of her own
femininity.

It was an odd feeling, that recognition of sensuality,
and it was certainly new for Rori. She was bewildered by
it even as she was intrigued. Her breasts felt fuller, heav-
ier, their peaks hardening in the coolness of the night
air. The motion of the water about her hips almost felt
as if someone was touching her, stroking her, and it left
her strangely weak-kneed.

Unnerved by the emotions that were tingling through
her, Rori tried to concentrate on the real reason why
she'd come here in the first place. She was here to take
a bath, and that was what she was going to do. Ignoring
the slowly awakening sensual feelings that were besieg-
ing her, Rori began to wash.

The silk of the soap as she ran it over her skin made her even more conscious of her body, of its softness, of its gentle curves. Rori had never really thought of herself as a woman before, but now the full impact of actually acknowledging her femininity left her uneasy. She'd hidden behind the boyish identity for so long and had been so happy doing it that she'd never given much thought to being a girl. Until this moment, her life had been relatively simple. Now, however, it seemed that everything had gotten much too confusing, and it was all because of Chance.

Chance . . . Annoyance surged through her at the thought of the arrogant Easterner. But even as she felt irritated with him, she couldn't forget how magnificent he'd looked when she'd seen him naked earlier that afternoon. She'd never thought she would think a man beautiful or even care, but Chance was, and she did care. *Damn him! How could she hate him and yet find him so terribly attractive?* The question seemed unanswerable, and an exasperated sigh escaped her.

Rori couldn't help but wonder what Chance was going to say once he found out she was a girl. It amused her to think about it, and she smiled to herself at the thought of his surprise. She'd bested him in everything. She'd shown him just how good she was! If it hadn't been for her fall at the slide area . . . Rori put that thought from her, for she didn't want to think about her lapse in judgment and how that had caused them more than a day's delay.

Realizing that she'd been away too long, Rori dove beneath the water again to rinse off. She stood up slowly, her back to the bank, completely and blissfully unaware of the man who stood there in the shadows, gun in hand, watching her in anger.

* * *

Chance didn't know what had awakened him. He just knew that one moment he'd been sleeping soundly, and the next he was wide awake. Cautiously, still pretending sleep, he shifted positions in his bedroll to get a better view of the camp. Through slitted eyes, he studied everything. Nothing seemed out of order. Nothing seemed different. Burr was unmoving, and even Big Jake lay still and quiet near where Rori, too, slept on.

Reassured by the dog's lack of interest in their surroundings, Chance figured he was mistaken, that nothing out of the ordinary had happened to wake him. Relaxing his guard, he had just closed his eyes when he heard something in the direction of the creek. It had almost sounded like a laugh to him, but he knew that was ridiculous, for who would be out in the desert in the middle of the night laughing? Anyone who was trying to sneak up on them certainly wouldn't be chuckling down at the watering hole.

With the utmost of care, Chance moved slowly, sliding his hand out to his holster nearby and grabbing his loaded sidearm. When he had a firm grip on the weapon, he made a lightning move from his bedroll, coming to his knees a short distance away, the revolver held in readiness.

Chance was prepared for the worst. He was prepared for an attack, possibly by the men who'd tried to kill him in town or the Apache, but nothing happened. There appeared to be no one around. He held his position for a moment, waiting, listening.

Jakie heard Chance's unusual movements and lifted his head to observe the man. He saw him crouched nearby, seemingly ready for an attack, and he wondered at his actions. Giving a limp wag of his furry tail, Jakie lay back down and closed his eyes once more.

Chance saw the dog's calm behavior and felt a bit foolish. Surely if there was anyone around, Big Jake would have heard them first and warned everyone of their presence. Obviously, he'd made a mistake, he thought a bit self-consciously and thought of how Rori would have chortled with glee over his error. He grimaced, thankful that he hadn't managed to wake the boy up.

Still, Chance didn't believe that he'd imagined the sound he had heard coming from the direction of the pond, and he decided to take a quiet walk down to the water's edge to see if anyone was there.

The moonlight was magic on the face of the desert, caressing all with its pale glow. Transformed by the night's gentle touch, the rocky landscape no longer appeared harsh and threatening. Instead, the cactus looked like staunch sentinels standing silent guard over the vastness of their domain.

Chance was wary as he drew near the watering hole, and he kept his gun in readiness in spite of Jake's obvious lack of concern about intruders. He moved stealthily, staying hidden in the brush and creosote trees just in case.

As he moved closer, Chance could hear a slight splashing in the water, and he knew something or someone was there. His grip tightened on his weapon as he crept ever nearer, wondering just what it was he was going to discover. With a slow hand, he brushed the limbs of a low-growing tree aside and stared down at the pool.

Chance wasn't sure what he'd been expecting to see, but the sight of Rori taking a bath was the last thing he would ever have imagined. The whole situation would have been funny, if it hadn't made him feel like such a damned fool. No wonder Big Jake hadn't been concerned! Rori was the one down at the watering hole, not some murdering thief in the night. Here he'd been ready to shoot whatever intruder he found there, and the intruder turned out to be the obstinate, aggravating boy!

Chance wanted to throttle him for his stupidity in pulling this trick. The ornery kid could have gotten himself killed! And after all the fuss he'd made that afternoon about his own bathing, what the hell was he doing taking a bath?

Chance's anger grew as he stared at the smart-mouthed brat, trying to decide what to do. The temptation to embarrass him was too great to pass up after all that had passed between them that afternoon. The scrawny kid was standing totally naked with his back to him in waist-deep water, and Chance knew that if he moved quickly he could take him completely by surprise. Then, he thought vindictively, he could give him the kind of scrubbing he well deserved.

Chance laid his gun aside, and without another thought, he charged into the water and grabbed the boy by the shoulders before he could react. It occurred to him vaguely that the boy felt awfully soft and fragile beneath his own hard, calloused hands, but he didn't stop to think about it. He just picked him up enough so that he lost his footing and then dunked him but good.

Rori gave a small shriek of fright and outrage as someone grabbed her from behind, but before she could scream for help she was pushed forcefully underwater. For a moment, she actually feared for her life—feared that the robbers from town had found them and were going to drown her. But when the powerful hands that had held her quickly released her, she got mad instead, surfacing sputtering mad.

"What the . . . ?!!" Rori spat out in furious indignation

as she came up and turned on her attacker. She forgot for just that instant that she was buck naked; all she could think of was how angry she was. "YOU?!!!"

"You're lucky I didn't shoot you, you little idiot! I came down here thinking we had some unwelcome company and . . ." His laughter stopped abruptly as his gaze dropped from Rori's outraged expression to the perfection of her rounded breasts, bared now in all their feminine glory to his gaze. He froze.

The silvery moonglow cast the entire scene in a surrealistic light, and Chance blinked, not quite believing what was before him. It was definitely Rori who stood there, but not the Rori he knew. The Rori who stood before him was female . . . a flesh-and-blood female. He blinked again, trying to form a coherent thought between what he thought he knew and what he was actually seeing. Rori . . . a girl . . . Why had she pretended to be a boy all this time, and why hadn't he noticed before?

No wonder he had thought her so soft. She was soft. No wonder he'd thought her thin. She was thin for a boy, but perfect, he realized now, in a feminine way.

Humiliation flushed through him as he remembered all that had been said and done between them, and his eyes narrowed as anger replaced embarrassment. He didn't know what kind of trick they'd been playing, but if there was one thing in this world Chancellor Broderick didn't stand for, it was being made the fool.

Rori read the suddenly threatening look in his eyes and realized the tenuousness of her position. She cried out softly in a strangled voice, trying to back away, "No!"

Rori's gasp of horror shattered his temporary immobility, and Chance grasped her by the upper arm and hauled her closer, slamming her slender form against his chest.

"No, hell!" he snapped, his dark eyes boring into hers.

He was livid, but he wasn't sure why. His grip on her arm was painful, but he gave no thought to easing his hold. He wanted, no, *needed* to understand exactly what was going on here, and he had no intention of letting her go until he got some answers. "You tricked me . . ." Chance seethed.

"I didn't trick you! I never hid anything from you! You were just too stupid to notice I was a girl, that's all!" Rori came back at him, struggling with all her might to get away from him. There was something about being held this way . . . her nakedness against his fully clothed body . . . that caused her to panic, and she began to tremble uncontrollably.

"Scared, are you? You damn well should be!" Chance taunted in cold fury, sick and tired of her insults.

His hold on her was bruising, but he had no intention of letting her go. Somewhere in the back of his mind, as he dealt with her desperate fight to escape, he was aware of her silken limbs beneath his hard grip, of the feel of her breasts crushed to his chest through the dampness of his shirt and the wriggle of her unclad hips against his powerful thighs. But he was trying to ignore that aware ness for now. His anger was feeding his actions at this moment and nothing else.

"Let go of me, you no-good bastard!" Rori choked out with more bravado than she was feeling. Terror, icy and deep, claimed her. Chance's expression was so terrible . . . She'd seen him angry before, but nothing like this. Burr had warned her about the viciousness of men, white men in particular. That was why he'd always wanted her to act the boy, to be the boy, but now it was too late . . . Fear chilled her to her very soul.

Her verbal attack turned his temper white-hot. Chance found he wanted to punish her for her deceit, no matter what the reason for it.

"Not on your life, little girl," he sneered. "I'm going to do what I should have done a long time ago!"

"What?" Rori whispered, her features going suddenly pale.

"I ought to take you over my knee and spank you, but I've got a better punishment in mind for you. I'm going to give you the bath you deserve!!" Chance snarled. He remembered her continual protests against him touching her and understood now why she'd been so adamant about him keeping his distance. No wonder she hadn't wanted to ride double with him! She'd been afraid he'd find out the truth. Well, he knew the truth now!

Chance pinned her to him with one arm as he reached down to untie the rawhide thongs that held her hair bound in braids. But Rori wasn't about to accede to his control, and she continued to squirm in her attempts to get away.

"Be still or I will beat you!" he commanded, clamping a restraining hand at her waist to hold her roughly against him.

"I won't!" she hissed. "You have no right to treat me this way! You . . ."

"Oh, I have every right," Chance bit out. "You've done nothing but antagonize me from the first minute we met. It's time I put you in your place once and for all."

His fingers were not gentle as he pulled the thongs from her hair and ran his hand through the plaits, combing the raven tresses into a heavy curtain about her shoulders. Rori tried to keep her face averted from him, but when Chance burrowed his hand in the thickness of her hair at the nape of her neck and tugged, forcing her to look up at him, she had no choice. Tears stung her eyes from the pain of his hold.

Chance hadn't expected to see such a change in her. He hadn't expected to see her transformed into a beautiful woman just by letting her hair down, but the difference in her appearance was amazing. Even the fading bruise on her cheek could not disguise the truth any longer. One moment she'd been the obstinate, mutinous boy who'd aggravated him every minute since they'd left Phoenix, and now she was a woman . . .

"My God . . ." Chance muttered in a deep guttural voice as his gaze swept over Rori's upturned features. He studied the wide emerald eyes, sparkling now with unshed tears of humiliation and pain, the delicacy of her nose and mouth, and he wondered how it was he'd been so blind . . .

"So you found out I'm a girl, so what?" Rori challenged, still hoping to escape his further wrath.

"I don't like being made a fool of," he growled as he began to scrub her scalp and hair with the soap. He took great delight in the effort and, remembering his anger, dunked her thoroughly to rinse the lather from her hair.

"Stop it!" she raged.

"I'm not going to stop until every inch of you is clean, including your mouth if you don't shut it!" He held the bar of soap up threateningly, and she quickly shut up.

Chance knew he should stop, but somehow as he continued to touch her, exploring her face, neck, and shoulders, his anger subtly altered. The awareness he'd denied before in the heat of his fury, he could no longer ignore. A fire burned within him, a fire that drove him to explore every inch of her silken flesh.

Chance eased his grip on her waist as he moved lower with the soap, rubbing it over the rounded swells of her upthrust breasts. The burgeoning orbs glistened in the moonlight as he lathered them, and he felt himself grow heavy with desire as the peaks hardened beneath his ministrations. Chance's touch became less demanding and more tender. He noticed distractedly that her efforts to escape had ceased for the moment, and so he released his hold on her waist and cupped his hands to dip up enough water to rinse the creamy foam from her skin.

Rori didn't know how it had happened, but she was mesmerized. Chance's threats had frightened her, but his touch had created such an overwhelming sense of excitement within her that it had overruled everything else she was feeling. Logically, she knew she should continue to try to get away from him, but the enjoyment of his wet, slippery caresses held her still. She thrilled at the feel of his hands upon her. She was enjoying the wild sensations that having him touching her created. Her head was thrown back now, her eyes closed, her breathing slightly labored as she gave herself over to the sensuality of the moment.

Chance paused to look down at her, and he had to stifle a groan. Droplets of water on her breasts beckoned to him to kiss them away, and all thought of who she was and where they were fled his mind. The soap slid unnoticed from his hand as he bent to her, his lips seeking out those peaks of pleasure.

The contact was so unexpected, so alien and so shocking to Rori that she reacted without thought. Jarred back to reality, she shoved at Chance's shoulders with all her might, and sent him tumbling backward into the water. It took her a second to realize that she was free of him, and then she ran for the bank, hoping to escape before he could come after her.

One moment Rori had been in his arms, willing, and the next Chance had found himself near drowning as she fled his embrace. He recovered quickly and charged after her.

"Oh, no you don't!"

Rori had no breath to shout at him, and she glanced back over her shoulder at him as she scrambled for safety. In a furious lunge, he launched himself at her

fleeing form and managed to tackle her just as she was
about to get out of the pond. They landed heavily in just
a few inches of water. Wild with fear and uncontrollable
terror, Rori tried to crawl away from him, and she made
it a short distance up the bank before he was on top of
her again, rolling her over to face him. The long, hard
length of his body was pressed fully to hers, pinning her
effectively to the ground.

"You're not getting away from me. Not now . . ."
Rori could feel the strength of him between her
thighs and knew real panic.

"No!" She flailed at him, hitting him wherever she
could in hopes of trying to dislodge him. "Don't . . ."

Rori's efforts were futile against Chance's superior
strength. He ignored her pleas, easily pinning her arms
above her head.

"That's the last time you'll ever take me by surprise,
little girl." He smiled wolfishly down at her. "The last
time . . ."

Then with measured intent, Chance lowered his head
to claim her lips in a kiss that was meant to master, to
subjugate, to teach her who was the man and who was
the woman.

Chapter 11

Rori had started to protest just as Chance moved to
kiss her, and he took full advantage, capturing her open
lips in a domineering exchange. When he boldly took
full possession of her mouth, his tongue delving into its
honeyed sweetness, Rori went rigid in shock. She had

never imagined he would kiss her this way. She groaned in outrage as she twisted and bucked beneath him, trying to get him to break it off.

Chance was not about to be denied, though. Sensing her upset, he changed his tack, easing up on the kiss, yet not freeing her completely. His mouth, once bent on conquering hers, became teasing. His body, once meant to pin her to the ground and hold her immobile, now shifted, molding itself intimately to her softer curves. He still held her hands pinioned above her head, but now used only one of his to hold her. His free hand he used to caress the slimness of her rib cage and then slip up higher to capture the fullness of one breast.

"I hate you!" Rori cried hoarsely, breaking away from his kiss. Shock waves were resounding through her at the boldness of his touch.

Chance only chuckled at her declaration, though, for the peak of her breast was taut against his palm. She might fight him and try to deny what she was feeling, but her body's response betrayed her words. She was responding to him . . .

Rori was frightened and confused. Every nerve in her body was alive and tingling from his caresses, and an ache, deep and coiling, was growing like a slow-spreading fire low in the womanly heart of her. She instinctively wanted to move against Chance, to rub her hips against his, for they were fitted tightly, erotically against her. It felt so good to be near him, but somehow, despite all the wild excitement that coursed through her, she knew it was wrong . . . all wrong!

"You have to stop!"

"Why?" Chance asked huskily, kissing her again. Images formed in his mind as he continued to caress her. Images of Rori watching him as he bathed, images of Rori caught staring at him so blatantly earlier that day. "You want me. Admit it," he coaxed.

Rori groaned inwardly. He wasn't even supposed to know that she was a girl, let alone touch her this way . . . and yet it felt so good to have his hands upon her and to be this close to him. Had she always instinctively known that it would be this way between them? Was he right? Had she always wanted this . . . him?

Chance broke off the kiss to gaze down at her. There was still a small grain of logic alive within his thoughts warning him that this was wrong, telling him that this was Rori . . . a young girl . . . a child, really, and that he should get as far away from her as he could. But as he stared down into her wide, wonderful green eyes and saw the tumultuous emotions reflected there, he was overcome by a sudden rush of tenderness. Confusion was clearly mirrored in the depths of her gaze, along with the desire she felt for him, but was trying to deny.

"You're beautiful," he murmured, pressing his lips to her throat.

Rori almost laughed at his words. Her? Beautiful? But the feel of his lips on her neck and shoulders wiped all thought of speaking from her mind. A shiver of excited anticipation caused her to arch up into the hardness of him, begging, no, demanding something more from him.

When she offered herself to him in that age-old innocent way, Chance was lost. The throbbing in his loins was clamoring for immediate release, clamoring for oneness with this woman/child. It was elemental. She was woman. He was man. He trailed his kisses lower, caressing her shoulder and then down . . . down to suckle at her breasts.

One last burst of fear caught Rori.

"Chance . . . I . . ." She tried to tell him how afraid she was of all the new sensations that were shuddering through her. Her breath caught in her throat at the feel of his hot, wet mouth moving erotically over her sensitive flesh, and ecstasy flooded through her. "Oh, please . . ." Rori groaned, but she wasn't sure if she wanted him to stop or continue.

Chance knew the tumult of emotion she was feeling, for the heat of his own need was pressing hard against the nest of her softness. He released her hands and continued to lave her breasts with kisses until she was moving restlessly beneath him, her hands clutching at his back in desperation. He found suddenly that pleasing her was utmost in his mind. He wanted her to know the ecstasy of loving. He wanted to take her to the heights.

"Easy, little love," he murmured, one hand moving ever lower to claim the very essence of her.

Though Rori knew the rudiments of the sex act, she had not really expected that Chance would actually touch her there. Still, when he did it, she did not try to block him, but opened to him as a flower in bloom. It seemed natural and right to her. She wanted him . . . had wanted him for so long. She ached to hold him close . . . to have him satisfy the sweet pain that throbbed within the heart of her.

At Rori's complete acquiescence to his touch, Chance reacted on instinct. He wanted her—God, how he wanted her—and she was warm, wet, and wild for him. He delayed no longer in freeing himself from his pants and fitting himself to her. His lips met hers, his tongue surging within, just as he positioned himself against the portals of her femininity.

Rori's eyes rounded as she felt the bold strength of him seeking entrance to her body. *He was so big!* The thought echoed through her mind. She remembered her scathing insult of that morning and knew she'd been wrong, very wrong.

Lost in the fire of the moment, Chance thrust forward, sheathing himself in Rori's virginal sweetness. The pain for Rori was brief, but knifelike in intensity.

She went rigid, tensing against his alien invasion of her body.

The shock of discovering her untouched state left Chance bewildered and confused, but he could no more stop making love to her than he could have stopped breathing. He wanted her as he'd never wanted another. He had to love her.

"Easy, sweet," Chance murmured thickly, surprised to find that he wanted to ease the agony she was feeling. He continued to stroke and caress her, wanting to replace the pain with pleasure, wanting to reawaken the desire she'd felt. "The pain will pass . . . just relax . . ."

Chance could feel the tension slowly ebbing from her, and he bent to kiss her. As his mouth moved over hers in a flaming exchange, Rori felt the excitement blossom within her again, and she moved her hips slightly, testing the discomfort—fearful, yet wanting to know more.

"You're right . . ." she whispered in amazement, breaking off the kiss as she found the worst had passed, and there was no more pain.

"It can only get better, love, I promise," he vowed in a hoarse voice.

Chance began to move then, his control broken. His hard-driving body was a passionate, fiery brand against hers, claiming her as his own as he plunged deep within her. Caught up in her own desire, Rori clung to him, understanding to meet his pleasure-giving thrusts without being told. She wanted this as much as he did, and her heart soared at the thought of being in his arms. She could feel the thrilling delight building and though she didn't know what waited for her beyond that cresting peak, she gave herself over to Chance's expertise without question.

Rapture claimed them both at the same time, sending them rocketing to the heights of ecstasy and beyond. Chance had never known passion so fulfilling. He clasped Rori to him in a possessive yet tender embrace, and for that short period of time before awareness returned, he was enraptured.

Rori was stunned by the wonder of what had happened. She lay quietly in his arms savoring the feelings that filled her. It had been more than she'd ever dreamed . . . it had been perfect. She sighed and nestled against him contentedly.

As with all things, nothing lasts forever. Just the softness of her sigh brought the harshness of reality crashing back in on Chance, and he stiffened. *What had he done?* Chance jerked back, away from Rori and stared down at her flushed, contented features. She looked like a child as she gazed up at him questioningly, and major guilt seared his soul. *Good God! What had come over him? How could he have been so stupid? This was Rori . . . she was only a child! Dear Lord, he'd only just discovered she was a girl and then promptly stolen her innocence. What the hell was the matter with him?* Chance glanced nervously back toward the camp, fully expecting to see Burr coming after him with a shotgun and knowing he deserved it.

Rori saw his furtive look back toward camp and saw the play of guilty emotion on his face and grew suddenly furious. So he was ashamed of having made love to her, was he? How could she have been such an idiot?!

"Get off of me, you . . . !" Rori spat, shoving at his shoulders and pushing him away from her.

"Rori? What . . . ?" Chance had been so caught up in his concern about her that he had no idea what she was talking about.

"You arrogant ass! I said get off of me!" Rori finally managed to disentangle herself from his embrace.

"But I thought . . ."

"You thought what, white man? That we might do it again as long as nobody saw you?" She quickly grabbed her clothes and began to dress. She was angry with him and mad at herself. She'd always known it was dangerous to let him touch her, and yet when he had, she hadn't fought him off nearly hard enough. *Hell,* Rori thought in disgust, *she'd thrilled to his caresses! She'd fallen into his arms like a lovesick puppy, damn him!* And now that he'd taken her, he was sorry that he'd done it. She could see the regret in his eyes. Was it because she was part Indian that he was sorry he'd touched her?

"What are you talking about?"

"I'm sorry I ever let you near me!" Rori lashed out at him, angry with him for being ashamed of her and hurt because she cared.

The regret Chance had been feeling over the taking of her innocence disappeared before her hostility, and all the tender feelings he'd been harboring vanished.

"No sorrier than I am!" he returned, wondering how he could have forgotten what Rori was like even for that short period of time.

"Well, you don't have to worry about this ever happening again," she continued, refusing to let him have the last word, refusing to let him see how much he'd wounded her. "Tonight was the biggest mistake of my life, and I plan to make sure it isn't repeated. From now on, just keep the hell away from me!"

"It'll be my pleasure," Chance told her sarcastically, a little upset that she was so eager to be away from him and that she so obviously wanted nothing more to do with him. This had never happened to him before. He had always been the one to end associations with his female friends, but then, he thought, Rori was not like any other woman he'd ever known. Straightening his clothing in abrupt angry motions, Chance wished that he'd never jumped into the pond to teach Rori a lesson in the first place.

At Chance's cruel words, Rori's eyes flashed emerald fire, and her heart twisted in anguish with emotions she didn't understand.

"If you value your hide, you won't tell my grampa about any of this," Rori threatened, suddenly fearful of what Burr would say if he found out.

"Don't worry, Rori. I'm not about to tell him anything. This isn't something I'm exactly proud of."

Her gaze flew to his face, but his features were stony and his eyes cold. One part of her wanted to launch herself back into his arms, to tell him that what happened between them had meant the world to her. Another part of her, a more realistic, more logical part, told her that his indifference was the best thing that had ever happened to her, that the man wasn't worth a hill of beans, and that she should forget him—the sooner the better.

Yet, even as she acknowledged that her more logical side was right, Chance's confession that he was sorry for having made love to her hit her hard. She didn't say another word as tears burned her eyes. She turned away from him, finished dressing, and stalked off back to camp. Rori dropped down on her bedroll, and, still fighting the tears that threatened, she began plaiting her still damp hair with numb, shaking fingers. *Damn him . . . damn him . . . damn him . . .* The words ran in a continuous litany in her mind.

Big Jake, as if sensing something was wrong, got up from where he rested and moved silently to her side. He sat down beside her in such a way that he ended up leaning against her.

"Ah, Jakie . . ." Rori slipped an arm around the brute of a dog and buried her face in his soft golden coat washing that gentle fur with her tears, and he gave a low whine of sympathy.

"You understand, Jakie . . . I know you do. I just wish I did . . ." Agony born of confusion tore through her, for she knew, had Chance asked her, she would have stayed in his arms all night.

Knowing that he might return to camp at any time,

Rori forced herself to stop crying and released Jakie so she could finish fixing her braids. Jake didn't leave her, though, and when her hair was done, he stretched out beside her on her blankets. He curled up close, and she gathered him even nearer, hugging the big animal to her heart as best she could manage.

"The faster we get to sleep, Jakie, the faster this whole thing will be over with, and he'll be gone. We'll be rid of him," she confided, and as she thought of being parted from Chance, her tears began again.

Chance's expression had remained blank as he'd watched Rori walk back to camp. As he followed her movements, noting now the gentle sway of her hips and the hint of her curves beneath the soft buckskin, he wondered how he could ever have mistaken her for a boy. Chance had always considered himself a man-about-town, and it surprised him to discover that he wasn't as observant as he'd prided himself on being.

Oddly, Chance found himself worrying about how much longer Rori would be able to get away with pretending to be a boy. No doubt, the loose-fitting garments and bruised face had helped with her disguise, but if the truth of her femininity came out, she might find herself in real trouble in town.

When Chance realized the direction of his thoughts, he frowned. What did he care what happened to her? Rori was as obstinate and ornery as the day was long. If anyone ever needed protection in a confrontation with her, it would be whoever chose to take her on, not Rori.

Chance still couldn't believe what had happened to him . . . that he'd lost complete control and made love to her the way he had, but then they'd been striking sparks off each other from the very beginning. He wanted to believe that it had just been the surprising shock of discovering she was a girl that had ignited their moment of passion in the pond. Surely, it had been nothing more, just a momentary thing.

Yet, even as he sat there, alone in the moonlight, Chance was remembering the exquisite feel of her satiny skin beneath his hands and the glory of her hair as it had hung unbound around her shoulders. He thought of her kiss and of the way she'd responded to him so openly and lovingly. He thought of the beauty of her breasts and how perfectly they had fit into his hands. He remembered the feel of her smooth, slender legs against his. Desire stirred within him again, and he scowled in agitation. He might desire her physically, but he was never going to act on that desire again. From now on, he would have nothing more to do with Rori. She was trouble, plain and simple.

Chance searched out his gun where he'd left it by the bushes and then sat down on the bank to stare out across the quiet water. A long time later, when his clothes were reasonably dry, he returned to his own bed, and even then sleep still proved elusive. Finally, just before dawn, he managed to drift off, but as he did, his last thought was of Rori and the glory of being one with her.

By the time the sun began to brighten the eastern horizon, Rori was already up. As she made her way through the camp to where Patch was tied with the other horses, she cast a covert glance at Chance and was aggravated to find that he was sound asleep. The idea that he could actually fall asleep while she'd tossed and turned restlessly all night infuriated her, and she silently cursed him with every vile cussword she knew.

Obviously, the passion that had exploded between them had meant nothing to him. It had been an accident . . . a fluke, and it was over, just like that.

Rori knew that she could parade before him in a fancy dress like his wonderful Bethany wore, and he still probably wouldn't even notice her. The thought pained her, but it was a pain she was determined to ignore. She wouldn't allow herself to feel anything for him! She wouldn't!

"Rori?"

The sound of Burr's voice startled her, and she jumped nervously. "What?"

"I was just wondering what you were doing up so early. It isn't even sunup yet," he pointed out as he joined her by Patch.

"I woke up and couldn't sleep any more, so I got up to see how his leg was," she answered simply, hoping he wouldn't notice anything different about her this morning.

In the ghostly glow of the still-rising sun, Burr could see the beginnings of dark shadows beneath her eyes and knew she wasn't telling him everything. He wondered why, because they were usually totally open and honest with each other.

"Something troubling you, girl?" Burr pressed, wanting to help if he could.

"Nope. Not a thing, Grampa," Rori denied quickly.

"You all over what we talked about a while back?"

"Yep. That's why I'm anxious to get started today. I want to get up to the mine and be done with it."

"How's Patch looking?"

"He's healthy and ready to go, just as soon as we are," Rori told him as she stood up and dusted off her hands on her pants. She was relieved that they wouldn't be forced to spend another day at the watering hole. She wanted to get on the trail away from the memories that haunted her here.

Burr gave a curt nod. "I'll wake Broderick and we'll go." He headed off to do as he'd said, knowing that there was more to Rori's mood than she was telling him, but also knowing that she wouldn't tell him what the trouble was until she was ready. *The girl is too close-mouthed,* he thought to himself in irritation and then realized with some chagrin that she took a lot after him.

Burr had no trouble waking Chance, and as soon as he'd gathered his things together, they were on their way farther up into the mountains. Rori had ridden out the minute she saw that Chance was stirring, and she maintained that lead all day. The last thing she wanted to do was to talk with him or be with him in any way. She wanted to stay away from him until they got to the mine, and then she wanted to get away from him just as quickly as she could.

When Chance discovered that Rori had already ridden out ahead of them, he'd been strangely disappointed. He found himself trying to catch a glimpse of her as the day progressed and was constantly frustrated for she was nowhere in sight.

"Don't you worry about Rori when he's this far ahead of us?" Chance was careful to make sure he still referred to her in the masculine with Burr.

"Rori knows the area as well as I do," Burr dismissed his concern.

"What if Patch should turn up lame again?" he asked.

"If Patch needs to rest, Rori'll rest him. Don't go worrying none. Rori won't run the horse into the ground. We'll get you up to Doug right on schedule."

Chance was glad that Burr had interpreted his worry as concern about being delayed in getting up to the mine. He didn't want the old man to think that he was interested in Rori, because, of course, he wasn't. He didn't care where she was or what she was doing. Chance couldn't help but ask himself, though, why he was constantly scouring the distance for some sight of her slender form mounted on the powerful pinto.

Chapter 12

Hal and Tom exchanged disbelieving looks as they rode up to the slide area.

"Did they git over it?" Tom asked as he studied the seemingly insurmountable incline.

"Had to," Hal spat. "Weren't no tracks goin' out. There must be a way through. We just gotta find it. Let me take a look around for their prints and see what I can figure out." He dismounted and started checking the hard ground.

Tom's shoulder was a little better, but it still pained him. He was not looking forward to a jarring ride up the steep hillside. "Is there any way around it?"

"Nope. We double back, we lose 'em completely. We gotta stay with 'em."

"I was afraid you were gonna say that."

"Your shoulder that bad?"

"It's been better, but it ain't no worse. Don't worry. I'll stay with you. I want that little Indian bastard bad," Tom vowed.

"And I want that map," Hal said seriously. He paused in his efforts and stared up one incline. "Looks like they all went up here. It may look bad, but if they made it, we can make it."

"Let's ride."

The going was treacherous, the footing still loose and

tricky. They came close to falling twice, but continued on, refusing to quit. By the time they reached the top successfully, their horses were winded, but still they went on.

Hal knew the watering hole was just a short ride away and that they could rest there. They were pleased when they found the remnants of Broderick's camp just on the other side of the slide. Encouraged, they rode even harder, knowing that every mile they covered brought them closer to their quarry.

It was midafternoon when they finally reached the pond, and their horses were desperately in need of rest. Tom took care of watering and feeding the mounts as Hal searched the area for some sign that Broderick had been here. When he found their burned-out campfire and realized that it wasn't twenty-four-hours old, he grew excited.

"Tom! C'mere!" he shouted from where he squatted by the ashes.

"What is it?" Tom hurried to his side.

"They were here all right and not too long ago! Look here . . ."

"How far ahead are they?"

Hal glanced up at the sky and judged the time of day. "I'd say they rode outta here about dawn, so figure they got a good half day's ride on us."

"Damn!" Tom swore. "I wish to hell the horses were rested."

"Don't worry. We'll rest 'em real good tonight and head out first thing in the morning. You know we got the advantage, don't you? We know where they are, but they don't know about us."

Tom grinned evilly. "I can't hardly wait to get my hands on that dirty little breed."

"Our time's a-comin', all right," Hal smiled as he

stared off in the direction Rori, Chance, and Burr had gone some nine hours before. "Yes, sir, it sure is."

Nilakla shaded her eyes against the setting sun and gazed off down the valley. Her instincts kept telling her that someone would be coming soon, and usually her instincts were right. So far, though, there had been no sign of anyone. She was glad, for the thought of Doug's brother coming for him shattered her heart. The less she thought about their inevitable parting, the easier it was for her to face each day, cherish it, and live it to the fullest.

"What is it, Nilakla?" Doug called from where he stood just inside the mine's entrance. "Do you see something?"

"No, nothing," she answered, trying to keep the joy she was feeling from showing in her voice. This meant they would have one more day together! As hard as Doug was praying for his Chance to show up, it wouldn't do if he discovered that she was praying for just the opposite.

"Damn," he swore, frustrated. "It's been so long . . . so many months now . . . I'm beginning to wonder if Chance is coming at all . . ."

Nilakla shrugged and wisely held her tongue as Doug disappeared back into the bowels of the mine. She had just started down from her lookout point when it happened, and she gasped in surprise. *Their child had moved!*

A look of pure wonder crossed her lovely features, and her hand flew to her stomach, covering the spot where she'd felt the quickening. She waited breathlessly for it to happen again. The movement had been so light it almost seemed like she'd dreamed it, but all was quiet. No further motion occurred.

Nilakla knew it had happened, though, and she felt

a great sense of peace well up inside her. She was really having Douglas's child. The future without him suddenly didn't seem so completely forlorn and hopeless. At least, when he'd gone from her, she would still have his child . . . their child . . . conceived in love. Her weary heart warmed at the thought, and serenity filled her soul as she started back to the mine to begin cooking their evening meal.

Over a thousand miles away, Agatha sat alone in her parlor with only one low lamp burning. Her nerves were stretched taut, her mood sour. Nothing! She'd heard nothing from either Chance or Doug, and it was driving her absolutely mad!

Agatha knew the conditions in the territory were primitive, but she'd held out hope that Doug might have had the opportunity to write to her again. There had been no correspondence, however, from him or from Chance. She supposed she shouldn't worry so much, but they were all she had left in the world. They meant everything to her. If anything happened to them, she didn't think she could go on.

Lonely as she was, Agatha wished now that Chance had taken her prodding seriously and had found himself a wife. She'd been after him for years to settle down and start a family, but he'd always managed to avoid it one way or the other. It angered her now that he'd been so selfish, but she knew in her heart that she was being the selfish one. If Chance hadn't married, it was because he hadn't met the woman he wanted to spend the rest of his life with yet.

Agatha did sense that there might be something to his association with Bethany Sutcliffe. The girl was a beauty, and they would surely make handsome children together, not to mention the financial coup that would be accomplished by the joining of the two families. It certainly was a match worth encouraging, if and when he ever got back . . .

Not *"if,"* she scolded herself angrily, *definitely "when."* Chance would come back just as he always did, and he'd have an unrepentant Doug in tow just as he always did. Agatha smiled warmly to herself. It was a good thought, and she would hold on to it.

"Madam, you have a caller."

Bailey's surprise announcement startled her from her reverie. "At this hour?"

"Yes, ma'am. Miss Bethany Sutcliffe is here and would like to see you."

"Bethany?" Agatha repeated with a small frown, wondering suddenly if the beautiful young woman had heard something from Chance and feeling a small stab of jealousy at the possibility. Grande Dame that she was, though, she allowed no discontent to show in her manner. "Please, show her in."

Bethany knew she was being outrageously brazen in approaching Agatha Broderick this way, but she was desperate for news of Chance. He'd been gone for weeks now, and she still hadn't heard a thing. Not that she'd expected to after the way they'd parted, but she always held out hope. There was no news of him through the usually very active society gossip mill either. It almost seemed as if he'd dropped completely off the face of the earth, and she was worried.

"Good evening, Mrs. Broderick, I'm so glad you're in tonight."

"Good evening, Bethany. This is an unusual surprise."

"I know I shouldn't have dropped in on you like this, but I'm so worried . . ."

Agatha suddenly grew fearful. *Dear Lord, did the girl know something? Had something happened to one of the boys?* "What is it, dear? What's wrong?"

"It's Chance . . ."

Agatha's heart constricted, but before she could speak, Bethany went on.

"I haven't heard from him in all this time, and I'm so concerned about him. I was just wondering if you'd heard anything, anything at all?" She gave the older woman her most pleading look in hopes that she could convince her of her sincerity, although there wasn't any need of her to play-act. She was really worried about Chance, but she also wanted to ingratiate herself to his mother so that, when he did return home, she'd have an advantage.

"I haven't heard from my son, but then I hadn't expected to," Agatha responded with dignity, not letting on how close she came to being distraught. It was good that Bethany hadn't heard anything. No news was certainly better than bad news. "Arizona is not Boston, you know."

"I know," she demurred, "but you see . . ."

"Yes?"

"Well, Chance and I had a bit of a fight that night at the Richardsons'."

"You did?"

"He didn't tell you?" Bethany was leading the conversation to find out just how much she knew.

"No. We rarely discuss such things."

"I see . . . well, I was upset when I found out that he was leaving again so soon. I'd waited so long for him to return from his last voyage, and then for him to turn around and leave again . . . I'm afraid I'm quite ashamed of the way I acted when he told me."

"I understand your predicament, my dear," Agatha sympathized. "His departure was rather sudden, but sometimes there are things that can't wait . . . things that have to be taken care of."

"I know that now . . . Let's just say that I'm sorry for

being so upset with him and that I can hardly wait until he comes home so I can tell him." At this point, Bethany knew she had nothing to lose in confiding in her. "You see, Mrs. Broderick, I'm in love with Chance."

"I can see that, Bethany." Agatha smiled warmly at her. Perhaps, she thought, it was time she did a little matchmaking on her own since Chance didn't seem so disposed. "Are you expected anywhere else this evening?"

"No."

"Then why don't you join me in a cup of tea? This might be a good time for you and me to get to know each other better."

"Thank you, Mrs. Broderick, I'd like that. I really would." Bethany had never imagined that things would move along this quickly, but she was not about to argue with success. She was going to marry Chance no matter what, even if it took kowtowing to his mother. Mentally patting herself on the back, she settled in for a long, intimate evening with her new ally in her plan to get him to the altar.

The days had passed quickly as Hal and Tom had kept up a torturous pace trying to close the gap on Broderick. Though originally they'd been excited about being so close, now they were growing increasingly frustrated. No matter how fast they had ridden or how many hours they had stayed in the saddle, they seemed to gain little ground.

Many days had gone by before they finally caught sight of their elusive quarry. Tom saw them first some miles ahead on the almost nonexistent trail that led up the steep, rocky, cactus-studded mountainside. Blood-lust filled him immediately when he picked out the smaller form of the breed riding a short distance ahead of Broderick and the old man.

"I can pick him off from here," Tom swore, reaching for his rifle.

"No, damn it! Hold it a minute!"

Tom looked at Hal in disbelief. "What d'ya mean 'hold it a minute'? I owe that little bastard! We been followin' them for days now just to kill 'em, and I mean to do just that!"

"Don't worry, you'll get your chance. Just use your head!" Hal criticized his companion's impulsiveness. "What if you take a shot and miss?"

"I won't," he replied stubbornly. He wanted to kill the kid and be finished with it.

"But you might, and then where are we? If they find out we're here, they'll start hidin' from us. We lose out. Let's do this cautious-like. Let's do this my way."

"Which is?" Tom always worried when Hal started plotting.

"We want the gold, right?"

"I want the Indian more," he insisted stubbornly, and Hal was growing exasperated.

"We can have them both," he argued back. "All we gotta do is hang back, yet keep them in sight. Instead of stealing the damned map, we'll let them lead us up to the mine. Then, when we get there, we attack."

"It sounds too simple."

"It's simple, but it'll work as long as they don't know we're trackin' 'em. We gotta stay back and stay low."

Tom glanced ahead and frowned. He was anxious for his revenge, but the thought of easy riches lured him. "What if there's guards at the mine? Then what?"

Glad that he was winning Tom over, Hal quickly spoke up. "If there are, we'll kill 'em. But I gotta feelin' there ain't nobody knows about this gold but us and the miner and them three up there."

"All right," Tom agreed. "I ain't no fool. I ain't against easy money. Let's ride. We don't want to lose 'em now."

Hal breathed a sigh of relief that he'd curbed his friend's rashness and then urged his horse onward, keeping a close watch on Broderick and the others.

The days had passed in tedious exhaustion for Rori. In order to avoid Chance, she'd forced herself to be the first one up and out of camp in the morning and the last one to bed at night. Whatever free time she had was spent tending to Patch in an area well away from the men or merely sitting off by herself with Big Jake. She was glad that they had kept up their rugged pace and were now less than a day away from Doug's mine. She could hardly wait to bid Chance a final good-bye.

Rori wanted to get away from the arrogant Easterner who'd made everything so complicated for her. She wanted him gone from her life, and once he was she didn't ever want to see him again. Rori was certain that the only way she would really be happy again was to rid herself of his presence. Once he was out of sight, she felt sure that she wouldn't think of him, she wouldn't miss him, she wouldn't desire him . . .

Rori groaned inwardly at the last thought. Lord knows, she shouldn't have wanted anything more to do with Chance, but the wonder of being in his arms had been so exciting . . . Each day, it had taken all of her willpower to keep from watching him constantly. Each night when she'd tried to fall asleep, she'd remember his touch and his kiss, and rest would elude her. Memories of his heated embrace and the glory of his body joined to hers were burned into her soul, and she wondered if she'd ever be rid of them.

As much as she knew she hated Chance, Rori couldn't understand why he had such an effect on her. She despised him, and yet just thinking about being with him made her feel all weak and funny inside. That was why she had avoided him at every turn. He'd said that he'd been sorry for making love to her, and she was not about to let him know that it had meant anything to her. To hell with Chance Broderick!

Rori knew she should be thrilled that, in another day, Chance would be out of her life forever. For some reason, though, she was miserable. Still, proud and stubborn as she was, there was no way Rori was going to want anybody who didn't want her. When the time came and she rode off with Burr, she vowed to herself that she wouldn't look back . . . ever.

As the trail broadened and then leveled out a bit, she put her heels to Patch's side. It was an unconscious gesture, but it was necessary to her survival. She needed to keep her distance from Chance. She couldn't afford to let him get too close to her ever again.

Burr saw Rori pick up the pace, and he shook his head slightly in bewilderment. Ever since they'd left the watering hole she'd led them a merry chase, always moving at top speed and always staying way out ahead of them. He understood Rori well enough to suspect that she was being driven partially by guilt, for it had been her horse that had held them up that extra day and they needed to make up the time. However, he also had a feeling, no matter what she said, that she was making the superhuman effort just to prove to Chance that she could do it. Rori was a stubborn one that way. Even so, the idea that she was driving herself almost to the point of exhaustion didn't sit well with him. If they hadn't been so close now, he would have dressed her down about it. As it was, he'd decided to just keep his mouth shut and wait until they reached Doug's mine the following day.

Burr's suspicions that something was going on between her and Broderick had faded during the past several days. The two hadn't spoken more than a few words or come within ten feet of each other since leaving the watering hole, so he figured he'd been wrong. Whatever it was that was troubling the girl, he just hoped she got over it soon. He sure didn't want to make the return trip out of the mountains at the same breakneck speed. Urging his mount to a faster pace, he drew up alongside Chance.

"We should be gettin' there tomorrow," Burr informed him.

Chance had had a feeling that they were getting close, and he smiled widely. "That's the best news I've had in a long time."

"If we're on the trail by sunup tomorrow, we should make it by dinnertime," the old tracker went on.

"Let's just hope everything is all right with Doug."

"Should be," Burr said with some confidence. "There aren't many folks who know their way around these parts. As hidden as the mine is, it's certain no one's going to accidentally stumble across it."

"I hope you're right."

"I am," he said firmly. "Doug's careful. He doesn't take any chances."

Chance fell silent, again struck by Burr's description of his brother. It had never been like Doug to think things through. Doug always acted first and worried about the consequences later. Unless he'd done a complete about-face in the time they'd been apart, Chance fully expected to find his little brother in deep, deep trouble when he arrived.

Chance gazed around, studying the harshness of the desert landscape. It had been rough traveling in the beginning, and it had grown steadily worse with each passing day. He knew it was the gold that had drawn Doug here, but he wondered what it was that had made Doug stay.

While he could appreciate the rugged beauty of the area, Chance knew he couldn't stay any longer than was necessary to help Doug. There were too many things depending on him back in Boston. He had a business to run. He had people waiting for him to return. Their mother was not the most patient woman in the world, and Chance was sure that she was probably champing at the bit by now, waiting for word. Then there was Bethany, too . . . She crept into his thoughts—beautiful and perfectly coiffed and gowned. He remembered what she'd said about needing him and waiting for him, and he knew he should feel flattered. Bethany Sutcliffe was many a man's dream, and she would certainly make the perfect society wife. Yet, as he tried to recall the kiss they'd shared in the garden, another woman and another kiss dominated his thoughts.

Rori . . . Chance glanced forward to where she rode, so proud and straight in the saddle ahead of them. He was torn between the urge to strangle her or the desire to grab her off her horse and kiss her. The first he knew he couldn't do; the last he knew he wouldn't do. He'd tried his damnedest to forget what had happened at the watering hole, but no matter what he did, the memory of their explosive union haunted him.

Chance went over that night again and again in his mind, trying to make sense out of it, but there was no logic that could explain it. What had happened between Rori and him had been elemental attraction . . . man for woman. It still astounded him that he'd reacted so completely out of character. Chance had always prided himself on being in complete control at all times, but he had exerted no control over himself that night. He had started out meaning to punish Rori and had ended up making mad, passionate love to her.

Chance had never known such excitement, not even with experienced lovers like Bethany. As physically arousing as Bethany could be, compared to Rori she seemed jaded and hard. There had been something fresh and wonderful about Rori. Her very virginity had made her special.

Chance wondered if he would have been able to stop himself had he known she was an innocent, and recalling that night, he knew the answer. The ecstasy they'd shared had been special, and he doubted that he would ever know it again.

Rori hated him. Chance knew he deserved her hatred, but not for the reason she thought. She'd thought he was ashamed of having taken her because she was part Indian, and that couldn't have been further from the truth. He hadn't been proud of what he'd done, because he felt that he'd taken advantage of her innocence. She'd been untouched until he'd come along, and in just those few moments of wild desire, he'd taken her most precious gift.

Night after night, he'd lain awake for hours thinking of her. Images of her slender form had seared his memory. Everything about her that night had been magical . . . the discovery of her femininity, the soft feel of her skin beneath his hands, the passionate response she'd given to his every kiss and touch. Rori had been perfect and . . .

Damn! Chance swore silently to himself as his jaw tightened in anger. He would not, could not, allow himself to think of Rori this way. She'd made it clear how she'd felt about what had happened between them. It was obvious from the way she'd been acting since that night that she loathed the very sight of him.

No, Chance reaffirmed to himself, *making love to Rori had been a big mistake, and it would never happen again. Rori was just a child!* It was ridiculous to torture himself this way, going over every detail of their white-hot encounter in his mind. Tomorrow, they would reach Doug's mine. Tomorrow, he would pay Burr and Rori for their help in making the trip, and they would leave. Tomorrow would be the last day they'd ever be together.

The sudden, unexpected sense of loss that assailed Chance at the prospect surprised him. Why should he care that Rori would be leaving? Why did the thought of never seeing her again after tomorrow bother him? Rori meant nothing to him. He had to take care of Doug and then get back to Boston . . . and to Bethany. With an effort, he turned his thoughts back to his brother, but even as he dwelled on Doug, his gaze rested on Rori.

Chapter 13

It was late, and the men were both asleep. The moon had already set, and a blanket of deep darkness had fallen across the land. At the edge of the camp, just beyond the flickering glow of the fading firelight, Rori paused. Protected by the shadows of the night, she relaxed her guard, allowing all the anguish and confusion she'd been feeling to show on her expressive features as she observed Chance from afar.

Rori longed for the uncomplicated days before she'd ever met Chance when she could go to bed carefree and fall asleep immediately. She knew it wouldn't happen tonight, though—not tonight, and probably never again. The torment of her tumultuous emotions made sleep impossible.

Tomorrow . . . tomorrow it would all be over. *That was what she wanted, wasn't it,* her aching heart demanded. Tomorrow, he would be gone from her life. *She'd been waiting for the moment, hadn't she?* Tomorrow, she would leave with Burr and never see Chance again. *That would make her happy, wouldn't it?*

Rori bit back a sob born of complete, frantic bewilderment. In a confession that was wrung from her, she faced the terrible truth about what she was feeling for this man who'd come into her world and turned everything upside down . . . this man who just by a smile or a look could send her senses reeling . . . this man whose very touch left her weak and willing. She loved him, she realized painfully, but it was hopeless.

Burr had told her time and again that men were no good and that white men in particular were far from honorable. He'd warned her never to trust them and above all never to love them, but it was too late now. She did love Chance, desperately.

Rori remained motionless as she stared at Chance across the small clearing. She knew as she watched him sleep that she would never again share his passion or know the bliss of his touch. The thought tormented her. She wanted him! Oh, how she wanted him!

Go to him, her heart goaded her. *Go to him one last time before he's gone from you forever. Hold him one last time. Love him one last time.*

The need to be with him was overwhelming, and she was like sand before the force of the wind, swept away by the dictates of her untamed heart. Hesitantly, Rori took a step forward into the circle of the campfire's glow.

* * *

Chance had been lying there for what seemed like endless hours, trying to get to sleep. His thoughts tonight were the same as they'd been every other night since they'd left the pond—they were of Rori. For a man who was used to being in control, it drove Chance to distraction that he couldn't restrain himself from remembering that night. He'd tried just about everything he could think of to turn his thoughts away from Rori, but inevitably, they always came back to her.

Disgusted, Chance told himself that Rori was just a child, but his memory and his body knew otherwise. She was childlike only in her innocence. No mere child could have wreaked such havoc on his self-control. There was something about her . . . something so rare . . .

An image of Rori lying naked beneath him flashed in his mind, and a surge of heat flooded his loins. Aggravated, annoyed, and generally irritated, Chance shifted restlessly on his blanket, wishing he could get to sleep and put himself out of his misery.

Later, he wouldn't know what it was that made him look up at that particular moment, but the reason why it happened wasn't important. All that mattered was that as he glanced out across the campsite he saw Rori move forward into the light of the fire.

Across the distance, their eyes met and held. Chance could read in hers all the confusion and bewilderment she was feeling, and the realization that she still desired him sent his own passions soaring. Held pinned where she was by the heat of Chance's smoldering gaze, Rori remained motionless. She hadn't expected him to be awake. She hadn't expected him to see her, and now it was too late. She waited breathlessly, hoping, dreaming . . . Chance waited, expecting Rori, woman-child that she was, to bolt from him like a frightened doe, but to his surprise and delight she stayed.

Logic dictated he remain where he was, but Chance was a man out of control. He had dreamed of her, wanted her, desired her . . . Chance rose slowly, brushing aside his blanket. He did not storm Rori, but went to her cautiously. He said nothing, not wanting to risk spoiling the moment, so tender, so fragile, between them.

When Chance stopped directly before her, Rori tilted her head back a little to look up at him. Common sense told her that she should run from him, hide from his overpowering nearness, but she didn't. She wanted him, and she would never run from him.

Rori reached out with a tentative hand to touch his cheek, and as she did, he grasped her wrist in a firm, strong hold. His touch was hot and sent shivers of excitement down her spine. She remembered the strength of his hands and the pleasure they could give her.

Rori did not protest as Chance led her away from the revealing light, away from the sanctity and safety of the camp, away from the protection of Burr's slumbering presence. Neither one of them spoke. Neither one of them wanted to shatter this fragile, almost crystalline closeness that existed between them.

Chance didn't stop until they were away from the encampment at a secluded spot where they would be neither seen nor heard. He released her wrist and turned to her then, gazing down at her with something akin to amazement. How was it that this mere slip of a girl—a girl who dressed like a boy, rode like a boy, shot like a boy, and cussed like a boy—could affect him this way? What was it about this raven-haired vixen that had stirred his desires to a fever pitch?

In Boston, the women chased him with practiced precision and expertise. He allowed himself to succumb to their charms as it suited him, used them in mutually pleasurable pursuits and then ended the associations when the thrill was gone. But Rori . . . Rori was so different, so unbelievably extraordinary that he was at a loss to completely understand it. Chance only knew that he wanted her with a gut-wrenching need that surpassed anything he'd ever experienced before.

Chance studied her upturned face in wonder, feeling almost as if he were seeing her for the very first time. Her dark eyes were shining like stars, and even in the darkness he could tell that her cheeks bore a gentle flush of excitement. Her lips were parted and he could hear the unsteady rush of her breathing as she waited for what they both knew was coming next.

Chance longed to run his hands through the black velvet cascade of her hair again. Lifting one thick braid from where it rested against her breast, he freed it from its binding and combed his fingers through its ebony silkiness. He repeated the gesture with the other one and when her hair hung about her shoulders in a sable cape, he cupped her face with his hands and sought her lips with his own.

His kiss was ecstasy for Rori, yet she remained standing rigidly before him, fearful that he would end it too soon. She wanted to savor the moment, to relish the delight of his mouth moving teasingly over hers. She didn't want to do anything that might cause him to stop.

Chance sensed that there was something bothering her, something that was causing her to hold herself back from him, and he raised his head to look down at her. "Rori?" Her name was a husky whisper on his lips.

His voice was deep and sensual and sent shivers of sensual awareness coursing through Rori. She couldn't speak. She was afraid to . . . afraid that she'd blurt out everything she was feeling and embarrass herself miserably. She raised her eyes to his in an unspoken plea for understanding as she unconsciously swayed toward him.

Chance saw the wild mix of confusion and desire in her dark-eyed gaze, and he knew just what she was feeling. Whatever this thing was between them, it was beyond restraining, beyond control. It was primitive and demanding. Chance waited no longer, but gathered her close.

"Ah, Rori . . . I know . . ." The confession was wrung from him. His lips met hers then softly . . . exploringly . . . questioningly . . .

Rori melted against him, clinging to his broad shoulders and relishing the feel of his hard body beneath her hands. *He said he knew . . . he said he knew . . .* It struck her as wondrous that he understood what she was feeling. *If he understood,* she reasoned with naive logic, *then he must be feeling it, too. He must love me, too!* The revelation wiped away any vestiges of doubt she'd had about loving him, and she gave herself over to him fully, without reservation.

Chance felt her surrender, and a thrill coursed through him to his very soul. He slipped one hand up to cup the nape of her neck as his mouth slanted demandingly across hers. His tongue sought hers in a sensuous duel, encouraging her to kiss him back in the same way, encouraging her to more boldness. Rori was breathing hard as the exchange ended, and when Chance trailed heated kisses to her ear and down the side of her neck, she instinctively arched against him as tingles of excitement shivered through her.

Chance grew mindless in his need to be close to her. He wanted to strip away all of their layers of clothing and ease her gently to the ground. He wanted to explore every inch of her with caresses meant to give pleasure as well as to please. He wanted to kiss her until she was senseless with desire, and then he wanted to slake that desire.

Had Chance thought about it, he would have realized that, for the first time in his life, he was more concerned about someone else's needs than with his own. But

Chance was beyond thinking. He was beyond anything but feeling. His hands drifted down her back to her hips to pull her fully against the thrusting strength of his thighs.

Rori felt the heat of his arousal and trembled in anticipation. She lifted her lips to his again, wanting to tell him with her kiss that her desire matched his in every way. This time she took the initiative, her tongue darting into his mouth in invitation.

At her sensual provocation Chance's already flaming passions exploded into a wildfire of fervid excitement. One hand slipped beneath her shirt to seek out her breasts as he still held her tightly against him with the other. He began to move against her in a teasing, taunting rhythm, letting her know with his body just what it was he wanted, needed from her.

A gasp of exhilaration escaped Rori at the sensations his surging hips created deep within her. She felt hot and restless and needed oh-so-desperately to move with him and against him. As she picked up his motion, fluidly moving her body in time with his, the tension between them grew almost unbearable.

Chance, knowing that she was driving him to the edge of oblivion, stopped all movement and just held her tightly to him. Rori's heart sank as he ceased his thrilling rhythm, and she tried to entice him to move again by rotating her hips against him. He groaned at her seductive ploy, but exerted his iron-willed self-control.

"No, sweet one, not yet . . . not yet . . ." he murmured hoarsely, shifting slightly away from her.

"Chance?" Rori suddenly feared that she'd done something wrong.

"Hush, love."

He silenced her with another kiss, a passionate, drugging kiss that wiped from her mind any thoughts that things were not right between them. When the kiss ended, he helped her shed her shirt, and she shivered to be so exposed to his gaze. Her protective instincts told her to cover herself, but her desire to prove her femininity to Chance encouraged her to be proud of her body.

Chance's dark eyes lingered on her bared breasts, tracing their loveliness, their golden, creamy fullness and their darker, duskier crests. She was so lovely . . . so beautiful. He kissed her once more fleetingly on the lips and then lowered his head to take one pert peak in his mouth. His hands rested possessively on her slender waist, holding her still before him.

Rori stared down at his dark head pressed against her bosom and knew a heart-swelling depth of emotion more vibrant, more shattering than anything she'd ever felt before. Of their own volition, her hands came up to cradle him to her. Encouraged by her move, Chance began suckling at the hardened nipple, and pleasure, so sweet, coursed through Rori, making her think that her knees were going to buckle beneath her.

Chance heard her sharp intake of breath and felt a surge of pride in knowing that he was pleasing her. Rori swayed against him as the ecstasy of his tender ministrations became too much to bear. He raised his head, then claimed her lips for a blazing kiss.

Together, they sank to their knees and then lay upon the sandy earth. Chance pressed heated kisses to her throat and bosom and then moved lower to trail them across her stomach above the waist of her pants. Rori's fingers tangled in his hair as he tormented her so, and when he finally lifted her hips and slipped her buckskins from her, she sighed. It felt so right and so good to be naked beneath him.

Chance moved to kiss her again, and she reached for him eagerly. Her hands worked feverishly at the buttons of his shirt as the kiss continued, and when at last he was naked to the waist, Rori could not stop touching him. She loved the feel of his hot, hair-roughened skin beneath her hands. She loved the feel of his firm, sculpted muscles. He was perfect in every way to her, and she loved him . . . she loved him . . .

Chance paused in their lovemaking only long enough to shed the rest of his own clothes and then went back into her arms. They came together in a fiery inferno of desire, each caress fueling another and another. Pleasure coursed through Rori's veins as he molded her to him, letting her feel the hard, ready length of his manhood.

Rori opened to him like a flower before the sun, parting her thighs in readiness for his possession. Chance fitted himself to her, his hands caressing her, preparing her for his entry into the dark heat of her body. He positioned himself and was surprised, and pleased, when Rori boldly reached down to guide him to her. Her hand was cool upon his hot, demanding flesh, and he reveled in her touch. She took him deep within the heart of her, tensing only momentarily as she accustomed herself to the still unfamiliar feeling of his body buried in hers.

Chance felt her body accept him and then close around him in a silken sheathing that wrapped him in molten rapture. He shuddered. His entire body was like a tightly coiled wire ready to snap, yet he exerted superhuman control over his raging desires and remained unmoving within her. Chance would not rush; he would not let this pass too quickly.

Rori held him close, cherishing his nearness, his very maleness. When he began to move, she met him thrust for driving thrust. When he began to touch her again, seeking out her most sensitive places, she returned the joy, caressing his back and hips. Daringly, Rori slipped a hand between their mating bodies to touch and explore their tender joining.

Stirred by her tantalizing caress, Chance's passion was driven to a fever pitch. He groaned and crushed her to his chest as he surged against her. They melded together, one body, each aware only of the other, each seeking only to please the other. The flashpoint came for them both, exploding in frenzied, overwhelming ecstasy. They spiraled upward, each rhythmic thrust taking them higher and higher until their glory burst upon them in a rush of breathless excitement.

Rori clung to Chance, sobbing as the feverish madness ebbed slowly from her. She felt him shudder as she held him and knew a new sense of womanly power. It was deep and abiding and left her feeling heady with the discovery that she could please him just as much as he could please her. She wanted to stay in Chance's arms forever. She didn't care about anything but being with him and pleasing him. She loved him. He meant the world to her.

Chance cradled Rori's slender body to his as the splendor of their enchanted joining quieted. He mused dazedly on how right it felt to hold her, their bodies still locked in love's embrace. He felt sated, yet still hungry for her. He wanted to keep her with him and . . .

As Chance's thoughts were drifting in aimless pursuit of the elusive dream that was teasing the edges of his consciousness, a desert breeze caressed him, cooling the heat from both his sweat-damp body and his passion-seared mind. He was startled to recognize the direction of his thoughts, and he berated himself for his idiocy. What could he be thinking of?

A relationship with Rori was impossible, no matter how right it felt. He admitted reluctantly to himself, now that he was logical, that he did care for her, but he knew it would be cruel to use her. He was going back to Boston just as quickly as he could manage it. If he continued to seduce her this way, making love to her at every opportunity, he would destroy her when he finally left. For all that she responded to him as a woman, he knew emotionally she was still a child. He couldn't risk hurting her that badly. He couldn't do that to her. He would have to fight what his senses told him was right and deny the elemental bond of attraction that existed between them.

Chance knew it wouldn't be easy. He would be lying if he said he didn't want her. He did want her. In fact, it was all he could do to keep from taking her again, right now, as they lay so intimately entwined on the hard ground. He silently cursed himself for behaving like an animal with Rori, taking her there in the wilderness with no thought to her comfort. Yet, he knew he'd been obsessed with having her and that nothing would have stopped him from taking her in that moment. Troubled, he levered himself up on his elbows to ease most of his weight from her, and looked down at her.

In the way of young girls and their first loves, Rori was in heaven. Her heart's desire had come true. Chance did want her. There was no doubt in her mind that Chance loved her. When he shifted his body slightly away from her, but did not leave her, it was another sign to Rori that he never wanted to be apart from her again. She was certain that everything was going to be wonderful between them from now on. Rori gave a deep, excited sigh as she gazed up at him, the adoration she was feeling for him shining in her eyes.

"Oh, Chance, I just knew you were pretending when you were ignoring me," Rori said in breathless, youthful excitement. She thought all of her dreams were coming true. "You really did want me." She sighed again ecstatically.

Oh, my God, Chance thought in desperation as he saw the tender emotion that was mirrored in her innocent eyes. How could it have come to this? He had known it was going to be difficult when he left her, but now he knew it would be far worse than anything he'd ever considered.

"Everything is just perfect between us," Rori whispered with heartfelt devotion. "I love being with you . . . you make me feel so special. I know things have been awkward between us for the last few days, but it was only because we were trying to deny the truth of what we were really feeling. Now, everything's changed. Now, we can spend more time together and . . ." As she was speaking, she lifted one hand to touch his cheek.

Chance physically flinched as she touched his cheek, as much from the physical contact as from her words. *Dear Lord, she expected this to go on and on and* . . . Chance moved completely away from her then, sitting up.

"Wait a minute, Rori," he said as sternly as he could.

"What is it?" Rori asked in all innocence. She had not yet picked up on the nuance of his move and expected only avowals of devotion from him.

"We have to talk."

"I know. Isn't it wonderful?" The newborn woman in her was regarding him with a lovestruck expression.

"Rori." His tone was even more stern and a bit exasperated. "We have to talk about this . . . This has got to stop."

She frowned, puzzled. "Stop? What do you mean?"

"I mean this is wrong, all wrong."

"Wrong? How could our making love be wrong?" Rori was starting to grow tense as she sensed she was not understanding him completely.

The way she said "making love" struck Chance almost painfully. He cared for her, and when she looked at him that way, there was no way he could deny himself, not when he knew how loving and passionate and giving she was. But he also knew that he had to discourage her once and for all, and he had to do it right now. He couldn't let this go on. He had to put an end to it. It would be far worse for her if he didn't.

"Rori, you're such an innocent that you don't understand." He deliberately made himself sound callous. "What happened between us here was not love. It was lust, pure and simple." Chance said the last as he got to his feet and began to dress.

"But you wanted me . . ." she insisted, remembering their explosive passion, still not comprehending what he was saying.

"I won't deny it. I do want you, but it's purely a physical thing between us. There's more to love than just this attraction we have for each other," Chance told her. He was filled with anguish as he saw the reality dawning in her eyes.

Rori recoiled visibly at his words, and she stared at him in disbelief as what he was saying to her took root in her consciousness. The pain was so great, she felt as if he'd slapped her, and in that instant, Rori came fully into her womanhood. She stared at the man before her as if seeing him for the first time. Her expression hardened, growing aloof and cold. Bitterness welled up inside her, and she realized what a fool she'd been. He had used her, and she had let him. The first time she could have forgiven herself for, it had been more accidental than anything, but *tonight* . . . Tonight she'd given herself to him fully, and he'd taken all that she could give.

"Do you understand what I'm saying, Rori? This shouldn't have happened, and we're both going to have to make sure it doesn't happen again. But I guess since we're so close to Doug's, we really don't have to worry about it. After tomorrow, you'll be on your way back home."

Chance sounded like he was dismissing her, as if she really wasn't important in any part of his life at all.

It was that truth that destroyed the childish hopes and dreams that had been nurtured within her. With the grace and control of a sleek animal of the wild, Rori came to her feet. She stood proudly before him as she reached for her clothing, and she dressed quickly with an economy of motion.

Chance waited, wondering what she was going to say, wondering if she was going to cuss him out like she usually did and tell him he was a damned liar or if she was just going to pull her knife and try to kill him. He waited, knowing he'd hurt her, yet knowing it was something that he'd had to do.

"You're right," Rori finally spoke up, but she said it quietly with none of her usual feistiness. "This was very wrong. I shouldn't have let it happen."

Her expression had gone from such open delight to such shuttered blankness that Chance knew he'd succeeded in what he'd planned. But even as he congratulated himself on having put a stop to the irresistible madness between them, he felt oddly, terribly empty inside. He watched Rori walk away from him into the night, her back straight, her head held high, and he knew he would remember this moment for the rest of his life.

Chapter 14

Nilakla's heart was heavy as she focused through the field glasses on the group of three riders making their way over the rugged, mountainous terrain. They were still too far away for her to be completely sure that it was

Burr and Rori bringing Douglas's brother, but she had a feeling that it was for she could make out the coloring on one of the horses and it was a pinto just like Rori's.

As she lowered the field glasses, Nilakla found herself wishing that it wasn't them. She knew this was foolhardy, dangerous, and selfish on her part, because if it wasn't Chance and his guides who were coming, then it was trouble, but at this point she didn't care. She didn't want her time with her love to come to an end, and that was what his brother's arrival would mean.

Nilakla sighed, resting a hand slightly below her heart over her unborn baby. In just a few more months she would give birth to their child, yet Douglas would not be there. She knew Douglas had never intended to stay in Arizona with her. She knew he had never made any promises to her of lifelong devotion. Yet, from the moment they'd met and she'd fallen in love with him, all she'd longed for was to spend the rest of her life with him.

Nilakla still remembered that fateful encounter at Burr's cabin. She had gone to visit Rori, and Douglas had been there. She had loved him from the first moment she'd seen him, and that love had only grown stronger during their time together. Douglas was her reason for living. He was the reason she'd given up her family and left her village. The love and passion she felt for him were consuming, making up for the fact that he had never told her he loved her. Nilakla had always hoped and prayed that her love would be strong enough to change him, but she realized miserably now that she'd been wrong. She wondered how she would ever live without him.

She moved slowly on her way back down to the mine. She was dreading telling Douglas of the riders, but knowing there was no way to avoid it.

"Douglas . . ." she called out as she entered the dig-

gings and made her way down the tunnel through the
dank, lantern-lit gloom.

"What?" Doug responded from some distance away.

"There are riders . . ."

Doug had been working since dawn at his backbreaking labors, and the going had been particularly frustrat-
ing that day. The news that someone was coming filled
him with exhilaration. *Chance! It had to be Chance! He'd
arrived at last!* Doug dropped what he was doing and
rushed to Nilakla.

"How far?"

"They're still quite a distance away."

"Is it Burr?" he asked, taking the field glasses from her
as he eagerly hurried outside.

"I'm not sure." Nilakla had seen the excitement in his
face, and her spirits sank even lower.

As they exited the mine, Doug automatically reached
for the protection of his rifle where it lay near the entrance. He'd become a cautious man since coming to
live in these mountains. He wouldn't set the weapon
aside until he was certain of exactly who it was approaching.

"Get extra ammunition," he instructed.

Nilakla hurried to comply. As she went to get the ammunition for him, though, she remembered how green
he had been in the beginning and how he had come to
learn the wise caution he now used.

Though it was sinking low in the western sky, the sun
was still harshly bright. Having come out of the semidarkness, it took Doug a minute before his vision adjusted. When it did, he climbed the narrow path to the
highest observation point to look for the riders. Doug
spotted them quickly and watched suspiciously as they
approached.

Doug knew he couldn't afford to let any strangers get
too close. Burr and Rori were the only ones who knew

the exact location of the lode besides himself, Nilakla, and his family, now that he had sent them the map. He hoped this wasn't someone just accidentally stumbling upon them. He'd gotten a lot like the other prospectors in the mountains. He didn't take too kindly to trespassers. His grip tightened on his rifle as he continued to follow their progress.

After observing them for nearly half an hour and noting that they seemed to know exactly what direction to take, the group finally close enough for Doug to recognize them, and he felt like shouting for joy. It *was* Chance! He'd made it! Now his own difficulties would be over! With Chance here to help, they were unbeatable. They'd be able to get the gold out and be on their way back to Boston in no time. Thrilled, Doug raced down from his lookout to tell Nilakla the news.

"It's them! I knew Chance would come! I knew it!"

"I am glad for you, Douglas. I know how much your brother's help means to you." Nilakla tried to sound happy, but, in reality, her heart was breaking. She wanted to cry out to him that this was not a joyous occasion, that something beautiful was going to be lost when they came. But she knew it was useless, Douglas couldn't see it. He didn't understand.

"Everything's going to work out just like I planned," Doug was saying as he started down the trail to greet them. "Everything's going to be fine now."

Nilakla struggled to control her own misery as she watched him move off excitedly. It wouldn't do for him to know that she was upset. She wouldn't reveal these thoughts to him. Douglas knew that she loved him with all her heart. There was no more she could do or say to bind him to her. Taking a deep, steadying breath, Nilakla prepared herself to face the others.

* * *

"Doug's seen us," Rori shouted back over her shoulder from where she rode ahead of them. She was delighted at the thought of seeing him and Nilakla again. She needed their warmth and friendship right now, probably more than she ever had before.

"We're that close? Where is he?" Chance was surprised.

"You know, you wouldn't last a minute out here on your own, white man," she said coldly, giving him a derisive look as she pointed toward a dangerous-looking precipice some distance ahead. "He was watching you for almost half an hour, and you didn't even know it. He's heading down here now. He'll be here soon."

Chance found her deliberately provoking attitude grating, but held his silence as they picked their way through the narrow, nearly impossible trail. He certainly didn't want to get in any verbal battle with Rori, knowing how quick-witted and sharp-tongued she could be. He was tense enough with worrying about Doug and trying not to think about what had gone on the night before.

"It's about time you got him here!" Doug emerged laughing from the rock just beside Rori.

"Doug!" Rori didn't even have second thoughts, but launched herself into his waiting arms.

Obviously delighted at seeing her, he swung her around and planted a huge kiss on her lips. An unexpected jolt of jealousy jarred Chance and rendered him speechless as he watched the two of them, his expression hard. Did Rori play the woman for every man but him? Why was it that she could be so open and affectionate with Doug? Was there something between them?

Burr had watched Chance's reaction to the little harmless scene with open interest. The stony yet startled look on the Easterner's face had convinced Burr that Chance hadn't learned the truth about Rori during their trip. With that worry off his mind, Burr almost chuckled out loud as he imagined Chance's thoughts upon seeing his brother kiss an Indian boy.

Doug set Rori down before him for a mock critical appraisal. "Still haven't grown up for me, have you? Don't you ever get tired of being a tomboy?" Doug teased good-naturedly, his dark eyes twinkling.

The shock of discovering how much he and Chance really looked alike startled her, and she had to force herself to remember that this was Doug, her longtime friend.

"Never!" Rori declared with more passion than normal. "Besides, you already have Nilakla. What would you want with me?"

It was the same teasing argument they had every time they were together. Doug found her innocence enchanting and loved her in much the same way he would a younger sister, and Rori had always thought him a handsome man, but knew that he loved Nilakla. They were comfortable and happy as friends, and they wanted it always to be that way between them.

"I know that somewhere beneath all that buckskin there's a beautiful woman just waiting for me . . ." He gave her a playful, dismissing swat on the rear.

Though Chance found he was still annoyed over the kiss Rori had given Doug, he realized suddenly that, in order to protect her, he had to act as if he was surprised that she was a girl.

"Why is it I get the feeling that I've been played for the fool?"

"Chance . . ." Doug turned to his brother for the first time, his eyes shining at the sight of him. "Why would you feel you're the fool?"

"Well," he drawled, "since everybody let me go on thinking that Rori was a boy . . . no particular reason."

"All this time you two were together, and you thought Rori was a boy?" Doug hooted in laughter.

Rori's emerald eyes were glittering as she added, "Some people are obviously more easily fooled than others." She wondered as she spoke if she was talking about Chance or herself, for she had played the fool the night before.

"Not *my* brother." Doug was still laughing. "Not much gets past Chance, especially not women."

His words were like arrows in Rori's heart. Her gaze accidentally collided with Chance's, and she felt a wave of pain wrench through her. Angrily, she tore her eyes away from his. To her dismay, Chance went right on talking easily with Doug. Obviously, nothing was bothering him, nothing at all.

"You know how difficult it is to trick me, don't you, little brother?" Chance leveled a cool-eyed stare at him.

"That I do." Doug chuckled, remembering the many times he tried and how he'd failed on each and every attempt.

"You know, you don't sound much like someone who's in deadly danger," Chance concluded dryly, crossing his arms over the pommel as he continued to hold him pinioned with his stare. He had expected Doug to react nervously, like a small boy caught with his hand in the cookie jar. Instead, Doug answered him very calmly and without guilt.

"'It's deadly enough, Chance, believe me, but we can talk about that later." He met his gaze fully and unflinchingly. "I'm just glad you're here," he went on with a solemn earnestness.

There was still no trace of the desperation Doug usually showed whenever he summoned him to the rescue, yet Chance sensed he was very serious about the danger. He stared at the man who was his brother and felt as if he was looking at a stranger. There was something different about Doug and not only in his physical appearance. Gone were the fancy gentleman's clothes that in the past he'd always set such store by. He was dressed now much like the miners he'd seen in town—denim pants, a nondescript dark cotton shirt, and scuffed boots. And there was a difference in his expression. Something in Doug's eyes showed a true change in him . . . a maturity that had never been there before. Despite the fact that he was dirty and sweaty from working all day, that his blond hair was overlong, and he sported better than a day's growth of beard, Chance could tell that he'd grown up.

"I'm glad I'm here, too, and I'm even gladder to see that you're still in one piece. From the tone of your letter, I was afraid I might not get here in time to save your hide." Chance swung down from his mount, and they embraced warmly as brothers should.

"Save my hide?" Doug scoffed good-naturedly when they moved apart. "As long as it took you to get here, I could have been dead and buried with flowers growing over me by now!"

"I got here as quickly as I could. I was only back in Boston three days before I left for Arizona. Your letter made it sound like you were in big trouble."

"Judging me by my past performance, I can see where you would have come to that conclusion. This situation is just as serious, Chance, but in a different way," he confided solemnly. "Let's go on up to the mine, and I'll explain everything." He then turned to Burr. "Burr, thanks for bringing him to me."

"You're welcome," the old man replied as he dismounted and they shook hands.

"Did you have any trouble on the trail?" Doug's concern was very real.

"We ran into a slide, but other than that it was smooth going for the most part," Burr answered.

"Good."

"How's Nilakla?" Rori asked, eager to see her friend. Nilakla was the only woman friend she had, and she was looking forward to visiting with her.

"She's waiting for us now." Doug nodded in the direction of the mine.

With Doug guiding them, they started up the path leading their mounts. Had Rori and Nilakla been less upset and the men less caught up in the reunion, they would have thought to keep an eye out to see if anyone was following them. As it was, they disappeared up the unmarked track to the hidden diggings, unaware of the two bandits shadowing them some distance down the trail.

"Where'd they go?" Tom asked Hal worriedly. "One minute they were there, and the next minute they're gone . . ."

"Don't go gettin' in an uproar," Hal told him, his eyes narrowing as he studied the mountains ahead. "This damn well might be it."

"You think it's up there?"

"It's sure hidden enough. We'da ridden right on by if we hadn't seen them disappear. Come on, we'll get up there a little bit closer and see what we can make out. They couldn't have gone too far."

"Let's ride," Tom agreed. If the end was in sight, he was ready.

Nilakla waited alone at the diggings. She was prepared to hate Chance even without having met him, and she chewed on her bottom lip nervously as she thought of the upcoming introduction.

"Nilakla!" Douglas called her as they entered the clearing. "Come meet my brother!"

He sounded so happy, so content, that her heart ached. She turned, ready to meet the man who would end the joy in her life.

Chance was walking alongside Doug, leading his horse behind him. When he caught sight of the lovely young full-blooded Indian maiden, he knew immediately why Doug had been so attracted to her. She was stunningly beautiful. He thought his brother a very lucky man and said so.

"I understand now the reason the territory has held you so long," he said to his brother quietly, and then turned to speak to Nilakla. He gave her a warm, welcoming smile as he extended his hand to her. "Hello, Nilakla. I'm Chance. It's nice to meet you. I've heard many wonderful things about you."

Nilakla blinked and took his hand, melting a bit in her resistance before his friendly manner and easy smile. "You have?"

"Burr and Rori told me all about you on our trip here, although they neglected to mention just how pretty you were. But I can see that for myself," he charmed her.

"Thank you," she replied, returning his smile in spite of her original intentions.

"Nilakla!" Rori called as she and Big Jake came up the trail.

"Rori!" the other woman cried in delight as she ran to see her friend. She was fond of the younger girl and always enjoyed her visits. They hugged each other and then she had to take the time to pet Big Jake who was hounding her for some attention.

"You've known Rori and Burr for some time?" Chance questioned.

"Just about since I arrived here. They're very special people, and I care for them a lot."

"I can see that," he answered, wondering just how much his brother "cared" for Rori after seeing the kiss they'd exchanged. As soon as he thought it, Chance berated himself for it. Obviously, Nilakla was Doug's woman, not Rori. Still, the jealous thought nagged at his usually unperturbable psyche.

While Burr took care of everyone's horses, the two women began to prepare the dinner meal, and Doug showed Chance the mine. When they reached the valuable ore he had stashed in the very depths of the cool, dark tunnel, Doug lifted the lantern high so his brother could see the quality of the gold.

"It looks to be one of the richest strikes in the territory," Doug explained. "That's why I've had to be so careful."

Chance could not believe how fabulously wealthy the vein was, and he felt a surge of pride in his brother's achievements. Doug had accomplished all this on his own. He doubted there were few others who could have done as well.

"So what do you do now?"

"That's where you come in. That's why I needed you. If the news of this location had slipped out, I'd probably be dead already. Now that you're here to help me, the odds are improved, and we should have no problem getting the gold out of here."

"You think the two of us can handle it?"

"Has anyone ever stopped us before?" Doug countered with a confident grin.

"Not that I can recall." Chance clapped him on the back as they started from the mine.

As darkness claimed the desert land, they gathered around Nilakla's small cooking fire for the evening meal. Chance studied his brother in the red-gold haze of the firelight, and he liked what he saw. Though they had only been reunited a short time, he had already discovered how greatly Doug had changed. No longer was he a wild dream-chaser. He'd found his dream, and he'd struggled to make it into a reality. The hard, backbreaking work had made a man out of him, and Chance was very proud of him.

"Not everyone could have done what you've done, Doug," Chance told him as they finished eating. "I'm proud of you. I know you've worked hard for this, and you deserve it."

"You are?" Doug stared at him incredulously. Chance had actually said he was proud of him! For a minute, he felt much like the gangling, awkward youth who'd always tried to live up to Chance's accomplishments, but had never quite succeeded. That quickly passed, and he swelled with a sense of achievement. When Chance met his gaze, Doug saw open respect and admiration reflected in his brother's eyes.

"I am, and Mother will be, too—not to mention everybody else you've ever wanted to impress in Boston." Chance grinned, lifting his tin coffee mug in salute.

"What are you going to do now?" Burr asked.

"Cash in my chips," Doug said with a smile, "and head back to Boston."

"You're leaving?" This surprised the old tracker. "You really want to go back?" He'd always felt an unspoken affinity with Doug, and he couldn't understand why he would want to return to civilization. Didn't he know he'd always be miserable there, and what about Nilakla? Burr glanced at her covertly and saw the strained, sad look on her lovely face.

Doug nodded. "There's a lot I still want to do, and now I can do it on my own without relying on my family."

"That's what family is for," Chance spoke up.

"Maybe, but I had to prove to myself that I was man enough to do this, and now I have."

Rori had been sitting with Big Jake near Nilakla just listening to them talk, but with the announcement that Doug planned to leave, she frowned in confusion. Doug was planning on returning home to his family in Boston, yet he made no mention of Nilakla. Nilakla had dedicated her whole existence to Doug, and now he was just going to leave her behind when he left . . .

Rori had always thought Doug was a wonderful man, but suddenly she was seeing him through the eyes of a woman, and she didn't like what she saw at all. He had used Nilakla for his own needs, and now that he had what he wanted, he would leave her behind. Burr had always warned her not to trust men, and now she understood why.

Unconsciously, she hugged Jakie to her. He and Grampa were the only men she could ever trust with her love. They were the only ones she knew would always be there for her. There was no one else she could ever rely on or risk loving. Her encounter with Chance had proven that to her . . .

Her gaze was drawn magnetically to Chance then, and she stared at him in the glow of the fire, remembering the way he'd looked at her the night before and how passion had erupted so wildly between them. Chance had been right. It should never have happened. She'd been a fool to give herself to him, just as Nilakla had been a fool to give herself to Doug. But she knew better now. She would never, ever make that mistake again.

Chance seemed to feel her eyes upon him, and he looked up to find her staring at him with cold disgust. Even though he knew he deserved it, it bothered him, and *that* bothered him. He shouldn't care what she was thinking about him. It was just like he told her last night. He had wanted her, lusted after her, he'd had her, and that was it.

As Chance ran those thoughts through his mind,

forcing himself to think of the bitter ending, images of her sweet and gentle in his arms, assailed him instead. He saw Rori whisper something to Big Jake, and it seemed as if even the damned dog was regarding him differently, too. When Doug suggested they take a short walk together and catch up on what was happening back home, Chance gladly jumped at the opportunity. They left the others and strode side by side from the camp out into the darkness.

"How soon do you want to leave?" Chance asked when they were alone under the stars.

"The sooner the better," Doug told him.

"Is Nilakla coming with us?"

Doug looked slightly surprised that he'd even asked. "No. She wouldn't be happy in Boston. You know how it would turn out. I refuse to let her be subjected to the cruelty that would come of it. Nilakla's a very gentle, loving woman. I don't want anything to hurt her." As Doug said it, he realized that he might be hurting her more by leaving than all the cruelties society might inflict on her in Boston. Still, he refused to change his plans. He was going home. That was all that mattered to him.

Chance was thinking of going back home, too. He realized that Doug was completely right about not taking Nilakla back with him. It would never work. The life there was far too different.

Chance thought of Rori and knew that he'd done the right thing by ending the passion between them when he had. He did care about her in his own way, and he hadn't wanted to hurt her, but it had been best to put a stop to everything before it had gotten too involved. This way she wouldn't be hurt when he left. In fact, she hated him so much she was probably looking forward to his going. That thought annoyed him, but remembering how she'd looked at him earlier that evening, he knew it was true.

Chapter 15

Taking care to go in the opposite direction that Doug had gone, Nilakla wandered off into the night seeking some time alone, some time to sort out her thoughts. Her eyes were brimming with unshed tears as she made her way to a quiet spot some distance from the mine. There, alone and forlorn, she finally gave vent to the pain and sorrow that had consumed her.

It was over. There was no longer any hope left in her heart that Douglas might change his mind and stay. After listening to him speak of Boston with his brother and seeing the happiness that shone on his face at the thought of going home, she knew their time together was over.

Now, it was just a matter of waiting until he left her, and Nilakla wasn't sure how she was going to live through it. Just the few hours tonight had been torturous for her. The prospect of standing by and watching him prepare to go away completely devastated her.

It was obvious that Douglas no longer needed her. Nilakla bit back a sob at the thought, and her pride surged forth. She realized with agonizing clarity just what she had to do. She would not wait around for him to leave. She would not be able to bear it. Instead, she would leave first, tonight, when everyone was asleep, and she would not be missed for many hours.

Nilakla felt certain that Douglas would not come after her, and that was the way she wanted it. After all, what would be the point? He wanted to go, and he was going. There would be no reason for him to worry about her. She could take care of herself quite well.

Her mind made up, Nilakla felt somewhat better. She would go back to Douglas now and share his love one last time. Then later, while he slept, she would disappear into the night and out of his life. It would be best this way.

Nilakla started back to the diggings, but decided to stop first at the small pond that served as their watering hole to bathe her face. She did not want anyone to know how upset she was. She was startled when she found Rori there with Big Jake. Nilakla tried to keep her face averted so Rori wouldn't see the ravages of her tears, but her friend's next words told her that she'd already seen the truth of her sadness.

"Nilakla . . ." One glance at her friend in the moonlight had revealed that she'd been crying. Rori knew it was because Doug was leaving, and she wondered if she could help her. "Is there something wrong? Is there anything I can do?"

"No, Rori. There's nothing wrong." Although she knew Rori meant well, she didn't want to talk about it. She just wanted to be left alone.

"You're sure?"

"I'm sure."

"Oh." Rori paused. The coolness in Nilakla's tone was unmistakable. "All right."

Rori took the hint, moving off in the darkness to allow Nilakla her privacy. Anger overtook her as she walked off with Big Jake, and when she was far enough away to talk to him without anyone hearing her, she grumbled, "I just don't understand it, Jakie! Why would Doug leave her when he loves her like he does? It doesn't make any sense. They've been together for such a long time, and now he's just going to pack up and go . . ."

For a moment Big Jake gazed up at her, his expression sympathetic, then suddenly he looked past her, cocked his ears, and growled. Rori knew he'd sensed someone coming, and she turned just in time to come face-to-face with Chance.

"Chance . . ." Rori gasped his name as she stared at him. Her emotions tumbled wildly within her. Despite her anger, her heart lurched and her pulse quickened. How she hated him, and yet . . .

It wasn't fair that he could still affect her this way. She didn't want to feel anything for him, but when he was near she couldn't seem to help herself. She'd managed to ignore him all day, letting the bitter memories of the night feed her hurt and anger. Yet, alone with him now under the stars, the memory of his passion returned full force. Rori fought it frantically with every ounce of her willpower.

"You! What are you doin' out here all alone? Aren't you afraid you might get lost?" she taunted.

Chance had been startled when he'd come across Rori. His guard was down and memories of last night jarred him. Vivid memories of how perfect their union had been ignited a flame within him. Her sarcastic challenge, however, cooled the unexpected and unwanted desire, and he was relieved.

"You don't have to worry about that, Rori," Chance replied evenly. "Doug showed me how to get back."

Rori gave a sharp, derisive laugh. "I wasn't worryin' about you gettin' lost, white man. I was prayin' that you would. Both of you, in fact. Where is Doug? Off packin' his bags already?"

"What the hell's the matter with you?" he demanded.

When he raised his voice, Big Jake bristled and gave a low, warning growl deep in his throat.

"Hush, Jake," Chance ordered, and the dog was silenced.

The anger Rori was feeling over Nilakla's hurt coupled with her own pain, and when Jake responded to Chance's command, she couldn't take any more. Having built to a crescendo her frustration and fury erupted into violence. Without another word, she threw herself at Chance, pummeling him with her fists.

Chance was caught off guard by her surprise attack, and Rori managed to land a few solid blows before he finally snared her wildly flailing arms and pinned them behind her. With a considerable amount of force, he slammed her against his chest.

The contact between them was electric. Anger vanished before the overpowering wind of passion that swept through them both. His dark-eyed gaze was glittering and dangerous as he stared down at her. A tiny, sane voice somewhere in the back of his mind warned him to release her quickly, to let her go, that it was foolhardy to hold her that way, but Chance ignored it.

Rori stared up at Chance, her lips parted as she gasped for breath against his rough handling. Her eyes grew wide as she saw desire flicker in the depths of his gaze and felt his body go tense against hers. She knew she should fight this. She knew she should continue to struggle, but somehow her body wouldn't obey her mind. Ashamedly, Rori felt her nipples tauten as the heat of him seared her even through all the layers of their clothes. She fought to keep from moaning as his thighs surged against hers.

Chance lowered his head without conscious thought, and his mouth descended over hers in an explosive caress. His tongue delved deeply between her parted lips, seeking her tongue in a dueling, sensual dance of arousal. Rori hesitated and then met him fully in that exchange. In an imitation of love, Chance began the pagan rhythm with his kiss, thrusting and retreating, coiling and coaxing, until Rori was moving hungrily against him.

It was only when Chance freed her hands and she looped her arms around his neck to draw him closer that reality returned. He went rigid, furious with himself for almost having forgotten his vow to stay away from her. Why was it every time he came within ten feet of her, all he wanted to do was lay her down and make love to her? What was it about Rori that drove him to distraction?

Reality dawned on Rori as she felt the sudden tension in Chance, and she blanched as she realized the terrible mistake she'd almost made. She jerked away from him just as he moved away from her. Her gaze clung to his face, and she saw there only a total calm. He seemed completely in control, and it infuriated her. She glared at him fiercely.

"I hate you, Chance Broderick," Rori swore viciously. "As long as you live, don't you ever put your hands on me again!"

"You're the one who attacked me, Rori," he drawled sarcastically. Without another word, because he was afraid he'd take her in his arms and kiss her again, Chance stalked away without looking back.

Neither Chance nor Rori saw Burr watching them from a short distance away. When they had both gone, Burr emerged from where he'd been sitting enjoying the quiet peace of the night. Now, however, he didn't think the night was so peaceful anymore.

Burr considered the kiss he'd witnessed and wondered how many other kisses there'd been and when they had started. It had obviously not been their first. He'd watched Rori after Chance had left her, and, knowing her as he did, he'd easily seen through the anger she'd projected. He realized solemnly that what he had feared most in the beginning had come to pass. Whether she acknowledged it to herself or not, Rori had fallen in love with the Easterner. The only relief Burr felt about the whole situation was that Chance obviously wasn't in love with her. Burr only hoped that he was too much of a gentleman to have taken advantage of her innocence.

Sighing raggedly, the old tracker started back to the mine. He had agreed to relieve Doug at midnight and take the late watch, and if he was to get any sleep at all, he had to get it now. Somehow, though, Burr knew that he'd get very little rest that night.

"Look, it's simple," Hal told Tom in a whisper as they crouched not too far from the narrow track leading up to the hidden diggings.

"I'm glad you think so," Tom countered. "We don't know how many men are up there or anything."

"It don't matter if we can take 'em by surprise, fool. Now listen! We wait till after midnight when we know they'll all be asleep. Then we sneak in and get the drop on 'em."

"How can you be so sure we'll surprise 'em?"

"You think they're lookin' for us? You think they know we're around here? Believe me, if they even suspected we were this close they'd be out here lookin' for us right now," Hal said convincingly. "Listen, we got 'em. All we have to do is sneak up there and blow 'em all away!"

"After midnight?"

"After midnight."

They exchanged savage smiles and settled back to wait for the midnight hour.

* * *

All was quiet when Doug returned early from keeping watch. Burr had surprised him by showing up ahead of time, and he'd been grateful. He'd been longing to make love to Nilakla all night.

As was their custom whenever they came to the mine, Burr and Rori had bedded down outside, and Chance had joined them there. Assured now that they would be alone, Doug felt the heat of anticipation warm his blood at the thought of Nilakla waiting for him. He entered the mine and went directly to where she lay, seemingly asleep.

Doug hesitated, not sure whether to disturb her or not, but as he knelt down beside her, Nilakla opened her eyes and lifted her arms in invitation to him. He said nothing, but went to her, taking her in his arms and holding her close. His lips sought and found hers in a deep, seeking kiss.

Driven by her desperation, knowing that this would be the last time she ever loved him, Nilakla gave free rein to her emotions. She wrapped her arms around him and drew him near to her heart. With every kiss and caress, she let him know that he was her one and only love. Their clothes discarded, they joined together in a breathless union.

As Nilakla moved with Doug in perfect rhythm, she felt certain that her heart was breaking. For this moment and this moment alone, he was hers. When he left her tonight, he would be leaving her forever. She fought back the tears that threatened as she hugged Douglas to her, kissing him hungrily, savoring every second of their being together. Then, it was over as in a cataclysm of excitement they reached the peak as one, and spiraled slowly downward still clasped in each other's arms.

"You're wonderful," Doug whispered as he pressed one last, soft kiss to her lips and then moved away to sleep.

Nilakla did not answer, for her throat was burning from the effort to control her emotions. She wanted to cry out her love for him and beg him to stay. Miserable and feeling very alone, she wrapped her light blanket around her and stared off into the enveloping darkness. She remained that way, waiting anxiously to hear the steady rhythm of Douglas's breathing so she would know he was asleep. Only then could she leave without detection or farewells.

It was less than an hour later when Nilakla made her way from his side. She stood over him in the darkness, watching him sleep, memorizing that one last sight of him before she crept from the mine. Nilakla paused at the opening to study the clearing, and when it appeared that Rori and Chance were both sound asleep, she headed toward the horses. She saw no sign of Burr, and she wasn't worried. Usually when the men kept watch, they stayed up at the lookout point a fair distance away.

As Nilakla started toward the small corral where the horses were kept, Big Jake stirred and his restlessness caused Rori to sit up and look around. Sleep had been impossible for her tonight. Her fight with Chance and their subsequent kiss had wreaked havoc on her senses, and she'd been tossing and turning ever since she'd lain down.

"Nilakla?" she whispered as she saw her friend.

"I'm just going to . . ." Nilakla lied, hoping Rori would just lie down and go back to sleep.

"I'll go with you," Rori replied in hushed tones so as not to disturb Chance. The last thing she wanted to do was to awaken him.

Almost screaming her frustration at Rori's unexpected companionship, Nilakla kept on going, needing to get away from the men before she could explain what she was really going to do. They walked together in silence, with Big Jake trailing after them. Rori only spoke when she realized they were heading for the horses.

"Why are you going over here?"

Nilakla turned to her friend in the early-morning darkness and knew there could be no lying. "I will tell you if you will keep what I tell you only in your heart."

Rori frowned. "What is it?"

"I'm leaving, Rori."

"You're leaving," she repeated dumbly. "Now? In the middle of the night?"

"It's the only way. Douglas is going home. There is no reason for me to stay here any longer. I am going back to my village to my people. I will be happy there."

"But . . ."

"Don't say it. There is no more to say. This is the way it has to be." Nilakla turned her back on her then and entered the corral to get her horse.

Hal and Tom crept ever nearer, guns ready, trigger fingers itching for action. Tonight was the night they'd been waiting for.

"There!" Hal told Tom excitedly. "Did you hear the horses?"

"Yeah, I heard 'em! Let's go!"

They charged quietly ahead, making their way toward the sound of the restless mounts. They reached the corral and hid behind several big boulders near the back of the enclosure. They could hear voices, but they couldn't quite make out who they were or where they were coming from. All they knew was that they sounded a lot like women.

"There!" Tom pointed to where Nilakla was in the corral putting a bridle on her horse.

"It's a damned Indian woman and look there, Tom!"

"There's that little bastard! I'm going to get him right now . . ."

"Hold your fire for another minute," he cautioned. "One shot will wake the others up. Let's sneak in a little closer and see if we can get 'em without shootin'."

Eager to have it over with one way or the other, Tom let Hal take the lead as they moved in to trap the squaw and the half-breed.

"Hold it right there!" Hal leveled his revolver at Nilakla as Tom strode toward Rori with bloodlust in his eyes.

Nilakla only stood and stared at the two in bewilderment, but Rori recognized the two bandits and reacted instantly.

"You!! Get them, Big Jake!! Kill!!"

The dog had heard the menace in the strangers' voices, and at Rori's order charged Tom without hesitation. Tom, however, was not about to be caught unawares this time. With a vicious swing, he clubbed the attacking animal on the head with the butt of his gun, and Jake dropped to the ground like a dead weight.

"Jakie!" Rori cried out as she saw him fall.

"Shut up, you red son of a bitch or I'll kill you right here!" Tom was about to grab her by the arm when Burr appeared out of nowhere.

"Hold it!" Burr hollered.

As Burr shouted his warning, though, Hal swung around. Nilakla threw herself at his gun in an effort to push it out of the way, but he shoved her to the ground with little trouble and fired. The bullet struck Burr, and he fell, collapsing as his own rifle discharged harmlessly into the night.

"Grampa!!" Rori screamed. In the space of a few seconds, she had seen the person she loved most and her beloved pet murdered before her very eyes. "No! No!" She tried to run to Burr, but Tom grabbed her roughly by the arm and started to drag her with him.

Chance had come awake when he'd heard Rori's cry, and he'd just started to get to his feet when the shots rang out.

"Doug! There's trouble!!" he shouted as he snatched his rifle and ran in Rori's direction.

Doug woke immediately at the sound of the shots being fired. He reached instinctively for Nilakla and was surprised to find her gone. He was already on his way from the mine with his own loaded rifle when Chance yelled his warning.

Chance raced toward the corral, keeping low and trying to hear what was going on.

"Tom! Let's get the hell outta here while we still can!" Hal shouted as he hauled Nilakla to her feet. "You takin' the little bastard with you or are you gonna kill him here?"

"He's goin' along for now. I want to enjoy what I'm gonna do to him! What about the woman? You takin' her?"

"Yeah. She's goin' with me," Hal leered. "Come on, we better move!" He pulled Nilakla along with him as he threw wide the corral gate releasing all the mounts into the night, then forced her to run beside him through the night to where their own horses were hidden.

Remembering how accurate Rori was with her knife, Tom stripped it from her and then prodded her in the back with his gun. "Move it! Now!"

Rori knew she was dead if she gave him the slightest provocation, but, oddly, it didn't faze her in the least. She wasn't afraid of either one of them. In fact, she felt nothing but contempt for them and a blinding fury that demanded revenge. Burr was dead . . . Jakie was dead . . . nothing mattered to her except getting even with these two for what they'd done. She didn't know how she'd do it, but somehow she was going to make them pay.

Chance made it to the corral just as the desperadoes led the women away through the rocks. He got off several shots, but they were already out of his range of fire. He started after them, but they returned a barrage of bullets and forced him to take cover. Doug, who'd come racing up, threw himself down beside him.

"Where are they?"

"They headed off up there with Rori and Nilakla!" Chance told him, indicating the direction they'd gone. "They looked like the same two I saw in town."

The news that they'd taken the women struck horror in Doug's soul. "Let's go! We can't let them get away!"

They raced after Hal and Tom, but they were too late. They heard them galloping off into the night as they ran through the maze of rocks trying to catch up with them. Swearing their frustration, the brothers hurried back toward the mine. Their only hope was to find Burr and get started after them as quickly as they could.

"Where's Burr? He had the watch, didn't he? And what about the dog?" Doug asked.

"I don't see them." Chance felt a terrible sinking sensation in the pit of his stomach. He remembered hearing Rori's anguished cry for her grampa. "But I heard Rori call out to Burr right after some shots were fired . . ."

They exchanged solemn glances, their fear for the old man reflected clearly in their strong, handsome faces. Sprinting back to the corral, they began to search. Chance found Big Jake lying quietly near the corral, and he knelt down beside the dog believing him to be dead. He was thrilled to find that Jake was still breathing.

"Come on, you miserable hound! Wake up so you can growl at me some more!" Chance threatened the mongrel in a cajoling tone as he ran his hands over his body trying to find his injury. The lump at the base of his skull was the only wound he could find. He was about to go for water to try to revive Jake when Doug's call stopped him.

"Chance! Hurry!"

Still clutching his gun, Chance rushed to the sound of his brother's voice and found him kneeling over Burr.

"Burr . . ." Chance dropped down at his side. "How bad is it?"

"It ain't bad at all," Burr groused, struggling to sit up.

"Burr, you might want to rest a minute. That bullet grazed your head. It might make you dizzy or . . ." Doug was trying to slow him down, but he would have none of it.

"If you think I'm going to let a little thing like this stop me, you're a damned fool. Those bastards took my granddaughter!" He was oblivious to the pain the bloody gash on his forehead was causing. He was worried about Rori. He glanced at Chance for a moment, trying to judge his reaction to what had happened. When he could read nothing in Chance's inscrutable gaze, he turned a condemning look on Doug. "Hell, they took your woman! What are you two doing still standing here? Get the horses! We've got to find the girls and fast! Or maybe you two fancy city boys don't know what men like that do to beautiful young women?"

Chapter 16

Galvanized to action by Burr's caustic comments, Chance and Doug went after the horses. Both men were relieved to find that the relatively tame animals hadn't strayed too far in the night. They maneuvered them back into the corral as quickly as they could, for time was of the essence. Rori and Nilakla's lives depended upon their rescuing them as fast as possible.

Chance did not speak as he worked beside Douglas saddling the mounts they would need for their pursuit. His thoughts were all centered on Rori as he tightened the cinch on his horse and then dropped the stirrup back in place. With an economy of motion, he checked his rifle to make sure it was loaded and then slid it into its sheath. A strange sense of desperation plagued him. Was Rori safe or had her volatile temper flared and gotten her into trouble? Had she tried to fight them and ended up hurt, or worse yet . . . dead somewhere out there in the night? A gut-wrenching anxiety drove Chance to hurry . . . to rush to find her before anything terrible happened. Chance didn't understand why he felt that way and he didn't question it, he just knew that he had to save her.

Chance's hand drifted down to his revolver where it rested in his holster low on his hip. He hadn't drawn a gun with murderous intent in some time, but tonight, right now, if he had the opportunity, he was going to shoot first and ask questions later. Those bastards had tried to kill Burr and Jake and had kidnapped Rori and Nilakla. This was no time for niceties. Chance was going to find them, and when he did . . . His expression was dark and brooding as he concentrated only on his goal. He was going to find Rori and bring her safely back. Nothing would stop him in that quest . . . nothing.

Doug was startled to find that his hands were actually shaking as he worked at readying his horse, and he set his jaw against the fear that threatened to overwhelm him. *Nilakla . . . Nilakla . . .* How could this have happened to them? Just a few short hours before they had shared such loving delight and now . . .

Doug went cold inside at the thought that something might happen to her. Nilakla was so warm and giving, so completely unlike the murderous villains who'd taken her. He hoped frantically that he could find her before they had the opportunity to harm her.

A fierce protectiveness surged through Doug, and he was surprised by the strength of the emotion. Just hours before he'd been all set to pack up and leave the territory, to bid Nilakla good-bye and never see her again. But now, the realization that she might be in danger made him face just how much she truly meant to him, and it was a startling revelation. *He loved her.* It was the first time he'd ever openly acknowledged the true depth of his feelings for her, and it jarred him. He wondered how he could ever have thought of leaving her behind.

Doug knew then that he had to tell Nilakla of his love. He had to let her know just how much she meant to him. Possessed by a new driving sense of urgency, he rushed to finish saddling the horses and then started to gather up the other things they would need. As he packed extra ammunition, Chance spoke up.

"I've got the feeling that these are the same two men who attacked me in my hotel room while I was in town."

"I didn't know you'd had trouble in town. What happened?"

"Evidently, somehow those two found out about the map. They were waiting for me in my room one night."

"How'd you manage to fight them off?"

Recalling the vicious assault in his room, Chance unconsciously touched his now-healed wound. "If it hadn't been for Rori, I'd be dead right now . . ."

"Rori? What was she doing there?" Doug was surprised by this. Rori in Chance's room?

Chance explained the situation, recalling how well she'd handled herself in the brawl. "She's damn good with a knife. She saved my life. I hope to God she's got her knife with her now."

"Rori's a fighter, all right. She's had to be to survive the kind of life she's led," Doug agreed.

"I know," Chance said, recalling all that Burr had told him. "It must be rough for a girl growing up like this."

"Even though she's eighteen, I don't think Rori even knows she's a girl yet," he responded as he turned away to throw his saddlebags on his horse's back.

Chance was shocked by Doug's remark. Rori was eighteen?! Never in his wildest dreams had he imagined she was that old. He'd thought he'd been robbing the cradle in his desire for her, but eighteen . . . ? Good Lord, Bethany was twenty, and they'd been seeing each other for some time now. Why had he thought Rori was so young? Just because of her innocence? Chance realized now that that made her even more special. Suddenly he couldn't wait another minute to go after her.

"Let's get going. We can't afford to let them get too big of a head start on us."

"You're right. Let's find Burr and ride."

Burr was glad that he'd managed to shame the two younger men into moving. He didn't doubt for a minute that they wanted to go after Rori and Nilakla, it was just that he had to get them away from him so they couldn't see how severely he'd been injured. A dizzying nausea bombarded him, and his head was throbbing until he was almost blind with pain. Still, Burr forced himself to move. Rori was in serious danger, and he wouldn't stop to worry about himself until she was safe.

Burr found his rifle lying nearby, and he bent over slowly to pick it up. As he straightened again, he heard a soft whimpering sound coming from nearby.

"Jake?" The sound of his own voice reverberated agonizingly through his head.

Again the whine came to him from the direction of the corral. Each step was pure torture for Burr, but he didn't stop. He spied Big Jake trying to get to his feet. Each time the dog made it, though, his legs seemed to collapse under him.

"Easy, Jakie. Easy, boy," Burr reassured the struggling pet, knowing exactly how he was feeling. He knelt down beside Jake and began to talk to him encouragingly as he petted him. "Take it slow, Jake, and it'll happen. We have to be strong, you and me. We have to be tough. Rori needs us."

Jake gazed up at Burr, his big brown eyes filled with pain.

"Where'd they get you, boy?" Burr asked as he checked him for wounds. "Just this lump on your head, eh?" He chuckled softly, taking care not to touch the swelling he'd found at the base of the dog's skull. "Guess they didn't know how hardheaded you really are, Jake. You're just like me, aren't you, big guy?" As he spoke the words, Burr had to close his eyes against the fierceness of his own pain.

Jake watched Burr for a moment and, as if sensing his agony, gave a soft whine and licked his hand.

"You're a good dog, Jake," Burr told him gruffly, glad for his undemanding companionship. As Jake pushed himself up to a sitting position and gave a weak wag of his tail, Burr was thrilled. "Good boy!" His spirits rose as he watched the brave animal fight his way back. "I need you to help me find Rori, Jake. We haven't got much time."

Jake gave a soft bark, sounding just like he knew what Burr was saying. He got to his feet then and shook himself off. Though he was unsteady for a moment, it passed.

"Rori, Jake. We have to find Rori," Burr urged.

Memories of Rori's call for help came flooding back to him then, and Jake growled viciously. With a loud bark, he ran in the direction the two desperadoes had taken the women. He paused near the rocks to look back at Burr, obviously wanting him to follow.

"I'm coming, boy!"

"Tom, hold it!" Hal called out as he reined in his weary mount. They'd been riding for what seemed like hours, and the breakneck pace they'd been keeping, along with the fact that they were riding double, had nearly exhausted their horses.

"What is it?" Tom asked as he halted beside him.

"We gotta stop for a while and rest these horses or we're gonna find ourselves on foot tomorrow. There ain't no way we can keep goin' like we been."

"You think we're far enough away?" He glanced back into the darkness, worrying that the others would be hot on their trail.

"Sure," Hal sneered. "They had to catch their horses before they could even think about comin' after us. Besides," he added cunningly, eyeing the steep cliffs and ravines that surrounded them, "if we find a good place to hole up, we can be ready and waiting for 'em when they finally do show."

Tom chuckled evilly. "Good. I can do some of my set tlin' up with the breed here while we wait." He had Rori in front of him on the horse, and he linked a cruel forearm around her throat and yanked her back so he could see her face.

Rori managed to keep from showing her fear, but it didn't stop his tormenting.

"Yes, siree," Tom went on, "you may not be scared yet, but you're gonna be before I get done with you. I'm gonna enjoy this."

Hal was smiling, too, at the thought of drawing out the men from the mine and ambushing them here on the trail. "This is workin' out better than our other plan. We'll pick 'em off as they're comin' up the trail after us. Then it'll be easy to double back and get the gold."

"What about her?" Tom nodded toward Nilakla as she sat silently before the other man on his horse.

"She's my entertainment while we wait. I ain't had no red meat for a long time." He reached around Nilakla to grasp one of her breasts painfully. She gave a small cry of terror at his brutal touch, but he only increased the pressure.

"When was the last time? That squaw and her white man all those years ago?"

"Yep," Hal agreed. "I still remember her. She was a fighter, and that made it fun." He fondled his captive more brazenly. "Are you gonna be a fighter, honey? Are you gonna make it good for me? You make it good for me, and I might let you stay with me for a while," he leered.

"We can share her after I get done takin' care of him," Tom said avidly, giving Rori's neck another wrench.

"We got time. They won't be comin' till after sunup anyway. Ain't no way they can track us in the dark," Hal told him confidently.

Rori had been fighting to control her temper ever since they'd dragged her from the camp. Biding her time, she'd been watching and waiting for the chance to either get one of their weapons away from them and attack them or to make an escape. Their talk about the squaw and her white man destroyed what little restraint she had left. Could these be the same men who had killed her mother and father?

The possibility created a volcanic rage in Rori. A violent need for revenge overwhelmed her. Somehow she would make these two pay for what they'd done to her family. She might not be able to kill them both before they killed her, but she would damn well give it a try. She wouldn't die easy.

As Tom urged his horse on, Rori erupted into violence. She jerked sideways to tear herself loose from his hold just as she kicked his mount sharply in its sides. Rori tried to make a grab for Tom's weapon as the horse bucked and bolted, but luck was not on her side. She lost her seat as she tried to seize his sidearm, and she crashed heavily to the ground.

"Rori!! Run!" Nilakla yelled.

Rori had no chance to get away, though, for Tom recovered control of his horse quickly and rode her down with ease. He threw himself from the back of the horse and tackled her as she ran. Grabbing her with vicious hands, he turned her over. Rori kept fighting, refusing to surrender, wanting to hurt him in any way she could. She bit and scratched, kicked, clawed, and hit out at him with all her might.

"I hate you, you murderin', thievin' bastard!! I'm going to see you dead!" Rori screamed.

"Like hell you are!!" Tom was furious. This half-breed had given him more trouble than he'd ever put up with from anyone else. He'd had enough. He pulled his gun and was ready to shoot her point-blank when Hal's reprimand stopped him.

"Rori!" Nilakla cried, thinking her friend was going to die right there before her eyes.

"Don't shoot that damned gun now!" Hal commanded angrily. "You want them to hear us and know which direction we took?"

"Aw, hell," Tom swore. Frustrated, he grabbed Rori up by the shirtfront and hit her square in the jaw, knocking her unconscious. "That'll shut you up for a while," he gloated. He shoved her limp form away from him, and as he did, her shirt tore beneath his hand. "Son of a bitch!!"

"What's the matter now?" Hal demanded in irritation as he kept a tight hold on Nilakla. He was anxious to find a good hiding spot so he could get on with what he really wanted to do.

"The damned breed's a girl!" He stared down at the beauty of her bared breasts in confusion.

"What?" Hal roared in amusement as he nudged his horse closer. "Well, I'll be damned! It was bad enough when you thought she was a boy, and she cut you up real good in town! But you been bested twice by a female, Tom, and a red-skinned one at that!"

Tom cursed his companion vilely as he studied Rori with evil intent. "And all this time I've been thinkin'" the little bastard needed killin' . . . but now I'm thinkin' different."

"Well, think about that later," he told him. "Let's go find us a place to hole up."

Tom picked Rori up easily and slung her facedown over the horse's back before mounting behind her. They rode on down the rocky trail about another mile before coming to a lookout that gave them a good view of the terrain they'd just covered. When sunrise came, the desperadoes knew they'd be able to see anyone within miles.

"This should do it," Hal announced, pleased with the location. "We could hold off a whole damn army from here." He reined in and dismounted.

Nilakla was frozen with fear as Hal dragged her down from the horse's back. He loomed threateningly over her, his expression wild and lust-filled.

"Get over there and sit down by them rocks. If you try to run, I'll kill you." His voice was harsh as he shoved her toward the far side of the clearing.

Nilakla had no doubt in her mind that he would do exactly what he'd said, so she hurried to do as he'd ordered. She had one hand resting protectively over her unborn child as she dropped to the ground to wait. Horror shook her as her imagination ran wild with visions of what these two might do to them. She began to shiver in fear. She wanted to live! She wanted to have her baby!

Nilakla knew that the men would be coming after them. But the trouble was, she didn't know if they would make it in time, what with Burr having been shot and the horses scattered. Nilakla knew she and Rori would have only one chance to save themselves on their own. Furtively, she touched the small knife she had strapped to her waist. Hal had not noticed it while he was holding her on the horse, and she was grateful for at least that much. It would offer little in the way of real protection from the two brutes, but it was better than being completely unarmed. Huddled there, Nilakla watched helplessly as Tom rode toward her with Rori, an evil grin on his ugly face.

Tom was excited. He'd been waiting a long time for this, and he was going to enjoy it. He stopped right before Nilakla and released his slight hold on Rori, letting her tumble to the ground.

Rori had just started to come around when she landed heavily on her back in the dirt. The torn material of her shirt was splayed open, giving Tom an unimpeded view of her bosom as she lay there trying to gather her wits about her.

"Get up," he ordered.

Rori blinked in bewilderment as she tried to figure out what was happening. When she didn't move immediately, Tom's expression turned black, and he climbed angrily down from his horse. Nilakla couldn't just sit by and watch as someone tried to hurt her friend. She rushed to Rori's side and attempted to help her. Tom would have none of it, though.

"Get the hell away!" He shoved Nilakla violently, and she fell backward, landing heavily against the rocks.

"Now, get up." He turned his attention back to Rori.

Rori had managed to get to her feet and was crouching before him looking much like a wild animal. Her eyes were wide and wary, her teeth bared in a feral grimace. Her shirt hung open, but she paid it no mind even though her breasts were clearly revealed. She might have lost the first battle, but she was determined not to quit trying.

Had Tom known her better, he would have recognized the danger in her stance, but his ignorance was to her advantage. "I said get up, you red bitch, and I meant it." He was bending down to grab her by the arm and jerk her to her feet when she launched herself at him.

Rori went for his eyes, but she missed and only managed to claw his cheek. Tom reacted furiously, knocking her down and kicking her savagely in the side. The force of the kick sent her sprawling on her back beneath the horse. The animal grew skittish at the disturbance, and she was forced to scramble from beneath him to avoid being trampled. Holding her side in agony, Rori rolled safely away. But even though she managed to escape the horse's deadly hooves, there would be no escape from her tormentor. Tom was there waiting for her.

"You ain't goin' nowhere so don't even think about it." He gripped her arm and dragged her to him, his gaze hot and heavy on her breasts.

Rori was gasping for breath, trying to fight against the pain in her side when she saw the heated lust in his expression.

"You lay a hand on me or my friend," Rori finally spoke up, her voice hoarse, "and you're a dead man."

"Is that so? And just who's gonna kill me? You?" he taunted.

"I almost did once," Rori countered recklessly, and he slapped her across the mouth.

"What's the matter? Can't you control this little one?" Hal drawled sarcastically as he came to Tom's side. He admired some spunk in a woman, but he didn't take backtalk from anyone.

"I can take care of this one in more ways than one," Tom snickered as he brushed aside the tattered shirt and fondled her breasts.

"Get your filthy hands off of me!!"

The men only laughed at her useless fury. "You got to understand, squaw, that we take what we want."

"If I ever get the chance, I'll put a knife in your heart . . ." she swore, shaking with frustrated rage as Hal, too, began to touch her. Rori said no more, but lifted her chin defiantly. Her dark eyes glittered mutinously as she spat on them.

"Why, you little . . ." Tom backhanded her, bloodying her lip. "You ain't gonna be doin' much of anything, 'cept what I tell you to do." Tom snarled. "Now, get over there with the other woman and stay put while we take care of the horses."

Rori made it to Nilakla's side and dropped down to sit beside her. She watched the two men through slitted, hate-filled eyes as they tended the horses.

"Rori, you're bleeding," Nilakla whispered as she reached out to touch her friend's torn lip.

Her bleeding mouth was the least of her concerns, and she wiped at it distractedly with her shirtsleeve. "We've got to get out of here . . ."

"I know, but how?"

"I'll think of something." She glanced around trying to judge the area.

"Rori, I still have my knife," Nilakla confided excitedly. "It's small, but it's better than nothing."

Rori's eyes lit up. Unarmed, she was just a woman, but if she had a knife and the element of surprise on her side, she could fight as good as any man. "Give it to me."

Nilakla slipped the small knife from its place in her waistband and covertly handed it over to Rori. "What are you going to do?"

"What do you think?" Her gaze was cold and deadly even as she smiled slightly at her friend.

"What do you want me to do, Rori?" She noticed the

men were just finishing up watering their mounts. "We haven't got much time."

"We're gonna have to make a run for it," she whispered, visually searching for a quick route that would offer them some protection should the men start shooting. "We have to get the hell out of here while we can."

"All right."

"When we run, head back the way we came. Chance and Doug will be coming after us . . ." Rori felt a searing pain of loss at the thought that Burr and Jake would not be with them. They were dead . . . killed at the hands of these men. She fought to put the emotion from her. She could not afford to be weak now. If she wanted to escape and survive, she knew she had to think clearly. "We aren't gonna get a better chance than right now," Rori told Nilakla, her eyes narrowing as she picked the quickest, safest escape route. "We gotta go while they're busy and while they think we're afraid."

"But I am afraid," Nilakla told her friend, smiling slightly.

"So am I." Rori grinned back. "But I'd rather get shot trying to get away from those two than suffer through what they've got in mind for us."

"Me, too."

"When I say go, head over there." Rori nodded toward the side where it was safest to go. "It's pretty rocky, and we should be able to get some cover."

"All right," Nilakla agreed, her heart hammering in her breast as she waited for Rori's signal to run. Escape was their only hope.

Chapter 17

Following Big Jake's lead, Burr, Chance, and Doug rode relentlessly through the night. Each man was haunted by the danger the women faced, and with every passing mile, their tension grew stronger, their nerves stretched taut.

Despite the pain he was in, Burr was ever alert. He couldn't give in to his weakness now. Rori needed him. Burr kept his eyes trained on Big Jake as the dog followed the trail left by the fleeing outlaws. Burr calculated that they had only about a forty-five-minute head start on them, and as treacherous as the terrain was, if they weren't familiar with the lay of the land, they wouldn't be traveling too fast.

Still, as dawn neared, their position became more vulnerable. Burr knew they would have to be more cautious in their approach. As craggy and mountainous as this area was, he knew it would be an easy thing to set up an ambush. They'd have to be vigilant. They would be of little help to Rori and Nilakla if they were shot down trying to rescue them.

A searing, blinding pain shot through his head, and Burr grabbed his saddle horn to keep from losing his seat. He was grateful for the covering darkness, because he didn't want Chance or Doug to see him and realize how bad he really was. It would pass, he told himself.

There would be time later, after they rescued the women, to worry about himself. Right now only Rori and Nilakla were important.

Burr remembered Atallie and Jack and the horrors they'd suffered. Though it had been a long time ago, the memory still had the power to hurt him, even now. He couldn't let that happen to Rori and Nilakla. He had to help them. Setting his jaw against the continuing physical and emotional agony that besieged him, he kept a firm hand on his reins and kept riding.

Doug followed closely behind Burr, his rifle ready in hand. He trusted the old man's tracking abilities and knew that if it was possible to find Nilakla and Rori they would.

Doug kept a sharp eye on their night-shrouded surroundings as they rode, but he let his thoughts drift, recalling in vivid detail all the happenings of the past twelve hours. He wondered how it was possible for things to change so fast. Just a short time before, he'd thought his life was perfect, and now . . .

The gold. The realization hit him forcefully. All of this had happened because of the damned gold. Doug's grip on his reins tightened, and his horse, sensing the change, moved uneasily. He forced himself to relax his hold, calming his mount, but his thoughts did not lighten. Silently, he castigated himself for what he knew now was the cause of all his troubles—selfishness and greed.

It was hard for Doug to admit to himself that he'd been wrong, but admit it he did. His whole purpose in coming here had been to get rich. He'd wanted to prove that he could make it on his own, that he was as good a man as Chance. Now, he realized, there was more to it. Money didn't make the man. What kind of man would he be if he deserted the one woman who truly loved him, the woman who had given up everything for him and asked nothing in return? The woman he loved . . .

Doug gave a slow shake of his head. He wanted Nilakla to be his wife, to be with him forever. It no longer mattered to him what people back in Boston thought—only Nilakla mattered. The thought that she might die because these men were after the mine filled him with self-loathing, and he knew he would give it all up just to have her safe again.

Doug vowed to himself then that, if he did find her and she was all right, he would give up the mine completely. He'd take the gold he'd already mined and get Nilakla away from there so she'd never be in any danger again. He wanted to take care of her forever, to have children with her, to spend all his years with her.

A new sense of maturity filled Doug, and he felt a firm resolve take hold of him. He knew exactly what he wanted to do with the rest of his life now, and he was going to do it. All he had to do was find Nilakla . . .

Doug tensed in the saddle and tightened his hold on his rifle as his gaze swept over the night-shrouded mountains. All he had to do was find her . . .

Chance rode along quietly near Burr, his gaze trained on Big Jake as the dog hunted out the desperadoes' scent on the rocky ground. Chance knew he should have been relieved that they had chased them this far and not found either Rori or Nilakla dead alongside the trail, but at the same time it worried him. Why had they taken the women, and what did they want from them? Were the outlaws strictly after the gold and so were planning to use Rori and Nilakla as hostages for the fortune, or had they merely taken the women to abuse them before they killed them, as had happened to Rori's mother? That possibility sickened Chance, and knowing how Burr felt about the past, he wondered how he was managing to hold up under the strain.

Chance thought of Rori, of their first encounter in town and how she'd successfully fought him off. Silently, he prayed that she'd be able to defend herself against the two who held her captive. He knew she was rough and tumble; Burr had raised her that way. She was scrappy and proud and wouldn't bend easily to anyone else's will, and he feared that her attitude would antagonize her captors. Chance worried how she'd do in a fight against a man if he decided to use his full strength against her, and he hoped to God that she'd never have to find out.

Tense with worry, Chance urged his horse to a little faster pace as he followed Burr and Jake. They had to find Rori and Nilakla tonight, and they had to be safe. If they weren't . . .

Rori led the way, moving slowly at first, creeping toward what she thought was their best escape route. They didn't want to draw any attention to themselves by running quickly, and yet they knew that they had to make their move as fast as they could before Hal and Tom finished rubbing down the horses. They edged slowly toward freedom, waiting for that moment when both of the men were screened from view by the mounts. Then Rori guessed they could make a clear run for it, and she dashed headlong for the cover of the rocks with Nilakla close on her heels. They were there before Hal and Tom had time to react.

"Tom!" Hal bellowed furiously as he rushed from

where he'd been standing behind his horse and drew his revolver.

Tom looked up just as Rori and Nilakla disappeared from sight, and he shouted his wrath at their bold daring. Hal fired quickly, but his shot ricocheted harmlessly off a boulder as Nilakla disappeared into the rocky landscape. He charged after them, gun in hand, determined that they weren't going to get away. Tom drew his gun and joined Hal in the chase. There was no way he was going to let that half-breed bitch escape. This was the last time she was going to humiliate him.

The gunshot echoed through the stillness of the night, and Chance, Burr, and Doug went rigid at the sound. Their expressions turned grim as they looked around trying to figure out which direction it had come from.

Big Jake had no such difficulty. His keen sense of hearing told him immediately where the shot had been fired, and he took off up the mountainside at top speed. Though the pain in Jake's head was constant, the desire in his heart to save Rori was more powerful.

"Follow Jake!" Burr shouted when he saw the dog take off. "They're up there." He pointed the way and jabbed his horse sharply in his sides to get him moving.

"Did Rori have a gun?" Chance called to Burr as he kept up with him.

"No," the old man answered tautly. "She only carried a knife."

"That's all Nilakla had with her, too," Doug told them.

All three men were deeply shaken by the fear that either Rori or Nilakla had been shot down in cold blood by one of their captors.

* * *

Rori and Nilakla were running as fast as they could, dodging this way and that among the rocks and low-growing shrubs. They were thankful for the covering darkness, knowing that without it, Hal and Tom would probably have shot them dead by now. Panting in exertion, they charged onward, never looking back. Neither woman had any idea where they were going, they only knew that they had to keep moving.

They had made it almost a half mile when Nilakla suddenly lost her footing and fell heavily.

"Rori!" she gasped, half whispering, half crying.

Rori stopped immediately and raced back to her friend's side. "Nilakla! Are you hurt?"

Nilakla was sobbing and had one hand resting on her stomach as she tried to catch her breath. "I don't know . . . the baby . . ."

"Baby?" Her eyes rounded in shock at this news. "You're going to have a baby?"

She nodded, her eyes welling with tears.

"Then you have to get up and move! We can't let them catch you! Come on!"

Nilakla tried to get to her feet with Rori's help, but her ankle gave out on her. "I can't do it! My ankle . . . I've hurt it somehow . . ."

"Damn!" Rori swore, looking around for some place where she could hide. There were only rocks and a low-growing creosote bush nearby. "There! Crawl under the bush! Quick!"

"But . . ."

"Don't argue, just do it! I'll keep going. Stay there and don't move! Chance and Doug should be out there somewhere. I'll find them if I can." She helped her to the cover of the bush. "Here, take this." Rori handed Nilakla back her knife.

"But you'll need it . . ."

"Keep it, and if they come anywhere near you, use it."

"What will you use?"

"I can at least run away from them," she told her. "Now, get in there and don't say a word! Don't even breathe loud!"

Nilakla gave her a quick hug and crawled into the hiding place. Rori took one look back and knew she had to get away. She had to get the men to chase after her and lead them away from her injured friend.

"Rori!" Nilakla whispered. "Be careful!"

Rori didn't hear her, though, for she had already disappeared into the night. As she ran, she prayed that Hal and Tom would follow after her and miss seeing Nilakla completely.

When they'd first run from the lookout, Tom and Hal had managed to catch glimpses of the women, but as they'd raced back down the mountainside, they'd temporarily lost sight of them. Knowing it was impossible for them to have gotten away, the outlaws slowed their pace and began to scour the area in search of them.

"They're here somewhere." Tom spoke softly, not wanting to give away their own position should their captives be nearby.

"Keep quiet, and we'll hear 'em movin' around." As Hal spoke, the faint sound of brush moving came to them, and they looked up in time to see Rori darting away.

"There she is!" Tom exclaimed as he took off after her.

"I'll go this way!" Hal shouted. "The squaw's got to be ahead of her. We'll circle in on them."

The two men raced off into the night. Driven by his need to catch the little half-breed, Tom scrambled excitedly after Rori.

The seconds seemed like hours to Nilakla as she huddled there beneath the camouflaging branches of the creosote bush. She held her breath in terror as Tom came crashing by her, but when he barreled on past without stopping, she was encouraged. Nilakla knew that Hal was still out there somewhere, so she remained frozen where she was, waiting, watching, and praying that Rori would get safely away. She clenched the small knife in her hand and was ready for the first time in her life to use it as a weapon against another person. Survival was all that mattered to her now. She would not die without a fight.

Rori came charging down the incline at top speed. She was trying to elude the two who hunted her, but at the same time angle back the way they'd come in hopes of finding help . . . of finding Chance and Doug. The sound of booted footsteps closing quickly behind her alarmed Rori. Straining to the limit, she tried to regain the lead she'd had on her pursuer, but her strength was failing. Her lungs burned as she fought for breath, and her legs felt leaden.

Tom was surprised to find that he was gaining on Rori. An evil laugh escaped him as he drew within arm's reach of her. The sound of his wicked glee sent shivers of dread coursing down Rori's spine. It almost seemed to her that she could feel the heat of his breath on the back of her neck. Realizing just how close he was, she gave one last burst of speed, but it was too little, too late. Tom grabbed Rori by the hair from behind and jerked her forcefully to a stop. She screamed in pain at his brutal hold.

"Thought you was smart, did you? Thought you could get away from me, did you?" He savagely twisted her head back to glare down at her.

The sound of Rori's agonized scream alerted Burr to her closeness.

"That was Rori!!" He turned his horse violently in her direction, leaving Chance and Doug to follow. Burr reined his mount in as he brought his gun to bear on Tom. He would have fired, but could get no clear shot at him while he was holding Rori. "Let her go!!" Burr demanded, his voice ringing out across the black Arizona night.

"Grampa!!" Rori cried out in joy. She had thought him dead . . . she had thought she would never see him again . . . Her spirits soared. Her grampa always managed to make things all right.

Rori's joy was short-lived as Tom reacted fiercely, turning and firing.

Just as the gun went off, Jake came hurling out of nowhere in a snarling, raging attack. The force of his assault knocked Tom backward and forced him to loosen his hold upon Rori.

Rori jerked herself completely free as Jake continued to battle with the bandit, snapping and biting him wherever he could. She saw Burr then, fallen from his horse, and rushed frantically to him. One look was all it took for her to realize how serious the gunshot wound was. She didn't notice the sound of other horses nearing as she grabbed Burr's gun and turned on Tom. Gripping it with both hands, she tried to get a clear shot at the badman. She wanted to kill him! She wanted to see him dead for all that he'd done to Burr and her! But there was no way she could fire while Jake was wrestling with him.

Chance and Doug rode up at that moment, their guns drawn and ready. Chance took one look at Rori, her clothing torn, her expression reflecting pure hatred for this man, and he knew he had to kill the bastard, to see him in hell. Chance didn't know what vile things this man had done to Rori, but he wasn't going to let him get away with it.

"Jake! Get out of the way!" Chance ordered, and the big dog jumped obediently back.

Tom still had his gun, though, and he fired in Rori's direction. She dove for cover just as Chance got his shot off. The bullet blasted into Tom's chest. Cautiously, keeping his gun trained on the desperado, Chance dismounted and went to check and make sure he was dead.

"Rori, where's Nilakla?" Doug asked worriedly as he kept an iron hand on his reins, his horse dancing nervously because of all the gunshots.

"She's back down the trail hiding!" Rori threw over her shoulder as she ran to her grampa, her throat tight with fear and her heart thudding furiously. "You've got to go help her!"

"Are there others?"

"Yes," was all she could manage as she dropped down on her knees beside Burr.

Doug dug his heels into his horse's flanks and wheeled his mount around, ready to rush off in search of her.

"Be careful, Doug!" she called as he galloped off.

Rori's concern for her grandfather drove all other thoughts from her mind. A deep, cold chill filled her as she realized the extent of his injuries. He was unconscious, barely breathing, his breath rasping harshly in his throat. Blood soaked the front of his shirt.

"No, Grampa! You can't die!" She cried in heartbreak and despair. "Grampa, what am I going to do without you? You can't die! You just can't!" Tears of anguish coursed unheeded down her cheeks as she bent over Burr's unconscious form.

Having made certain that Tom was dead, Chance holstered his gun and hurried toward Rori. As he drew nearer, he heard her plaintive cries and realized that Burr must have been seriously hurt. He stopped a short distance away and watched her as she hovered over her grandfather in anguished heartbreak. The happiness he'd been feeling over her well-being vanished, replaced by a deep wave of sympathetic grief. In a moment of understanding, Chance recognized that the old tracker was the only person in the world Rori had to rely on. She had no family—she had only Burr.

Chance had never known such desolation. He'd always been surrounded by family and friends. He could barely fathom the depths of her despair, but he himself felt a heart-wrenching pain. He felt a sudden overwhelming need to take her in his arms and hold her, to protect her from this terrible agony. His need to comfort her overpowered his hesitancy, and he took the final steps. He reached down and took her by the shoulders, drawing her up to him.

"Rori?" He said her name softly.

She was aware of nothing but pure pain; her heart was torn to shreds.

"Grampa, Grampa," she mourned. Her body shook like a leaf in a high wind, and she clung in desperation to the only solid thing left in her world. She looked up at him, her wide eyes reflecting the misery she was feeling. Tears coursed down her cheeks as her gaze locked with his. It was a moment caught in breathless time, when there was no battle, there was no war, only pain and consolation.

"You've got to help me, Chance," she begged. "My grampa's dying . . . I can't get the bleeding to stop, and the bullet went so deep . . ."

Chance's heart lurched painfully in his chest as he stared down at her tear-stained face. For the first time, he was seeing Rori completely defenseless, and it struck him almost painfully. She was so sweet and so young and so totally vulnerable.

"He can't die, Chance! I won't let him die!" Rori vowed with a fierce determination born of fear. What would she do without him? Where would she go?

"Let me see what I can do," Chance offered, dropping

down beside Burr. It was then that he got a good look at the old man's wound. He had seen many like Burr's during the war, and he knew there was little they could do for him there in the wilderness. He needed a surgeon's care and fast, but there was no hope of that. "He needs a doctor, Rori. Where's the nearest help?"

"There's only the Pima village," she answered.

"How far is it? Will they help us?"

"It's several hours ride due west, but it's still closer than town. Nilakla has relatives there. They'll help us."

"As soon as Doug finds Nilakla and brings her back, we'll make a travois and take Burr there," Chance promised her. Yet, even as he tried to sound supportive, deep inside him, he worried that Burr wouldn't survive the rest of the night.

Chapter 18

Nilakla heard the gunshots and knew true terror. Her imagination conjured up horrible images of Rori being shot and Nilakla knew she couldn't stay in hiding any longer. She couldn't remain there like a frightened animal praying for help that might never come. She had the knife, and she had to go help her friend.

Though her ankle was swollen and painful, Nilakla didn't let it stop her. She climbed from beneath the creosote bush and started off in search of Rori. Traveling as quickly as she could, Nilakla tried to stay low as she hobbled along. Her nerves were stretched taut as she moved across the treacherous terrain. She kept the knife clenched tightly in her fist, and at every unusual sound, she swung around in fearful expectation. Nervous sweat beaded her forehead, and she found that she was shivering despite the heat of the night.

Faintly, in the distance, Nilakla heard the sound of approaching horse's hooves. She held her breath as she looked around quickly for a place to hide. She had no idea who might be coming. The thought that Hal or Tom might somehow have doubled back and gotten their horses sent her racing for cover behind a big boulder nearby. Afraid that even the slightest sound might give her away, she remained perfectly still as she pressed herself tightly against the rock and waited.

Doug was getting frustrated and very worried. He'd been watching and listening for some clue to Nilakla's whereabouts ever since leaving Chance and Rori, and so far he had met with no success. A cold sense of dread was beginning to take hold of him as he continued his fruitless search. He was starting to fear that the other outlaw might have already found her. Doug's heart rebelled at the possibility. She had to be all right! She had to!

"Nilakla?" He called out, knowing it was risky, but he was so desperate in his concern that he was willing to take the chance.

Nilakla heard him call her name and couldn't believe it was actually Doug. She hesitated, her actions tempered by both caution and confusion. Remaining where she was, she waited until he had ridden on past her so she could get a good look at him before revealing herself. Nilakla recognized his tall, broad-shouldered form immediately when she crept forward to catch a glimpse of him, and she cried out his name in joyful relief. She was safe at last!

"Doug!"

"Nilakla!" Doug caught sight of her then and practically threw himself from the saddle in his haste to go to her. "Thank God I've found you. Are you all right?" He took her in his arms.

"I'm fine," Nilakla assured him. She knew she shouldn't let him hold her, that it was over between them but there was no way she could deny his touch at that moment.

"I was so worried about you," he confessed earnestly as he held her close. Doug lifted his hands to frame her face. He gazed down at her raptly, then slowly lowered his head to hers and claimed her lips for a long, lingering, cherishing kiss. Doug put everything he was feeling into that exchange—all the love, worry, and joy. He never wanted to be away from her again.

Nilakla almost surrendered to her need for Doug, but she forced herself to remember that she meant nothing more than a bed partner to him. As his lips plied hers in tender persuasion, she strove to remain passive and unresponsive. It was over between them.

Doug had been ready to bare his soul to Nilakla, but her coolness in his embrace puzzled him. He drew back to stare down at her, and she moved completely away from him.

"Nilakla? What is it? What's wrong?" Doug feared the bandits had hurt her somehow, done something unspeakable to her.

"Nothing's wrong," she lied, thinking that things were really a mess right now and how much better it would have been if everything had gone as she'd planned. She had wanted to leave him without making a scene. She had wanted to ride off into the night so she wouldn't have to deal with a tearful good-bye, but now her plan was ruined. She was trapped and she was going to have to face him.

"Good," Doug said as he tried to take her back in his arms. He wanted to profess his newly discovered love to her. He wanted to tell her that he loved her and would never leave her. But Nilakla refused him.

"No, Douglas."

"No?" He looked at her in bewilderment.

"I don't want you to hold me. I don't want you to touch me."

"What are you talking about? Have they harmed you in some way?"

"No, Douglas, they didn't hurt me," she answered, thinking that nothing the outlaws could have done would have hurt her any more than his plan to leave her.

"Then . . . ?"

"It's done between us, Douglas."

"What are you talking about?" His consternation was very real.

"Had they not come into our camp and taken us, I would be gone now, and everything would be all right."

"Gone? Gone where?"

"Back to my village and my people. Our time together was at an end, and I thought it best to leave quietly. Your brother had come, and I knew you would be leaving soon so . . ."

"But, Nilakla," Doug began, believing that if he told her the truth of his feelings for her she would understand and stay with him, "I love you."

It was the first time Doug had ever confessed his love to a woman. He had expected that everything would be wonderful once he did. Nilakla's reaction to his declaration, however, was nothing like he'd imagined. There was open disbelief mirrored in her dark eyes, and it startled him. *He loved her! Why didn't she believe him?*

Nilakla had waited for so long to hear Douglas tell her that he loved her that now she found it very hard to believe. Though in her heart she wanted it to be true, her mind told her there had to be another explanation for this sudden change in him, and she was sure she knew what that reason was. He had found out about the baby! What other possible reason could there be? He didn't want her love. All he wanted from her was their child, and no doubt he thought this was the way to get him.

"I want to believe you, Douglas, but I don't," Nilakla told him as she met his gaze squarely. "You can take everything you want from this land with you when you go back East, but you will never take my child from me."

Doug was completely shocked. *Nilakla was pregnant? She was having his baby!?!*

"I'm going home to my people, and I will have my child there," she continued defensively. "I want him to be surrounded by people who love him."

Doug went from stunned to elated, and he smiled crookedly. "That's how a child should be raised, love," he agreed, thinking of his own childhood. He lifted a hand to tenderly caress her cheek. "You'll make a beautiful mother, and our baby will be perfect."

She stared at him distrustfully, not that he hadn't always been kind and gentle with her, but why should he be showing such interest? Why did he care? He was leaving. He would be going back to Boston with Chance just as soon as he could. That hadn't changed.

Doug watched her changing expression, read the conflict there, and felt a great tenderness well up inside him. As much as it hurt him now to admit it, he understood what she was feeling. He realized that he'd never given her any real reason to believe that he loved her. During the course of their relationship, he'd seldom been a giver.

Reflecting on it now, it seemed to Doug that all he'd ever talked about was striking it rich and going home to Boston. No wonder Nilakla doubted him. Doug knew he had a big job cut out for him if he was going to convince her of his sincerity, if he was going to prove to her that she meant everything to him. It would take time, for she was wary of him, much like a deer in the forest, but he had nothing to lose and everything to gain by being patient. Nilakla and their child were his life now—nothing else mattered.

The bullet slammed into the boulder beside them, shattering the momentary quietude that had existed between them. Doug instinctively threw Nilakla to the ground and shielded her body with his own as he tried to decide from which direction the shot had come.

"Were you hit?" Doug asked in a hoarse tone. The fear that he'd felt over her disappearance was totally eclipsed by the terror that gripped him at the thought that she might have been shot while standing right beside him. Doug cursed himself for letting his guard down for even that short time. He had been so caught up in the thrill of knowing that she was carrying his child that he hadn't been thinking of the danger. That foolishness had almost cost them their lives.

"No," Nilakla whispered.

"Chance got one of them, but this must be the bastard who got away. Stay down, no matter what," he ordered harshly in her ear and then scrambled quickly away from her, his gun drawn and ready.

Hal had seen what had happened to Tom in his showdown with Burr and Chance. Realizing that he was outgunned, Hal had hightailed it back the way he had come. He was desperate to get safely back to his horse. Moving quickly and silently through the night, he'd headed up the mountain toward the lookout spot. As he neared the point where he had split off from Tom, he had heard voices and recognized one as the other Indian woman's.

Logic told Hal that he should get his horse and get out of there since he knew the location of the gold mine and could easily come back another time for his riches. But Hal was unable to pass up the chance to seek some

revenge on the women. He had climbed to a higher
vantage point, and then had crept closer to the edge of
the overhang so he could get off a good, clean shot at
those below.

When he'd spotted Nilakla with Doug, he'd taken
quick aim and fired. When his shot missed them by just
inches, Hal grew furious. His advantage of surprise was
lost, and he knew he'd better get out of there as fast as
he could. He ran from where he'd been hiding and
headed straight for the small clearing where they'd left
the horses.

Doug saw the furtive movement on the ridge overhead, and he made a daring dash for higher ground. He
wanted to trap the cowardly killer and face him down on
his own terms. Doug took care not to make himself an
open target as he shifted positions and kept down low
among the craggy boulders and outcroppings. He was
almost halfway up the steep incline when he saw Hal
making a run for it.

"Hold it right there!" Doug ordered, training his gun
on the fleeing bandit's back.

Hal heard him call out, but did not stop. Instead, he
pivoted and fired haphazardly as he kept running. He
knew his only hope now was to get to the lookout place.
He could hear Doug coming after him in endless pursuit, and he stopped at the crest of the jagged mountainside to fire at him again. That was his fatal mistake, for
the rising sun was just beginning to brighten the eastern
horizon, leaving him perfectly silhouetted against the
paling sky. Doug returned his fire, winging him, knocking him off balance, and sending him tumbling backward out of sight down the far side of the mountain.

Doug waited, not trusting that Hal had really fallen.
His breathing was still labored as he slowly climbed the
rest of the way to the top, searching guardedly for some
sign of the villain. As the sun slipped above the horizon,

bathing the desert world in its fierce golden glow, Doug saw what was left of Hal at the craggy bottom of a fifty-foot sheer drop. There was no doubt that the man was dead, for no one could have survived that bad a fall.

Doug stood for a moment, looking down at the body, and then turned his back on the scene. He slowly holstered his gun as he headed toward where Nilakla, and his future, waited for him.

Rori was keeping vigil at Burr's side now wearing Chance's big shirt over her own torn and tattered one. At the sound of an approaching horse, she looked up to see Doug returning with Nilakla, and she was thrilled. She wanted to run to her friend and welcome her back, but she didn't dare leave her grampa's side. Though she and Chance had done all they could, Burr had not regained consciousness since he'd been shot. Rori knew that his only hope for survival was to get him to the Pima village as soon as possible.

Nilakla saw Rori kneeling beside her grandfather's still form. Without a word to Doug, she dismounted and went to her. "How is he, Rori?"

Rori lifted her gaze to Nilakla's and the Indian woman saw reflected there all the anguish and sorrow the younger girl was feeling. "I don't know," she told her in a hushed, tear-choked voice. "He hasn't moved or spoken . . . We have to get him to your village. It's the closest place and there might be someone there who could help him."

As Doug joined them, he quickly assessed the situation and then spoke up. "I'll ride to the mine and get what we need to make a travois. There's no other way Burr can be moved safely."

"Thank you," Rori said as she turned back to Burr, keeping his hand held tightly in hers.

"Thanks, Doug. I'll stay here with them," Chance told his brother as he watched him mount up again, "but hurry. I don't know how long he can hold on. How far a trip is it to the village?"

"It'll take half a day at the pace we'll have to keep," Doug answered, and Chance nodded his grim understanding. "I'll be back," he promised, and they exchanged knowing looks as he rode off.

It was early afternoon when they finally came within sight of the Pima village. Nilakla rode ahead to announce their coming. Doug had wanted to ride along with her, but she had refused his offer. She did not want her people to think that she and Douglas were one. She was returning to her home now and planned to stay there.

Nilakla's refusal to let him accompany her into the village to meet her people hurt Doug, but he fought it down. He had a long way to go to win back her trust and love, and he realized that this was just the starting place. He would take it one day at a time.

Doug rode along slowly with Chance and Rori as they maintained the plodding pace necessary for the travois that Rori had insisted she, and she alone, pull.

Chance, wearing the extra shirt Doug had brought him from the mine, had been quietly observing Rori, and he sensed she was nearly half crazed with worry for Burr. The old man had shown no signs of regaining consciousness during the entire, arduous trip, and Chance was beginning to wonder if he ever would. He had tried to talk with Rori several times during the course of their cross-country trek, but she had barely responded to him beyond answering a "yes" or "no" to simple questions. He had finally given up the effort and had just ridden silently along at her side.

Rori was oblivious to anything except the need to reach the village. Her emerald eyes seemed huge in her face, their depths haunted by her unspoken fear. Her mouth was set in a grim line, and tension radiated from every part of her slender body. Her movements were mechanical as she subdued her desire to panic. She wanted to kick her horse into a run and rush Burr to the village, but she knew such a rough ride would only make things worse. With a patience and iron will Rori didn't know herself capable of, she held her runaway emotions in check and kept her gaze locked on the encampment up ahead where help awaited them.

Though his heart leapt with excitement at the sight of his only child, his daughter Nilakla, riding back into their midst, Chief Lone Hawk kept his rugged features schooled into a stony expression. Long months ago, he had tried to stop her from going away with the white man she'd called Douglas, but she had defied him. She had ridden away with the white man without a word, and he had heard nothing from her since.

Lone Hawk wondered now why she was returning. Had the white man used her and then left her as the chief had originally feared he would? Was Nilakla being forced to swallow her fierce pride, that was so like his own, and return to live with her people? Though he could not appear too welcoming after her blatant show of defiance, the chief was thrilled to see her. He had missed his spirited offspring.

Nilakla rode forward to face her father for the first time since she'd willfully rebelled against him and had chosen to go live with Douglas. She kept her head held high as she met his fathomless, obsidian gaze without flinching. "Father," she greeted him cautiously.

"Nilakla," he returned stiffly.

"I have come because I am in need of your help," Nilakla told him quickly. When he didn't respond, but continued to regard her with a wooden expression, she went on. "Burr, the old white man whose son married Atallie, has been shot. My friends are bringing him here now. We need your help, Father, or he will surely die."

"There were no white men who could help you?" Lone Hawk asked tersely.

"It was white men who did this to him," she answered just as brusquely.

He met her eyes and, seeing the concern there, gave a quick nod. "We will do what we can for him. He is known to us and is a good man."

"Thank you, Father. I will ride out and tell them of your generosity."

As Lone Hawk watched her gallop away, he wondered how long she would stay and if he would miss her as much the next time she left.

Nilakla was torn as she hurried back to tell the others that they were welcome in the village. She had deliberately gone to the camp alone because she had needed time to herself so she could think. Whenever Douglas was around, she had little peace of mind.

Her emotions were in an upheaval, and she was trying to make some sense out of her feelings. Her heart was telling her that she should stay with Douglas until the bitter end when he left for Boston, but her mind was telling her to return to the home of her father. She would be safe there. She would have her child and be happy.

Even as she thought it, though, Nilakla knew the last was a lie. She would never find happiness without Douglas. He was her happiness. He was her life.

Caught in a dilemma that would mean heartbreak

either way, she wasn't sure what to do. He had told her that he loved her, but what good was a vow of love when he planned to leave her as quickly as he could? Love only thrived if it was shared and nurtured. As much as she wanted to believe that he cared, she dismissed the hope that there had been any truth to his words.

Nilakla caught sight of him then and her breath caught in her throat. He was so tall in the saddle and so devastatingly handsome that all she wanted to do was be in his embrace forever. Her heart aching in anticipation of their coming separation, Nilakla wondered how she was ever going to be able to be parted from him.

"Chance . . ." Doug had been giving his future serious thought during the journey, and he knew it was time to tell his brother what he was going to do.

"What is it, Doug?" Chance asked as they dropped back slightly behind Rori.

"I've come to a decision . . ."

"What kind of decision?"

He looked his older brother squarely in the eye. "I'm not going back to Boston with you."

"You're not? Why?" Chance was surprised and more than a little confused by this news. "I thought your whole purpose in coming out here was to strike it rich on your own and then go back home to show everybody that you'd made it. Why have you changed your mind now that you've accomplished what you set out to do?"

Suddenly, Doug found that the need to be rich and to impress the good people of Boston didn't matter to him anymore. All he cared about was Nilakla and making a life with her and their child. Doug gave him a wry smile. "But I didn't make it all on my own. I had Nilakla. It took nearly losing her to make me realize how much I love her, Chance. What I feel for her is worth more than gold. I could go back to Boston and live like a king on the fortune I've found, but I know now that I'd be miserable without her. Money means nothing if you don't have love . . ."

"Have you told her yet?"

"No," he replied, and at Chance's puzzled look, he quickly explained what had happened between them earlier.

"What are you going to do about it?"

Douglas flashed him a roguish smile. "Have you ever known me not to get the woman I wanted?"

Chance chuckled to himself as he thought of Doug's days as an eligible bachelor in Boston and his many exploits with the women there. "No."

"I don't intend to lose her, Chance. I love Nilakla, and I'm going to spend the rest of my life with her." He broke off as he saw Nilakla coming their way, and he put his heels to his mount to catch up with Rori so he could hear her news.

Chapter 19

The Pima village was alive with activity as they drew near, but as soon as the dogs became aware of their approach, all that changed. Charging forth from the encampment, they barked a raucous warning to all who would listen. Young children who'd been laughing and running among the tipis stopped their play to watch the strangers' progress into the village. The women who'd been tending to the cooking and other chores stopped all work to stare in open curiosity and concern. The warriors and old men who'd been sitting in the shade resting all got up to see what the excitement was about. White men did not often come to their camp, and they were wary as they watched them move past. When they recognized Nilakla and saw them stop before Chief Lone Hawk's lodge, their concern eased. If their chief accepted these strangers into their midst, then they had nothing to fear.

"Father, we thank you for your welcome," Nilakla said as they drew up before Lone Hawk.

The chief nodded. "Burr is a friend. Take him there." He indicated the tipi nearest his. "I will send Rain Cloud to you."

Rori was the first to dismount when they reached the other lodge and she ran immediately to Burr's side. He showed no sign of improvement. His face was still deathly pale, and his breathing was shallow and labored. Chance and Doug quickly came to her aid, untying the bonds that had held him immobile during the trek. They lifted him as gently as they could and carried him inside.

Rori started to follow them, but Nilakla stopped her, taking her by the arm. "Give them a minute to get him settled," she advised.

"But I want to be with him," Rori argued stubbornly, fearful that Burr might die if she wasn't right there by his side to give him the strength to go on.

"You will be," she promised. "Just give them time to make him comfortable."

Rori understood what she meant, and she lingered there by the horses, waiting for Chance and Doug to emerge.

As Chance and Doug were laying him down upon the mat that served as a bed in the lodge, Burr gave a low groan.

"Burr . . ." Chance leaned over him anxiously, hoping

to see some sign that he was coming around. "Burr, it's Chance . . ."

As if from a great distance, Burr could hear the other man's voice calling to him. A part of him wanted to surface from the blackness that engulfed him, but another part of him fought it, knowing that with renewed awareness would also come excruciating pain.

"Fight, Burr!" Chance insisted. "Think of Rori. Don't give up!"

Rori . . . Agony washed through Burr as full consciousness returned, and a moan escaped him. The pain . . . God! The pain!

Rain Cloud, the short, heavyset medicine man of the tribe, entered the lodge. "Lone Hawk tells me there is a man here who has been shot."

"Yes . . . please, we need your help." Doug quickly moved away from Burr's side to give the medicine man access.

Rain Cloud said no more, but went to the old tracker and dropped down beside him opposite Chance. He went straight to work, cutting away what was left of Burr's shirt and removing the makeshift bandage Rori and Chance had fashioned in the desert to help control the bleeding. One look at the lethal wound told him there was no point in doing more. The white man would not live much longer.

Burr had come fully back to consciousness now. He glanced weakly around for Rori, but did not see her in the tipi. Ignoring the medicine man's ministrations, he focused on Chance where he knelt beside him. "Chance . . ." he rasped. "I need to see Rori right now . . . get her for me . . ."

"I'll get her for you in a minute, Burr, just let the medicine man see what he can do for you," Chance told him.

Rain Cloud lifted his sad, dark-eyed gaze to meet

Chance's, and he slowly shook his head negatively. The old man's condition was completely hopeless.

Chance stiffened as he realized that his worst fears were confirmed. He knew he should send for Rori at once. Burr was dying.

"Don't horse around with me, boy!" Burr managed with as much force as he could muster. "I don't have much time."

"Burr . . . I . . ."

"Listen to me, boy," he said hoarsely as he waved away the medicine man's efforts and reached out to grab Chance's arm with a strength born of desperation.

Chance fell silent as he listened respectfully. Burr eyed him judgingly, knowing he was his only hope. He prayed silently, fervently, that he was doing the right thing.

"I'm leaving you the one thing in my life that means anything to me," Burr told him in a husky tone. At Chance's confused look, he went on. "You've got to take care of Rori for me. As much as she acts tough, she can still be hurt and hurt bad. I'm begging you, boy, the world's a hard place, and Rori doesn't have anyone to stand beside her now."

Chance was stunned by his request. Take care of Rori for him? Rori hated him. Still, he knew there was nothing else he could do. The old man was dying and needed the reassurance of knowing that she would be safe.

"I'll do whatever is best for her, Burr. I promise," he replied.

"I can't ask for any more than that." The fierce light that had shone in Burr's eyes faded as he heard him agree. The effort had cost him much, and a sudden, wearying weakness overwhelmed him. He let his hand fall away, and he closed his eyes. "I need to see Rori . . ."

Chance thought he was dying then, and he turned

to Doug and in a low, intense voice ordered, "Get her, Doug. Now!"

Rori had been waiting anxiously outside the tipi with Nilakla ever since Chance and Doug had carried Burr in. When Rain Cloud had entered, she'd tried to follow, but again Nilakla had restrained her. Each moment that passed added to her terrible sense of panic.

Feeling her friend's sympathetic gaze upon her, Rori moved off a little ways to be alone. Big Jake trailed after her and lay down at her feet as she stared off across the sun-drenched landscape. Rori thought of how much she loved Burr and how empty her life would be if anything happened to him. Burr was the only parent she'd ever known, the only person who'd ever loved her. The thought of losing him, of losing the one solid thing in her life, left her frantic.

Dear God, she prayed fervidly but silently, *please let my grampa be all right. Grampa's a good man, he doesn't deserve to die like this . . . I promise I'll be good, I'll do anything, if you'll just let him get better. Please make him well. He's never hurt anybody in his whole life. Don't let him die, please don't let him die . . .*

The agony of her fear gripped her soul. Burr was her whole world. He meant everything to her. If he died . . . As unbidden thoughts of trying to go on without him seared her, tears burned her eyes and coursed hotly down her cheeks in a testimony to her wretchedness. *Grampa has to make it, he just has to!*

"Rori . . ." Nilakla's call drew her from the depths of her torment.

Rori looked back quickly and saw Doug, standing near the lodge with Nilakla, beckoning for her to come. She raced to him, her heart in her throat. "Grampa . . .

is he . . . ?" She looked worriedly from the tipi to Doug and back again.

"No . . ." was all Doug had time to say before she rushed past him inside with Big Jake on her heels.

Burr had heard the sound of her voice and called her name, "Rori . . ."

She was there, then, at his side, taking up his big hand in hers. She leaned forward and pressed a kiss to his weathered cheek, unaware of Rain Cloud backing slowly from the tipi. Chance stood in paralyzed silence as he watched her.

"Grampa!" Rori cried. "Thank God! I was praying so hard and . . ." She was so taken by the fact that he was conscious at last that she didn't realize he was mortally wounded. Her spirits soared, her prayers had been answered! Everything was going to be all right!

"Rori, girl . . ." Burr's gaze was fevered as he turned to her, cherishing the sight of her, loving her more than she could ever know. "I love you, child."

His eyes met hers, and in them she could read all the pain and torture he was suffering. She was shocked by how terribly weak he looked and how frail. He suddenly seemed old, his vitality drained, his lifeblood having poured from him.

"Oh, Grampa, I love you, too," she whispered in a strained voice.

"Listen to me, Rori . . ."

"Yes, Grampa . . . anything!" Rori told him, stricken.

"I tried to do the best I could by you, girl, but I wonder if I did you right . . ." Burr was thinking about her, so innocent and unworldly, and worrying about what would happen to her when he was gone. He thought of Chance and trusted that he would care for her.

"Of course you did," she choked. "We've always been fine, Grampa. We've always been happy."

"You're wrong, child. I should have raised you to be a lady. I should have taught you what you need to know to survive . . ."

"You did teach me everything I need to know," Rori defended staunchly, oblivious to his meaning. "I can track and ride and hunt and shoot . . ."

"Ah, Rori, there are so many things I should have done, so many things left undone . . ." His eyes misted as he thought of his long-dead son and daughter-in-law. He deeply regretted that he'd never been able to find their killers. A wracking, violent fit of coughing seized him and left him strengthless in its aftermath.

Rori saw how weak he was getting and grew desperate to encourage him to hang on. She knew that he'd never stopped trying to find her parents' murderers through the years, and she hoped that telling him of their deaths would help, even if the vengeance hadn't come at his own hand.

"Grampa, those men who took Nilakla and me . . . they're dead."

"Good," he rasped, glad that they'd been dealt with harshly.

"They deserved killin', too . . ." Rori was fierce as she told him about the outlaws. "They were the same ones you been lookin' for all these years. The same ones who murdered my mother and father," she finished.

Burr's eyes brightened with an inner glow as they bored into her own. "How could it be after all this time? How do you know?"

"They were talkin' about it while we were with 'em. They were talkin' about how they killed a squaw and her white man years ago, and how they were gonna enjoy hurtin' us, too. It was them, Grampa, and Chance and Doug killed 'em. I just wish I'd been the one to pull the trigger."

"They're dead . . ." Burr repeated dazedly. He had

carried the burden of Jack's and Atallie's deaths all these years. He had felt frustrated and helpless over his inability to find their murderers. "It's good, Rori. It's good."

It seemed to Burr that a great weight had been lifted from him, easing the fiery agony that tortured him in both body and soul. The tranquility of inner peace embraced Burr, and he no longer fought against it. He embraced it with all his fading might, seeking rest, seeking contentment, seeking serenity.

Rori saw the urgency fade from him. She felt his life force paling, and she knew. Tears flooded her vision, and she bit her lip to keep from crying. Burr knew her too well, though, and he let his gaze meet hers directly.

"Don't cry, child. Be strong. Death's just another part of living . . ."

"But, Grampa . . ."

"I love you, Rori . . ." Burr told her in a pained whisper as his awareness of his surroundings faded. The anchor of Rori's loving devotion tried to bind him, but his spirit drifted away. His thoughts raced through the years, conjuring visions of ships and seas, of deserts and mountains, of loved ones and his most cherished Rori, until he slipped silently through the gates of life, escaping the torment of his fallen body to grasp the glory of the tranquility beyond.

"Grampa . . . ?" It took Rori a moment to understand that the end had come, that he'd met his peace. She clung to his hand, refusing to release it, refusing to admit that he had gone from her.

Hadn't she promised God she'd be good? Hadn't she vowed to do whatever He wanted her to do, if only He would let Burr live? Rori lifted her tear-ravaged face toward the heavens, cursing the fates that had taken her grampa from her. She couldn't comprehend how a man as good as Burr could be taken away.

Rori's despair was complete. She could see no rhyme or reason to life. She could see no point in it. There was only pain and sorrow. She was forlorn, grief-stricken, lost in the depths of her own private anguish. Rori barely realized that she was crying until, as if from a distance, she heard herself sobbing. *Don't cry, child, be strong . . .* echoed faintly through her mind. Rori clutched Burr's hand in both of hers, pressing it to her bosom. She rocked back and forth, unknowing and unable to hear even her own sounds of grief.

"Grampa . . . Grampa, don't go . . . don't leave me. I love you, Grampa," she moaned.

Chance could feel her pain tear at him. He felt the hot sting of tears in his own eyes, and he ached to comfort her somehow. If only he could hold her . . . take some of her pain as his own . . . ease her misery . . .

The agony was too much for Rori, the misery too brutally real, the unending torture of it too savage. She couldn't bear it. Loving and losing someone hurt, and she never wanted to hurt like this again.

She sought oblivion. If she couldn't feel anything, then nothing could hurt her. Rori dragged herself away from the pain, refusing to think about it, damming it up inside her, protecting herself from its cutting edge. A numbness of heart and soul began to seep into her, and she welcomed it with open arms.

Big Jake sensed her distress and moved close to her. He lay down beside her and rested his big head on her thigh as he gave a low whine.

"Jakie . . . we're alone now," she told him in a strangled voice. "It's just you and me, Jake . . . It's just you and me." Rori leaned down to bury her face against the softness of his fur.

Nilakla had heard Rori plaintively cry out her grampa's name and sensed that the end had come. She

entered the tipi to find Burr lying motionless in death
and Rori there at his side, hugging Big Jake.

"He's dead, Nilakla . . ." Chance said in what seemed
like a calm voice, never taking his gaze from Rori.

The pain that had been etched into Burr's face while
he'd still been alive had been erased by death. He
looked quiet, as if he was sleeping, and Chance hoped
Rori could see it that way one day . . . that he was just
sleeping.

"I'm sorry, Rori. So sorry . . ." Nilakla went to her and
drew her up into her arms. She comforted Rori much
as she would have a child, stroking her hair and hugging her close.

Chance watched helplessly, wanting to be the one
who said words of comfort, wanting to be the one who
shared his strength with her.

Overwhelmed by the myriad of powerful emotions
that threatened to shatter her into a million jagged frag-
ments of pain, Rori clung to the blessed numbness that
had fallen over her. She remained silent, not bothering
to answer Nilakla. She concentrated instead on being
strong, because that's what Burr expected. She wouldn't
think about anything else right now, and she wouldn't
cry. She wouldn't worry about what she and Jake were
going to do next. Burr had always told her that tomorrow somehow always took care of itself, and she believed him.

Chance stepped out of the tipi to face his brother,
and they exchanged saddened looks. They both liked
and respected Burr, and they hated to think that he
was dead.

"It's over . . ." Chance finally spoke. Rori had to be
devastated. He found he was anxious to go back to her,
but he waited, allowing her time with Nilakla.

The unspoken truce that had been struck between them earlier when Burr had first been shot was fragile at best, but Chance found himself hoping it would last. He had his doubts, though, for he didn't know what Rori was going to do when she discovered that her grandfather had entrusted her to his care. Chance wondered vaguely why Burr had extracted the promise from him and not from Doug.

"What are you going to do about Rori?" Doug asked, noticing that Chance seemed to be lost deep in thought.

"I don't know," he answered honestly. He had given Burr, a dying man, his word that he would take care of Rori, but he hadn't the slightest idea how to begin. Did he take her home to Boston with him or did he leave her there in the territory with someone to watch over her? "What do you think?"

"Have you thought about taking her back to Boston with you when you go?"

"No," Chance replied. He tried to imagine Rori fitting into the strictures of polite society there and grimaced inwardly. Where Boston ladies were quiet and genteel, Rori was loud and outspoken. Where Boston socialites were always perfectly coiffed and groomed, Rori didn't know the first thing about feminine garments and next to nothing about hairstyles and perfumes. He didn't even consider that possibility seriously, because he didn't want to see her hurt. "I doubt she would ever be happy there."

"You're probably right. The Boston elite can be heartless. That's why I'd never live there with Nilakla. What if Rori came to stay with the Pima?"

"They *are* her mother's people," Chance agreed thoughtfully, wondering why nothing seemed to be the right solution for Rori.

"She could stay always with Nilakla and me if she

wanted," Doug offered. "I'm going to propose to Nilakla as soon as I can. I'm sure she'd have no objection to Rori living with us."

"At the mine?" Chance frowned at the prospect.

"No. I've been doing a lot of thinking, and I've decided to close it down."

"Why?" It startled him to discover that Doug didn't care about the riches, that he was ready to give it all up.

"It's too dangerous, Chance. Look at what just happened . . . the girls were kidnapped and Burr was killed, and it was all because of the damned gold. I love Nilakla too much to ever put her in this kind of jeopardy again."

"What are you going to do? Where are you going to live?"

"I'm going to take the gold I've already mined and use it to buy a ranch closer to town. There should be enough money left over to keep us comfortably until I can make the ranch start paying. We could make room for Rori if she'd want to stay with us."

Chance regarded his brother with deep, abiding affection. Doug had grown into a fine man, and he appreciated his offer. "I'll talk to Rori about it as soon as I can."

Later that day, they buried Burr some distance away from the village on a low rise that offered a stunning view of the desert valley. Rori remained quiet through it all. She was bereft and wholly despairing, but she refused to give vent to her inner sorrow. She was dry-eyed and seemingly composed as she stared down at the rock-covered patch of ground where they'd just laid Burr to rest.

Chance had been watching her closely ever since she emerged from the tipi with Nilakla, hoping for an opportunity to speak with her alone. But Rori had stayed close by her friend's side the entire time, her usually sparkling eyes dull, her expression curiously vacant, her manner subdued.

Chance knew Rori had to be in shock. He had wanted to comfort her, to hold her close and tell her that it would be all right, but he knew it would be a lie. Nothing in Rori's life would ever be the same again. Still, he knew he had to try. He cared about her. She was so young and innocent, and he couldn't bear to see her in pain.

As everyone else moved away, Chance stayed behind. It was time for them to talk. Since Doug had decided to remain with Nilakla in Arizona, there was really no reason for Chance to stay on any longer. But he knew that before he could even think about returning home, he would first have to see to Rori's future.

"Rori?" He spoke her name softly when they were alone.

Rori glanced up at Chance, really seeing him for the first time since they'd reached the village. Her weary heart ached as she stared at him. So much had happened and in such a short period of time. Rori thought of how good it had felt when Chance had held her after the attack on Burr, and she suddenly wanted to lose herself in his embrace, to lean on him and draw on his strength. But her sanity had returned now, and with it the memory of the last time they'd made love. She realized, painful though it was for her, that Chance had only helped her because he was being kind, nothing more. Chance didn't love her, didn't really care about her. He never had, and he never would.

Staunchly, Rori denied the longing she felt for him. It wasn't love she was feeling, she told herself. She wouldn't, couldn't love him, for love invariably meant pain. She had loved Burr and he was gone, and she knew Chance would be leaving soon, too.

"What do you want?" Rori asked.

"I need to talk with you."

"About what?"

"Rori, I spoke with Burr before he died . . . before you went in to see him this afternoon." When she didn't say anything, but just continued to watch him with wide, wary eyes, he went on. "Burr made a request of me . . ."

"What kind of request?" She was suddenly suspicious.

"Rori," he said quietly, trying to anticipate how she was going to take the news, "Burr asked me to take care of you for him."

Chapter 20

For just one brief instant, Rori's battered spirits soared—*Chance was going to take care of her* . . . She had a fleeting vision of being safe and secure in his arms, of sharing his kisses and knowing his love, but as quickly as the thought came, she banished it. Chance didn't love her. He'd told her so. She was being foolish to even dream about such a thing.

The memory of his rejection stirred her ire, and she was glad to have her anger to hang on to right now. It was going to be just her and Jake from now on. She wouldn't depend on him or anyone else!

"I don't need no *takin' care of*!" Rori declared hotly. "Least of all by you!"

"Rori," Chance began again with exaggerated patience, sorry that the tentative peace between them was gone, "I gave Burr my word. I'm responsible for you now."

A tidal wave of crippling misery overwhelmed her.

The tears that had threatened Rori for so long came close to falling, and she blinked furiously to control them. Her heart was breaking. While it was true she'd lost her grampa and was essentially alone in the world, she still didn't want to be anybody's charity case or responsibility. She could take care of herself. It was obvious to her that Chance thought of her merely as a task he was obliged to see to its proper end, and she chafed at the thought. Her pride was all she had left now, and it reasserted itself with a vengeance. Giving herself a hard, mental shake, Rori lifted her chin mutinously to glare at Chance, her emerald eyes shooting icy daggers at him.

"Forget it, Broderick," she told him angrily. "There ain't nobody responsible for me 'ceptin' myself! My grampa raised me to take care of myself."

"That may well be, but . . ."

"There ain't no 'buts' about it, white man. I'm fine. I got Big Jake, and he's all I'll ever need. You just go on about your business and don't worry about me."

"Burr wanted me to see that you were safe and protected."

"Well, that's real wonderful, but let me tell you somethin'. I am safe . . ." She gestured toward the peaceful Pima farming village. "And I'm damned well protected!" Rori pulled her knife in a wicked, slashing motion. "Or have you forgot just how good I am with this?"

"It didn't help you much last night, did it?!" Chance retorted angrily in growing exasperation. Didn't Rori realize all he wanted to do was help?

"Look, Broderick, I don't need you!" Rori exploded, just wanting him to get out of her life. She fought against the memory of his lovemaking and his tenderness to her after the shooting. She reminded herself forcefully that she was only an obligation to him, that he felt no deep emotion for her other than mild concern, and he only felt that because Burr had managed to get a deathbed promise from him to watch over her. What else could Chance have done, but agree to it? "I'm letting you off the hook. You don't have to worry about me. I don't need your help."

"Well, your grandfather thought you did!" Chance found his temper flaring at her stubbornness.

"Well, he ain't exactly here anymore to worry about it, is he?"

"That's precisely my point!" They were glowering at each other, toe to toe, neither willing to give an inch. "He asked me to take care of you, and I intend to do just that!"

"The hell with you! You ain't got no claim on me! I ain't goin' anywhere with you, least of all back East!"

"I wasn't planning on taking you back East with me, Rori," Chance announced, thinking that this news would cheer her. He assumed she was reacting so angrily because she didn't want to leave Arizona, and he wanted to assure her that she could stay there. He knew she must love the land just as much as Burr had.

His statement had quite the opposite effect on her. It devastated her. Deep inside Rori, there had still been one tiny spark of innocent hope that she meant more than just responsibility to Chance . . . after all, they had made love . . . But his declaration that he fully intended to leave her behind doused that last glowing ember of sweetness. The truth came crashing in on her with painful clarity. She meant nothing to him. He would see her safely taken care of, and then he would leave the territory as quickly as he could and never look back, never think of her again. Probably the only reason he and Doug hadn't already left was because he had to settle things with her first.

"Good! I'm glad you weren't plannin' on it, 'cause I wouldn't have gone!"

"Rori, if you'll just listen for a minute . . ."

She continued to glare at him, but said nothing more.

"I thought that you might want to live here with your mother's people," Chance offered, thinking the quiet farming village would be a protected place for her.

Rori couldn't believe what he was saying to her. He actually thought she could settle with the Pima and be happy.

"Or," he continued on, "I spoke with Doug, and he said that you would be welcome to live with him and Nilakla."

Live with Doug and Nilakla? Why would she want to? She could do fine on her own. It occurred to her then that Doug was supposed to be going back East with Chance when he left. "I thought Doug was going back with you."

"He's decided that he wants to stay here in the territory. He plans to marry Nilakla and start up a ranch with the money he's made at the mine. He told me earlier when we were talking about you that there would always be room for you, if you decided you wanted to stay with them."

Rori was happy that things had turned out well for Nilakla. She knew how deeply she loved Doug, and how much it would have hurt her had he left. Now, with the baby coming and Doug deciding to stay on, they would make a wonderful family. It pleased her that Doug realized his love for her friend before it was too late for them to find true happiness together.

But as for herself, she grew resentful of Chance's almost casual discussion of her own life. Who did he think he was? He had told her before that nothing existed between them, that this emotion they felt for each other was simply lust and nothing more. So why did he

think that he had any right to order her around? He
didn't have any claim on her.

Her pride surged forth, stiffening her determination
to distance herself from him. Sure, Burr had made him
promise to take care of her, but so what? She was capable of handling her own destiny. She didn't need
Chance Broderick sticking his nose in her business.
She wanted him out of her life, and, if pretending to go
along with one of his solutions would satisfy him, she
would do it. Once Chance was on his way back to
Boston, she could do whatever she wanted and he'd
never know.

"I couldn't live with Nilakla and Doug, not with them
just being married and all," Rori answered coolly, believing that she'd outsmarted him. "I'll stay here in the
village."

Rori had gone from being hostile to consenting so
quickly that Chance studied her suspiciously. When he
could find nothing devious in her expression, though,
he dismissed the thought that she might be up to something. Rori had probably just come to her senses and
recognized that the village would be the best place for
her. Here she would be accepted and would, no doubt,
in time fall in love with some Pima warrior and marry.
Her future would be assured.

"I'll speak with Lone Hawk," Chance said slowly.

"Thank you." Rori was calm as she turned and walked
away from him with Big Jake at her side.

It was a very civil ending to their encounter, yet it left
Chance wondering why he felt so damned rotten when
everything had turned out so well.

After leaving the gravesite, Nilakla had started off
toward the village to find her father. She was ready to
reconcile with him, to let him know that she wanted

to come home to her people. Doug's earlier confession of love had confused her a bit, but it hadn't deterred her from her plan. What did it matter that he told her he loved her if he wasn't going to stay?

"Nilakla!"

At the sound of Doug's urgent call, Nilakla turned to find him coming after her. She studied him as he strode purposefully toward her, his striking good looks leaving her breathless as always. In desperation, she realized that, even now, he still had too great a hold on her heart.

Her sense of self-preservation told Nilakla to stay away from him. His nearness was too overpowering, his kisses too potent. If he touched her, she knew she would probably melt at his feet, and she couldn't allow herself to be that weak. She had to be strong, for herself and her child. She wanted Doug to go so she could start trying to forget him and get on with her life.

"I'm on my way to see my father," she told him in a tone meant to discourage him. "What is it you want?"

"I want you, Nilakla," he responded.

"For what?"

"First, to talk." His dark eyes sought out and held hers. "I have something I have to say to you."

"There's really nothing left to say. I'm staying here to raise my baby . . ."

"Our baby . . ." he interrupted. The desire to take her in his arms and kiss her senseless was fierce, but he restrained himself. He had to tell her what was in his heart first. Later, there would be time for loving.

"And you're going back to Boston with Chance," she finished.

"That's where you're wrong, love," he said seriously as he took her hands.

Just the touch of his hands on hers sent excitement coursing through her, and she silently pleaded with the gods to give her strength enough to resist him. She thought about breaking away from him but didn't want to let him know that he could affect her so easily. Instead, she stood quietly, waiting for him to finish. "What do you mean?"

"I know you didn't believe me when I told you earlier that I loved you, but, Nilakla, it was the truth. I love you."

Doug was so earnest about what he was saying to her that her pulse quickened at his statement. Still, as much as she wanted to believe it, she wouldn't allow herself that luxury.

When she didn't respond to his statement, Doug went on. "It took almost losing you last night to make me realize how much you mean to me. The thought of living without you left me frantic, love. I don't want to be apart from you. I want to stay with you always."

"You do?" she whispered, hoping against hope.

"I do. I've already spoken with Chance and I've told him that he'll be traveling back to Boston alone."

Nilakla stared at him in stunned surprise. *Douglas wasn't leaving her! Douglas was staying here!* It was her most ecstatic dream come true, but she couldn't believe it was really coming to pass; she was afraid to believe it.

Doug read the last fragment of doubt in her expression and hastened to clear everything up between them. "I know you think that it was my finding out you were pregnant that forced me to admit my feelings for you, but you're wrong. You mean the world to me, Nilakla . . . you are my world. Our baby is just that much more love in my life."

She was quiet, studying him, doubting him, loving him.

"I've decided to close down the mine, I'm going to take out the gold we've already dug and use it to buy us a ranch somewhere closer to town."

Nilakla stared at him in mute surprise. "You're going to close down the mine?"

"It's too damned dangerous," he explained tenderly. "I'd be a fool to put my wife and child in this kind of situation ever again."

"Your wife?"

Doug gave a self-conscious laugh as he realized that he'd been so busy explaining everything that he'd forgotten the most important thing. "Nilakla, will you marry me?"

Nilakla's disbelief and distrust had faded before his earnest, solemn explanations, and at his proposal her heart swelled within her breast until she thought she was going to burst from the thrill of it all. Douglas did love her! He wasn't going to leave her! He wanted to marry her! They would be married and live happily together forever!

"Oh, yes, Douglas! Yes, I'll marry you!!!" She went into his arms, and they kissed in passionate devotion.

Doug had hoped that she would believe him, and he gave a quick prayer of thanks that she hadn't rejected him outright before giving him the opportunity to explain himself. Every word he'd told her was the truth, and he knew he would never leave her.

They were married the following day according to Pima custom. It was a joyful occasion. Doug and Nilakla were rapturous about their newly declared love for each other, and the rest of their lives stretched before them in an unending blending of days spent loving.

Chance watched his brother's obvious delight and was glad for him. As he celebrated Doug's newfound happiness later that night at a wedding feast, he knew his own time in Arizona was coming to an end. Soon he was going to have to start home.

As Chance wandered away from the reveling, he wondered idly where Rori was. He had caught a glimpse of her, during the wedding itself, but she had not attended the feast tonight. In truth, now that he thought about it, he realized that he had seen little of her since the day before when he had taken her to meet with Chief Lone Hawk.

Chance thought of the chief and knew that Nilakla's father was truly a kind man. He had accepted Rori warmly into their midst and generously provided her with a lodge of her own even though she had no relatives among the tribe. Rori had been subdued during the encounter, and it had surprised him.

Chance wondered how she was going to take to the Pima way of life. They were primarily a farming community. The men worked the irrigated fields while the women worked at making baskets and pottery. For an instant, he questioned his judgment in leaving her behind in such foreign surroundings. However, he knew Rori was a smart girl, and he felt certain that given time, she'd adapt. It would be good for her to be with people and socialize. Living as she had with Burr, she'd never really made any friends, and he hoped she would find some here and begin a whole new life. Thinking of her, believing that he'd made the right decision for her future happiness, Chance wandered away from the camp for a few minutes of quiet reflection alone beneath the stars.

Rori lay on the mat in her tipi, longing for the days to pass. She felt as if she was suspended in a limbo of sorts waiting for the rest of her life to begin, and she didn't believe that would happen until Chance was gone. Only then would she be able to escape from this prison called a village.

Though Rori had put on a show of humility and thanks to the chief for his generosity, the truth was she had no intention of staying once Chance was gone. She hated women's work, she hated pottery, she hated basketry. She wanted to be free and wild like the land she was raised in, but she knew she would have to bide her time until Chance left. Once he was on his way back East, she'd be able to do whatever she wanted, and he'd never find out because he would never bother to check on her.

The last thought upset her, and she became irritated with herself. He'd made it no secret that he didn't care about her, so why should she let it bother her that he would never think of her once he'd gone from the territory?

Rori tossed restlessly on the bed as she closed her eyes and sought sleep, but images of Chance assailed her, leaving her wide awake and miserable—images of Chance kissing her, touching her, making love to her . . . A dull ache grew in her heart, and she found herself longing for him in spite of everything.

Rori swore vividly out loud. She was angry with Chance for what he made her feel, and she was angry with herself for feeling it. She couldn't want him! She wouldn't! It was useless to even think about it. He was leaving. If she allowed herself to care, she would only be hurt.

"Jakie . . ." She whispered his name as she saw him watching her from where he lay.

At her call, the big dog got up and lumbered slowly to her. He flopped down lazily beside her on the mat, getting as close as he possibly could. Rori needed the intimacy, was glad for it, and she hugged him to her.

Things were happening so quickly that she wasn't sure what to think or do. Reluctantly, Rori admitted to herself that she was scared. What would she and Jakie do once they left the Indian village? She knew they could go back to the small cabin she and Burr had occasionally called home, but she wasn't sure what would happen after that.

The frightening feeling of being totally alone settled over her in a smothering mantle, and unable to deny it any longer, she gave vent to her tears. She cried softly into the night, until at long last, exhausted, she finally fell asleep.

"What are you doing out walking around?" Chance asked Doug when he met him as he was returning to the village.

"I was allowing my wife a few minutes alone before I go to her," he told his brother, his eyes alight at the thought of his new bride and the excitement of the night ahead.

"I see." Chance chuckled. "I don't know that I could be as patient as you are."

"Don't be fooled, I'm anxious. It's just that we've got the rest of our lives to be together, and I wanted tonight to be special."

"That's true," he agreed as they walked slowly through the village toward Doug and Nilakla's lodge. "Have you given any thought at all to bringing Nilakla home for a visit?"

"As a matter of fact, I have. I do want Mother to meet her. I think she'll like her."

"I know she will," Chance assured him. "Why don't you make the return trip with me?"

Douglas would have liked to make the trip right away, but due to Nilakla's delicate condition, he decided to wait. He didn't want to put her in any stressful situations until after the baby was born. "We'll come later."

"Why not travel with me now?"

"Because Nilakla's pregnant," he explained, not sure

how his brother would take the news, "and I'm afraid that such a long trip might cause problems."

Chance was surprised, but pleased by the news. "Congratulations, Doug. That's wonderful!"

"Thanks. I'll wait until the baby's old enough to travel and then I'll make the trip back."

"That's a good idea." He grinned, fancying himself as an uncle and wondering how their mother was going to react to being a grandmother.

As they spoke, neither man noticed Nilakla emerging from the lodge that was now hers and Doug's. She was looking for Douglas, for she missed him and wanted him with her. They didn't realize that she was coming their way, and they didn't know that she could hear some of what they were saying.

"*. . . wait until the baby's old enough to travel and then I'll make the trip back.*"

Agony shrieked through Nilakla as she froze in her steps. The fear that her original assumption had been right and that everything he'd told her had been lies jolted through her. It was obvious from his statement that he planned to stay with her only until she had the baby and then he was going to take their child and leave.

Nilakla backed silently away, returning unseen to the seclusion of their tipi. Though her heart was breaking, she knew she wouldn't turn Douglas away. She loved him madly, and if she was only to have these months with him, then she would take them and live them to the fullest. There was only one thing she could hope for—that he would come to love her so deeply during the months that she carried his child that he would never be able to leave her.

As Nilakla returned to the lodge, Chance was saying, "Have you decided yet when you're going back to the mine?"

"I'd planned on going back tomorrow. We should be able to carry everything on three or four packhorses. The trip should take a day or two, and then you can be on your way."

"Fine."

Doug glanced toward his lodge and smiled at the thought of his bride awaiting his arrival. "Well, I think it's time for me to turn in for the night . . ."

"I'll see you some time in the morning."

Chance watched his brother walk away, ready to begin his new life as husband and father, and he could sense how happy and fulfilled Doug was feeling. Chance felt a strange sense of emptiness in his own life as he thought about his brother's excitement. Doug had only been away from Nilakla for a short time, and yet he'd been champing at the bit to get back to her.

Doug's desire to be with Nilakla made Chance wonder why he wasn't even a bit lonely for Bethany after all these weeks. Certainly, she would make him a good wife, but if he felt no deeper emotion than that for her, he was skeptical that any union between them would be successful, no matter how good a financial merger it might seem to be.

Chance tried to conjure up a picture of Bethany in his mind, but he could manage only a general vision of petite, blond perfection. Then, as he was pondering the excitement of her kiss, he found that instead of seeing her delicate loveliness, the image of a dark-haired, innocent, green-eyed beauty superimposed itself in his mind. Rori . . . her raven tresses tumbling about her shoulders, her emerald eyes flashing at him, her body responding wildly to his . . . Rori desolate and crying in his arms over her fallen grampa . . .

Desire, hot and unbidden, surged through Chance at the thought of Rori, along with another deeper emotion he didn't recognize and couldn't name. The force of what he felt startled him, but he refused to take it seriously. It was just lust, nothing more. He'd known that from the very beginning. But even as Chance tried to dismiss his feelings for Rori as unimportant, he found himself wondering where she had disappeared to that night.

Chapter 21

Nilakla was waiting eagerly for Doug when he finally entered the lodge. Her breath caught in her throat at the sight of him. To Nilakla, Douglas was the epitome of male beauty, and she knew no matter what the future held that she would make tonight a night he would always remember.

Doug was excited about joining Nilakla for their wedding night, and at the sight of her reclining nude on the mat that was to be their bed, he paused, enthralled. He knew in that instant that he'd never want another woman. Nilakla was perfection, and he loved her with all his heart and soul.

Their eyes met across the width of the darkened room, and Nilakla, reading the sudden heat in his expression, lifted her hand to him in invitation.

"I love you, Douglas, my husband," Nilakla told him in a husky voice. "Come let me love you . . ."

Doug's mouth went dry as his gaze dropped first to her slightly parted lips. Nilakla saw his interest, and she ran just the tip of her tongue over her slightly fuller bottom lip in a slow, sultry gesture. Entranced, he let his gaze move even lower, and he stared hungrily at her

lush beauty. Her dark hair was unbound, falling about
her shoulders in a satiny black cascade that veiled her
breasts teasingly, allowing him just tantalizing glimpses
of their succulent glory. Her slender waist blossomed to
the gentle roundness of her hips, and her long and
shapely legs were coyly posed, shielding her womanhood from his view.

Mesmerized by Nilakla's loveliness, Doug moved forward toward her, stripping off his shirt as he went. She
was his wife, his love. He wanted her. He loved her as no
other, and he would only be happy in her arms.

"I love you, Nilakla," he told her hoarsely, choked by
the power of the emotions that were welling up inside him.

His declaration should have thrilled her, but it didn't.
Instead, it only served to remind her of her doubts
about his sincerity. She didn't reveal the pain his words
were causing her, nor did she reveal the tears she was
crying inside. Instead, despite the anguish she was feeling, she smiled.

"Then love me, my husband . . ."

Doug could wait no longer to join her on the bed. He
lay down beside her and took her in his embrace. He
held her tightly as his mouth moved over hers in a possessive, demanding kiss. Her lips parted to his questing
tongue, and they shared that even deeper exchange.
They breathed as one, each sharing the other's breath
in an odd intimacy that evoked a primitive heat in
Douglas.

When his mouth left hers to explore the shell-like
curve of her ear and then trace molten excitement
along the sensitive cords of her throat, a shudder of
pleasure wracked Nilakla. She arched seductively
against his hard male body, wanting more from him,
much more. The crests of her breasts hardened as he
continued to plunder the sweetness of her throat and

shoulders, and she moaned in joyous agony. She wanted him to kiss her breasts, to touch and caress her until she was mindless to anything but the splendor of their joining.

Doug could feel her excitement building, but he was not going to give her what she wanted just yet. He continued his sensuous play with practiced expertise, arousing her to a fever pitch, making her want him wildly. The thrilling torment he inflicted upon her only encouraged her to return the favor.

Nilakla's hands were restless as she caressed him. She was impatient to know the heat of his flesh upon hers, so she did everything she could to encourage him to hurry. Her touch was bold as she sought his manly strength, and the power of Doug's response to that caress pleased her. Brazenly she began to remove the rest of his clothing, and when he would have helped she pushed him back down upon the bed to stop him. Nilakla's movements were definitely designed to seduce as she undressed him. When she'd discarded the last of his offending garments, she began to kiss and caress him with fiery abandon. Her hands and lips trailed over him, seeking out his pleasure points and coaxing him to greater and greater heights of arousal.

Finally, Doug could stand her rapturous torture no longer. He pulled her to him for a kiss and then rolled over, bringing her fully beneath him. Nilakla gave a throaty laugh as Douglas moved between her legs, and she lifted her hips to accept him deeply within the hot confines of her body. The moment of their joining was electric, and the ultimate pleasure could no longer be denied. He began to move in a steady, thrusting motion, but Nilakla was hungry for him. Her hands sought his hips, guiding him, encouraging him, until Doug was lost in the frenzy of their mutual need. They lost track of everything except the wanton splendor of their mating.

This was where they both knew they belonged—locked in each other's arms, sharing the gift of love. This was their heaven.

They reached ecstasy's pinnacle and hung there suspended in heart-stopping excitement. Their rapture faded slowly. Wrapped in the bliss of love's blending, they began the descent back to reality.

"Will it always be this way?" Doug managed to ask after a long, quiet moment. He still had not released her and, in fact, did not even want to consider letting her go just yet. Nilakla felt too wonderful in his arms, her silken limbs entwined with his, the heat of her body still holding him captive.

"Yes, Douglas, always," she whispered dazedly. What had passed between them had been so breathtakingly beautiful that she was afraid to talk about it further, lest they destroy some of its perfection.

"If that's true, we may never leave this lodge again . . ." he responded in exhausted good humor.

His words touched Nilakla with a poignancy that almost brought tears to her eyes. She knew that if there was some way she could have held him captive in that tipi forever to keep him from leaving her, she would have done it. "That would be heaven for me, Douglas. There is nothing I'd rather do than love you . . ."

Doug answered her with a passionate kiss. When the fire of his desire stirred again, he did not deny himself, but swept her away with him on a tidal wave of ecstasy.

Long hours later, Nilakla lay beside her sleeping husband, her head resting on his shoulder, her hand resting on the broad expanse of his chest. She could feel the steady, solid beating of his heart beneath her palm and said a prayer that her love would be strong enough to bind him to her for all time. Tears dampened her cheeks, but she didn't care. At long last, she slept, and her dreams that night were visions of them in the future, living happily together with their baby, a complete and loving family.

The following three days passed in a blur of activity for Doug and Chance. The day after the wedding they'd ridden out late for the mine. They'd made the trek there without incident, and they headed back to the village, the packhorses ladened with their few personal possessions and the gold.

"I guess you'll be wanting to leave now . . ." Doug remarked as they rode into the Pima village.

"It's time," Chance agreed, knowing that their mother was still awaiting word from them and feeling the responsibility of the business weighing heavily on his shoulders.

"How soon do you want to go?"

"I want to check on Rori and make sure she's all right, and then I'll be ready."

Doug nodded. "It may take Rori a while to get used to the lifestyle here, but I'm sure she'll be fine."

"I hope so . . ." Chance was less certain than his brother that Rori would do well living within the restrictions of Pima life, but he was trying to be optimistic. She obviously hadn't wanted to live with Nilakla and Doug, and she had been outraged at the thought of going East with him. *No,* Chance reasoned, *the village was the best place for her . . . the only place for her.*

"We'll plan on riding out some time tomorrow, then," Doug concluded. He wasn't thrilled at the idea of being away from his new bride so much, but it was important that he get into town and find out what lands were available. The thought of founding a Broderick dynasty in Arizona appealed to him, and he was looking forward to buying a ranch and developing it into the best the territory had ever seen.

"I'll talk with Rori tonight, and I'll be ready to leave when you are," Chance decided. He was anxious to find out how she was faring. During the course of their trip back into the mountains, he'd often found himself thinking of her, wondering what she was doing and how she was adjusting. Now that he was back, he planned to satisfy his curiosity.

Rori was sitting with Nilakla and a group of other women, listening to their chatter of babies, pottery, and baskets, and quietly going out of her mind. She silently cursed the circumstances that had brought her to this fate and cursed Chance Broderick. As frightening as her future seemed if she left the village and struck out on her own, it couldn't be worse than the present torture of trying to take part in the women's work. She felt nearly insane with the desire to run from them screaming her lungs out. She was meant to be out riding and hunting and tracking, not sitting here by the cookfires.

"Look, Nilakla! Your husband returns!" Dawn Blossom, a middle-aged, heavyset mother of five, whispered to them excitedly as she caught sight of the two white men returning.

Nilakla was quick to look up, and when she saw her husband riding into camp, she left the women without word and ran to greet him.

Rori had glanced up at Dawn Blossom's exclamation and just as she did, Chance looked her way. Their gazes collided and locked, and Rori felt the shock of his regard all the way to the pit of her stomach. She swallowed nervously as she wondered why just one look from him should affect her so. She wanted to glance away, but found she couldn't. It was as if she were pinned and held immobile just by the force of his gaze.

Rori watched almost helplessly as Chance made some

remark to Doug and then turned his horse in her direction, coming toward her at a walking pace. Instinct told Rori to avoid him, but she felt unable to move, unable to run. She waited where she was, a captive of his gaze.

"Rori," he greeted her with a slight nod.

"You're back," she replied, keeping her tone flat and trying not to think of how marvelously handsome he looked and of how she suddenly longed to have him greet her as Doug had greeted Nilakla—with a wildly abandoned kiss and embrace.

"Obviously," he drawled as he swung down from the saddle and brushed off some of the trail dust. "I need to talk with you for a few minutes."

"Why?" she challenged, not wanting to be alone with him for any reason. He was too virile . . . too attractive . . . and she remembered too much.

"Rori . . ." His tone held just the slightest hint of annoyance.

"All right." She gave him a resentful glare and got begrudgingly to her feet. Though she had really wanted to stay away from him until he'd gone, she reasoned just talking to him couldn't hurt anything, and it had to be better than the alternative—staying here and listening to talk of babies, baskets, and pots!

"Thanks."

Chance handed his horse over to one of the young boys who vied for the chance to take care of him and then walked with Rori out of the encampment so they could have a few minutes alone to talk.

"I didn't get the opportunity to speak with you before Doug and I left for the mine, and I just wanted to see how you were doing."

"I'm fine," she answered brusquely, not wanting to encourage him. What she did was her business, not his.

"You're sure?" he probed, wanting to be certain.

"Look," Rori turned on him sharply, "why is it that,

for some reason, you think you have the right to know everything that goes on in my life?"

"You are my responsibility," Chance countered.

"I thought that was all settled. You thought I should stay here, so I'm stayin' here, and everything's wonderful. Right?"

"That's what I wanted to know, Rori. Is everything working out for you? Do you think you'll be happy here?"

Happy? The word reverberated through her soul, and Rori almost laughed out loud at the absurdity of it. *Happy?* Burr was dead, and she had no one but Jake. And she wondered if she'd *ever* be happy again.

"Of course." Rori kept her expression stoic, deliberately looking away from his probing dark eyes. "Why?"

"I just wanted to make sure," Chance began, noticing how she was avoiding looking at him. He wanted to draw her to him, comfort her, and tell her that things would eventually get easier for her, but there was something in her manner that put him off. She was her usual angry prickly self, but there was something more . . . an unnatural coldness that troubled him about her. "I'm leaving for Boston tomorrow, Rori, and I needed to know that you were going to be all right here."

She was stricken by his words. *He was leaving tomorrow* . . . She had never really believed the moment would come. She had never really believed that he'd go, but he was—tomorrow.

Chance thought he saw a fleeting flicker of some emotion—it looked almost like sadness—in her eyes, but it vanished just as quickly as it had come, making him doubt that he'd ever really seen it. Her next words, as brash as ever, served to further convince him that he'd been mistaken.

"Well, rest your conscience, white man. I'm going to be just fine."

"You're sure?"

"What did I say?" Rori challenged, wanting him to just leave her alone. "You go on back where you came from. Jakie and me are real happy here." The lie almost stuck in her throat, but she was willing to say just about anything to get rid of him.

"All right." He backed off, recognizing her hostility and knowing from experience not to push her. "I'll see you sometime tomorrow before I leave."

Rori gave a careless shrug of her shoulders as she started to walk away. "Don't matter to me."

"I'll see you tomorrow, Rori," Chance called after her. He was pensive as he watched her move off, trying to figure out why it bothered him so much that she didn't seem to care even a little bit that he was leaving.

Later that night, curled up with Big Jake in her tipi, Rori mulled over her conversation with Chance and tried to fight down the feeling of desperate panic that threatened. He had seemed so coolly indifferent while they'd talked. It was obvious that he thought it was his obligation to make sure that she was cared for because that was all he'd wanted to talk to her about. At no time had he said anything remotely personal or told her that he was going to miss her.

It seemed to Rori that Chance was acting as if their two nights of ecstatic lovemaking had never happened or, if they had, they had been supremely unimportant in the scheme of his life. To him, those encounters had meant nothing. To Rori, they would be what she built the rest of her life on.

Rori couldn't believe that Chance was actually leaving forever, and she found she was miserable at the thought. Though she had told herself over and over not to care for him, that he had used her and that he would never love her, she had failed miserably. Every time she set eyes upon him, she was reminded of the ecstasy of his touch and their passionate lovemaking, and she wanted him again.

Rori was angry with herself for her weakness where he was concerned. Perhaps if he had never kissed her or touched her, she might have been able to banish him from her thoughts, but now she doubted that that would ever happen. It was almost as if Chance had become a part of her . . . a part that after tomorrow would be missing. As much as she'd been wanting him to go, deep in her heart Rori wasn't sure if that was good or bad.

"I don't know what to do, Jakie . . ." she murmured to her lifelong friend as she contemplated her dilemma. "I don't want to want him, Jakie, but I do . . . I really do . . ."

Despite the activity of the day, Chance was surprised to find that he could not sleep that night. He felt restless and troubled, and he wasn't sure why. Somehow in the back of his mind, he connected his disquiet to Rori, but he couldn't put a name to the reason for his misgivings.

Chance rolled to his back on the hard mat and folded his arms beneath his head. Through the small hole at the top of the tipi, he could see a small patch of star-spangled night sky. He stared up at it, not really seeing its beauty as his thoughts centered on Rori and the mystery of his uneasiness.

Chance didn't understand his sudden concern for her. He had done everything he'd promised Burr he'd do. He'd assured her future with the tribe, and it was obvious to him, judging from her reaction, that she was content in the village. *Hell,* he swore to himself, *she'd told him so straight to his face!*

Chance knew Rori wasn't a shy, retiring miss who would keep her mouth shut if something was bothering her. If she'd been upset about anything, he was certain she would have let him know it. He found himself grinning at the thought. Rori certainly did have a knack for speaking her mind.

For the first time, Chance actually admitted to himself that he was going to miss her. Though Rori had meant nothing but trouble for him since the beginning, he'd come to enjoy that trouble. Since Burr's death, though, except for their few mildly aggravating discussions, she'd been very subdued.

Chance realized that she'd never really mourned her grandfather's passing. She'd been distraught when he'd first been shot, but he hadn't seen her shed a tear since, not even when they'd buried him. He knew it wasn't healthy to keep grief bottled up inside, but he could think of no tactful way to broach the subject to her. Rori seemed inordinately pleased that he was leaving, and he feared she would just erupt with anger should he "try to stick his nose in her business" again.

It occurred to Chance that he rarely saw Rori anything but angry. The first time they'd met she'd been fighting those boys in town. She'd turned her fury on him then for "not mindin' his own business," and they'd been fighting each other ever since . . . except for those two glorious times when they'd made love.

The realization that he thought their encounters glorious shocked him. He'd tried to convince himself all along that lust was the only thing he was feeling when he'd made love to Rori. But Chance knew that lust was quickly satisfied and eventually faded with the passing of time. To his consternation, he was beginning to recognize that what he was feeling for Rori seemed to be growing and thriving, and that unnerved him.

He shouldn't care about her, he told himself. *But he did,* his conscience answered, *and not just as an inherited responsibility.* Chance recalled the last time they were together, and heat flooded his loins, leaving him heavy with his need for her. In agitation, he rolled over onto his stomach and fought to bring his surging desire for her under control. He couldn't deny that he wanted her, but he would deny himself the right to take her. He would protect her . . . even from himself.

Chance knew that this was Rori's one opportunity for a happy future, and he wanted her to have that. He wanted her to fall in love and marry and have children. He wanted her to have a good life.

Why then, he wondered in annoyance, *did he feel so downright miserable over the thought of her marrying another man?* Completely baffled, Chance refused to even think about it anymore. Closing his eyes, he sought rest, but the throbbing hunger in his body left no doubt in his mind that it would be a long and sleepless night.

Chapter 22

Chance was leaving . . . Chance was leaving . . . Chance was leaving . . . The refrain played in Rori's mind as she watched the sun crest the eastern horizon. The night had been long, lonely, and dark for her, and despite the bright sunlight, the day promised to be even more so.

Rori was listless as she left her lodge and wandered

through the still quiet village down to the edge of the small creek that ran nearby. She sat down on the bank and stared out across the water, her thoughts a-jumble. Confusion reigned supreme in her mind. Conflicting emotions tore at her, and she wasn't sure what she was really feeling anymore. All she did know was that Chance was at the center of it all.

He was going home, back to Boston and to the woman he'd spoken of so often—Bethany. Jealousy ripped through Rori at the thought of him with another woman. She was certain that Bethany was beautiful. A woman would have to be to capture the interest of a man like Chance.

Rori realized then that she had never really done anything to improve on her own looks. She was still wearing her buckskins, still pulling her long hair back in two braids, and she hadn't had a bath since that time with Chance. The water's edge beckoned, and Rori moved down to it to gaze at her reflection. To her dismay, she looked exactly the same as she always had. She looked like a boy. No wonder Chance was eager to leave and go back to Bethany.

The thought of Bethany waiting back home for him was sour in her mind, and Rori found herself wondering just how lovely Bethany really was. She glanced down at herself again, staring at her wide eyes and raven hair, and she challenged herself to try to look her best for just one day.

Not that she really cared what Chance thought or about his women back in Boston, Rori told herself, but she knew she'd get a great sense of satisfaction out of showing him just how good she could look, how very womanly she could be, if she put her mind to it. When a quick look around affirmed that she was alone, Rori stripped off her well-worn clothes and stepped into the water. She unbraided her hair and then slipped beneath the surface to wet it down. She hurriedly washed as best she could and then emerged from the stream to tug her clothing back on.

Dawn Blossom had given Rori a traditional Pima cloth skirt and blouse to wear when she'd first learned that she was going to be staying with them. Until this moment Rori had disdained the thought of ever wearing the garments. She'd cast them indifferently aside after putting on a show of thanking the woman. Now, she couldn't wait to don them. She was going to show Chance Broderick! He might never think of her again after he left today, but at least once he was going to see her looking like a woman.

For a moment, Rori tried to understand why it even mattered to her. It seemed almost silly to even care what he thought. He was leaving, and she wanted him to leave and never come back . . . didn't she? Exasperated by her inability to sort it all out, Rori did the only thing she could if she was to have any peace of mind. She stopped thinking about it. She set her sights instead on the goal of looking the best she possibly could when she went to tell him their final good-bye later that day.

Chance moved to take Nilakla in his arms and plant a brotherly kiss upon her cheek. "You're a beautiful woman, Nilakla, and Doug's lucky to have you."

The Indian woman flushed with pleasure at his compliments as she gazed up at her husband adoringly. "I'm the lucky one to have Doug for my husband and you for my husband's brother."

"Take care of him."

"I will," she promised.

"And come to Boston as soon as you can."

Nilakla's spirits plummeted, but she hid her upset

behind a wide smile. "I would like that," she answered, really meaning it.

Chance looked around, ready to say good-bye to Rori. He hadn't seen her all morning, and now that he and Doug were packed and ready to ride out, he was worried that he was going to miss her entirely.

"Has anybody seen Rori?" he asked.

"She was in her tipi earlier," Nilakla answered. "I'll go see if she's still there." Just as she started to go after her, Rori came out of her lodge with Big Jake at her side. "Here she comes now."

Chance looked up, his gaze seeking Rori out, and he stared at her in disbelief, not quite sure it was really her. Rori looked stunning . . . she actually looked like a woman . . . Her ebony hair was unbound and hung, shiny and silken, down past her shoulders. The sleek raven tresses seemed to beg for a man's touch, and Chance remembered, against his will, just how wonderful they had felt beneath his hands. She wore a loose-fitting light-colored blouse that was scoop-necked in style, and a dark, full skirt that came just to her ankles.

Chance knew as he watched her move toward him that no one could have mistaken her for a boy now. She looked lovely. She was a beautiful woman. Somehow being forced to admit that to himself made Chance realize how much he still desired Rori physically. He didn't want to feel this way about her; he'd fought it every inch of the way, but to no avail. He did want her.

Though Rori gave the impression of walking toward him with a confident stride, in truth there was nothing confident about her. She was quaking inside at the thought that this would be the last time she would see him—ever.

Her gaze clung to him, committing to memory everything about the way he looked. He was wearing a black shirt, and pants that fit his muscular physique perfectly.

His dark hair gleamed in the brightness of the noonday sun, and his teeth flashed whitely against his tanned face when he smiled in her direction.

Rori felt her knees go weak when Chance smiled. She wanted to believe that that smile had been just for her, but logic told her she was wrong. If he was so glad to see her, why was he leaving? The only reason he was smiling, she told herself, was because he was happy about going home. Still, her pulse quickened as she drew nearer to him, and her heart began to pound in an erratic rhythm. Dismally, Rori wondered if she would ever get over him once he'd gone away.

They probably would have continued to stare at each other without speaking had Big Jake not broken the deadlock. With a loud, happy woof, he charged forward to greet Chance, his tail wagging forty miles a minute.

Happily distracted, Chance dropped to one knee to say good-bye to the big, oafish hound. "You're a good boy, Jakie, and you stay that way," he told him as he ruffled his golden coat. "You take care of Rori now, you hear?"

Jakie gave a sharp bark, making it almost seem like he knew what Chance had said to him. Chance gave him one final pat on the head and then got back to his feet. As he straightened up, his eyes met Rori's and, again, he saw mirrored in the emerald depths of her gaze a flare of emotion that he couldn't quite identify. As if sensing that he had seen too much, Rori quickly shuttered her expression. Chance was left to puzzle over what he thought he had or had not seen. Because he believed she couldn't stand the sight of him, he had expected her to be joyful at the thought of him leaving. But the emotion he'd seen reflected in her eyes had been far from happy, and he wondered . . .

"The traditional dress suits you," he finally spoke up. "It does, Rori. You look lovely," Nilakla told her

friend, unaware of the fine thread of tension between
Chance and Rori.

"Thanks. Dawn Blossom gave them to me," she
replied. "I thought it was time I dressed like a Pima,
since I'll be one of them from now on."

Perversely, Chance found himself trying to imagine
which young buck from the tribe was finally going to
win her heart. He'd have bet quite a few would be more
than willing to try to impress her once they got a good
look at her dressed this way.

"You take care of yourself," Rori said with a casualness
she wasn't feeling. On one hand, she was wishing he
would just hurry up and go—get it over with; yet, on the
other, she was wishing he would stay so they'd never
have to be parted.

"You, too, and be sure to keep Jakie out of trouble."
Chance felt awkward, like a damned fool. Here they
were, standing around like strangers making idle talk,
when all he really wanted to do was to take Rori in his
arms and kiss her senseless.

Trouble was, Chance knew he couldn't do it. Rori deserved better than that. What they'd shared had been a
fleeting thing, a brief fiery flare of passion that led
nowhere and would have to be forgotten. He had his
future, and she had hers. Still . . .

Almost as if drawn to her magnetically, Chance took
a step closer. With the utmost of tender care he cupped
her face with both his hands and pressed a soft kiss to
her forehead.

Rori trembled as his lips touched her, and she bit
back a sob of anguish. How was she ever going to live
through this? First, Burr had left her, and now Chance
was going, too? How was she ever going to survive without them . . . without him?

When Chance drew away, his gaze probed hers once

more, but it was a fruitless effort. Whatever emotions she was feeling, she wasn't about to reveal them to him.

"No knife, little one?" he managed to sound teasing as he thought of all the times she'd pulled a weapon on him and threatened him for touching her.

"I don't need one now," Rori countered lightly, struggling with all her might to keep up the carefree façade and not break down and cry. "I'm safe here and happy, too."

Her flippancy troubled Chance, and he stepped away from her, breaking all physical contact. "That's all I ever wanted for you, Rori . . . your happiness."

"Chance? You ready?" Doug had already kissed Nilakla good-bye and was mounted up and waiting for him.

"Yeah, I'm all set," he answered, then turned to Rori one last time. "Be happy, Rori."

"I will be," Rori replied, giving a slight lift of her chin as if defying him to doubt her. "Good-bye, Chance."

"Good-bye, Rori." The words were final, and he swung up on his horse's back. He stared down at her for a minute and then put his heels to his mount's flanks and moved off after Doug.

Rori stood rooted where she was for a long time, watching Chance until he was out of sight.

"You're going to miss him, aren't you, Rori?" Nilakla ventured, noticing how intent her friend was.

Rori shrugged, but didn't respond. She wasn't sure she could trust her voice enough to speak, and if she did manage to speak, she wasn't sure she was an accomplished enough liar to convince Nilakla that the arrogant white man meant nothing to her.

Without another word, she turned away from her friend and went back to her lodge to be alone. Deep inside, she felt she was a failure. Even looking her absolute best, she still hadn't been able to distract Chance from leaving.

Rori was miserable as she and Jake entered the tipi, and she closed the door behind them. Though it was still relatively early in the day, she didn't care. She didn't want to see anybody or talk to anybody. She just wanted to be alone.

For an instant, anger surged through her. In a white-hot fury, she stripped off the Pima clothing and tore at it as hard as she could, ripping it to shreds. What did she care if the skirt and blouse were the only ones she had? She never planned to dress that way again anyway! Tomorrow she was leaving this place and striking out on her own, but for now . . .

The anger passed as quickly as it had come. Rori stood nude and suddenly vulnerable in the center of the tipi. Refusing to cry, still trying to be strong, she grabbed up her earlier discarded clothes and yanked them on. She dropped down to sit on the bed and, with shaking fingers, began to plait her hair. That done, Rori lay down and closed her eyes, and Jakie came to rest close beside her.

It was then, as she lay grief-stricken and defenseless, that wave upon wave of pain washed over her. It was an aching, wrenching pain that tore at her very soul. Sorrowfully, Rori wondered if she would ever be able to survive the agony of it all . . . the agony of being so alone . . .

"What are you going to tell Mother?" Doug asked in a lighthearted tone.

"I'm going to tell her the truth—that we handled it just like we always do," Chance shot back with a grin.

"I'm sure she'll want all the details."

"She always does." Both men laughed, for they knew their mother well.

"Tell her that I love her and that I'll come home for a visit as soon as I can."

"She'll be thrilled, and when she finds out that she has a grandchild on the way, I may be hard put to keep her in Boston. You'd better make sure you have a guest room at your ranch. I've got a feeling you're going to need it."

Though Chance's mood seemed lighthearted, in truth it wasn't. Rori was on his mind . . . aggravating, irritating, annoying Rori. Damn! Why was it that she, of all females, had the power to drive him crazy? Chance had never known another woman like Rori, and in a way, he doubted if he ever would. She was unique.

It still amazed Chance to think that he'd been in such close contact with her for so long and had never realized that she was a girl. Now that he knew, he couldn't imagine ever having been fooled. She moved with an innate grace and definitely was not built like any boy he'd ever seen. Of course with the cut and bruise on her cheek, it had been hard at first to see that feminine loveliness, but now there was no mistaking it. Rori was a beautiful woman, and whoever claimed her for his would have a prize worth treasuring . . .

Chance let his thoughts drift over what he thought would be her future. She would marry some young, virile warrior and have his children. Then she would grow old here with the tribe, happily doing the domestic things that the Pima women did. She would make baskets and pots, she would tend to her children and grandchildren and, above all, she would be safe in the village . . .

Chance knew he should have been satisfied with that destiny for Rori, but something kept nagging at him. He kept seeing her as she had been when he'd left her.

She'd been very womanly, very lovely—downright gorgeous, in fact—and very, very . . . sad . . . It came to Chance then, as he kept going over and over their final conversation in his mind, trying to put a finger on what it was he'd seen in her eyes, that Rori had been filled with sadness. She'd been totally miserable and yet had tried to cover it up with a nonchalant attitude.

Chance wondered why she'd put on the act and then realized that she'd probably done it just to get rid of him. For the first time, he suspected that she was not really happy where she was and that she could never be truly happy there. He'd been so concerned with making sure that she was safe that he'd forgotten what a free-spirited creature she was. Rori could no more survive in the village climate he'd put her in than Jakie could survive being locked in an airless box in the middle of the desert on a hot summer's day.

Chance silently cursed himself for his selfishness. He'd been so caught up in what he wanted to do that he hadn't considered what was really best for Rori. He knew now that there could be no going back to her days of innocence with Burr. He wouldn't leave her there in the village. He would go back and get her and take her to Boston with him. Chance knew it wouldn't be easy. He knew she had a lot to learn, but he also knew that Rori was as smart as a whip.

Even as Chance told himself that he was doing it because he'd promised Burr and he wanted her to have a better life, a small voice in the back of his mind told him he was just fooling himself. He wasn't taking her back to Boston with him because of any promise he'd made to Burr. He was taking her back because he was already missing her and he wanted her with him. In spite of all of his efforts to the contrary, Rori had come to mean something to him, and he wasn't ready for it to end between them yet. Although consciously he tried to deny it, he felt driven to return for her.

"Doug . . ." He slowed his horse.

"Yeah?"

"I'm going back."

"Why?"

"I forgot something."

Doug gave him a funny look, for he knew they'd taken great care when they'd packed that morning. "What?"

"I forgot Rori."

"Rori?" Doug was surprised by his statement, but before he could get any more out of his brother, Chance had wheeled his horse around and headed back. He stared after him for a minute and then raced to catch up. He had no idea of what was going on between Chance and Rori, but he wondered why his brother would want to take her back East with him. They had already discussed how difficult that would be when he was considering taking Nilakla back, and now Chance wanted to take Rori?

"Chance!" He shouted to him as he got closer, and he was pleased when he slowed down to allow him to catch up.

"Yeah. What do you want?"

"Chance, how can you even think of taking Rori along with you? We talked about this before. We both know how hard it would be for Nilakla, and Rori's no different."

"I made a promise to Burr to do my best by her, Doug, and I intend to do just that."

"I thought you were happy with the idea of leaving her with her mother's people?"

"If she'd had blood relatives there, I would have felt better about it, but, think about it, Doug. Rori's all alone in that village. Even though she put on a good front when we left, I had a strange feeling that she was not happy there . . . not happy at all."

"You're sure this is what you want to do? It's going to be hard, you know."

"I know, but I'll take care of her," Chance answered somewhat fiercely.

At his determined reply, Doug sensed the undercurrent of his brother's feelings and understood. Somehow, wild little Rori had managed to entangle herself in the ever-elusive Chance's emotions. He almost smiled at the thought. He had fallen in love with Nilakla so unexpectedly, and now Chance . . .

Knowing his brother as he did, Doug said nothing about his suspicions. It wouldn't do to tell Chance that he was lying to him and to himself about his motives. Instead, he rode silently along at his side, wondering what Rori's reaction was going to be to his return.

A few villagers looked up as they rode back into the village, but no one said much. Chance took the lead and drew his horse to a stop in front of Rori's lodge. He didn't speak, but dismounted and strode forward to throw wide the doorflap. Without waiting for an invitation, he walked right on inside.

Rori was lying on her bed depressed and lonely, trying to get up enough energy to pack her few belongings and leave the Pima encampment. When she heard the sound of horses outside, she wondered who it might be riding by, but she never imagined it would be anyone coming to see her. After all, who did she know? No one.

"Rori . . ." Chance called her name as he entered unannounced.

Rori had never dreamed that Chance might possibly

come back for her. His good-bye had been too final, too devastating. She stared at him in mute surprise, her defenses down.

Chance took one look around the lodge and knew that he'd been right. The clothes she'd worn were now lying in a ruined heap in the middle of the floor. It had all been an act. She was unhappy, and it was all his fault.

Rori was tired of fighting the loneliness and misery that had been her constant companions since Burr's death, and for just that one moment in time, she allowed herself to believe that Chance had come back because he wanted her. As she stared at him across the room, her heart was thudding in a painful but hopeful beat. His next words to her were so callously and demandingly spoken, however, that they jarred her from her young girl's sweet reverie.

"You're coming with me," he ordered flatly in a tone that brooked no argument.

But Chance had forgotten that he was dealing with Rori. Nobody ordered Rori around—nobody.

At his commanding attitude, her eyes narrowed in suspicion. As much as she would have loved to have thrown herself into his arms, kissed him passionately and agreed to go anywhere he wanted her to go, Rori refused to give in to the desire. She knew Chance. She knew him well, and she didn't trust him. She thought he might be up to something, but she couldn't imagine exactly what it might be. His words echoed through her, and she glared at him as she got quickly to her feet to face him, arms akimbo.

"You can go to hell!" Rori snapped back at him furiously. "I ain't goin' anywhere with you, Broderick!"

Chapter 23

"You want to bet?" Chance didn't know why Rori's vehemence surprised him so much, but it did. He supposed it was because she was looking so lost and defeated when he'd first walked in that he hadn't expected her to react so angrily to his proposal.

"There ain't no bettin' about it," Rori countered. "I'm perfectly happy here in the village."

"You may lie convincingly, Rori, but the evidence tells the true story," Chance told her coolly as he reached down to scoop up her discarded women's clothing.

"I don't know what you're talkin' about." She glared at him with open antagonism as he fingered the tattered skirt and blouse.

"Well, unless some young warrior tried to join you and you had to fight him off, I'd say you were real upset about something not too long ago." He held the garments up for her inspection.

"It was Jakie . . ." she lied. "We were playin' and he accidentally grabbed at the skirt and ripped it."

"The blouse, too?" Chance asked, his eyes reflecting his obvious disbelief of anything she had to say.

"There ain't no point in talkin' about this," she said sullenly.

"You're right. Just get your things and let's go."

"I told you," Rori enunciated every word with care, "I ain't goin' with you."

"And I told you, you were. I'm your guardian, Rori, and you'll do as I say." Chance was getting angry over her stubbornness. He didn't understand why she was fighting him when it was so plain that she was unhappy here.

"Says who?"

"Says your grampa, that's who," he spoke curtly.

"Well, my grampa's dead."

"I know, and before he died, he asked me to watch out for you, and I promised that I would. Now, get packed."

Rori was sputtering with rage. "You did watch out for me. You got me all settled in here, and I intend to stay! You just go on and go and leave me alone."

"I wish to hell I could!" Pushed to the brink by her continued resistance, Chance responded angrily before he knew what he was saying.

His declaration sounded to Rori like he hated every minute of what he was doing, but in truth, Chance was trying to deny the driving force that kept Rori in his thoughts constantly. Every time he turned around she was there in his mind, haunting him.

"So who's stoppin' you?! Go!" She fought back, hurt.

Chance was at his wit's end, and he grabbed her up by her shirtfront and jerked her to him. They were standing nose to nose as he ground out, "The only way I'm leaving here is with you, with or without your consent. Now, you can come along peacefully or I can rope-and-hog-tie you and throw you over my shoulder." Abruptly, he dumped her back down to her feet.

"You wouldn't?" Rori's green eyes widened at the threat she didn't understand. If he hated having her with him, why was he bothering to take her?

"What's it going to be, Rori?" Chance took a menacing step toward her.

"I thought you wanted me to be happy?" She backed slightly away from him.

"I do." He followed her retreat.

"Well, I ain't gonna be happy with you!"

Those words stopped him. "You'll learn how," he replied stonily, not revealing that he was truly hurt by her statement.

"But I don't want to learn!" she cried, desperate for a way to get out of going with him.

"Too bad." He would tolerate no refusal in his determination to have her with him. "Let's go."

Rori felt like screaming. She didn't want to go with Chance. She'd thought that he was out of her life forever and that it was time for her to go on without him. He'd told her that he didn't love her, so why had he come back here now, insisting that she accompany him to Boston?

"Rori . . ." The ominous edge to his voice set her to moving, for Rori had no doubt in her mind that Chance would do what he'd threatened.

"Why are you doin' this?" she demanded as she moved grudgingly to pack her few meager belongings . . . her saddlebags and Burr's. Tears threatened, but there was no way she was going to let him see her cry.

"I told you. I made Burr a promise, and I intend to see it through. You're my ward, Rori, my responsibility until you come of age, and I'm not a man who takes his responsibilities lightly."

That was about the worst thing Chance could ever have said to Rori, but he was completely unaware of the devastating effect his words had upon her. Rori fell completely silent after his last remarks. There was nothing more she could say. If she refused to go with him, he would simply overrule her and carry her off. There wasn't a single thing she could do about it, either, for no one in the village would dare try to stop him. Burr had, in effect, turned her over to Chance's keeping, and she was stuck with the arrogant Easterner.

"I'll be ready in a minute. Why don't you wait outside?" she suggested, hoping he would do it so she could sneak away while he wasn't looking.

But Chance knew better than to give her any time alone. He knew Rori, and he intended to keep an eagle eye on her. "That's all right," he said easily as he folded his arms negligently across his broad chest. "I'll wait here until you're done."

Rori gritted her teeth as she turned her back on him in a huff. She began muttering angrily under her breath as she started to gather her few things, "You may think you've won, but the first chance I get I'm going . . ."

Before she knew what happened, he was beside her, grabbing her by her upper arm and spinning her around to face him. "Like hell you are! The only place you're going is back to Boston with me. Do you understand that?"

Rori glowered up at him, but didn't respond.

"Do you understand me, Rori?"

"Yes," she answered resentfully.

His concession won, he still didn't feel he could trust her. "If I have to, Rori, I will tie you up every night just to make sure you don't run. I'm not going to let you out of my sight. We are going to be traveling together, eating together, and sleeping together."

Rori swallowed nervously. "I understand."

"Good." Chance released her arm. "Now, get your things."

He bent down to pet Big Jake, his manner casual and

at ease, and Rori returned to what she was doing, silently cursing him for his composure.

When word came to Nilakla that her husband had returned with his brother to the village, she hurried to find him, wondering what had gone wrong. She had not expected Douglas to return for many weeks, and she feared that they had run into trouble on the way to town. She found him heading from Rori's lodge to their own.

"Douglas?" Nilakla called his name worriedly as she ran into his welcoming embrace. "Has something happened?"

"No," Doug assured her, and then gave her a warm kiss. It surprised him to find out just how much he'd missed her in the short time he was away. "Everything's fine."

"Then why have you come back?"

"Chance found that he wanted to take something else along with him," Doug told her, his eyes glowing with good humor.

"What?"

"Rori."

"Rori?" Nilakla repeated slowly.

"I do believe my older brother has met his match." Doug chuckled as he slipped an arm around her waist and led her on to their lodge.

"You mean Chance has fallen in love with her?" She smiled at the thought.

"I think so." He grinned. During his bachelor days in Boston, Doug had modeled himself after his big brother. Chance had had tremendous success with the women, and he'd always wanted to be just like him. It looked to Doug like Chance had finally found the one woman who'd stand up to him and give him just as good as she got. "With Rori along, this trip back to town promises to be mighty interesting."

Nilakla gave a delighted laugh. "He will be perfect for Rori."

"Once he realizes how he feels," Doug added. "We Brodericks are a little hardheaded about such things. Just look how long it took me to recognize what a good thing I had."

His words were bittersweet to Nilakla. While she wanted with all her heart to believe they were true, she still remembered the conversation she'd overheard. As they entered their tipi, she turned to him and linked her arms behind his neck.

"The only thing that matters, my husband, is that you finally did realize it. I only hope your brother is as smart."

"He is," Doug said distractedly as she pulled him down for a deep kiss. Wrapped in each other's arms, they promptly forgot about anything but their own love.

When Rori had finished gathering her few possessions, she stalked from the tipi, calling to Jakie to follow her. Jake had been in heaven as Chance was scratching his ears, and he gave Chance a confused, remorseful look before lumbering reluctantly after his mistress. Outside, Rori started off immediately to get Patch.

"Where do you think you're going?" Chance demanded.

"To get my horse," she answered from between gritted teeth.

"Leave Jake and your saddlebags here. That way, I can be sure you won't run."

"Why you . . ." she seethed, ready to cuss him out.

"I wouldn't say it if I were you," he told her, grinning mockingly as he anticipated the direction of her thoughts.

They stared at each other assessingly for a moment before Rori was forced, once more, to back down.

"Go on, Jakie. Go to Chance," she directed, and started to walk away again.

"The saddlebags, Rori?" He knew he was pushing her, but it was time to put a stop to her rebelliousness.

Rori didn't say a word, but hurled them at him with all her strength. Chance caught one and dodged the other, laughing all the while. "Good girl. Now hurry up. We've got a long way to go."

Rori turned and stormed off without another word. Chance watched her stomp away, her arms swinging furiously at her sides, her shoulders set in annoyance, and realized that they had a long way to go in more ways than one.

Doug and Nilakla found him waiting there for Rori when they emerged from their own lodge.

"Well?" Doug asked. "How did it go? What did Rori say?"

"She's agreed to come along."

"That easily?" Doug fought down a smile.

"That easily," Chance answered, but he was tempted to laugh in derision over his own gross exaggeration of the truth. There was never anything easy about dealing with Rori. As always, she'd been as prickly as a saguaro, and while that made her difficult to deal with, at least she was acting a little more like her old self.

She'd certainly managed to puncture Chance's ego in this latest encounter. Never in his life had Chance had to force a woman to be in his company. It didn't sit well with him that he'd had to do it now, with her. His manly image suffered greatly when he remembered that he'd had to threaten her with violence in order to get her to agree to travel back East with him.

Chance found he could ignore his bruised ego,

though, for all that mattered was Rori was going with him. Now he could rest assured that she would be fine.

"What are you going to do with her once you're there?" Doug inquired, trying to envision Rori among the Boston elite.

Chance had the good grace to look a bit distressed. "I hadn't really thought that far ahead . . ."

"Well, first things first," he counseled him. "You'd better get her dressed right."

"Is there a dressmaker in Phoenix?"

"If there isn't, we'll find you one. The way I figure it, you've got about six weeks at the most to get her ready to meet Mother—and the rest of Boston," Doug told him, no longer able to suppress a grin.

"Rori'll do just fine," Chance responded, trying to sound confident. All he had to do was convince Rori that she wanted to be a lady. Once he'd accomplished that, the battle was half over. Rori was smart, and Chance knew she could do anything she set her mind to.

"I know she will," Nilakla spoke up.

"Just remember, though, Rori's used to having a lot of freedom," Doug advised. "It's going to be really difficult for her to learn everything she's got to know."

"She's special, Chance," the Indian woman added. "Take good care of her."

"I plan to," he replied, wondering what they were getting at. Didn't they realize that he had her best interest at heart and that was why he'd come back here in the first place? "Rori's my ward, and I intend to provide for her until she comes of age."

Doug and Nilakla exchanged a knowing look, but Chance was oblivious to it or the reason for it. He was too busy watching Rori as she rode slowly toward them on her pinto.

* * *

Rori had taken as long as she could to mount up. She hadn't wanted to stay at the village, but then again, she definitely didn't want to go with Chance. The thought scared her for more reasons than one, but prideful as she was, she wasn't about to let on. She'd never let Chance Broderick see her frightened. Never! She'd show him!

While Rori had had a few minutes to herself, she'd tried to figure out why Chance had come back for her. She wanted to think that, dressed in women's clothing, she hadn't been the failure she'd imagined earlier that day. Her womanly vanity was urging her to believe that Chance had realized how beautiful and irresistible she was and had decided that he couldn't live without her.

Although Rori longed for that to be true, her ever-present common sense told her that she was being ridiculous. There was only one reason why Chance had come back. When she hadn't been strong enough to hide the depths of her loneliness and despair from him, he'd felt it was his duty to take her with him. He believed her to be his responsibility—nothing more, nothing less.

Her heart ached in acknowledgment of the truth she could not deny. Chance did not love her, would never love her. He'd told her so. It was ridiculous for her to even think that something would come of his taking her along. He was obligated to take care of her. That was all.

Rori sighed deeply, momentarily resigned to her fate. Still, she harbored the hope that once they were out on the trail, she might be able to escape Chance and go on about her life as she'd originally planned. She didn't want to spend time with Chance when his very nearness made her crave that which she couldn't have. It would hurt too much to be with him all the while knowing that they could never be together again. She didn't want to care about him, yet somehow she couldn't stop . . .

Rori glanced up and saw Nilakla waiting with the men and Jakie. She dismounted and rushed to hug her friend who moved away from the men to greet her so they could have a private moment to talk.

"Did Chance tell you?" Rori asked, a definite catch in her voice.

"That you're going with him?" Nilakla returned, and at Rori's nod, she added, "Yes. Are you glad?"

Their eyes met, and Nilakla could see the young girl's confusion mirrored in her emerald gaze. "I don't know . . ."

"Chance will be good to you . . ."

"Hah!" She gave a sharp laugh. "You don't know Chance very well if you believe that."

"He's a good man, Rori, and I know he would never hurt you," Nilakla said the last with very real confidence. "He only wants what's best for you."

"Then why won't he let me go?"

"Would that be best? To leave you out here all alone?"

"I'd be fine." Rori bristled.

"I would hope so, but what if something happened to you? How could Chance ever forgive himself?"

"How would he even find out?"

"He does care what happens to you, you know," Nilakla chided her gently, hinting but not giving anything away. However, Rori's emotions were too bruised to understand what she was saying.

"All Chance cares about is honoring the promise he gave to my grampa. That's all."

"But, Rori, he didn't have to make that promise . . ." She would have said more, but Chance's call interrupted them.

"Rori, we have to go." He took his time throwing her

saddlebags onto one of the packhorses, allowing her a few more minutes alone with her friend.

"Oh, Rori . . . I'm going to miss you!"

"And I'm going to miss you, too," she returned, hugging her close in a desperate embrace.

"I'll see you again, won't I?" Nilakla asked as the men mounted up and edged their horses toward them.

"I hope so, Nilakla . . ." They hugged each other warmly, and then Rori stepped away, mentally preparing herself to begin a whole new life. "You take care of that baby . . ."

"I will."

Rori glanced up to see Chance and Doug waiting patiently for her to finish her good-byes. Her vision blurred with tears, and she almost stumbled as she walked back to her horse. She swung up on Patch's back without another word. Putting her heels to his sides, she rode away from the Pima village without looking back.

Jakie had been sitting next to Chance's mount, but when he saw Rori gallop off, he raced after her at top speed. Wherever she went, he went.

Doug leaned down from where he sat on horseback to give his wife one last kiss. "I'll be back just as soon as I can."

"I'll be waiting," she promised, her love for him shining in her dark eyes. "Hurry . . ."

"I will."

With that, Doug and Chance started from the encampment on their way to town for the second time that day. They set a steady, ground-eating pace across the arduous terrain, but Rori always managed to stay a distance ahead of them.

"I thought you said she'd agreed to go."

"She's going, isn't she?" Chance snapped. He was annoyed by Rori's determination not to ride with them, but he didn't understand why.

"I wonder why she isn't riding with us." Doug tried to lead the conversation, but Chance was in no mood to discuss it. He didn't want to tell his brother that he'd had to threaten her to make her come along.

"Ask her."

"I will later, if we ever catch up with her."

"Oh, we will," Chance remarked, knowing she'd damn well better be with them when they made camp later that night.

It was near dark when they finally stopped for the night near a small watering hole. Rori already had the fire started by the time the men got there.

"This good enough, Doug?" She pointedly ignored Chance. She wanted to establish that she was still in her own domain, her own element. All too soon she would be surrounded by new people, places, and things. Right now, she needed the reassurance of knowing that she had some kind of control over her life, however small.

"This is fine."

Chance remained silent as he went about tending his horse. Doug was still busy seeing to his own and the packhorses, when Chance set about laying out his bedroll. He made a point of deliberately spreading it out right next to Rori's.

Rori couldn't believe what he was doing. Of all the area there by the fire, he'd chosen to bed down beside her . . . Hell, he was practically on top of her!

"What the hell do you think you're doin', Broderick?!" Rori demanded.

"Lesson number one, my dear, a lady never uses foul language," Chance responded calmly.

"Why, you no-good . . ."

"Rori . . ." He used that commanding tone again. "I said a lady never cusses. Remember that!"

"I ain't no lady, and I'll damn well cuss if I want to!" she came back at him obstinately.

"Your first statement couldn't have been more true," Chance replied curtly, deliberately raking her with a cold look, "but let me assure you, Rori, you're going to stop cussing, and you're going to stop now."

His icy, assessing gaze hurt Rori. She knew she didn't look like a lady now, but how could she? These were the only clothes she owned. Guiltily, she remembered the shredded garments back at the camp, but she quickly put the thought from her mind. Her bottom lip stuck out a bit as she glared at him sullenly.

"Like h—"

"Don't say it!" he ordered. "From now on, if you so much as utter one cuss word, I'll use the soap on you, and I don't mean for a bath."

Rori grimaced, swallowing nervously and trying to keep from gagging involuntarily at the thought. When she didn't say anything, Chance considered it a minor victory.

"Good. I'm glad to see that you catch on quick."

"You still didn't answer my question," Rori challenged angrily. She was irritated that he'd backed her down on cussing. She'd cussed since she could remember and always with Burr's blessing. Still, Rori wasn't foolish enough to want to have her mouth washed out with soap.

"Oh? You mean what am I doing with my bedroll?" At her nod, he gave her a derisive smile. "I'm getting ready to bed down, what else?"

Chapter 24

"But why here, by me?" Rori demanded in outrage.

"I told you before we left the village that we were going to be traveling together, eating together, and sleeping together. Did you think I was lying?"

Rori blanched. She had never thought he would plan on sleeping with her. She had thought he meant that they would be forced to sleep at the same campsite, but not . . . together. Rori wasn't sure whether to be excited or angry.

"But you said that was all a mistake . . . that it would never happen again . . ." Confusion rocked her. Did this mean that he really did want her?

Chance saw the very real distress in her gaze and assumed it was because she despised him so much. "I said "sleep' Rori," he told her impatiently, "and that's exactly what I meant. Nothing else."

He meant for his statement to ease what he thought was her worry, but instead, it hurled Rori to the depths of misery. He didn't want her . . .

"Well, why don't you just go *sleep* somewhere else?!" she reacted angrily.

Chance's expression turned mocking. "Sorry, Rori. Until you promise me that you'll never try to run, we will be sleeping together."

"But I don't want to sleep with you!"

"It's up to you," he told her, shrugging. "The choice is yours. Just give me your word that you won't run, and I'll move my bedroll over there." He gestured to the far side of their camp.

Rori knew the easy way out would be to promise that she would never try to get away from him, but the way she felt right then, she couldn't. Her pride refused to allow her to give in to him, and her pride was all she had left at this point. When Rori didn't answer him, Chance continued on with what he was doing.

Doug had been busy with his horse and had missed the exchange between them completely. When he finally came to join them and saw their bedrolls together, he was secretly pleased. He knew already that they loved each other, the trouble was *they* didn't. They were sitting on opposite sides of the campfire studiously trying to ignore each other. Still, Doug figured it would only be a matter of time before they finally admitted it, to themselves and each other. He only hoped that he would be around when it happened.

He joined them at the campfire. They ate the meal in relative silence. The tension that existed between Chance and Rori was almost a tangible thing.

Some time later, Chance and Doug stretched out on their blankets. Rori, however, stayed by the fire, trying to drag out eating her food for as long as she could. She didn't want to lie down beside Chance. She didn't want anything to do with Chance! Only when her eyes began to close of their own volition did she realize that she was finally going to have to admit defeat. She was about to give up her vigil to stay awake and surrender to the inevitable, when Chance spoke up.

Chance had been lying there, watching Rori. He could tell that she was desperately trying to stay awake so she wouldn't have to come to bed with him, but exhaustion was claiming her. While he admired her for her sheer grit, when he saw her nod off, he'd had enough of her stubbornness.

"Rori, get over here right now!"

She hated to admit it, but she knew he was right. She couldn't sleep sitting up, and if she tried to go anywhere else to lie down, he was sure to come after her. Defeated, but at this point too tired to care, she got to her feet and moved to her own blanket.

Rori dropped down beside Chance and quickly pulled the blanket up to her chin as sort of a flimsy barrier against him. She'd hoped to go right to sleep, but being this close to Chance set her senses reeling. She didn't want to think about him lying just inches away from her. She didn't want to remember all the times he'd kissed her and had touched her, but she did. Rori fought back a groan. Why did this man affect her so?

Rori was annoyed that she found herself wide awake and tense. She was desperate for a way to keep from thinking about Chance, and she lay there wracking her brain in an effort to find something to distract her. In a flash of brilliance, it came to her. She knew exactly what she needed to help keep her mind off him.

"Jakie!" she called out to her pet, and the big mongrel came to her immediately. When she patted the small space she'd left between her and Chance, the dog stepped over her to curl up comfortably between them.

Rori was feeling quite smug at her ploy. She was used to having Jake near, and this was perfect. She'd show Chance he didn't bother her in the least. She was going to go on just as if nothing had happened. All set to enjoy a good night's rest, she started to roll over on her side away from him to get comfortable.

Chance couldn't believe her antics. He figured she was probably intending to distract him with the dog while she made her getaway, and he wasn't about to give her even that much of a chance. The minute she tried to roll over away from him, he reached out and grabbed her by the wrist.

Rori sat up quickly at his steely touch, struggling to get free as she glared at him. Then she saw the rope in his hand, and she began to tremble. "What are you doing now?" she squeaked.

"I told you, Rori. Unless you promise me that you aren't going to run away, I'm going to have to make sure you don't get the opportunity," Chance explained in a cool, logical tone as he made short order of expertly tying their wrists together.

Big Jake merely lay there between them unconcerned.

"You're out of your mind!"

"Can you think of a better way for me to keep track of you? I need my rest, Rori. This way, if I keep you bound to me, if you so much as move a muscle during the course of the night, I'll know it."

Rori was furious. She felt like a horse on a tether. She flopped down on her back, her left wrist tied firmly to Chance's right, and tried to sleep. But even with Jake between them her awareness of him was more potent now than it had been before. Memories of his lovemaking assailed her. She grew flushed and feverish. Her body was betraying her, and there was nothing she could do about it.

Rori knew she shouldn't want Chance, but she did. Rori knew she should hate Chance, but she didn't. Every inch of her flesh was tingling with an excited need for him, yet, he lay beside her seemingly unaffected. He was as relaxed as her damned dog! Chance's breathing was easy and steady, and he gave no indication whatsoever that he was even aware she was near.

Rori was in misery. She would have tossed and turned, but the restraint effectively prevented such free movement. Finally, she closed her eyes and prayed desperately for sleep to release her from the erotic prison her body had become.

Even though Chance gave the outward impression of being unaffected by Rori slumbering beside him, he was in total discomfort. He'd told himself over and over again that it was no good to want Rori, but as he lay next to her, he could almost taste the sweetness of her kiss and feel the heaven of her embrace as her body had sheathed his. Passion suddenly shot through him as he envisioned the last time they'd made love.

Chance silently cursed his own weakness in dredging up those memories. He was her guardian now, he berated himself. He was responsible for her and couldn't violate that trust no matter how much he physically desired her. She had been entrusted to his care, and he would not take advantage of her.

Chance had always prided himself on being in control of his emotions. Though it took considerable effort on his part, he finally managed to bring his surging need under rigid domination. He lay there, fighting to maintain an outward appearance of calm, and wondered how long it would be before Rori finally gave up on her pride and promised not to give him any trouble. Chance hoped it would be soon, for he didn't know how long he could go on having her so close beside him. He knew he could control his desires when he was awake, but he wasn't sure he wouldn't reach out for her unconsciously in his sleep, and he knew that wouldn't do at all. Stifling a sigh, Chance lay beside her, feigning sleep and remembering . . .

That night, Chance had no idea how stubborn Rori really was. Oh, he knew she had a nasty temper and that she could be obstinate to the point of aggravating, but he had no idea as to her staying power. As the nights and days passed in unparalleled misery for the both of them, neither one was prepared to back down. If anything, they each became more and more determined to stick to their guns.

Though neither Rori nor Chance would admit it, the whole ordeal was pure torture. Neither slept well and, as a result, tempers ran short during the day.

At first, Doug looked on without comment. He didn't understand exactly what they were trying to prove by their self-imposed torture. After about a week, he could no longer restrain himself from bringing it up. He and Chance were riding quietly along while Rori rode out ahead with Big Jake keeping a goodly distance between them.

"I don't understand something," he remarked in an almost casual tone that warned Chance immediately that something was coming.

"What?" he asked curtly.

"What are you trying to prove with Rori?"

"What do you mean?"

"I mean, why are you forcing her to sleep with you every night?"

Chance's good humor was frayed already, and when Doug made it sound like he was forcing Rori to meet his sexual demands, he exploded. "I'm not 'sleeping' with her!" He let his brother know in no uncertain terms that he had not made love to her.

"I know that," Doug told him disparagingly. Chance's fury with him for even suggesting such a thing only reinforced his belief that his brother was denying himself that which he wanted most. Had Chance and Rori been sharing love's passion and not fighting against it so hard, Chance would not have been so short-tempered or looked so haggard.

Doug found the entire situation just short of hysterically funny. Back in Boston, Chance had been a carefree bachelor. He'd had any woman he'd wanted. They'd thrown themselves at him with gusto, for he was Chance

Broderick—rich, handsome, and single. Chance had cut a wide swath through the social circle, never promising anything beyond momentary satisfaction, and yet the women had flocked to him. Now, here he was trapped by a guileless virgin, and Doug knew his brother had no idea how to handle it. It was interesting . . . most interesting.

"Don't you think this has gone on long enough?" They both knew he was talking about tying her to him every night.

"I don't trust Rori. I don't trust her one bit. She's headstrong and impulsive."

"Yeah, so?"

"So until she promises me she won't run away, I'm keeping track of her every movement."

"Why would she, and where the hell would she go?" Doug asked.

"Ask her," Chance returned. "She's the one who threatened to do it back in the village."

"She did? I thought you told me she'd agreed to go along with you without any argument."

"Look, Doug, I told Burr I'd do what was best for her, and I firmly believe that she'll have a better chance at life back in Boston. What's she got here? Nothing . . . nobody . . . At home, I'll see to it that she has the best of everything, meets the right people, attends the right functions . . ."

"But what if that's not what's best for Rori in her own mind?"

Chance, too, had been troubled by that thought, but he was so firm in his conviction to have her with him that he refused to worry about it too much. "I'll make sure she's happy."

Doug wanted to tell Chance that he couldn't force Rori to his way of thinking, that he couldn't force her to enjoy what she didn't want to enjoy, but he remained silent. He'd seen his brother in determined moods like this before, and he knew there was no arguing with him or convincing him differently. When Chance decided to do something, he did it. Doug supposed that was why he'd been such a success in his business endeavors. He only hoped that his bulldoggedness would work for him now with Rori. Doug decided he would watch and wait and smile a lot when neither one of them was looking.

Rori deliberately rode out as far ahead of the men as she thought she could get away with. The greater distance she put between her and Chance, the better. Her defenses against him were weakening, and she hated herself for it. She was almost to the point of giving in to him just so she could escape the agony of bedding down next to him.

Rori hadn't gotten a good night's sleep during the entire trip. Every night, her wrist bound to Chance's, she lay awake for hours, staring up at the stars and wondering how she'd gotten herself into this. When she finally did fall asleep, usually just a short time before dawn, hers was not a restful slumber, but one filled with tortured memories of Burr entwined with sensual images of Chance. Still, despite the torment of her predicament, Rori couldn't bring herself to admit to Chance that he'd won. She wouldn't give him the satisfaction of knowing that sleeping beside him disturbed her in the least.

When they made camp that night, Chance considered what Doug had said. In a way, he realized his brother was right, but there was no way he could end the situation between him and Rori without losing face, and he wasn't about to let her get the upper hand on anything. Chance didn't stop to ask himself why it was so important to him that he keep her under his control. He just knew he had to do it.

* * *

Rori was exhausted as she checked on Patch one last time that night after they'd eaten dinner. She knew she should stay up and try to avoid all contact with Chance, but the hope of getting some sleep drove her to her own blanket. Long before either of the men even thought about retiring, Rori had fallen sound asleep.

Much later, Chance and Doug said their own good nights and bedded down. Doug, too, was tired, and he fell asleep almost immediately. Not Chance, though. He was determined to bind her to him even though she was sleeping, but as he reached for her arm, he found himself mesmerized as he watched her sleep.

Jake was slowly making his way to join them.

"Not tonight, Jakie boy," Chance told the hound in a low voice.

The dog looked from his blissfully sleeping mistress to Chance and obediently moved off to lie down nearer the fire.

Chance remained braced up on one elbow, studying Rori in repose. There was no doubt she was a beautiful woman, and he could feel the stirring of desire deep within him. Chance did not understand this need he felt for Rori.

Chance had always considered himself a man who knew his own mind. He also considered himself a man of action. He met all of life's problems head-on and could usually solve any dilemma to his own satisfaction, but Rori left him stymied. Not that she was a problem, exactly, but the emotions he felt for her were conflicting and confusing. One minute he would find himself ready to throttle her, and the next he'd be longing to hold her and comfort her and ease all of her sorrows and fears. Chance grinned wryly to himself. If nothing else, since he'd met her his life had not been dull.

Chance was overwhelmed with a sense of tenderness for her. Things had been so rough for her lately. He knew he was being hard on her, but he had to show her that he was the boss. He had to teach her to listen to him and do things his way when he knew he was right. He reached for her hand so he could tie the rope to her wrist, and when he grasped it easily in his, she murmured something softly in her sleep.

The sound of her sleep-husky voice sent a shiver of sensual recognition through Chance, and he gritted his teeth against it. He waited a bit nervously for her to come awake, and when she didn't, he breathed a deep sigh of relief. He was in no mood for an angry confrontation with her tonight. He needed some rest, too.

Chance stared down at her, marveling at the freshness of her loveliness. As much as he wanted her, Chance knew he would not take advantage of her. She was his ward. He was her guardian. He couldn't let it be anything more. Still . . .

He glanced down at the rope in his hand and threw it aside in disgust. There would be no need for *that* kind of restraint tonight. The only restraint he was going to need was on his own raging desire.

The temptation to bend down and kiss her was overwhelming, but he refrained. Instead, he slipped an arm around her and drew her gently to his side being careful not to awaken her. Still fast asleep, she murmured softly as she curled instinctively against him.

The innocent sensuality of her move sent shock waves of passion surging through Chance. He shuddered as he fought for control. Closing his eyes against the excited torment, he asked himself why he'd been so stupid as to think that he'd be able to hold Rori close without wanting her. It had been this way between them since the first moment he'd discovered her true identity, and he was beginning to wonder if it was ever going to end.

Chance's jaw clenched as he struggled to remain passive with her in his arms. The temptation was great to make love to her right then and there. He knew she might fight him for a minute, but he knew how to make her want him. It would be a simple matter to . . . Chance stopped himself before he even really began to plan her seduction. He was on his honor to care for her, and if he made love to her now, he would be betraying his word to Burr.

Chance was tense and downright miserable holding Rori, yet it never occurred to him to even think of letting her go. Rori lay nestled comfortably against him as he stared up at the night sky asking himself how many endless hours were between now and the sanctuary of daylight.

Rori awoke slowly feeling greatly contented, although she wasn't sure why. She felt warm and protected and safe, almost like she was in a heavenly haven. *Why,* she thought dreamily, *it's almost like before Burr died . . .*

The last thought jerked her painfully back from her dream world to the harshness of reality. Her mind was foggy, and it took her a moment to focus on where she was and what she was doing. Burr . . . Chance . . . going back East . . . It all came flooding back in on her then, and she realized that she must have gotten her first real night's sleep since the tragedy. She was glad, for she felt more rested than she had for a long time. Rori sighed and opened her eyes.

Rori didn't know what she expected to see, but it wasn't Chance's chin. She stiffened in horror. What the hell had happened here? What was she doing sleeping in Chance's arms with her head resting intimately on his shoulder? Thankful that he was still asleep, Rori shifted positions a bit and carefully looked around. To her absolute dismay, she discovered that she was lying curved against his body as naturally as if it happened every night, and there was no sign of Jakie. Where was that damned dog? He was supposed to sleep in between them!

It was then that Rori realized that he hadn't tied her wrist to his the night before, and that confused her. Had she been so sound asleep that her resistance to him was weakened, and she'd gone into his arms willingly? The possibility distressed her. She didn't want to show any weakness around Chance. She couldn't afford to.

Rori was worried about what might happen between them in the future if she'd gone willingly into his arms last night while she was asleep. At the realization that she couldn't trust herself when she was sleeping, Rori made up her mind then and there to put an end to the situation. She knew she really had no choice where her future was concerned. Chance Broderick was a formidable foe. If she ran, he would come after her. There would be no defeating or escaping him. He intended to take her back to Boston with him, and she was going.

Resigned to her fate, Rori moved gingerly away from him and began to fix breakfast. When he awoke, she would make the promise he'd been waiting for. She would promise not to try to get away. She would go with him without a fight. Her heart cried out to her that she was being foolish, that she would only be hurt, but Rori knew there was nothing else she could do.

Chance had not fallen asleep until just before dawn. When he awoke a short time later, he realized immediately that Rori was gone from his side. He jerked up into a sitting position, expecting the worst, expecting to find that she had fled the camp while he'd slept. Instead, he discovered that she was busily tending the breakfast fire. Relief flowed through him, and he gave a ragged sigh. He ran a hand through his hair as he got to his feet and stretched.

"Good morning, Rori," he greeted her.

Rori had had her back to Chance as he'd awakened,

and at the sound of his greeting she went still. "Chance," she responded curtly, glancing around at him. She thought it embarrassing that she'd slept so intimately with him last night, and she hoped he wouldn't bring it up this morning.

"I'm surprised you're still here," he broached the subject immediately.

"There was no point in runnin'," she said, her resentment obvious in her tone.

"You realize that now?" He was surprised.

"You have your promise, Chance. I won't run," Rori told him flatly, knowing that she had to escape his nearness.

His elation over having won the showdown with her was less than he'd expected, because now he knew that he had to keep his promise to her. He had to let her sleep alone. Logically, he told himself that it was for the best, but that didn't stop him from wanting her badly, and resenting the fact that he was a man of honor.

"And you have yours. Tonight I'll move my bedroll," he answered, mystified by the honor in him that drove him to keep his word. Why couldn't he be an unprincipled scoundrel like some of his contemporaries back in Boston? Annoyed, Chance realized with grim amusement that his mother must have raised him right. He decided then and there that he would have to talk to her about that the next time he saw her.

Rori nodded in response. From now on she would be sleeping alone. Yet, even as the idea pleased her, she wondered why she suddenly felt so terribly lonely again.

Chapter 25

Rori was tense, her mood strained, as she reined in beside Chance and Doug in front of the hotel in Phoenix. This was her first trip back without Burr and memories of him haunted her as she looked around. She had tried not to think of him too much during the trek from the village, but now there was no denying how much she missed him. She loved him dearly and would always mourn him.

As Rori dismounted, she cast a sidelong glance at Chance. He was paying no attention to her whatsoever, but was locked deep in conversation with Doug. She remained standing by Patch, the uncertainty of her position leaving her nervous and unsure of what to do next. They had barely spoken since the morning she'd made her promise to him. He hadn't told her anything of his plans, and she wasn't sure what was expected of her now.

"Rori, let's go inside," Chance directed as he and Doug tied up their own mounts and, taking their saddlebags along, started inside the hotel.

"Chance . . . wait . . ." Rori called out to him, distressed. She remembered the last time she'd entered the lobby and how the owner had tried to prevent her from going up to Chance's room, telling her that they didn't let "her kind" in there.

"What is it?" Chance walked slowly to where she was

standing with Jake, wondered what was bothering her, since she'd had very little to say to him over the course of the last week or so.

"You plannin' on us stayin' here?" The tilt of her chin was stubborn as she looked up at him.

"Yes, why?"

"Well, you and Doug can, but I ain't." Her pride dictated that she not go where she wasn't welcome.

"And may I ask where you plan to stay?" Chance did not understand her reason for balking at the accommodations.

"I'll find some place. I'll sleep out if I have to," she answered, "and you don't hafta worry. I won't run off."

"Sorry, Rori, but you're staying with me," he replied adamantly.

"But I don't want to stay here."

"Why not?" Chance was growing exasperated. He was hot, tired, and dirty. He wanted a comfortable bed, a bath, and clean sheets.

"I don't like it."

"It's the best hotel in town, Rori! I know it isn't much, but it's better than the alternative. Now, let's go." He turned away from her and strode with Doug into the hotel lobby.

Rori wanted to keep arguing, but she knew it was useless to try to explain to him. Chance was going to find out firsthand "why not" just as soon as she walked into the lobby anyway. Virgil Keeps would not let her stay in his hotel; she felt sure of it.

She sighed deeply as she was forced to surrender to his will and then advised her pet, "Wait here, Jakie." Grabbing her things from Patch's back, she hurried after Chance and Doug.

"Well, Broderick, welcome back," Keeps greeted his former customer warmly. He was an avid fan of money and genuinely fond of paying guests.

"Hello, Keeps," Chance returned. "My brother and I are going to need three rooms for tonight."

"Three?" He raised his eyebrows as he questioned Chance's statement. When Chance nodded that he had heard him correctly, he rumbled, "You got somebody else joinin' you?"

"Yes," Chance answered a bit curtly, not wanting him to know his private business.

"Fine, fine." Keeps was grinning as he turned the ledger around so they could register. As they were signing in, he looked up and caught sight of Rori standing just inside the doorway. He raced around the counter heading toward Rori, intending to throw her bodily out of his establishment. "Get outta here, boy! I've told you before I don't let your kind in here with good, clean-living white folks!"

He was just about to grab her when Chance spoke up. "I wouldn't do that if I were you, Keeps."

"Rori's with us," Doug said firmly.

"This breed's with you?" Keeps was stunned as he looked back and forth between the two white men and the grubby-looking Indian boy.

"Yes. The third room is for Rori, but if you have a problem with that, we can easily take our business elsewhere." His threat was subtle but effective as he reached into his pocket for the cash he needed to pay for the accommodations.

The greedy hotel owner quickly backed down. He gave Rori a hate-filled look and then turned back to fawn over Chance and Doug. "I suppose I can make an exception this time . . ."

"I was hoping you'd see things our way," Chance responded, glancing back at Rori, his expression telling her that now he understood her reasoning.

Rori had been ready for a fight when Keeps had come at her so threateningly. She knew the bigoted white man, and she knew he would stop at nothing to get her out of his hotel. Her hand had been on her knife, and she'd been prepared to use it.

However, when Chance warned the other man off relief swept through Rori followed by a new respect for the man who was her guardian. The realization that he'd stood up for her against this man surprised and pleased her. It was a rare day when anyone backed old Virgil Keeps down, and she had loved every minute of it. As Chance's gaze met hers, she couldn't resist giving him a quick, bright smile.

"Top of the steps and to the right, the three rooms at the far end of the hall," Keeps directed as he handed them the keys and quickly picked up the money Chance had tossed on the counter.

"Thanks," Chance said less than graciously as he and Doug started upstairs. "Come on, Rori."

"How long do you think you'll be stayin'?" Keeps asked as he watched Rori follow them.

"Don't know yet," Chance answered without looking back, "but when we decide you'll be among the first to know, Keeps. By the way, send up a hot bath to Rori's room right away, and then one for my brother and me later on tonight."

"Right away!" the hotel owner replied respectfully. He watched them disappear down the hall and wasn't sure whether to cuss or celebrate. He definitely needed the money, but he sure didn't need any damned Indian staying there.

Aggravated, Keeps sat back in his chair for a minute to hungrily count out the cash Chance had paid in advance. He was torn until he finally convinced himself that he could stand the breed's presence for a little while, since it meant renting three rooms extra a night. With dollar signs in his eyes, he hoped they'd be in town for at least a few more days. Stuffing the money down in his pants pocket, he hurried out back to see about the bath Broderick wanted for the boy.

Doug and Chance exchanged a few words, and then Doug went on into his room, leaving Chance to get Rori settled in. She reached for the doorknob to the room he'd indicated as hers, intending to open the door and barge on inside, when Chance stepped in front of her to stop her.

"A lady always waits for her gentleman to open any doors for her," he admonished gently, delivering another unsolicited etiquette lesson.

"But I ain't no lady," she pointed out with maddening logic.

"It's only a matter of time, Rori," Chance assured her. "We're about to change all that."

They were standing just inches apart, and Rori found that she was suddenly breathless. They hadn't been this physically close since that morning she'd awakened to find herself in his arms. She slowly lifted her gaze to his, trying not to let her unexpected excitement show in her expression. She didn't want him to know how he could affect her. She didn't want him to know that she craved his embrace.

"Why?" Rori finally managed to ask.

"Because if you're going to have a successful life in Boston, you have to master the social amenities and become a lady."

"I don't mean 'why' about learnin' all your 'social amenities' or how to become a lady. I just want to know why men think they have to open doors for girls. I've been opening doors for myself all my life. It's not hard to do."

"It's done as a sign of respect, Rori."

The explanation Chance offered sounded dumb to Rori, but she did not argue the point. She wanted to get away from him as quickly as she could. She waited impatiently for him to open the door and then proceeded inside, trying not to brush against him as she went. Once they were in the sparsely furnished, but relatively clean room, she turned to Chance.

"Well, now what?"

"What do you mean?"

"I mean, we're here in Phoenix. What do you want me to do?"

"The first thing you're going to do is take a bath when they bring it up. Then stay here in your room until I come back for you."

"All right," she answered as if it really mattered very little to her that he was going to leave her all alone.

"I'll be back," he told her, and he was gone, striding purposefully from her room.

Rori looked around herself at the single bed with its colorful, lightweight quilt, small washstand with a mirror hanging above it, and small dresser, and she thought it a rather comfortable room. To Rori these were luxurious accommodations, and she flopped down on the bed and stretched out across its softness. She folded her arms comfortably beneath her head and stared up at the ceiling.

Rori was just about to drift off when a knock sounded at the door. Thinking and hoping that it was Chance coming back already, she jumped up and ran to throw it wide. To her disappointment, it was the hotel maids bringing the tub and water. She let them in and said nothing as they prepared the bath. When they'd gone, Rori stood staring at it for a few minutes. She hadn't bathed since that last day in the village and strangely enough she found herself actually looking forward to the prospect of scrubbing off all the trail dirt.

Rori made short order of stripping off her filthy

clothes, and she even went so far as to unbraid her hair so she could wash it. The heat of the water was like a velvet caress as she stepped into the tub, and she sank down into it with a soft sigh. With relish, she picked up the soap that had been provided and began to scrub every inch of her body. She wet her hair and washed that, too. It wasn't long before she was done, and she climbed out to dry off, rubbing herself vigorously with a towel.

Rori was tired, and she hated the thought of putting her dirty clothes back on. Since Chance hadn't told her a time, she figured he wouldn't be back for a while so she had time to take a nap. Rori was heading for the bed when she caught sight of herself in the small mirror over the washstand. She paused and stared at the slender young woman who was reflected there. Her hair was ebony and hung in a sleek cape about her shoulders. Her breasts were round and full, her waist almost waspishly thin. Her hips were gently curved, and her legs long and shapely. There wasn't an ounce of extra fat on her body, and Rori guessed that she was attractive enough, although she had no way to really compare herself to anyone. All the white women she'd ever seen had been dressed from their necks to their wrists to their ankles, and it was impossible to render a judgment from that.

It occurred to her suddenly that she didn't know what Chance intended to do with her. He had said something about making her into a lady, but she had no idea what that meant or how soon he intended to start. She didn't know if he wanted her to continue to dress as a boy or if he was going to insist that she begin dressing as a female right now. Frankly, she would rather have continued her charade as a boy, but she didn't think that would work much longer, especially since they were heading back East. Shrugging, she went to lie down on the bed. She wrapped the cover around her and closed her eyes, meaning only to rest until Chance came back.

Chance stood in the middle of the dry goods store studying the selection of ladies wear and wondering what to buy.

"Can I help you with something, sir?" the middle-aged, balding clerk asked, eyeing Chance askance and wondering what he wanted with women's things.

"Yes, I need a wardrobe for a lady."

The retailer's eyes lit up at the thought of a sale. "What in particular did you need?"

"Everything," Chance answered firmly.

"Everything, sir?"

"Yes. I need a dress, undergarments, a nightgown, shoes . . ."

"Everything." He smiled broadly. "Let me show you what we've got . . . What size is your lady?"

Chance started to protest that she wasn't *his* lady, but thought better of it. It was no one's business but his own who he was buying clothes for.

"She's . . . um . . ." Chance grinned wryly as he tried to calculate Rori's proportions. As best he could, he described her figure to him. He gave an estimate of her height and her weight, the slimness of her waist easily spanded by his two hands and the fullness of her curves. The memory of pressing kisses to her tender flesh stirred in the back of his mind, and he fought it down.

"I see," the salesman replied as he began to show Chance a variety of items.

Chance was not pleased with the quality of the undergarments, and the only dress he had that might fit Rori was quite plain, but Chance knew he had little real choice here in Phoenix. He decided to take what he could get, but as soon as they reached St. Louis, he was going to buy her an entire wardrobe.

When Chance inquired about getting another day-gown made for her, the clerk gave him the address of a dressmaker in town. After paying for the things he'd selected, he left the store and went to the seamstress's house. The woman agreed to do a rush job for them, so Chance made an appointment for Rori for later that same day.

All in all, Chance was satisfied with the success he'd had shopping as he headed back for the hotel. At least now she had feminine clothes to wear while they were traveling.

He crossed through the lobby without even bothering to speak to Keeps and took the stairs two at a time in his eagerness to see Rori in the dress he'd brought with him. He knocked softly at her door and waited for her to answer it. When she didn't respond to his summons right away, he grew tense and immediately suspected the worst.

Had Rori promised not to run away while they were on the trail, only to leave now that they were in town? It seemed logical to Chance, and he angrily tried the doorknob. It was unlocked, as he'd expected it to be. She had probably just been waiting for him to disappear from sight before running away. He cursed himself for ever having trusted her as he opened the door and walked in.

Chance was stunned, to say the least, to find Rori wrapped in the quilt, sound asleep on the bed. He took another step inside the room and silently closed the door behind him, all the while rejoicing that she hadn't fled. He approached the bed slowly with measured tread, and as he drew near the side, he gazed down at her, enchanted. How lovely she was . . . how beautiful . . .

Spellbound, he set the parcel aside that contained the

clothing he'd bought for her and reached out to brush
the heavy silk of her hair away from her cheek. At his
gentle touch, Rori stirred and opened her eyes to see
him standing over her.

"Chance . . ." She whispered his name in a sigh. She'd
been dreaming about him, she realized, and here he
was. Almost without volition, she lifted her arms to him.
The movement let the quilt fall away, revealing to him
the beauty of her breasts.

Chance stood frozen where he was. The temptation
to take her while she was sleepy and didn't know what
she was doing was great. Heat surged through him as his
gaze lingered on her bosom. He longed to press his lips
to that burgeoning flesh, to cradle her softness against
him and know the joy of joining with her again. It jolted
him to realize what he was thinking, and he forced himself to step back away from her.

"For God's sake, woman, cover yourself!" he ordered
in what sounded strangled to him, but disgusted to Rori.

Embarrassed, Rori clutched the covers to her breasts.
"What are you doing in here?" she demanded, going on
the offensive, for she was humiliated by her own display
of longing for him. She didn't want him to know how
much she really needed to be held in his arms.

"When I knocked on the door you didn't answer . . ."

"So you thought you'd just barge right on in?"

"I thought you might have hurt yourself some way or
that you might have . . ."

She realized what he'd been thinking and grew furious. He still didn't trust her, even after she'd given him
her word! "You were afraid that I had run away, weren't
you? You didn't trust me to stick around without you
watchin' over me every minute, did you?"

Chance looked suitably contrite, his hunger to touch
her fading slightly before her indignation. Still, he
couldn't help but notice how lovely she was when she

was angry, how her green eyes flashed emerald fire at him and how her bosom rose and fell in agitation over his doubting of her.

When he didn't answer right away, Rori went on. "I may not be one of your fancy Eastern ladies, Chance Broderick, but my grampa raised me to value my honor. When I give my word that I'll do something, I do it!"

"I'm sorry for doubting you, Rori," he finally spoke.

She was still angry with him, but she let it go. Her point made. "What did you want? Did you just want to see if I'd taken a bath like you told me to? Well, I did."

"I can see that," Chance replied, glancing back at the tub and discarded damp towel. "I came back because I bought you some clothes."

"Clothes?" Rori wasn't sure whether to be happy or cautious. She'd longed for something clean to wear, but she wondered exactly what he'd gotten her. "You bought me clothes?"

"Yes." He reached for the package that contained the dress and undergarments and untied the string that bound it. Opening it up, he spread out the new garments on the bed before her for inspection. "Here."

Rori stared wide-eyed at the lovely things—daygown, chemise, stockings, shoes. "You bought these for me?"

"I think they'll fit. I was guessing your size."

She continued to stare at them for a minute, and then, her heart heavy, she shook her head. "Nope. I ain't gonna wear 'em. What I got is fine. I'll just wear my own clothes."

Chance had thought that he would please her with the dress and accessories. He didn't know a woman alive who didn't love getting new clothes, and he was completely baffled by her response.

"Rori, you're going to be traveling on stagecoaches and trains. You have to look the part of a lady."

"I don't have to do nothin'," she declared firmly, refusing to budge. "My clothes are fine."

Chance had had it. Enough was enough. "Rori, your clothes are fine for living in the desert, but I will not allow you to be the laughingstock of Boston. Do you understand me?"

"Do you understand me, Chance? I said 'no'!"

"Put on the dress, Rori."

"No."

"If you don't do it willingly, I'll dress you myself!"

"Go ahead, if you think you're man enough!" Rori knew the minute she said it that she shouldn't have dared him, for a fierce fire suddenly glowed in the depths of his dark eyes.

"You doubt that I can do it, Rori?" Chance grinned wickedly as he reached out and grabbed the top of the quilt. In one easy motion he stripped the cover from her, leaving her naked before him. Without pausing, he snared her wrist, jerked her up, and hauled her full against him.

The contact of her bare flesh against him was explosive. Chance knew he should have realized touching her would be a mistake, but he'd been too annoyed at the time by her challenge. The force of the emotions that rocketed through him startled Chance, and he stared down at her as she knelt before him on the bed.

Rori had intended to struggle with him, to fight him in his attempt to dress her, but suddenly this wasn't about getting dressed anymore. Suddenly, this was something totally different. She ran the tip of her tongue nervously over her lips as she tried to decide what to do.

Rori was completely surprised when Chance gave an audible groan and bent down to capture her lips with his. His tongue moved boldly to claim hers, delving deep within the honeyed sweetness of her mouth. It was a hot, devastating exchange.

Melting against him, Rori gave up all thoughts of fighting. She had wanted this—oh how she'd wanted this! She'd dreamed of being in his arms, of his wanting her again, and now it was happening. Chance had released her wrist, and she looped her arms around his neck now to draw him even closer. She could feel the heat and hardness of him and craved even more intimate contact with him.

Chance knew he should stop this madness, that he should turn around and walk out, but it was too late. He had wanted her for so long, needed to hold her and make love to her for so long that any thought of denying himself the joy of tasting of her love again vanished.

He moved to lie on the bed, drawing her with him. His mouth met hers time and again in fiery, passionate kisses that left them both breathless and straining together. His hands explored her silken curves with cherishing yet arousing caresses. They were man and woman. They desired each other. That was all that mattered.

Each touch led to another more bolder one. Soon Chance's clothing had been discarded, and he was next to her, his naked flesh pressed to hers, the heat of his maleness hot and hard against her thigh. His mouth explored the peaks and valleys of her bosom with hot, wet kisses that sent her senses reeling. His hands were everywhere, molding her soft curves to his hard leanness.

Rori thought she was still dreaming as Chance finally moved to make her completely his own. She gasped at the sensation of being one with him. It was so intimate, so wonderful that she felt tears burn her eyes. Rori knew she was letting herself in for a lot of pain by caring for him, but she could no longer doubt her heart's desire. She loved him. Clasping him to her, she moved at his urging, matching his rhythm with her own fierce driving need. This was Chance . . . he was all she wanted, all she needed.

Chance was beyond thinking as he plumbed the heated silken depths of her womanhood. It was an elemental joining . . . a craving that had to be satisfied. He was in ecstasy as he thrust into her welcoming warmth. It was perfection in all its rapturous splendor.

They climaxed together, scaling the peak of excitement in unison, the glory of their mating a vibrant, almost living thing. Waves of heart-stopping pleasure washed over them as Chance held Rori tight. Their bodies were fused, their limbs entwined. The only sound in the quiet of the aftermath of their passion was the harshness of their breathing.

Chapter 26

As the heated moment cooled, a shudder of awareness wracked Chance. Confusion shook him as he cradled Rori's slender body to his. They had made love . . . and he'd never known ecstasy so sweet.

Chance knew he should feel guilty, but what had happened between them was too beautiful to be marred by self-recrimination. He wondered what there was about Rori that could drive him to mindlessness with physical desire for her. Not even Bethany, with all her experience, had been able to arouse him to such heights of rapture. It was only with Rori that he could feel these things. Only with Rori . . .

A tinge of conscience pained Chance as he realized what he was doing. He was using Rori for his own pleasure, and he knew it wasn't fair. She deserved so much more than the momentary physical pleasure he could give her. She deserved a man who loved her and would marry her.

Chance's honor stung him again, and he knew he'd have to keep his distance from Rori in order to live up to the promise he'd given Burr. It was all too easy to enjoy the thrill of her lovemaking, but she was an innocent, unschooled in the ways of the world. He would have to teach her how to deal with men like himself, bachelors intent on seductions. He would have to show her how to fend them off without insulting them and how to use her womanly powers to gain what she really wanted in life. He didn't like the idea of trying to change Rori, but he tried not to think of it that way. Instead, he convinced himself that he would be doing her more harm if he didn't teach her what she needed to know to move into society gracefully.

Rori stirred in Chance's embrace. She was in heaven. Rapturous contentment filled her. This was where she wanted to be . . . in Chance's arms forever. She loved him. Her heart sang as she accepted the truth. She realized that she might be hurt, but the pain would be worth it just for the joy he had given her today. She had never dreamed such delight existed, and now that she knew it did, she never wanted it to end.

Chance opened his eyes to the brightness of the sunlit room. He knew he should say something, but he wasn't sure what. As he glanced around, he saw the new clothing he'd bought Rori strewn all over the floor beside the bed. He smiled as he realized how useless his threat had been.

"Rori . . ." he began.

Rori was tense as she waited for him to continue. She was expecting him to deny what had happened between them, and she was surprised when he didn't.

"Rori, I think you'd better dress yourself . . . unless you're still doubting my manhood?"

She heard the touch of humor in his voice and opened her eyes to gaze up at him. She found herself mesmerized by the tenderness in his expression. Her heart swelled with love for him as she visually traced each chiseled line of his handsome features. Yet even as she confessed to herself her adoration for him, she was saddened that she couldn't do as he asked. Her love for him was strong, and her newly discovered desire to please him was growing, but her pride held sway on this decision. She couldn't take the clothes from him—she just couldn't. As lovely as they were, and as much as she longed to wear them, she couldn't allow herself to become any further indebted to Chance. She had no money with which to repay him and no prospects right now of ever being able to earn any.

"Chance . . . I can't . . ."

"You're still doubting my ability to dress you?" he asked, trying to lighten the moment even though he found her continued refusals puzzling.

"No, no, it's not that. It's just that I can't take the clothes, that's all."

"Can't?" Now he really was confused. "Why not? They're here, they're paid for, they're yours. Wear them."

"But that's the problem! They're not paid for, not by me anyway. I can't accept them as a gift from you. I don't want you buying me clothes. It's hard enough for me to accept the fact that I'll be traveling back East with you. I can't let myself become indebted to you for a whole wardrobe of white women's clothing."

A whole wardrobe? He'd barely managed to buy her one day's essentials. Chance would have chuckled out loud had the moment not been such a serious one. He could tell that her pride was going to be a very important factor in their dealings with each other, and he made a mental note, from this moment on, to keep it foremost in his thoughts.

Chance pressed a soft kiss to her forehead before replying to her heartfelt statement. "Let's get one thing straight right now. In our world, there's no 'white' anything. We are who we are, Rori. All right?"

She nodded, but didn't speak, waiting to see what else he had to say.

"Secondly, you seem to have forgotten that I'm the one indebted to you. Without your help and Burr's I would never have found Doug. I owe you five hundred dollars."

"You do?"

"I do. So, if it's money that's been worrying you, don't give it another thought."

"It was," Rori confessed, the realization that she was not poor giving her spirits a definite lift. She did have money! She could reimburse Chance for all the things he'd bought!

"Then don't let it concern you anymore. Just let me take care of everything, and when we get to Boston we'll settle up. How's that?" he suggested.

"Fine."

"Rori?"

"What?"

"Will you try the clothes on now?"

"Oh, yes, Chance," she told him happily, sliding from his embrace to gather up the feminine garments. Suddenly she was eager to try on the new clothing. She wanted to impress Chance, to show him how good she could look when she dressed like one of his ladies.

Chance watched her every move with glowing eyes as she pulled the garments on. He regretted that they were not the most delicate of undergarments, but at least he knew they were better than what she had been wearing. His gaze was warm upon her as he caught an occasional glimpse of swelling breast and curvaceous thigh. He wondered distractedly how fantastic Rori would look in expensive, lacy lingerie, when she looked so absolutely beautiful in these plain things. Chance made a secret vow to himself to buy her some more delicate undergarments at the first opportunity.

As she donned the chemise, he had to fight down the urge to tear it from her body and make love to her again. He was glad when she finally stepped into the dress and put him a little out of his misery. She presented too much temptation to him dressed the other way.

Still, when Rori came to stand before him, wanting him to fasten the buttons at the back of the gown for her, he was hard put not to slip his hands beneath the soft cotton material and caress her silken flesh. He contented himself with the task at hand, though, and when he finished the last button, he stood up and pressed a gentle kiss to the back of her neck.

Rori shivered with delight at the touch of his lips. She could not believe the change in Chance or in herself. She no longer wanted to fight him. Now she only wanted to impress him. It puzzled her, but she liked the idea.

"Well? What do you think?" In a purely female motion, Rori stepped away to pivot before him.

Chance studied the rather plain but serviceable gown with a critical eye. He always appreciated a beautiful woman, and he had no doubt that Rori was the most lovely female he'd ever seen. He wished with all his heart that her first gown could have been something special . . . a ballgown of the finest silk, but he knew that would have to wait until they reached civilization. When the time came, he would see to it that she had the best wardrobe of any young woman in Boston. Rori was acting so delighted, though, that Chance realized this gown might as well have been an exclusive from Paris. The thought that he'd pleased her made him smile.

"You look lovely, Rori. Blue becomes you."

"Do you really think so?" She beamed, blushing at his compliment.

"I know so," he assured her. "I want you to have at least one more gown to take on the trip, so I made an appointment with the dressmaker here in town. We have to go see her in about an hour to have your measurements taken."

"What measurements?" Since this dress fit so perfectly, Rori didn't understand what was needed.

Chance's gaze dropped to her bosom, her slender waist, and then to the gentle swell of her hips. He decided then and there that he was not about to get into a detailed explanation on the art of dressmaking. "She has to know what size you are in various places so she can make the gown to fit."

"Oh."

"It's going to be a rush job on her part because we're leaving for Prescott tomorrow morning."

"Tomorrow?" She was surprised that they'd be leaving so soon, but realized there was no longer any need for them to remain here.

"The stage leaves at ten thirty. We go to Prescott, then on to Denver where we'll board a train for home." Chance could see that she was a bit intimidated by the itinerary.

"Home . . ." Rori repeated dully, swallowing nervously.

"My home, but it will soon be yours, too."

"It will?"

Their eyes met across the room, hers mirroring her sudden uncertainty at the whole new world he was offering her, his reflecting only calm assurance.

"You're going to do just fine there. Wait and see. Once you're settled in, you'll be the belle of Boston. You're a beautiful woman, Rori. Men will be swarming all over you just for one of your smiles. They'll be standing in line to court you, Rori, and you'll probably be swamped with proposals. You'll have the pick of the men in Boston." Chance wanted to convince her that she was going to be a tremendous success.

Rori's spirits plummeted, and she turned away from him to study her reflection in the mirror. She didn't want the pick of the men of Boston. She wanted Chance! She realized a bit sadly that nothing had really changed between them. He didn't love her; he only desired her.

The realization hurt Rori, but she refused to be heartbroken. Instead, her pride flared, and with it her spirits. If she was as pretty as Chance said, why couldn't she win his love? His proposal was the only one she wanted. He was the only man she loved. Her resolve stiffened, and she smiled in determination at her reflection. She was going to marry Chance Broderick. She didn't know exactly how she was going to manage it yet, but she was.

Rori had only a few short weeks left until they reached Boston and his precious Bethany, so she knew she had to begin her campaign to win his love right now. Since he seemed to feel that ladylike behavior was an important asset for a woman, she decided to become the most ladylike lady he'd ever met.

"Chance?" She turned from the mirror to face him, determined to use all her newly awakened feminine wiles in this pursuit. "How do you think I should fix my hair now? Should I still braid it?"

"Where's your brush?" Chance had no idea what was behind her sudden concern for her hair outside of the possibility that she was finally becoming aware of herself as a female. Rising from the bed, he pulled on his pants and then went to her.

Rori handed the brush to him and waited as he moved behind her. Chance had never thought brushing a woman's hair could be such a sensual act, but he found himself enjoying it. When he finished, her ebony mane was shining about her shoulders in silken splendor, and he had to fight to keep from running his hands through the satiny veil.

Slightly annoyed with the direction of his thoughts, Chance gave her the brush back and went to finish dressing. He yanked his clothes on quickly, wondering how he was ever going to control what he was feeling for Rori if he couldn't even brush her hair without wanting her. The only way he could handle the situation, he decided, was to avoid being alone with her. From now on, he would have to make sure that there was always a third person around to chaperone him. That would force him to keep his hands to himself. He felt fairly confident that he'd resolved his dilemma as he faced her again.

"Let's see if we can find Doug so we can tell him about our appointment with the seamstress and plan to meet him for dinner afterward."

"Just let me get these shoes on . . ." Rori sat down on the bed and hiked her skirt up above her knees as she pulled on her stockings.

Chance swallowed tightly as he watched her guide the stockings over her shapely calves. Finally, in desperation he wandered over to the window to look out at the street below. Only when Rori announced she was ready, did he turn back around. He offered her his arm and escorted her dutifully from the room.

It was nearly two hours later when they finally made it to the restaurant for dinner. The trip to the seamstress had gone well, and she had given them her assurances that the other daygown Chance had directed her to make would be ready first thing in the morning.

Rori's decision to become the most "ladiest" lady around fueled her attentiveness when they were seated in the restaurant. She was a bit startled when Chance insisted upon pulling out her chair for her, but acceded to his wishes without comment. Rori took her seat as gracefully as the awkward full skirt would let her, all the while telling herself that if he thought manners were important, then she'd learn every bit of manners there were. Whatever it took to win Chance, she planned to do. She wanted him, and she was going to get him.

Rori sat across the table from Chance and Doug as they waited for the food to be served, avidly listening to their discussion of the ranch Doug had heard was for sale. The other patrons kept glancing at her curiously, but she ignored them with ease, having already dealt with Virgil Keeps and his look of gaping surprise when she'd crossed the lobby on Chance's arm. Chance and Doug had assured her that anyone staring at her would be doing it only because she was beautiful, and the thought thrilled her, for she wanted to be beautiful . . . beautiful for Chance.

The two men were still involved in their conversation when the food was finally served. Rori was so hungry by this time she didn't care about utensils. All she cared about was eating. She dug into her meal with her usual gusto. But after a few minutes of stuffing down her food with her fingers, Rori realized that both men had stopped eating and were openly staring at her, Doug in amusement, a smile playing about his lips, Chance in consternation. She paused as she leaned forward to take a bite from the hunk of bread thick with butter that she held halfway to her mouth.

"Is something wrong?" she asked, her mouth still full from the last bite she'd taken.

"A lady never talks with her mouth full," Chance admonished.

"If I don't talk, how am I gonna find out why you're staring at me?" she demanded a bit defensively and then made a concerted effort to swallow what she'd been chewing.

"Lesson number one on eating," he began. "Never chew with your mouth open and never take a big bite of anything."

"You want me to eat like a bird?" Rori demanded, her stomach still growling hungrily. "I'm starving, and you want me to eat like a bird?"

"Eat all you want, Rori, just do it politely."

"Like a lady," she said snidely.

"Yes, like a lady."

She stifled a sigh, remembering her determination to learn all she could, as fast as she could. "All right. Tell me everything I need to know," she urged, surprising Chance completely.

He'd expected her to react angrily to his negative comments, and he studied her for a moment to make sure she was serious. Seeing the earnestness in her expression, he began, and by the end of the meal, both men were pleased with her progress.

"If you're always this quick at picking up on things, you should be more than ready for Boston when we get there," Chance complimented her.

"I agree," Doug put in.

Rori smiled widely at his praise. She knew she could do it! She knew she could!

It was dusk as they made their way back to the hotel, and then Rori spotted Big Jake sitting all alone at the side of the building.

"Jakie! C'mon, boy!" she called him, dropping to her knees to give him a big hug. "Mad at me, are you? I wouldn't have left you out here all night." She petted him and hugged him again before standing up.

They started inside, but Keeps was vigilant again, and when he saw the dog, he erupted. "Get that mutt outside. I ain't letting no damned dog in this place."

"Mr. Keeps," Chance's voice was chilling, "there is a lady present."

Rori was amazed when the hotel owner flushed.

"I apologize for my cussing, but I don't allow no animals in here."

Rori glanced down at Jakie and knew that wherever he went, she went. She couldn't bear to be without him. He'd slept with her ever since she'd first gotten him, and she didn't intend for that to change. Chance saw the love in her gaze as she stared down at her pet, and he approached the desk where Keeps sat glowering at them.

"The dog is with us, but I'll be more than willing to pay you for any inconvenience he may cause. Will an extra dollar cover it?"

Keeps almost licked his lips in anticipation of a dog as a paying customer. "That'll do it, but you clean up any messes he makes."

Chance tossed the money to him. It never ceased to amaze Chance just how powerful money was. No matter what the problem, money somehow always managed to solve it.

They said good night to Doug at his door and went on down the hall to Rori's.

"Thanks for helpin' me keep Jakie with me tonight, Chance," Rori told him as he unlocked her door for her. Her pulse quickened at the thought that he might want to come into her room again.

"Well, you two sleep tight, all right?" Chance pushed the portal wide so she could enter, but made no attempt to go in himself.

Rori's heart sank as he remained standing in the hall. "Chance . . . I . . ."

"Rori," he began in a gruff yet soft tone, "we can't let what happened this afternoon repeat itself. I'm your guardian. I'm supposed to protect you from men like me, not use you."

"But . . ." Rori wanted to yell at him that she didn't want to be protected from him, that she wanted to love him, but he didn't give her the opportunity.

"Shhh . . . don't say anything else. I'm going to take you back to Boston, and you're going to find a good man and have a good life."

Rori stared at him in aggravation for a minute. *I've already found a good man!* she wanted to shout at him, but she realized that it was still too soon to press her point. She rose up on her tiptoes to kiss him on the cheek and then turned to go inside.

"Good night, Chance." She closed the door behind her. She wanted him, her body ached to be held in his embrace, but her pride refused to let her beg him for attention. If he didn't want her tonight, fine, but that was all going to change very quick.

Chance stood there staring at her closed door for a moment before continuing on down the hall to his own room. He went inside and stretched out fully clothed on his bed, all the while fighting down the urge to go back to Rori and spend the night making mad, passionate love to her. He couldn't do it. He wouldn't do it.

A knock at the door summoned him from his restlessness, and he opened it to find the maid bringing him his bath.

"How hot's the water you got there?" he asked sharply.

"This is hot."

"Well, take it back and bring cold . . . and lots of it."

"Yes, sir."

The sound of the crash brought Chance bolt upright in bed, and he stared around his darkened room, trying to decide where the noise had come from. It occurred to him suddenly that it must have come from Rori's room. He struggled into his pants, grabbed his gun and bolted for the hallway. He charged out of his room just as Doug did. Both men were barefoot, shirtless, and their hair was sleep-tousled. They exchanged worried looks as they stood there in the hall.

"No! Don't! Stop it!"

They could hear Rori's cries, and without hesitation, they booted her door open. Chance's heart was in his throat at the thought that she was in danger. They launched themselves into the room, guns ready. They intended to shoot whoever it was who was daring to hurt her, and they both froze, feeling like complete fools as they took in the scene before them.

Rori looked up at them and scowled. She was kneeling next to the bathtub that was in the center of her room, and she was trying to keep Big Jake from jumping out of the water. She was wearing her old clothes and was soaked from head to toe. Soapsuds covered her, and it looked like there were more suds on her than on the bedraggled, soggy mutt.

"Chance? Doug? What are you doing?" Rori asked, struggling to keep her hold on Jake.

"What are you doing?" Chance thundered, embarrassed and more than a little angry now that he knew she was all right. She'd just given him the scare of his life.

Rori shrugged. "Givin' Jake a bath. I decided that he smelled kinda bad, and if I was gonna be a lady, he was gonna have to be a lady's dog."

Chance and Doug groaned almost in unison as they slowly straightened up and lowered their guns.

"Ladies don't give their dogs a bath in the middle of the night," Chance dictated.

"Ladies do when they can't sleep!" she retorted.

Realizing how ridiculous they all looked standing there, the two men backed from the room.

"Good night, Rori," they said pointedly.

"Good night," she called lightly after them.

Chance closed the door behind them as they went out into the hall. He was glad to find that they hadn't broken the lock during their hasty entrance. He and Doug said good night once again, and he returned to his own room.

When he was stretched out on his bed once more, Chance found sleep impossible. All he could think about was how upset he'd been when he thought someone was hurting Rori and how he'd been ready to kill to keep her safe. It was a long, seemingly endless night for Chance.

Chapter 27

Wearing her new green dress that had just been delivered barely an hour before, Rori stood quietly beside Chance as he spoke earnestly with Doug.

"It sounds like you've found what you're looking for."

"I'm going to ride out and take a look at it tomorrow. If it's as good a piece of land as they say and if the water runs year round, I'll buy it and start founding the western branch of the Broderick dynasty."

Chance chuckled. "Let us know what you do."

"Oh, I will. I'll write, and as soon as we can we'll come back to Boston for a visit."

The stage driver climbed up atop the waiting vehicle, and Chance knew the time had come for their final farewell.

"We'll be waiting to hear from you." He shook his hand and then embraced him.

Doug turned to Rori and hugged her, giving her his

usual robust kiss on the lips. "Don't be afraid, Rori," he told her so softly only she could hear. "Everything's going to work out just the way you want it to, you'll see."

His statement puzzled her, and she drew back to look up at him questioningly. She saw a gleam of understanding in his eyes, and she wondered if Doug knew more than he was saying about what was going on between Chance and her.

"Really, Rori," Doug repeated in earnest. "Be happy." He kissed her once more and then grinned at her consternation as he released her. "You're going to be the toast of Boston, darling. I can't wait until Mother meets you. Take care." He touched her cheek gently.

"I will. Good-bye, Doug," she answered, and then Chance helped her into the waiting stage.

After handing Big Jake up to the driver, who'd agreed to let the overgrown dog ride up top with him, Chance turned back to Doug. They shook hands once more. He would have let go of Doug's hand, but his brother held on an extra moment, just to get his full attention.

"Take good care of her, Chance. Rori means a lot to me, and I don't want to see her hurt."

"I'll do what's best for her," Chance answered, frowning slightly as he wondered if the subtle threat he thought he'd heard in his brother's voice was real or imagined.

"You do that. Just make sure you know what's best," Doug counseled. The driver made an impatient noise, and Doug knew Chance had to get aboard. "Get going. Nilakla and I will come as soon as we're able."

"Bye, Doug."

With that, Chance entered the stagecoach and closed the door behind him. The driver slapped the reins on his horses' backs urging them to their pace, and they moved off on the first leg of their journey home to Boston.

Doug watched them go, wondering how long it would be before Chance came to realize just how much he loved Rori. It was obvious to him that his brother was crazy in love with her. He'd never known Chance to care so much about one woman. Why else would he have paid extra to let Jake stay in her room with her and why else would he have reacted so strongly the night before when he thought she'd been in danger?

Chance loved her all right, Doug decided, he was just too dumb to realize it. Doug only hoped that he didn't take too long to discover the truth of his feelings. If he did, he had a feeling Chance would have a lot of additional competition for Rori's affections from the other bachelors in Boston. Rori was a rare find, and the man who won her would have a prize of great value.

When the stage had gone from sight, Doug turned away from thoughts of his old life and turned back to his plans for his future. Nilakla was waiting for his return. It was important that he see about buying the ranch and get back to her as soon as he could. He missed her terribly already and could hardly wait to be back in the warmth of her loving embrace.

Rori was nearly hanging out the window of the coach as she watched Phoenix fade into the dusty distance. She couldn't believe that she was actually leaving . . . leaving the territory . . . leaving the only life she'd ever known. Chance had told her that they would be in Boston in less than a month, and now that they had started on their way, it suddenly seemed all too real and all too threatening. Panic seized her. What was she going to do? How was she going to survive?

As quickly as the doubts came, Rori fought them down. This was what she wanted. She wanted to be with Chance. She wanted to win his love. She certainly wouldn't be able to do it if she stayed here and continued to live like she had. Now that Burr was gone, change in her life was inevitable.

Rori sat back on her seat and cast a nervous glance at Chance who was sitting next to her. She was surprised to find him gazing at her sympathetically.

"Scared?" Chance asked, seeing the sudden look of fear in her eyes.

"No," she answered. Then admitted, hesitantly, "Well, maybe just a little."

"Don't be," he said calmly. "I'll be with you every step of the way."

She graced him with a tentative smile. "I'm glad."

Her smile went straight to his heart, and Chance was hard put not to kiss her, right then and there. It was difficult enough for him, sitting right next to her, his thigh pressed against hers. With every jounce of the stage, he was reminded of her nearness, and he knew it was going to be a very long journey.

Still, the alternative of not sitting next to Rori was far worse for Chance. Their companions on the trek north were two scurrilous-looking cowboys, and Chance wasn't about to let them any nearer to her than he had to. He didn't like the idea that the two were going to be able to sit there and leer at her all they wanted. An emotion he couldn't name ate at him. Rori was so lovely and so innocent that Chance wanted to protect her from the seamier side of life. He wanted this to be a trip she'd remember forever, an awakening of sorts, as he showed her the rest of the world. He wanted everything to be perfect for her. Above all, he wanted her to be happy.

There were times during the two and a half, interminable weeks of traveling in the stagecoach that Chance thought the trip would never end. What he had hoped would turn out to be a great adventure for the two of them had turned into endless miles of torture. His motives had been noble when he'd started out on the journey, but trapped as he was with Rori in the close confines of the coach, it had turned into pure hell.

The enforced intimacy had only proven to Chance just how much he desired her, yet there had been nothing he could do about it. He'd wanted it this way. He'd wanted to make sure there were others around to unwittingly chaperone, but he was slowly losing his mind over the fact that they had not had a moment alone together since leaving Phoenix. Meals at the way stations were rushed and crowded, and the nights spent there were even more difficult, for women slept in one room and men in another.

Chance had to admit that Rori was faring much better than he was. She went out of her way to make friends with the others on the stage, and while he attempted to join in her merriment, he found himself subtly resenting the way the others responded to her. At each stop, when some passengers got off and others got on, Rori initiated conversations and kept things from getting too dull. She treated him with the same easy camaraderie she showed the others, and it annoyed Chance, though he wasn't sure why. He had expected Rori to have difficulty maintaining the feminine veneer she'd acquired, but somehow she was carrying the whole thing off with aplomb, and he was pleased about that, he thought.

What Chance didn't know was that Rori was as nervous and unsure as she had ever been in her life. She was terrified of making a major mistake and looking like a fool in front of Chance, but she tackled the problem the same way she did everything else in life, head-on. In her mind, she went over and over everything he'd taught her about ladylike behavior. When the stage made its stops, she waited for him to help her descend, and when they were ready to depart, she waited for him to help her back inside. When they ate, she handled her utensils with expertise and made sure to keep her bites tiny and feminine. Occasionally, she caught herself about to pepper her language with less than ladylike phrases, but somehow she managed to stop herself in time. The biggest problem she had was in adjusting to wearing skirts all the time. She was used to being able to walk freely without encumbrance, and the yards of material definitely hampered her movements. In a way, though, Rori realized it was probably a good thing, for she'd noticed in her observations of other ladies that none of them moved particularly fast. She would just have to remember to slow down, and everything would be all right.

Rori figured she was not doing too badly on the trip. She had made no major errors or blunders that called undue attention to herself. Only the tension that came from being constantly near Chance made it awkward for her. She loved him so much that it was difficult not to let it show. She tried to distract herself by engaging the other passengers in conversation, but Chance was always there beside her, his leg pressed against hers from hip to knee.

Rori was glad when they arrived in Denver, for she was hoping that there might be a layover there and some respite from being in such close quarters with Chance. To her dismay, their connections were perfect. The train that would take them to St. Louis was leaving that very same day.

Chance hurriedly made arrangements for Big Jake's transportation on the train and then sent a telegram to Boston informing his mother that all was well and that he'd be returning home soon. He did not give her an exact date of arrival, though, for he had some things he wanted to take care of in St. Louis and didn't know how long he would be. That done, they boarded their first-class car on the hotel express train and set out on the next leg of their journey home.

The opulence of the train car and the elegant meals served there by the courteous, uniformed porters greatly impressed Rori. She thoroughly enjoyed the trip except for the sleepless night she passed in the snug, curtain-shrouded berth that was so close to Chance's.

St. Louis. Despite the relative briefness of their day-and-a-half trip from Denver, Chance was beginning to wonder if they would ever get there. When they finally arrived, Chance whisked Rori and Jake off to the Planter's House, the best hotel in town.

Rori was completely amazed by the sights and sounds of the major metropolis. From the busy riverfront crowded with steamboats to the horse-drawn streetcars and the elegance of the hotel, she found herself overwhelmed with the new and different. She was leading Jake on a rope leash and staring around her as if she'd never seen the likes of it before, which she hadn't.

"Is Boston like this?" she asked Chance in amazement as they entered the sumptuous hotel lobby.

"Worse," he told her with a grin, "but don't worry. You'll be fine."

Rori had her doubts as she watched the bustle around her, but her tight hold on Jake's leash was the only outward sign she gave that she was a bit nervous. She listened distractedly as Chance made the unorthodox request to allow Jake to stay in her room, and she was overjoyed when the clerk finally agreed. They went to their room to freshen up, and it was only a short time later when Chance came for her.

Rori was feeling a bit self-conscious about going out in public. She had managed to brush out her hair and wash up a bit, but her simple dress definitely showed the wear and tear of the last few weeks of hard travel.

"Where are you taking me?" she asked as they left Jakie behind.

"You'll see" was all he replied, deliberately leaving her guessing, as he guided her from the hotel and down the busy streets of St. Louis. When he swept her into the William Barr and Company store on Fourth Street, she was astounded.

"Chance!" she gasped, agog at the sight of so many things for sale. "What is this place?"

"It's a dry goods store, my dear. Anything and everything a lady could possibly need is available here. Let's see what we can find, shall we?" With a possessive hand at her waist, he led her on.

The next few hours were a wonderland of discovery for Rori. She had never imagined such fine things existed, let alone that she would own any of them. Dresses were selected, along with lingerie, stockings, an assortment of footwear, handkerchiefs, hats, and every other conceivable item she might need to ensure her immediate acceptance in Boston. Chance wanted to be certain that she lacked for nothing.

"Are you sure I can afford all this?" Rori asked at one point as she eyed the mounting store of goods he was selecting for her.

"Of course you can," Chance told her confidently, and he was rewarded with a brilliant smile.

By the time they finished shopping, they had so many packages that Chance had to hire a conveyance to take them back to the hotel. Once they returned to Rori's room, she began to unwrap everything with the enthusiasm of a young child at Christmas.

As he watched her excitement, Chance couldn't help but wonder if she'd ever really received any presents. She seemed thoroughly delighted with each item they'd chosen, and she handled them with great care, touching the delicate things almost reverently and smoothing any wrinkles she found from the large selection of gowns he'd insisted she buy.

Chance was glad that he'd picked so many different dresses for her.

Her wardrobe was extensive now and would get her through just about any social situation she might encounter during her first few days in Boston. All she really lacked was a ballgown, but he wanted her first dressy gown to be special, something created especially for her. As soon as they reached Boston, he would have his mother set up an appointment for her with her own seamstress. He knew the woman was very talented with a needle and thread and could no doubt create the perfect style for Rori, something that would complement her dark beauty and fit her slender, enticing curves.

Chance found himself staring at Rori hungrily as she sorted through her new purchases. The memory of watching her try on all those gowns that afternoon returned, and he remembered the ones that had been discarded, too—the loose-fitting dress that she'd almost swum in and the one that had been far too tight in the bosom. Chance drew a strangled breath as he recalled how her breasts had come so close to overflowing the bodice of the tight gown with the square-cut neckline. Desperate to keep his mind off the memory of that tempting display of tender flesh, he decided to excuse himself, pleading the need to get cleaned up before dinner.

"Chance?" Rori's soft call stopped him as he was about to flee from the room.

Chance paused at the door, turning back to find she was coming toward him. "What?" he asked, anxious to be gone.

Rori linked her arms about his neck and started to pull him down for a kiss. She wanted to thank him for all he'd done.

The heady scent of the perfume he'd bought her earlier that day surrounded him and weakened the control he was exerting over his desire for her. Desperate to avoid the intimacy he was sure would destroy the last vestiges of his restraint, Chance turned his cheek to accept her kiss.

Rori seemed not to notice his diversionary tactic as she kissed him sweetly. "Thank you for everything, Chance. The clothes are beautiful."

"You're welcome," he grumbled in a hoarse voice, and then he hurried from the room.

Rori stared at the closed door once he'd gone, wondering at his odd reaction. She wasn't sure whether to be hurt by his avoidance of her kiss or encouraged by it. When she would have fretted about it, the female in her instinctively told her that she was doing fine. Hadn't he paid unceasing attention to her all day? Hadn't he picked out the prettiest and most expensive gowns for her when she would have chosen less stylish and less costly ones?

Wandering back to the bed where all the new gowns were spread out in a colorful, rainbow array, she studied them for a minute and finally selected the one Chance had said he liked the best. It was relatively demure in style, but of a vibrant turquoise color that Chance had said was perfect on her.

Since tonight was their first night in St. Louis, Rori had every intention of looking her most beautiful and her most feminine for him. Time was running out. In just a few more days they would be in Boston, and he would see Bethany again. She had to act fast if she was going to win his affections before they got there.

In his own room Chance took a cold bath.

* * *

Bethany didn't wait for the servant to open the door completely before she rushed into Regina's house unannounced.

"Regina!" she shouted excitedly.

"Bethany?"

The sound of her friend's response from the parlor sent Bethany racing down the hall to find her.

"He's coming home!" Bethany announced in ecstasy.

"Chance?" Regina knew Bethany had been impatiently waiting for his return.

"Yes. His mother got a telegram last night. He was in Denver and on his way."

"Bethany, don't get carried away now," her friend cautioned. "You know how you two parted."

"That doesn't matter anymore," she declared, conveniently forgetting the ugly scene at the Richardsons' all those weeks ago. "Chance is coming home, and this time he's going to marry me. There's no way I'm going to let him get away again. As soon as we find out the exact date of his arrival, I'm going to plan a big 'welcome home' celebration. It'll be wonderful, and by the time the night is over, he's going to be mine!"

Regina saw the determination in her expression and knew that when he got back Chance Broderick was going to have the fight of his life if he intended to hang onto his bachelorhood.

Chance knocked on Rori's door, expecting her to be ready to leave. Instead, there was silence at first and then what sounded like a muffled curse.

"Rori?" he finally called out, a bit worried as he knocked softly a second time.

Then the door flew wide, and he found himself face-to-face with a half-clad Rori. She didn't speak, but reached out to grab him by the forearm and practically drag him into her room. She slammed the door shut behind him.

"How do your precious little Eastern ladies manage to do this?" she demanded, her annoyance obvious. She was trying to hold the dress up in front while attempting to fasten the back of it on her own.

"They call for a maid," he answered, his gaze lingering heatedly on her bosom.

"Oh," Rori replied meekly, the thought never having occurred to her, and then she smiled. "Well, I guess you're going to have to play the part. Here." She pivoted before him, presenting him with her back. "I just can't reach the dam—I mean, darned things."

Chance cleared his throat in discomfort as he began to work at the closures near her slim waist. He itched to caress the curve of her spine and press a kiss to the back of her neck, but he refrained.

"Once we get back to Boston, we'll have to find you a maid," he remarked, thinking of how outraged his mother would be to find him in such an intimate setting with a young, marriageable maiden.

"Why?" Rori broke away from his ministrations for a minute to look at him, her emerald eyes wide and questioning.

"We'll be living in my family's home, and my mother will be guarding your honor like a she-hawk. I'm sure she'll be quite relentless in protecting you from me."

"But I don't want to be protected from you, Chance." Her words were so plainly spoken that there could be no denying their true meaning. Her eyes met his imploringly.

"You may not want to be, but you need to be," he answered gruffly, turning her around so he could finish what he'd started. "Now, no more talk about Boston. Let's enjoy our evening together."

"Do I have much more to learn before we get to Boston?" Rori asked, hoping her "lessons" would go on forever.

"You've mastered talking, dining, and walking. You still have to learn how to dance, but that can come later."

"I saw some people dancing in Phoenix once. I think it was at some kind of church thing, but Grampa and I didn't go. Will you show me how?" There would have been nothing Rori would have liked more than to be held in Chance's arms right then and there, but at her suggestion he quickly fastened the last button and stepped away from her.

"When we get home, I'll teach you." Chance knew he had to back out of the request or end up miserable all evening. There was no way he could hold her in his arms tonight after what he'd endured all day. It was best if he touched her as little as possible.

Disappointment wracked Rori at his refusal, but she didn't let it show. After all, he hadn't said "no." She just had to keep trying and hope . . .

Chance was staring down at her in her new, fashionable gown, and he was scarcely able to believe that this was the same ragtag little scoundrel who'd pulled a knife on him just a short time before. How could Rori have changed so completely? The only trace of the feisty, scruffy little Indian he could see was the brilliant emerald eyes. All else had changed, and changed for the better. The woman she really was had emerged from hiding, and the revelation was startling. Rori had been transformed into an absolutely beautiful woman. It was as shocking a transformation as that of a caterpillar becoming a butterfly. Chance suddenly found himself hoping that when she tried her wings she wouldn't stray too far.

Chapter 28

Bethany was in heaven. "Everything's set," she confided to Regina when they met for lunch. "According to his mother he'll be back for sure tomorrow."

"What took him so long to get here from Denver?"

"He had some kind of business to attend to in St. Louis, supposedly. Anyway, it doesn't matter. All that matters is that he's going to be here in less than twenty-four hours!"

"You're sure you've got everything ready for the party?"

"Everything," she replied with confidence. "The food, the musicians, the guests . . . all I need is the guest of honor."

"In more ways than one!" Regina teased.

Bethany beamed and gave a light laugh. "You're right." She then added in a conspiratorial tone, "I've bought the most magnificent gown ever! Wait until you see it!"

"Bethany, you're hopeless!"

"Hopelessly in love."

"Well, I just hope everything turns out the way you expect it to."

"It will. It has to."

* * *

"This is where you live?" Rori stood outside the Brodericks' Boston home, staring up at the stately, three-story brick mansion with something akin to amazement.

"This is my home, Doug's and my mother's and mine," Chance answered.

Rori had thought the hotel in St. Louis was big, but that was for putting up hundreds and hundreds of guests. This huge house belonged to just three people. She shook her head slowly in wonder.

"Well, shall we go in?" he suggested, realizing that they looked a bit odd standing here with Big Jake on the walk in front of the house.

Rori's eyes were alive with excitement and more than a little nervousness. She'd dressed with extra care that morning on the train to make certain that she looked her best for Mrs. Broderick. She didn't want to give Chance's mother any reason to dislike her.

"Is it all right to take Jakie in with us?"

"Of course. My mother loves animals."

"Well . . ." Still she hesitated. "Do I look all right? I mean, will your mother approve?"

"You look beautiful, Rori," Chance told her, his gaze warm upon her.

"Really?"

"Really."

His unflagging confidence buoyed her, and she gave him her brightest smile. "Then I guess we're ready, huh, Jakie?" She patted her pet on his massive head as he looked up at her questioningly.

Chance took her arm in a courtly manner, and they moved up the stairs to the front door. He didn't bother to knock, but opened it and pushed it wide so they could enter together.

"Mother! I'm home!" he shouted.

"Chance?" Agatha had been waiting all morning for his arrival, and her heartbeat quickened as she finally heard him in the hallway. "Chance, thank goodness you've come home! Douglas . . . I'm going to . . ."

Agatha came flying out into the main hall from the dining room where she'd been drinking a cup of tea. She was expecting to find both of her errant sons standing there looking suitably ashamed of themselves for causing her such distress. Instead, she came face-to-face with Chance, a huge monster of a dog, and the loveliest young woman she'd ever laid eyes on.

"I'm back, and I've brought along two very special friends, Mother," Chance told her.

Agatha blinked in surprise as she looked from her tall, handsome son to the beautiful girl at his side. She'd heard the note of pride in his voice and made the only response that seemed logical to her. "Dear Lord, you married while you were gone?"

"No!" Chance came back quickly, shocked that she would even have imagined such a thing. "No, Mother. This is Rori, and the big guy beside her there is Jake."

"Hello." Agatha approached with a warm, curious smile.

"Rori's a very special friend, and I need you to take her under your wing."

"Rori's a friend?" Agatha repeated in confusion as she met the girl's green-eyed gaze. Rori was not a beauty in society's terms, for right now custom dictated that women like Bethany who were petite and blond were all the rage, but she *was* special. Her flawless, dusky complexion, her waist-length ebony hair, and her eyes, so round, expressive, and vividly green, set her apart. She was stunning. Agatha frowned slightly. There was something so strangely familiar to her about the girl and yet . . .

"Actually, she's my ward," Chance explained quickly.

"Your ward." Her expression was bemused as she glanced up at her son. She saw something there in his eyes as he gazed at Rori, something different . . . Suddenly she was eager to hear what had brought these two . . . these three together.

"Rori." Agatha presented her with her full attention as she sweetly took her arm to guide her down the hall to the dining room. "Suppose you join me for a cup of tea."

"Is it all right to bring Jake along? I mean, your house is so lovely and I'd . . ."

"Please, bring him along. He appears to be quite well mannered."

"Oh, he is!" Rori assured her quickly.

"Then there should be no problem. This promises to be a most interesting afternoon, Chancellor. I'm especially curious to find out what has happened to my other son." She glared over her shoulder at Chance, who was following them. "He will be joining us shortly, won't he?"

"I'm afraid not, Mother," Chance responded, and at her distressed look, he added, "Don't worry, Doug's fine. I'll tell you everything as soon as we settle in."

And he did. It was almost half an hour later before he concluded his explanation of all that had taken place in Arizona.

"So Douglas won't be home for some time?"

"Not until after your first grandchild is born," Chance said with a smile. "But I know he's eager for you to meet Nilakla. He loves her very much, Mother. I know they're going to be happy."

"You say Douglas has changed?" Agatha asked shrewdly. She'd worried about her youngest, devil-may-care son for some time now.

Chance nodded. "All for the better," he assured her. "He's grown up. He didn't send for me because he was in trouble like all the other times. He sent for me because he'd made his fortune, and I was the only one he trusted."

Agatha sighed deeply. "I'm glad he's finally matured, but I'll miss him terribly. You say he loves this woman he's married?"

"Very much."

She smiled. "Then that's all, as a mother, I can ask for him. Now, as far as your decision concerning Rori . . ."

Chance waited nervously for her pronouncement. Knowing what a stickler she was on propriety, he was expecting to feel the bite of her tongue. He did not expect her praise.

"You did exactly the right thing." Agatha reached over and patted Rori's hand. She'd been observing Rori quietly as Chance had spoken and sensed that there was a great deal more to this young lady than met the eye. "Since you are officially Chance's ward, you will, of course, stay with us."

"Thank you," Rori breathed. She'd been a nervous wreck since they'd arrived, fearful of making a fool of herself in front of this lovely, gracious lady. Somehow, in her imaginings, she had never pictured Chance's mother as being so wonderful. In her mind, she had been a threatening authority figure. Rori was glad she'd been wrong.

"What is your full name?" Agatha questioned.

"Aurora."

"That's beautiful. It suits you," she pronounced. "And your last name?"

Rori's expression was blank. "I don't know."

"You don't know?"

"We always were just Burr and Rori. That's all. Grampa never said."

Sensing her discomfort, Agatha dismissed her interest. "Well, no matter. Aurora you shall be from now on. This is going to work out perfectly."

"Why? What are you up to?" Chance caught the twinkle in his mother's eye.

"I'm not up to anything, dear son, but there is a welcome home party planned for you tonight, and it will be the perfect time to introduce Aurora to everyone."

"Tonight?"

"When Bethany heard that you were returning, she couldn't wait to plan a celebration."

"Bethany," Chance repeated dully, not sure whether to be aggravated or just plain angry. Caught up in his own discontent, he missed the look of despair that flitted across Rori's face. "What time?"

"I believe it starts at eight."

"Then I think I'd better take Rori shopping."

Rori glanced at him in surprise. "But, Chance, we just . . ."

"Knowing Bethany as I do, this is going to be a very fancy party. You'll need a ballgown."

"I'll handle everything, Chance," Agatha spoke up with authority.

"There's no need, I can—"

"Chancellor, this is women's business. You go on and do whatever you have to do. I'm sure there's plenty of business for you to catch up on."

"Yes, Mother." Chance cast Rori a sheepish grin that left her amazed. She'd never seen him back down to anyone.

"That's a good boy. Now run along, and while you're at it, take care of Jake. It is Jake, isn't it?"

"Yes, ma'am."

"Well, take care of the dog, Chance. Aurora and I will be far too busy to worry about him right now. Come, my dear. I'll show you to your room so we can see what you've brought along with you, and we can then decide exactly what we need to buy."

Agatha was thrilled at the idea of shopping for Aurora. She had always wanted a daughter to pamper and spoil. The girl had a delightful figure, and she wasn't too short or tall. She would take her to her own dressmaker, Françoise, and see what she could come up with in time for the party tonight. Françoise was a miracle-worker with a needle and thread, and with an inspiration like Aurora, well, the sky was the limit in what she could do to help her look her best.

Besides, Agatha thought, she'd never seen Chance react this way to a woman before. Perhaps there was something more here than just a custodial relationship. Perhaps her oldest son had finally met the one woman intriguing enough to capture and hold his heart.

Agatha knew Bethany thought she was in love with Chance. As much as she liked Bethany and thought her a good marriage prospect for Chance, she felt certain that her son didn't feel the same. He had had numerous opportunities in the past to claim Bethany for his own, and yet he'd never done so.

This Aurora, however, was different from all the other women he'd known, and yet he'd agreed to become her guardian. That in itself was surprising and pleasing to Agatha. *Yes,* she mused, smiling, *it will be great fun dressing this young woman for the party tonight.*

Rori wasn't quite sure what was happening to her. One minute she'd been worried about meeting Mrs. Broderick, and the next, the older woman was insisting that she call her "Agatha" as she rushed her from the house to the dressmaker's.

With Chance nowhere in sight, Rori grew edgy, but Agatha sensed that and immediately put her fears to rest.

"I'm sure you've had a difficult time with all you've been through during the last few months, but all that's going to change now. You'll see," Agatha told her as they hurried across town in the Broderick carriage.

"The hardest part has been learning everything,"

Rori confided, "and there's still so much more I need to know."

"You're doing beautifully," she complimented.

Rori smiled, warming toward this open, friendly lady who seemed so genuinely concerned about her. "I'm glad you think so. I was worried about meeting you. I was afraid I'd make a bad impression."

"Nonsense," Agatha pooh-poohed. "We'll take one day at a time, and you'll see how easy it really can be."

"I hope so . . ." Rori let her voice trail off as she thought of her upcoming confrontation with the wonderful Bethany. This woman who was Chance's lover had haunted her ever since she'd first heard Chance speak of her many weeks ago. Seeing Bethany and Chance together tonight was going to be difficult, and she hoped she could carry it off without doing anything stupid.

With Big Jake sleeping beside him, Chance sat at his desk trying to concentrate on the stack of contracts and business letters that were piled before him. Yet, no matter how hard he tried, he couldn't focus his attention on his work. His thoughts, instead, kept drifting to the night ahead . . . and Bethany.

A few months ago he might have felt differently about the upcoming soirée, but now the only emotion Bethany and her plans stirred in him was irritation. He wondered why she'd taken it upon herself to give the party for him. He remembered their last time together before he'd left town, and it hadn't been a particularly endearing encounter.

Chance shook his head as he strode to the small liquor cabinet and poured himself a tumbler of bourbon. He didn't know why he was feeling particularly tense about seeing Bethany again. He just knew that he didn't relish the idea of being with her tonight. This was Rori's first night in Boston, and he'd wanted it to be something special for her. He downed the drink, and when he caught Jakie's questioning gaze upon him, he shrugged and gave him an almost silly grin.

"Sometimes, Jake, old boy, a drink is the only thing that helps."

With a sigh, Chance set the empty glass aside and returned to his desk. If nothing else, he thought, at least Rori would have the opportunity to meet all the other bachelors in town tonight, and that would be a beginning for her. Chance knew, too, now that his mother had taken charge, that Rori would be looking absolutely perfect tonight. There was no way any fashion error was going to get past Agatha Broderick. Confident that Rori's appearance would be faultless this evening, he turned his concentration to matters at hand. But as he attempted to get to work, the thought of Rori meeting other men kept distracting him and leaving him uneasy.

"Miss Aurora, your hair is delightful to work with," Jeannie, Agatha's maid, told Rori as she sat at the dressing table in her bedroom at about seven o'clock that evening. "Do you have a particular style that you like best?"

Rori was embarrassed to tell the maid that she'd never had her hair styled in her life, that she'd always just worn it in braids or loose down her back. "No. Please feel free to do whatever you want."

"Well, Miss Agatha told me to make sure you looked special for tonight, so let's see what we can do here." Jeannie pulled the silken ebony tresses up away from her face and pinned them in place with combs. She then set about curling the back so the heavy mass would fall about her shoulders in a cascade of soft curls. She knew the style was a simple one, but sometimes simple was better, for it would emphasize Miss Aurora's lovely features, not detract from them.

It took her nearly half an hour to arrange it to perfection, during which time Rori tried to keep from fidgeting. She'd never had to hold still so much in one day during her entire life as she had today. First, for what seemed like hours at the dressmaker's with Agatha and now with Jeannie. It was nearly driving Rori crazy.

Thoughts of the upcoming party and her inevitable introduction to Bethany refused to be banished, and Rori knew tonight would be the most important night of her whole life. Tonight she would meet her competition for Chance's heart. For a moment, doubts assailed her. What hope did she have of winning his love against a, no doubt, sophisticated woman like Bethany? The thought was paralyzing, but Rori fought it off. She was scared, but she refused to let it unnerve her. She loved Chance and she was going to get him. She set her jaw tensely as her determination grew.

"You don't like it, Miss Aurora?" Jeannie had glanced up into the mirror and had noticed the fierceness in Rori's expression. She worried that she wasn't pleasing her.

Rori blinked, focusing for the first time on her own reflection in the mirror and that of the suddenly very nervous maid. She was stunned by how marvelous her hair looked and how the style emphasized her eyes. "Oh, no, Jeannie. It looks wonderful!" She smiled at her reassuringly. "I was just thinking about something else, that's all."

"Oh, good," Jeannie sighed, relieved. "You looked so, well, upset. Is it anything I can help with?"

Rori had never confided in anybody in her life, and no matter how much she wanted to, she found she couldn't. "No. I guess I'm just a little nervous about tonight."

"There's no need for you to worry there. With Miss Agatha and Mr. Chance beside you, you don't have a worry in the world."

"I don't?"

"No, ma'am, Miss Aurora. The Brodericks are important people here."

"Oh."

"It's getting late. It's after seven already." Jeannie noticed the time as she glanced at the clock on the mantel above the fireplace. "We'd better see about getting you into that gown right now."

Rori rose from the dressing table as the maid hustled to get the dress ready for her to don. With the utmost care, she slipped into the gorgeous creation and stood quietly while Jeannie fastened it and then adjusted the skirts. The maid stood back to study her handiwork. Just as she was about to speak, a soft knock sounded at the door.

"Jeannie? Aurora? Are you ready yet?"

"Come in, Miss Agatha. I think everything's just about perfect."

The older woman entered as she was bid and quietly closed the door behind her. She was ready for the ball, having donned a fashionable, double-skirted evening gown of rose satin. Her hair, too, had been artfully arranged, and Rori thought she looked lovely.

"Oh, Agatha, you look positively elegant!" Rori gushed.

"Thank you, my dear," Agatha beamed. "Now, let's see how elegant you look." Agatha circled Rori, studying her critically, her expression thoughtful. When she finally spoke, it wasn't to Rori, but to Jeannie. "You've done a wonderful job. Aurora will be the belle of the ball tonight."

"I think so, too, ma'am."

"I will?" Rori looked from her benefactress to the maid questioningly.

"Françoise was worth every cent we paid her," Agatha declared. "That dress is absolutely stunning on you, Aurora. Have you seen yourself yet?"

"No, I . . ."

"Then you must take a look in the mirror right now. Take a look and see what Boston will see for the first time tonight."

Rori resisted for a moment, feeling slightly shy about it, and then lifted her gaze to stare openly at herself. She gasped in stunned surprise. The full-skirted, off-the-shoulder gown of white tulle and lace fit her like a dream. The bodice was relatively low-cut, highlighting the fullness of her breasts while accentuating her slender waist. Rori had never known she could look so feminine or so positively delicate.

"But it doesn't even look like me!" Rori protested, turning to Agatha with a troubled look upon her face.

"Ah, but it is you, Aurora," Agatha said serenely. "You are a beautiful young woman, and tonight the whole world will know." *Including my son,* she thought with unspoken delight. "Finish up whatever you have to do here, and then meet me in the parlor in, say, ten minutes. Will that give you enough time?"

"Oh, yes, ma'am. Miss Aurora will be ready," Jeannie promised.

"Good. I'll see you downstairs." Agatha swept from the room without a backward glance.

Agatha found Chance in the parlor, a glass of bourbon in hand. He reminded her so much of her long-dead husband at that moment, so tall, dark, and classically handsome in his evening clothes, that her heart actually ached. Chance was such a good man, and Agatha knew he deserved so much more in life than just his work. He deserved a wife and a family.

She thought of Bethany and of how the young woman had tried her best to insinuate herself into her good graces while Chance had been gone. She liked Bethany and knew she had all the correct social influence, but she wasn't sure she was the right woman for her son. The fact that Chance was drinking already and had not been the least bit enthused about the upcoming party clued her that something might be troubling him. Agatha hoped that her guess as to what, or who, that might be was correct.

"Good evening, dear. You're looking magnificently handsome this evening."

Chance gave her a crooked smile as he set his glass aside. "You're looking lovely as always, Mother."

"I wasn't fishing for compliments, my dear boy, but thank you all the same." She came into the room to join him, pressing a soft kiss on his proffered cheek. She rested a hand on his arm to get his attention as she spoke again. "I believe we have a small problem," she told him with an earnestness that caused him to immediately tense.

"Rori?" Chance asked. He hadn't seen Rori since she'd taken her over earlier that afternoon, and he'd been worrying constantly, wondering how she was. "What happened? What did she do?"

"Nothing 'happened,' my dear, and I don't know why you're so concerned about what she did. She didn't do anything but be a complete lady all day long."

Chance breathed a noticeable sigh of relief as he took a quick drink from his glass.

"It's just that she should have some jewelry to go with the gown we selected for her," she went on, "and I was wondering how you felt about her wearing your grandmother's pearls." Agatha had been thinking about the pearls ever since Rori had first tried the gown on at the dressmaker's that afternoon. She knew they would match the dress perfectly and positively glow against Rori's flawless skin.

Chance was surprised by his mother's suggestion. His grandmother's jewelry had been set aside for years now, waiting for Doug and him to marry so it could be divided between their wives. Yet now that he considered it, the thought of Rori wearing the lustrous pearls pleased him.

"I think it's a wonderful idea."

"Why don't you go and get them, darling? Aurora will be down in a few minutes, and you can help her put them on then." As she watched her son go, Agatha smiled to herself. She was becoming more and more convinced that her maternal instincts were right.

Chapter 29

Rori was having difficulty walking with all the petticoats and hoops on, and she paused at the top of the staircase, not about to take any chances on the steps. After a quick, conspiratorial look to make sure that there was no one around to observe her, she hiked her skirts up well above her knees with one hand, clutched the bannister with the other for balance, and started down the steps. It was a tricky passage with the new, heeled shoes on, but she finally made it down to the main hall. Dropping her skirts back down, Rori smoothed them out in a ladylike gesture. She squared her shoulders, gave her hair a gentle pat to make sure it was still in place, and then continued on to the parlor where she could hear Chance and his mother talking.

"It's getting late. Are you sure she's . . ." Chance was saying, glancing at his timepiece as he paced the room.

"She was almost ready to come down when I left her. Don't worry, Chance," his mother chided him, trying to control the smile that threatened. She had never seen her son so eager to be with a woman in his life.

"I think I'm ready."

At the sound of Aurora's voice in the doorway, Chance spun quickly around. He didn't know what he was expecting, but it was not this. Struck speechless, he stood immobile, staring at the vision of loveliness before him.

"Rori?" He finally said her name in hoarse astonishment.

"Good evening, Chance." She smiled, and then turned to his mother. "Agatha."

"Good evening, Aurora. Come join us."

"Thank you." She moved forward into the room very much aware of Chance's dark eyes upon her.

Chance could not look away. Neither could he say anything more. This was Rori? His Rori? His gaze devoured her from the top of her fashionable hairstyle to the tips of her slippers where they peeped from beneath the exquisite white gown she wore. How could this be Rori? Rori wore braids. Rori rode better than he did and shot better, too.

Chance was dumbfounded to say the least. He'd known that Rori had looked attractive in the dresses he'd chosen for her in St. Louis, but they were sacks compared to this. Dear Lord, he mused besottedly, she'd turned into the most breathtaking woman he'd ever seen.

"Chance, darling, quit gawking at Aurora, and tell us a man's opinion. What do you think?"

The sound of his mother's voice penetrated the dazed stupor Chance had found himself in, and he finally regained his senses. Realizing that she'd asked him a question, he turned slightly toward her and lifted his glass in a toast.

"Mother, you have outdone yourself."

"The credit all goes to Aurora, Chancellor, dear. She is, after all, the beauty. On a lesser woman, that gown would be totally ineffectual."

"Indeed it would be," he agreed huskily, his gaze swinging back to Rori. He set his drink aside and strode purposefully toward her.

Rori had been watching the whole exchange between the two and was beginning to feel like a half-side of beef hung out for display. "Does that mean you like the dress?" she asked Chance as he came to stand before her.

"I love the dress," Chance told her. "Now, turn around for a minute."

"Why? Is something wrong in the back?" Rori twisted to try to get a look behind her.

He gave a deep chuckle, and the sound skittered pleasantly down Rori's spine. "The back is fine, love. Just turn around because I asked you to."

"But . . ." Rori was puzzled by his request, but did as he asked.

"I have a present for you."

"A present? For me?" Rori asked. She rarely got presents, and she was practically dancing with excitement at the thought.

"You won't be absolutely perfect without these," he said in a low, husky voice as he drew the jewelry case from his coat pocket and opened it. He took out the single strand of luminous pearls and fastened them about her throat. "There."

"I knew those pearls would be elegant with that gown. She looks positively stunning," Agatha spoke up from across the room.

"I do?" Rori turned to face Chance.

"You do," he concurred. He held up two earrings

that matched the necklace. "Now, do you know how to put these on?"

"No . . ." she answered breathlessly as she reverently touched the pearls that weighed heavily about her throat and dipped between her breasts.

"I'll have to do it for you, then." Chance took her by the shoulders and turned her to face him. His fingers were strong and sure as he completed the task.

Rori shivered at the feel of his hands upon her flesh, and she lifted her emerald gaze to his as he adjusted the earrings. The moment was suspended in time. Man and woman. It was an unsettling instant that touched them both with a deep yet unspoken recognition of desire.

"There," he said unsteadily as he quickly withdrew from that simple contact. "Now you really are perfect."

It was all Agatha could do to control her delight as she watched the two of them together. She knew Chance well, probably better than he knew himself, and she realized as she played the observer that he was totally enamored with his young ward. The thought pleased Agatha to no end.

"We were just having a drink while we waited for you," Agatha said, deliberately breaking the strained silence of the moment. "Would you care to join us?"

Rori cast a worried glance at Chance. She had never had any liquor to drink in her whole life. "I've never really had liquor before."

"Then tonight is going to be an experience for you, isn't it?" Agatha broached, thinking how delightfully guileless Aurora was.

"I am a little nervous."

"You'll do fine," she told her confidently.

"There is one thing . . . I didn't have the time to teach her to dance," Chance admitted regretfully.

"Oh, my." Agatha looked perplexed for a moment, but then smiled. "Well, no matter. Things will all work out. You'll stay with either Chance or me all night, that's all."

"Do you really think it'll work?" Rori worried.

"Of course, it will work, and tomorrow, I shall arrange lessons for you with Monsieur LaPointe. He's absolutely the best, and by the time the next party arrives, you'll be able to dance rings around all the other young ladies."

"I hope you're right."

"Do you doubt me, child?" Agatha used her stern taskmaster voice.

"Oh, no, Agatha. It's just that you put so much faith in me. I don't know the first thing about dancing, and yet you think I'm going to be good at it right away."

"My dear, you can do anything you set your mind to. Do you want to learn how to dance?"

"Oh, yes!" The thought of being held in Chance's arms sent her pulses racing.

"Then you will," she concluded in a tone that brooked no argument. "Now, shall we go? It's fashionable to be a tad late, but not too much so."

"The carriage is waiting," Chance announced as he offered them each an arm and escorted them from the room.

"Now, Aurora," Agatha continued counseling her as they left the house, "drink only champagne while you're at the ball and just take ladylike sips of that."

"Yes, ma'am."

Bethany was slowly going out of her mind as she stood in the foyer of her home with Regina greeting her late-arriving guests. "I know damn well Chance's back! Where the hell is he?" she complained in an undertone to her friend.

"Chance will be here. Don't worry," Regina tried to calm her.

"Wouldn't you think he'd want to be among the first to arrive at a party given in his honor?"

"Maybe he had business to attend to. Who knows? Plus there was that rumor . . ."

"Rumor? What rumor?" Bethany was instantly alert.

"It's just hearsay, I know, but someone told my mother that they saw Mrs. Broderick out with a young woman shopping this afternoon."

"Mrs. Broderick shopping with a young woman?" She was perplexed. "Who was it?"

"I have no idea. I'm just telling you what I heard."

Bethany started to scowl, but a new batch of arrivals forced her to smile. With the composure of a good hostess, she greeted them warmly and directed them on into the ballroom where the party was in full swing, the music and dancing having already begun.

"Well, I can't wait here any longer," she declared angrily. "I'm going in to my guests. Are you coming, Regina?"

"Of course," she answered, but as they started to turn away from the main doors to join the party in progress, the Broderick carriage drew up. "Wait, Bethany! Here he comes now!" Regina hissed to her as she grabbed her by the arm.

"Chance?" Bethany's eyes shone at the thought that he'd finally arrived. "Do I look all right?"

"Like a dream, how else?" her friend answered honestly, having never seen Bethany looking more lovely than she did now in the triple-skirted, yellow grosgrain gown with lace overlay and very low-cut décolletage. "I'll leave you to him. Good luck." Regina absented herself from Bethany's side.

"Thanks." Wetting her lips nervously, Bethany smoothed one errant curl back in place, then watched as he climbed out of the carriage.

Chance looked so marvelously handsome that Bethany

felt her heart skip a beat. *Soon . . .* she told herself . . . *soon she would be in his arms, holding him, kissing him, loving him . . .* She waited impatiently for him to help his mother down, and she started to take a step forward when he turned back to the carriage again. She could tell that he was speaking to someone else, but she had no idea who it could be. Chance held out his hand as if to help someone else descend, and it was then that Bethany saw her.

All kinds of terrible thoughts raged through Bethany's mind as she stared at the slender, raven-haired young woman Chance was offering his arm to. The rumors had been true, but who was she?! Had Chance married while he was gone? Her heart ached at the possibility, and Bethany wondered how she would handle it, if that was indeed the case. As she watched them come up the walk, Bethany's killer instinct reared its ugly head. If this woman had stolen Chance from her . . .

"Good evening, Agatha. Chance, darling!" Bethany greeted them as they entered the house.

"Good evening, Bethany," Agatha and Chance greeted her, and then Agatha added, "We've brought an extra guest along, and we hope you don't mind. Aurora, dear, this is our hostess, Bethany Sutcliffe."

"How do you do?" Rori greeted Bethany, seeing in the lovely, blond woman everything she could never hope to be.

"Aurora has come back East with Chance and will be staying with us now," Agatha explained.

"How wonderful," Bethany gushed, thrilled to know that at least Chance hadn't fallen for another woman while he was gone. "Are you related, Aurora?" She turned to Rori, eyeing her critically, and in that moment, she assessed her as a very worthy rival for Chance's affection.

"No," Rori started to answer, but Chance stepped in.

"Rori is my ward, Bethany."

"Your ward?" She blinked in surprise at the irony of Chance Broderick being responsible for a girl's reputation. She would have laughed at the absurdity of the notion, but knew better than to show her claws before Mrs. Broderick. She put a hand on Chance's powerful forearm as she said with pointed intimacy, "You'll have to tell me all about it, darling, as soon as we get a moment alone."

"Shall we go on in and join the other guests?" Agatha suggested, wanting to put an end to the tête-à-tête that was making Aurora and herself feel uncomfortable.

"By all means," Bethany agreed. "Everyone's so glad you're back, and they're positively dying to hear all about Arizona." She took his arm and artfully stole him right away from Rori and his mother. She gazed up at him adoringly as she led him into the party, knowing that they as a couple would be the center of attention and not Chance and his "ward."

Rori stood awkwardly until Agatha patted her hand and drew her aside. Agatha had seen the predatory look in Bethany's eyes, and she knew what the other woman had planned for Chance, even if he didn't. Her own sentiments, however, were with Aurora. She didn't know what existed between the young girl and her son, but she sensed it was more than just a passing attraction.

"My dear, you are an innocent in the ways of women, aren't you?"

"What do you mean?" Rori asked, tearing her gaze away from the sight of Chance and Bethany as they disappeared into the ballroom.

"You've never come up against women like Bethany before, have you?"

"No . . . I . . ."

"Don't say a word," Agatha advised, "just listen. Women like our hostess there will do whatever they have to to get what they want. The thing to do is to outsmart them at their own game."

"But how do I do that?"

"You just go in there and have the best time you possibly can."

"But what about the dancing?"

"If a young man asks you to dance, tell him you're tired, but that you'd love to talk to him. Then ask him about himself. Believe me, you won't have to worry about dancing again all night long. If there's one thing men love, it's talking about themselves."

"It's that simple?" Rori was mystified by her advice.

"For tonight it is. You are the prettiest woman here, and the moment you go into that room with me, you're going to be the center of attention. Are you ready?"

The thought of Chance and Bethany still hurt, but Rori was determined not to let him think that she cared one way or the other. She would join the party and have as much fun as she could. "Yes," she told Agatha with a determined lift of her chin, "I'm ready."

"Good girl."

Together the two women stepped through the open double doors and into the ballroom.

It seemed that everything Agatha had told her would happen did. Not only did she cause a stir among the older woman's friends, but it seemed that every young man in the place flocked to her for an introduction. Agatha handled it all with a certain finesse, and soon Rori was safely ensconced on the side of the dance floor surrounded by potential beaux. Rori remembered all of Agatha's advice and was amazed at how easy it was to fend off their invitations to dance and engage the men in conversation. Agatha, she decided, certainly knew what she was talking about when it came to men.

* * *

"Chance is one sly dog," Evan Strickland declared as he stood across the floor talking with another bachelor of equally questionable repute. They'd been eyeing Rori ever since she'd entered the room some time before. "He goes out West because his brother needs help, and he comes back with the most beautiful woman Boston has seen in years."

"They say she's his ward, but I don't know if I believe it or not," Michael Samuels added lecherously.

"Believe it," Evan said firmly. "We all know Agatha Broderick."

"That's true enough," Michael backed down from his unspoken accusation.

"Whoever she is, she's absolutely gorgeous."

"Quit drooling, Evan. If she's connected with the Brodericks, you haven't got a chance. You know Chance won't let you within ten feet of her."

"It's true that Chance and I have had our differences in the past, but . . ."

"There's no 'buts' about it. He hates you, Evan. He won't let you near her."

"We'll see." Evan's eyes narrowed speculatively. "When I want something, Michael, I usually get it, and I think I want Aurora."

"You don't have a prayer," he announced negatively.

"Maybe, maybe not . . ." Evan answered coolly as he plotted his move in gaining an introduction to the beauteous newcomer.

"If Chance hadn't caught you cheating at cards that one night, it might be all right, but now . . ."

Evan glared at his companion dangerously. The memory of his ugly encounter with Broderick some time ago still had the power to humiliate him. "I was just slightly short of funds that night. I've since recouped my losses. My financial status is . . . well . . . comfortable right now."

"Right," Michael drawled, knowing how quickly and easily Evan went through money. "Well, I wish you luck with her and her guardian. If tonight's crowd is any indication, I think you're going to need it."

"I don't," Evan answered easily as he started across the dance floor to speak with the object of his newly inflamed desire.

Rori couldn't believe all the attention she was getting or all the compliments the men were heaping on her. She would have been enjoying herself had it not been for the sight of Chance and Bethany, arm in arm, laughing and visiting with a group of guests on the other side of the room. She hadn't spoken to Chance since Bethany had claimed him in the foyer, and the way he was ignoring her hurt. Every time she heard Chance's deep, mellow laugh or saw him smile at his sophisticated companion, she felt as if someone was twisting a knife in her heart.

Still, Rori followed Agatha's advice. She smiled and chatted and carried on her act of being a lady quite well, considering all she wanted to do was march straight across the room to Bethany and . . .

Rori sternly told herself to stop. She couldn't do anything to Bethany. She was a lady now, and ladies didn't do those things. A taunting voice in the back of her mind asked "why not," but her common sense told her a firm "no." Chance was proud of her because she'd become a lady. She couldn't let him down. Not now, not ever, no matter how much she wanted to revert back to her "old" self.

* * *

For all that she was smiling and acting like she was having a wonderful time, Bethany was fuming. Her every effort to manuever Chance alone had been frustrated, and she was desperate to be in his arms. It had been so long! When the music began again, this time a lilting waltz, she would not be denied. Tightening her grip upon his arm, she interrupted his conversation with his friend Rod.

"Chance, I do believe it's time we danced, don't you?" she asked archly.

Chance almost groaned out loud. He'd been quite successful at avoiding intimacy with her since they'd arrived, but it seemed she would be put off no longer. "Of course, Bethany. If you'll excuse us, Rod?"

Chance had no choice but to take her in his arms and guide her out onto the dance floor.

They swirled around the room, looking as if they were perfect for each other, her petite fairness complementing his tall, dark presence. Being held close to him was heaven for Bethany. She had waited for this forever, it seemed, and if she could do it, she was going to get him outside on the veranda before the night was over.

Chance, on the other hand, felt stifled and trapped by Bethany's clinging nearness. He had not been able to get away from her since they'd first arrived, and he wondered now if he ever would.

Chance found himself looking for Rori as they moved about the room in perfect rhythm. At first, he'd thought she was quietly passing the evening with his mother and her friends, but then he'd heard the light sweetness of her laugh. His attention honed in on where she stood, seemingly holding court.

Chance had expected her to be popular, but he'd never thought the men would be swarming around her like they were. He felt a pang of some irritating emotion, but he refused to put a name to it. Instead, he turned his attention back to Bethany, reminding himself that he was not to interfere. This was exactly what he'd wanted for Rori. This was exactly what he had hoped would happen. Yet, even as Chance told himself that over and over again, he wondered why it still bothered him so much that she seemed to be enjoying the attention of all those other suitors.

Chapter 30

"To what do we owe the honor and joy of your presence in our midst?" Evan asked Aurora outrageously as he joined the gathering of admirers surrounding her. He'd been watching and listening as he'd approached, and he noticed that none of the other men had been daring to really take the initiative with her.

"I beg your pardon?" Rori was taken aback by this stranger's boldness, and she looked up to see a smiling, fair-haired man coming directly through the group toward her.

"I've been told by reliable sources that your name is Aurora and that you belong to Chance Broderick. Is that true?" Evan deliberately led the statement to get a reaction from the lovely young woman as he elbowed his way to her side.

"I don't belong to anybody!" Rori denied hotly, wondering how anyone could think she belonged to Chance when he'd been off gallivanting around with Bethany ever since they'd arrived. "Whoever told you that was lying."

"No one told me that." Evan gave her what many

women considered a devastatingly flirtatious grin. "I just made it up to see if you really were unclaimed."

"You make me sound like a gold mine or a piece of property you can stake your claim on," Rori returned, amused by this man's brazen, unorthodox manner. The other men had been nice to talk to, but ultimately they were boring. This man, with his blond good looks and wicked glint in his eyes, at least promised an entertaining conversation.

"Could I stake my claim on you, Aurora?" Evan's blue eyes were dancing with devilish delight as they met hers.

"But I don't even know you, sir," she answered, feeling suddenly out of her depth and wanting to avoid his question.

"My name's Evan Strickland. I'm twenty-seven years old, and I've just fallen madly in love for the first time in my life," he professed baldly, drawing a chuckle of agreement from her other admirers.

Rori flushed in embarrassment. She wasn't quite sure how to handle such flowery compliments. She thought he was jesting, but then again, he seemed so ardent, she couldn't be certain.

"Would you care to dance? I've noticed that none of your other suitors here has managed to get you out onto the dance floor yet, but the waltz that's playing is slow and romantic. Won't you join me?"

"I am quite tired this evening, Mr. Strickland. I'd really prefer . . ."

"Call me Evan, and I won't take no for an answer." He took her hand before she could withdraw it and tugged her onto the ballroom floor.

Short of making a scene and embarrassing herself, Rori could do nothing but follow him. She cast an apologetic look to the other young men and then turned to her bold escort, wondering how to handle the situation. She was chewing on her bottom lip nervously, and Evan noticed the uncertainty in her expression.

"Is something wrong, Aurora?" he asked in a low voice so the others wouldn't hear.

"No . . . I . . . er . . . Evan, can I be totally honest with you?" Rori asked, tired of the game-playing she'd been doing all evening.

"I'd want nothing else from you."

"Well, the truth is, I don't know how to dance."

Again his puzzled gaze met hers. "Really?"

"Really."

"How could you have grown up to be such a beautiful woman and never have danced?"

"Where I grew up in Arizona, there wasn't much dancing."

"Would you like to try? Would you like me to teach you?"

"Right now?"

"Of course, when better to learn? We'll take it nice and easy, then no one will ever know that you're just a beginner."

"Thank you." She beamed up at him, her smile bright with excitement. Suddenly, though, she grew serious. "What do I do?"

"First, you relax. Then rest one hand on my shoulder and follow my lead. We're going to take rhythmic steps in time to the music and make circles while we're doing it. All right?"

Rori gave a little nod as she moved into his arms. She held her breath in excitement as Evan squired her out onto the floor. They moved a bit haltingly at first as Rori worked to understand the rhythm, but once she got the feel of it, she danced as if she was born to it. She laughed with delight as Evan spun her completely around, and she didn't miss a step as he expertly increased their tempo.

"You were meant to be in my arms, Aurora."

"It feels like it, Evan. Thank you," Rori replied, smiling and laughing lightly at the joy of being swept gracefully around the dance floor.

Chance had been waltzing with Bethany, trying not to look in Rori's direction, but when he heard her laughter so close to him, he glanced up to find her dancing with Evan Strickland. Fury jolted through him. *Evan Strickland! Of all the lowlife bastards in the world, what the hell was Rori doing dancing with him! Hell, what was she doing dancing at all?!*

Chance would have broken away from Bethany and gone after Rori, but he knew he couldn't do it without making a scene. In frustration, he continued to dance, waiting for the song to end so he could get her away from the miserable Strickland. Strickland was a weasel—a low-down, no good, skunk of a man. He made a practice out of using other people to his advantage. To the best of Chance's knowledge, the man had yet to do an honest day's work in his life. He'd inherited a small fortune from his deceased parents when he reached his majority, but had wasted that considerable amount in no time. In the years since, he'd tried to make a living by his glib tongue, sleight of hand, and quick wit. Women seemed to adore the devil-may-care attitude he represented, but the men knew him for what he really was—a rake and a wastrel. Chance had no use for Strickland, and he didn't want Rori anywhere near him either.

Chance would not admit to himself that Rori's dancing with another man bothered him. He would not admit that he had wanted to be the first man to waltz with her. Instead, he directed all his anger at the intruding Strickland, and he could hardly wait for the dance to end so he could maneuver Rori away from him.

Bethany noticed Chance's agitation over Rori dancing with Evan Strickland, and she grew annoyed. What was the matter with Chance? The girl was only his ward, wasn't she? Why was he so damned interested in what she was doing? Bethany had caught him glancing toward Aurora several times that night, his expression dark and foreboding.

At the time, Bethany had blamed his tenseness on herself, thinking she'd done something to irritate him, but now she was beginning to believe that Chance's black mood was because of his ward. Oddly enough, that discovery didn't ease the aggravation Bethany was feeling. If anything, it made it worse as she tried to figure out exactly what was going on between the two of them.

When the music stopped, Chance was pleased to find that they were standing close to Rori and Evan. He turned deliberately to speak with Rori, his gaze harsh upon her.

"Did you enjoy the waltz?" Chance asked her in an icy tone that surprised Rori. She'd expected him to be pleased that she'd managed so well.

"Yes, Evan was wonderful. He taught me the proper steps and how to move and . . ." Rori answered, not the least bit cowed by his attitude.

"So I saw," he cut her off tersely as Bethany came close to take his arm.

"Did you enjoy your dance?" Rori asked Chance pointedly, but it was Bethany who responded.

"Oh, yes," Bethany cooed, hugging his arm to her breast as she gazed up at him adoringly. "Chance is the most marvelous dancer."

Rori's stomach churned, and she felt like throwing up. Bethany made her positively sick with all her gushing over Chance. She wished there was some way she could knock that disgustingly self-satisfied expression off the other woman's face, but she could think of no ladylike way to do it. "So I've seen."

"You mean you didn't dance together when you were in Arizona?" Bethany lifted one expressive brow at Rori's revealing statement, and she gave a throaty laugh of relief. All night she'd had the suspicion that there was more to their relationship than just ward and guardian, but now it seemed she'd been wrong and she was delighted. She gave Chance a heated look, believing the path to his heart to be clear. "It's good to know that you weren't dancing with other women while you were gone."

Rori saw the look and couldn't stay quiet any longer. She hated this woman with a passion. "Chance didn't have much time for dancing, but he did speak of you often."

"I'm glad I was on your mind. I know I was thinking about you constantly," Bethany breathed huskily.

Chance could have groaned. He knew Bethany thought he'd been counting the hours that they were apart, but nothing could have been further from the truth. Suddenly, he felt very, very cornered and decidedly uncomfortable.

"You were on his mind, all right," Rori went on, desperately needing to put the blonde in her place. "Why, that night when I was in his room with him, right after he'd been stabbed . . ."

"You were stabbed?" Bethany gasped in horror.

Before Chance could answer, Rori continued.

"Well, it wasn't life-threatening or anything, just a little cut on the arm. Anyway, he was saying just how much he missed you and how much he would have liked to . . ."

"Rori!" Chance finally ground out in exasperation just as the musicians began another waltz. "I wouldn't want to bore Bethany and Evan with details of our exploits in Phoenix. Besides, this is our dance, isn't it?"

"Yes, it is," she declared, feeling particularly triumphant.

"Bethany, if you and Evan will excuse us?"

Rori was pleased to see a look of anger flit across the other young woman's face for an instant before being carefully hidden behind a mask of civility.

"Of course."

Chance didn't hesitate another second to whisk his ward out among the other dancing couples. His anger was such that his movements were tense and jerky. *Damn Rori, anyway! What the hell did she think she was trying to do, first dancing with Strickland and then blurting out about being in his room in Phoenix? Didn't she realize statements like that could ruin her reputation before she even had the chance to establish herself?*

Chance had been holding himself stiffly as they'd waltzed until he realized that this was not the time or the place to try to explain the intimate workings of gossip in society to Rori. He forced himself to try to enjoy the rest of their dance together. It surprised him to find that she was keeping up with him so easily, seeming to float along with his guidance, rarely missing a step. It felt right holding her this way, moving to the sensual sway of the melody.

Then Chance glanced down at Rori to find that her eyes were closed and her expression was almost rapt. It startled him even as it suddenly, sharply aroused him. His anger vanished, and in its place came a fierce, hot awareness of her as a woman. The heady scent of her perfume surrounded him. He became conscious of the slender curve of her waist beneath his hand and of her breasts swelling temptingly above her décolletage. He was mesmerized by her nearness, enthralled by the feel of her in his arms. He suddenly wanted to crush her to his chest and kiss her. Chance gave himself a mental shake, warning himself against those kinds of thoughts.

He had brought her back to Boston to help her start a new life, not to seduce her again. With an effort, Chance focused on her dancing and how well she was doing for only her second attempt.

"You've learned very quickly," he complimented, trying to keep his voice from sounding strangled as he dragged his gaze away from where the pearls nestled between the tops of her breasts.

At the sound of his voice, Rori's eyes flew open to find him gazing down at her. For a moment, she had allowed herself to forget everything but the wonder of dancing with Chance and being held by him. It had been so long . . . The fury she'd been feeling over the way he'd let Bethany hang all over him reasserted itself, burning through the haze of contentment that had surrounded her, and she stiffened in his arms.

"Thanks," she responded curtly.

"Rori . . ." Chance pressed, knowing that he had to set her straight about Evan Strickland.

"What?" she snapped.

"I want you to steer clear of Strickland. He's no good for you. Keep away from him."

Rori bristled. She was in no frame of mind to listen to any of his pronouncements from on high. Who did he think he was, trying to dictate who she could and could not dance with? "I'll make my own friends, Chance. I'm sure I don't need your advice about companions."

"What's that supposed to mean?" he shot back, trying to ignore the way their bodies were moving in unison to the gentle, swaying rhythm.

"It means that you're not such a great judge of character!" she told him pointedly, her eyes flashing fire. "Just look at who you're spending your evening with— Bethany . . ." Rori grimaced in distaste. "How can you stand her? All she does is gaze up at you with goo-goo eyes!"

"Goo-goo eyes?" Chance repeated, stunned, and then grinned at her ridiculous-sounding description.

"Don't you dare laugh, Chance Broderick! It's the way cows look at bulls when they're wantin' somethin', and, trust me, I ain't never seen a cow wantin' a bull more than that one," Rori finished in disgust, blushing a bit as she realized that she'd reverted back to her old way of talking.

Chance was suddenly serious again. "I don't need any criticism from you about my lifestyle. I am *your* guardian. *You are not mine.* Is that clear?"

Rori glared up at him mutinously, but didn't answer as they continued to dance.

"I want you to stay away from Strickland," he commanded.

"Sometimes we don't always get what we want in life," she retorted.

"I do, Rori," Chance told her sternly.

"Look, Chance. I make my own decisions."

"Just make sure they're the right ones, Rori, and we'll get along just fine," he bit out tersely.

The music stopped then, and, as if by magic, Bethany reappeared at Chance's side.

"Chance, darling, there are some guests who have to leave a bit early. Could you come and bid them good-bye?" She took his arm and drew him away with an apologetic glance toward Rori.

"Of course, Bethany. Rori, I'll speak with you later," he told her in a semi-threatening tone.

"Don't bet on it," Rori muttered under her breath so he couldn't understand her. She turned away from the sight of him with Bethany on his arm once again, strolling leisurely across the floor. Pasting a smile on her face, she deliberately sought out Evan.

* * *

Chance was never quite sure how Bethany managed it, but one minute they'd been bidding some departing guests good-bye and the next they were alone, outside on the veranda.

The night was a beautiful one. Stars spangled the black velvet sky, and a sliver of a moon hung heavily on the horizon. Bethany knew it was now or never. She had to lure him into her arms and make him profess his love for her. She was almost positive that he loved her, for he'd been very attentive all night long.

Bethany gazed up at him longingly as she moved closer to him. "It's a perfect night."

"Good sailing weather," he remarked casually, wondering why all he could think about was getting away from Bethany and getting back to Rori.

"Sailing weather?" Bethany asked flirtatiously as she nestled against him. "Would you really rather be sailing right now?"

A resounding *yes* thundered in his mind. He wanted to be anywhere, but here—sailing, back in the desert, anywhere! Still, gentleman that he was, Chance knew he couldn't tell her the truth.

It occurred to him then what he'd been avoiding for some time now. He didn't love Bethany Sutcliffe, and he never had. Chance knew that it was ridiculous to let her go on thinking that he cared. He had to end this, to let her down, but he had to do it as gracefully as possible.

"Oh, Chance, darling . . ." Bethany drew him back into the shadows and pulled him down for a flaming kiss. She'd been waiting forever to have a moment alone with him so she could kiss him. She put everything she had into the embrace, arching heatedly against him in a sensual offering that she hoped he would not ignore.

Caught by surprise, Chance responded for an instant, but then suddenly realized that this was all wrong. This wasn't the woman he wanted in his arms. This wasn't

Rori. The last thought shocked him to the depths of his soul. Rori? Was it Rori he really wanted? In confusion, Chance took Bethany by her upper arms and set her from him.

"Chance? What is it?" Bethany asked worriedly, thinking she'd done something wrong.

"Nothing, Bethany, or maybe everything. I'm sorry, but this isn't going to work."

"What do you mean?" Her heart constricted painfully in her breast.

"You deserve more than I can give you, Bethany."

"What are you talking about?"

"I don't love you."

"You don't?" She had feared as much all along, but had never had the nerve to face up to the possibility. "But we meant so much to each other."

"We shared passion, Bethany. That's all. I'm sorry." He gave a negative, regretful shake of his head and then turned, disappearing down the steps and away from the house and leaving her standing there, alone in the pale moonlight.

Evan had been thoroughly delighted when Rori had come back to him after dancing with Broderick. He'd plied her with champagne, seeing to it that her glass was continually filled. He thought her a delightful companion and couldn't wait to take her in his arms and kiss her.

Evan had made several inquiries about Aurora and had been slightly disappointed to discover that she had no funds of her own to speak of, but was totally dependent on the Brodericks for her well-being. He thought Aurora a woman he could fall in love with, but, unfortunately, the bride he chose would have to have a substantial fortune behind her if they were to live in the style to which he'd become accustomed. Still, Aurora's lack of funds did not diminish his interest or his desire for her, and he wondered hungrily if she could be encouraged into a dalliance. Certainly it was worth a try for she truly was a beauty.

"Would you care to step out into the hall for a breath of fresh air?" he invited after they'd shared several more champagnes.

Rori was flushed from the effect of the potent wine and thought his suggestion a good idea. "Yes, thank you, Evan. I would."

He guided her from the crowded ballroom out into the main hallway, but there were still several couples around. Frustrated, he walked her without apparent intent across the wide hall to the entrance to the study. To his delight, it was empty.

"There are some windows open in here. Perhaps there might be a breeze," Evan told her as he manipulated her into the privacy of the semi-darkened room.

Rori entered ahead of him and then she heard Bethany speaking.

Would you really rather be sailing right now? Oh, Chance, darling . . .

She looked out one of the floor-to-ceiling casement windows that faced the veranda on the front of the house to see Bethany in Chance's arms and him kissing her passionately. It was very obvious that the amorous couple thought they were unobserved there in the shadows of the night.

In that fraction of a second, Rori's heart was shattered. She backed miserably away, accidentally bumping into Evan. She turned to face him, struggling to keep from revealing too much to him.

"Excuse me . . . I just remembered that I have to see

Agatha about something . . ." Without waiting for him to speak, she fled the room.

Agatha had seen Evan and Aurora disappear out into the hall. Knowing the young man's reputation, she had decided to follow after them. She had just reached the ballroom door when she came across Aurora looking very pale and very distressed. Luckily, the hall was deserted at that moment, and no one saw them.

"Aurora, dear . . ." She put a supporting arm around her as she drew her aside for a moment of privacy. "Did Evan do something?"

"Oh, no. Evan was a perfect gentleman. I just . . . I'm not feeling too well. Would you mind if we left now?" Rori asked.

"Not at all. I'll just go find Chance and . . ."

"No!" She grabbed Agatha's arm to stop her. "No. There's no need to spoil the party for him. It is his party, after all. In fact, if you want to stay, I could just go on alone."

Agatha was far more perceptive than Rori gave her credit for, but she said nothing. "I'll just leave word for him that we're going. I'm sure he'll be able to find another way home."

Rori gave a tight nod as she fought for control. She wouldn't break down and cry! She wouldn't! She was relieved when Agatha returned a short time later with the news that their carriage had been brought around. The older woman was surprised that Bethany was not there to bid them good night, but said nothing as she ushered her young ward into the waiting conveyance and headed home.

Chapter 31

Rori thought the ride back to the Broderick house would never end. She tried desperately to keep from thinking of Chance and Bethany and the passionate kiss she'd witnessed, but it was impossible. The memory was burned into her consciousness, a vivid, painful reminder of Bethany's obvious victory and her own failure. When they finally reached the house, Rori wanted to bolt from the carriage, race inside and seek solace in the privacy of her room. The hindrance of her skirts, however, curbed her, and she was forced to descend from the conveyance with her newly acquired feminine grace and walk with Agatha at what she considered a snail's pace.

"Aurora, shall I send for the doctor to come see you?" Agatha asked, truly worried about her young companion. Aurora had been quiet all the way home, and she was concerned that she really might be ill.

"Oh, no," Rori answered hastily, knowing no doctor could cure what ailed her.

"Then would you care for a cup of tea before you go on up to bed? We could sit in the parlor and just relax for a while if you'd like," Agatha invited, wanting the young girl to open up to her and tell her what was troubling her.

"No, thank you, Agatha," Rori replied. She felt guilty

that she wasn't being completely honest with the kind woman, but she wasn't used to sharing her deepest feelings with anyone. Besides, her agony over having lost Chance to Bethany was far too raw to be dealt with openly just yet. She needed some time alone—time to sort out all that had happened and figure out what she was going to do next. "I think I just need to go to bed. I'm probably just tired from all the excitement."

"It has been a busy day for you," she agreed sympathetically. "I'll send Jeannie up to help you undress."

"No, really, that won't be necessary tonight."

Agatha could see the almost distraught look in her eyes and knew it would be best to leave her alone for a while. "Well, dear, you go on up and get a good night's sleep. But, Aurora . . . ?"

"Yes, ma'am?"

"If you need me . . . if you need anything at all, you have but to ask." Agatha sensed there was far more to her upset than just a slight malady or weariness, but unless she was willing to share it with her, there was nothing she could do.

Rori heaved a strained sigh of relief as she finally escaped to the sanctity of her own room, and she was thrilled to find Jake there, curled up at the foot of her bed. She closed the door behind her and dropped to the floor beside her dog, hugging him close, mindless of her expensive gown and fancy hairstyle.

"Jakie . . . oh, Jakie . . . what am I gonna do now?" she sobbed, finally giving vent to the misery that gripped her. She wrapped both arms around the big mongrel's neck and buried her face in his soft fur as she cried.

It was quite a while before she finally regained some semblance of control. She moved away from Jake just long enough to throw off her clothes. Dressed only in her chemise, she crawled up on the bed and patted the mattress beside her. The dog was eager to join her on the comfortable bed, and he jumped up with ease, snuggling close at her side where she sat.

"I don't know what to do, Jakie," Rori confided in a broken voice to her one and only friend. "Chance loves Bethany. I guess he always has." She sniffed loudly as she wiped the fresh tears from her cheeks. "You know, I thought I could make him love me. I thought if I was a good enough lady, he would love me and not her, but I guess I didn't do good enough."

Jake cocked his head and gave a soft whine.

Tears still streaming down her face, Rori clasped her knees to her chest and began to rock back and forth in anguish as she huddled there with her pet. "We have to leave, Jakie. We can't stay. I don't know where we're gonna go, but I can't just hang around here and watch Chance with her. She's so pretty . . . she's everything I'm not."

Again the dog whined, and this time he nudged her arm with his cold nose, forcing her to open up just a little and hug him again.

"Oh, Jakie, you're the only one left who really loves me." Rori's heart ached. "Grampa did, though . . . Grampa did . . ."

Getting up for a minute, she wandered miserably over to the big dresser where she'd placed Burr's things upon arriving. Opening the drawer, she drew out the small package of personal possessions that had belonged to her grampa. She had looked at them only once, right after he'd died, and hadn't had the heart to open them again since. Tonight, though, she needed them. She needed some reminder that she had been loved, that Burr had existed and that he had cared for her.

Climbing back up on the bed next to her expectant pet, Rori untied the string that bound the parcel and spread her grandfather's few belongings out on the bed before her. There wasn't much, just the few things he'd kept in his saddlebags, and she touched each item with cherishing hands. There was the crested ring he'd always carried with him, but never worn. There was the small portrait of her father with her grandmother when he'd been a small boy. She often asked about her grandmother, but Burr had never had much to say, only that she'd died of the fever when her father had been a small boy. There was the packet of old, now-yellowing letters, too, that Burr had always kept, but never read. Being unable to read herself, Rori had never given them much thought, but right now she longed with all her heart to be able to read them, just to have some contact with her own past.

"Oh, Grampa . . ." Rori sobbed his name heartbrokenly. "I thought I could do it, but I can't . . . I just can't . . ."

Clutching all his precious belongings to her breast, she finally gave vent to all the grief she'd carried deep within her. She had managed to distract herself during the trip to Boston by concentrating on becoming the perfect lady for Chance, but now that she'd failed at that, she had nothing left. She wept in mournful agony.

Agatha had intended to drink a calming cup of tea by herself in the parlor, but the memory of Aurora's strange mood upset her, and she decided to go upstairs to see how she was doing. As she neared her room, she could hear her crying, and the sound tore at her very soul.

"Aurora?" She called her name softly as she tapped lightly on the door, but Rori was too lost in the depths of her despair to hear her. Concerned about her, Agatha tried the doorknob and, finding it open, let herself in the room.

"I know you said you wanted to be alone, but . . ." As she entered the room and saw the young girl looking so completely miserable sitting in the middle of the bed with her dog, she almost cried herself. "Aurora . . ."

Agatha closed the door and went straight to her, sitting down beside her on the bed and taking her in her arms. She held her as a mother would a child, murmuring warm endearments to her and stroking the silk of her hair in a gentling caress.

"It's all right. Things aren't really that bad. Don't worry, I'm here and I'll do whatever I can to help . . ."

At long last, Rori quieted, and she was surprised to find that she was clinging to Agatha like a baby. She moved from her embrace and rubbed at the tears that coursed down her cheeks, embarrassed.

"I'm sorry . . ." Rori mumbled, humiliated at having been caught crying.

"Sorry? Sorry for what?" Agatha asked, handing her the lace handkerchief she always kept handy.

"I shouldn't be cryin' . . ." she sniffed as she blew her nose in a most Rori-like gesture.

"And why not?" Agatha demanded, startling her.

"Because, because Grampa said . . ." Rori answered, nervously twisting the handkerchief in her hands.

She patted her hands confidingly. "I know your grampa raised you, but you know, sometimes men don't always know what we women need."

"What do you mean?"

"Sometimes crying can help. I don't know why, but it does!"

"It does?" Rori was surprised to hear this. She'd always thought it was a weakness that had to be fought.

"Absolutely. Sometimes when things just get so terrible, crying is the only way to let it out. I know when my husband died . . ." Agatha's loving expression faltered as she remembered the pain of losing the only man she'd ever loved.

"Did you cry?" Rori asked with childlike innocence.

"A lot," Agatha replied honestly, "I did feel better eventually, but it took a while before I was able to get on with my own life. It may not seem likely to you now, but someday you'll be able to think about Burr's death and understand." She saw then that Rori was holding some things close, and she wanted to encourage her to talk about her feelings. "Did these things belong to your grandfather?"

Rori nodded dumbly as she realized that she was still clutching them to her. "Would you like to see them?"

"Very much."

She laid the letters, portrait, and ring back down on the bed to show Agatha. "This is Grampa's ring, but he didn't wear it much." Rori showed it to her. "This is a picture of my father and my grandmother, and these are some letters Grampa always kept. I don't know why he kept 'em. He never read 'em or anything." Rori did not notice that Agatha was intently studying the ring and the portrait.

"Aurora . . . may I see the letters?"

"Sure," she agreed, handing them over. "I've never read 'em, so I don't know what's in 'em."

"Why didn't you read them?"

Rori flushed. "I can't. I never learned how."

"Oh," Agatha replied in surprise, and then she gave her a reassuring smile. "Well, don't worry. That's easily remedied. Would you like me to read these to you?"

"Would you?" She brightened considerably. She might never have Burr again, but at least hearing about him would help ease the loneliness.

"Of course. Do you know who these are from?"

"No."

"Well, let me see . . ." Agatha took the missives and carefully separated them. She was startled to see the postmarks were from Boston. "Whoever wrote them years ago sent them from here."

"From Boston?" Rori's eyes widened.

"Let's see . . .

Dear Burton,

It has been so long since we've heard from you that we are becoming concerned. We know you were devastated by all that happened, but that's in the past now. Please come home. We miss you and Jack. There is a void in our lives that will never be filled until we have you back in our midst.

Your loving brother,
Joseph Prescott

"Dear God!" Agatha exclaimed. She let her hand that was holding the letter drop to her lap as the shock of what she'd just read became clear to her. Almost mechanically, she picked the letter back up. "What's the date on this?" She scoured the yellowed page for the date, then read it aloud in amazement. "September 9, 1847."

"What's the matter, Agatha?" Rori asked, concerned by her strange reaction.

"You say your grandfather went by just the name Burr?"

"Yes."

"I see." She hesitated, picking up the ring and the portrait once more.

"What is it?"

"I think we may have just discovered something very wonderful, Aurora."

"What?"

"I think you may not be the orphan you think you are."

"What do you mean?"

"I mean, the Joseph Prescott who signed this letter is still alive."

"Joseph Prescott?"

"He's your great-uncle, child. If I'm right, this ring bears the family crest and will be proof positive of your relationship. I thought the woman in this picture looked familiar, and now I know why. I knew her, not intimately, mind you, but years ago we did move in the same social circle. As I recall, her death was a real tragedy. She had a young son at the time. After the funeral, though, her husband and the boy both disappeared from Boston and never returned."

"Grampa . . ." Rori breathed in stunned wonder. "My name is Prescott?"

"I believe so. I think I'll send a message to Joseph requesting a meeting with him in the morning. This should be quite exciting. Joseph and his wife Charlotte were never able to have children, and according to the rumors circulating through the years, it seems they never gave up hope that Burton and his son would come back home."

"So I might have family after all?"

"Indeed you might, Aurora, my dear. The Prescotts are very well established here in Boston. This will be wonderful if it's true, but let's not get too excited until we speak with Joseph and Charlotte tomorrow. There may be some problems we don't know about."

"I understand," Rori said, trying to keep calm as the joy of thinking she might have kin sent a thrill coursing through her.

"Now, why don't you just get into your nightgown and try to get some sleep? First thing in the morning, we'll see what we can find out. All right?"

"All right." As Agatha started from the room, Rori called out to her, "Agatha?"

"Yes, dear?"

Rori ran to the older woman then and embraced her. She had never had any womanly guidance before except for her occasional talks with Nilakla, and it was a new but wonderful experience for her.

"Thank you."

Agatha felt tears burn her eyes. She hugged Rori close and pressed a motherly kiss on her cheek. "You're more than welcome. Now, get some rest. I want you up and bright-eyed in the morning."

"Yes, ma'am," Rori answered. When Agatha had gone, Rori donned her gown and climbed back into bed with Jakie. She hugged her dog close feeling more alive than she had in ages. She knew it might not be true, but if it was . . .

Chance entered Rori's thoughts then, and she realized how late it was. She knew he hadn't returned home yet, and she bit her lip to still her inner pain. She had to leave the Broderick house one way or the other, for she couldn't bear the thought of being near Chance, knowing that he loved Bethany. She had planned to leave, to run away if she had to. Now it seemed almost a godsend to discover that she might have relatives right here in Boston.

"Maybe everything will be all right, Jakie. Maybe it will . . ." she whispered to her sleeping pet as she, too, drifted off.

The sudden change in Aurora had left Evan totally confused. He'd given her no reason to suspect his motives and so could not understand what had caused her to flee the study. He'd started to follow her when she'd rushed out into the hall, but when he'd seen Mrs. Broderick coming, he'd known it was probably best to make himself scarce since he wasn't a favorite of the Broderick family. Evan returned to the ballroom through a different door and began to mingle with the crowd once again.

It was only a short time later that he saw Bethany enter the room alone. Curious as to what had happened to all of the Brodericks, he approached her.

"Where's our guest of honor? I thought you two were inseparable," he asked.

"I have no idea where he is now. He left a while ago." Bethany answered him brusquely, still hurt and angry over what Chance had told her.

"Did they all leave together? I haven't seen Aurora lately."

"No. He didn't leave with *his ward*," she replied tensely, thinking of Aurora and wondering jealously if he was with her right now.

Evan heard the bitterness in her tone and wondered at it. "He didn't?"

"No, he didn't. Why? Are you jealous of him? I saw you squiring his sweet little ward around. Are you afraid he's after Aurora?" Bethany challenged. She'd known him for years and knew pretty well how he thought. Evan never asked a question unless he wanted something.

"Are you?" he countered sharply.

"You're far too perceptive, Evan." Her blue eyes narrowed as she studied him.

"Do you want to talk about it?"

"I'm not sure there's anything left to talk about. I thought Chance loved me, but he told me tonight that he doesn't."

"Perfect timing on his part, right in the middle of the party you gave for him," Evan remarked dryly.

"Wasn't it, though?" Bethany agreed sarcastically.

"So you think this has something to do with Aurora?"

"It might. I'm not sure. I just know that I refuse to believe he doesn't harbor some feelings for me. We've meant so much to each other . . ." The fierceness of her bulldog tenacity came to the fore. "I've wanted him for far too long to give up now. I've waited for him for far too long to let him go so easily."

"But you can't make someone fall in love with you, Bethany," Evan scorned.

"Maybe, maybe not, but I can certainly try. All I have to do is get rid of the competition."

"Meaning Aurora."

"Meaning Aurora."

"Why don't you leave her to me? I could find her an enjoyable distraction."

Bethany had to laugh at him. "But she's not rich, Evan."

"I said she was a distraction. I didn't say I'd marry her. Besides, you may not have the problem you think you do. She made a point of telling me that she didn't care about Broderick that way."

"She did?" Her spirits were buoyed by the news.

He nodded.

"Then maybe I do still have a chance to win him . . ." Her eyes lit up with a spark of hope.

"Exactly, and I'll be more than glad to keep Aurora occupied so you can continue your pursuit of Broderick."

"That's quite a sacrifice on your part."

"I know, but a most enjoyable sacrifice."

"Well, if you can just get Aurora to fall in love with you, I'll take care of the rest."

"I wish you luck. Chance is not an easy man to sway once he sets his mind on something."

"I know," she answered grimly. "I know."

The sky in the east was just growing lighter as Chance descended from the hired carriage. He paid the driver and then started slowly up the steps to the house. He was drunk and he knew it and he didn't care. The night had been a long one for him as he'd passed it alone, drinking at one of the better saloons near the water-front. He'd been confused when he had walked away from Bethany, and he'd known he had a lot of thinking to do. He'd bought a bottle of bourbon and had found himself a quiet table away from the crowd where he could sort out his thoughts.

With each successive tumbler of bourbon, it had become more and more clear to Chance—he loved Rori. The realization had burst upon him like a flare in the night as he'd sat there all by himself in the saloon. Love was this wild, uncontrollable emotion that left him seething at the sight of her in Strickland's arms. Love was the reason why just being near her destroyed all his finer intentions and left him wanting her more than he'd ever wanted any woman. He loved Rori, and it seemed that he had almost since the first moment they'd met. He had just been too stupid to realize it. They had struck sparks off each other since the beginning, and it looked like they would continue to do so for the rest of their lives. He had grinned to himself at the thought of the rest of their lives, and he'd gotten up from his remote table and left the bar.

Now, as Chance entered the house, he knew he had to be quiet or face his mother's wrath. It had been bad enough that he'd deserted them at the party the night before, but to come in at dawn slightly drunk would never do. He headed up the staircase taking great care not to make any noise. He paused before Rori's room, wanting to walk right in and tell her that he loved her and tell her that everything was going to be just fine from now on, but he held himself back. He would tell her tomorrow. Tomorrow, everything was going to be wonderful. He was quite pleased with himself as he made it to his own room, and his last thought before he passed out was that he couldn't wait to talk to Rori and tell her that he loved her.

Chapter 32

Joseph Prescott's hands were shaking as he read the letter. Though he was nearly seventy years old, he was still as astute as he had ever been. The Brodericks were friends, and he trusted Agatha completely, but he wondered if someone was trying to play upon his sympathies and his bank account. It was known throughout Boston that they'd always hoped Burton and his son Jack would return. Had someone uncovered these letters and was now trying to use them to their advantage after having duped Agatha into helping them?

"Where did you get this?" Joseph asked in a strangled voice as his wife Charlotte, a tall, stately woman ten years his junior, stood at his side looking on.

"Is it authentic?"

"It is," Joseph answered.

"What about these?" Agatha opened the small package she'd brought with her and handed him the ring and the portrait.

"Dear God!" he exclaimed, giving his wife a tortured look before leveling a sharp-eyed gaze at Agatha. "They're Burton's. How did you come by them? Do you know where he is? Where Jack is?"

"Agatha, if you know where they are, please tell us. We've waited so long for some word . . . we've hoped and prayed . . ." Charlotte added, her gentle blue eyes alive with hope and excitement.

Agatha hated to tell them the bad part of her news, but she knew she had to. "Burton is dead and so is Jack . . ."

"No . . ." Joseph mourned. He had always held out hope that someday they would return.

"How did you find out, Agatha? Where did you get all of these things?" Charlotte wondered as she put a consoling arm about her husband's shoulders.

"I got Burton's things from his granddaughter."

"His granddaughter?" They both looked up, their expressions guarded. Their long, loving marriage had regrettably been a childless one, and the thought of a grandchild from Burton's side of the family thrilled them. Still, they had to be cautious.

"Yes. Jack married an Indian woman named Atallie, and they had a daughter. Her name is Aurora." She quickly explained the tragedy of Atallie and Jack's death, how Burton had raised her, and how Aurora had ultimately come back to Boston with Chance.

"Her name's Aurora . . ." Joseph repeated slowly as if testing the name. "We'd like to see her . . . to meet her to make sure. We always wanted a family . . ."

Agatha smiled, more confident now. She'd realized that the reason Aurora had seemed so strangely familiar to her was because her eyes were so much like the Prescotts'. At the time, the connection didn't occur to her, but now it seemed quite evident.

"Let me get her for you . . ."

"She's here?"

"Waiting outside in the hallway. I wanted to make sure you were receptive before bringing her in to meet you. Aurora's had a difficult time of it lately, and I didn't want her to be hurt anymore," Agatha told them with a smile as she turned and went to open the study door to admit Aurora to the room. "Aurora, please come in."

* * *

Rori had been waiting nervously in the main hall of the Prescott mansion since Agatha had disappeared into the study to meet with them. It seemed to be taking forever, and she was growing more and more tense with each passing moment.

Pacing the hallway, she tried to concentrate on her surroundings and on what might be transpiring behind the closed doors where Agatha had gone, but her wayward thoughts kept returning to last night and to Chance. She had no idea what time he'd returned home from the party, and that had left her upset despite the likelihood of her own good news. The memory of him in Bethany's arms was agony to her, and she could only think that he'd spent the night with her. Her heart weighed heavy in her breast at the thought—Chance loved Bethany.

Rori decided that maybe it was a good thing Agatha hadn't been able to rouse him that morning to tell him where they were going and why. Perhaps it was better this way, for if things worked out, she wouldn't have to see him again for a while. That would give her the time she needed to get control of her emotions.

Rori jumped nervously as the door to the study suddenly opened. When Agatha called out to her to join them, she took a second to compose herself and then moved into the room.

"Aurora, I'd like you to meet your great-aunt and great-uncle, Charlotte and Joseph Prescott," Agatha was saying with a delighted smile. "Charlotte and Joseph, this is Aurora, Jack's daughter."

The Prescotts stood hesitantly for a minute in the middle of the room as they regarded the lovely young woman before them. Only when Rori lifted her gaze questioningly to meet theirs, did they recognize her resemblance to Burton in her emerald eyes and know without doubt that she was their kin.

"Dear Lord, our prayers have been answered!" Charlotte moved quickly to her. "Aurora, you have no idea how we've longed for news of your father and grandfather, and now you're here. You've come home."

Rori was engulfed in a sweet, loving embrace as her great-aunt Charlotte took her in her arms. It was a tender moment, and Joseph joined them to press a kiss on Rori's cheek.

"Welcome, Aurora," he told her huskily, deep emotion shining in his eyes. "Welcome home."

Aurora's gaze met his, and he looked so much like Burr that she couldn't stop herself from hugging him when she and Charlotte moved apart.

"Thank you, Uncle Joseph." Her voice was tearstained. In his strong embrace, she felt the same cherishing affection Burr had always bestowed upon her. She knew he was right—she was home.

"Has Agatha told you everything?" Rori asked as they moved to sit down.

"Everything . . ." Joseph replied, the sadness of hearing of his brother and nephew's deaths obvious.

"We can't imagine what you've suffered losing your parents and then Burton, but we can help make the rest of your life one of happiness, Aurora—if you'll let us," Charlotte offered.

Rori was nearly choked with joy as she returned their embrace. "Yes, yes, oh, yes. Thank you . . ."

"Thank *you,* dear," Charlotte told her with heartfelt emotion. "Our lives have been so empty, but now we have you . . ."

Some time later, Agatha started on her way back home alone. Charlotte and Joseph had not wanted Aurora to leave. They had so much to catch up on that they had appealed to Agatha to let her stay. Seeing the young woman's happiness at having discovered relatives she'd never known existed, Agatha had agreed and had promised to pack up her possessions and send them along later that day. It was a joyous time for Rori and the Prescotts. Everyone was thrilled that things had worked out so well.

Chance woke up some time after the noon hour, and immediately regretted ever having opened his eyes. He knew there was a reason he wanted to jump out of bed and get going today, but for the life of him he couldn't think of what it was right now. His head was throbbing, his mouth tasted like half of the Union Army had trooped through it, and every inch of his body ached. Vaguely, he recalled a night spent alone in a saloon, but beyond that everything seemed pretty fuzzy. All he knew was that he was lying there, still fully dressed, and that he felt awful.

Chance levered himself up and then swung his long legs over the side of his bed. He rested his elbows on his knees and cradled his head in his hands as he waited for the room to come into focus. It took a minute for him to get his bearings, and when he finally did, he got slowly to his feet. He noticed uncomfortably that the odor of liquor and smoke still clung to his clothes and his stomach churned uneasily at the stench.

Chance figured it couldn't hurt to open the window, so he made his way to it and, without thinking, threw the drapes wide. The brightness of the noonday sun was a jolt of agony to his already beleaguered senses. He groaned out loud as he fell back across the bed and rested a forearm over his eyes to protect them.

"What the hell did you do last night, you idiot?" he asked himself disgustedly.

The answer came in a soft, gentle revelation . . . Rori.

She floated into his thoughts and brought him upright on the bed. Rori—beautiful, wild-spirited, passionate Rori—he loved her, and he had to tell her. Mindless to the stabbing pain in his temples, he bolted from the bed. He wondered what time it was, and when he focused on the mantel clock and saw that it was already afternoon, he started to rush from the room to find her.

Chance passed the mirror on the way out and came to a screeching halt. He looked terrible. His hair was a mess, he was unshaven, and his clothes were wrinkled beyond belief. He did not want to face Rori with the truth of his feelings for her looking and smelling like he did, so he threw off his clothes and set about getting cleaned up.

When Chance finally left his bedroom and started downstairs it was nearly half an hour later. He was fully expecting to find his mother and Rori at home. He suspected that they might be annoyed with him . . . Chance paused in his thoughts and reasoned that they were probably furious with him, but that would all be set to rights just as soon as he told Rori everything. After that it would be a simple matter to plan the wedding and then . . .

Chance was grinning widely, feeling confident and cocky, as he reached the downstairs hall. He hesitated at the bottom of the stairs to listen for the sound of their voices. When he discovered it was silent, he frowned and went looking for them. He found Jeannie in the kitchen.

"Where are my mother and Rori?" he inquired.

"They went out quite early this morning, Mr. Chance. Miss Agatha tried to wake you, but you were sleeping too soundly, I guess."

"I see," Chance answered, disappointed. "Do you know where they were going?"

"No, sir, and Miss Agatha didn't say when they'd be back."

"Oh." He'd been so excited that it aggravated him to have to cool his heels and wait for their return. "Thanks . . ."

His high hopes deflated, Chance retreated down the hall to the study intending to work until they returned. He stared at the stack of papers on his desk with little enthusiasm, but decided to at least try to accomplish something while he was waiting.

Agatha's step was light as she came up the steps to the house. Aurora would be fine with the Prescotts, she just knew it. Joseph and Charlotte were going to be wonderful to her, and she would have all the love she deserved.

Agatha was a bit annoyed with Chance, though. She could have sworn that he cared a great deal for Aurora. Yet at the party last night, he had paid scant attention to her, allowing all the other bachelors of Boston to court her without interference. Then, to top everything off, he had not returned home until the wee hours of the morning. Where had that boy been and what had he been up to?

Agatha wondered if she could have been wrong in her instinctive belief that Chance was in love with Aurora. She considered it thoughtfully for a moment now, but really felt that her initial intuitive reaction still rang true. Of course, she realized time would tell, and she entered the house, ready to order Aurora's things packed and delivered to the Prescott mansion.

Chance heard the door and came quickly out of the study. "Mother . . . Rori . . ." When he found his mother alone in the hall, he stared at her blankly. "Where's Rori?"

"Well, hello to you, too, Chancellor," Agatha replied sharply.

Chance had expected to taste of her disapproval. "Hello, Mother," he said contritely as he went to kiss her cheek. "Where's Rori?"

"It seems that's the second time I've heard that question."

"And?" Chance led a little anxiously.

She moved into the parlor with him trailing behind her and then turned to fix him with an icy regard. "Aurora is out of your reach, my clumsy son."

"Out of my reach? What are you talking about?" he demanded.

"I'm talking about the major discovery she and I made last night."

"Discovery? What kind of discovery?"

"Aurora, it seems, is none other but the grand-niece of Joseph Prescott. Her grandfather, who you knew as Burr, was really Burton Prescott, Joseph's long lost brother."

"What?" Chance was stunned by the revelation. *Rori was a Prescott?*

"Aurora had some letters and a few keepsakes that linked her directly to them. The family resemblance, by the way, is phenomenal." She was growing amused at the conflicting emotions that were flitting across Chance's for once unguarded features.

"Rori is a Prescott . . . ?" Chance said dumbly.

"Yes she is, and she's there with them now. They are just crazy in love with her already. You wouldn't believe how happy they were to find out that Burton had had a granddaughter."

"I'll bet," he replied distractedly. "Well, when is she coming home? I've got to talk to her and . . ."

"She *is* home, Chancellor. The Prescotts have welcomed her with open arms. Aurora will be living with them from now on."

"No, no, no. Wait a minute. I'm Rori's guardian."

"Not anymore. She has a family now, and, I must say, a most doting one."

Chance was completely bewildered. "Rori's gone to live with the Prescotts, and I wasn't even told about it?"

"My darling son," Agatha began. She had been waiting for this moment. "Had you decided to come home last night at a reasonable hour, you might have learned of it then or possibly this morning, had I been able to wake you. I tried four times to rouse you, you know."

He had the grace to look shamefaced as he remained silent.

"Now, if you'll excuse me, I have to see to having her things packed and sent over."

"Her things sent over . . . How did this all happen? When did this happen?"

"As you know, we left the party early last night. Aurora wasn't feeling well, and she was upset about something."

"She was?" Chance didn't know how he was supposed to have known that they'd left Bethany's early, but he'd worry about that later.

"Yes, so I sat with her in her room for a while, and we talked. She showed me some of the things she had from her grandfather, and there were some letters . . . Well, since she couldn't read, she had no idea what was in them. I had just started to read them to her when we made the discovery of Burr's true identity. The rest I've already told you."

"I'll be back." Chance was already striding from the room.

"Where are you going?"

"I have to talk to Rori. I'll see you later." And with that, Chance was gone from the house.

Agatha watched him go and smiled. She knew she'd been right all along. Chance did care about Aurora. Why else would he be rushing off to see her? However, she wondered what kind of reception her son was going to get. Aurora had seemed greatly relieved when he hadn't gotten up that morning. It had been almost as if she dreaded seeing him. Agatha had guessed then that Chance had been the cause of her upset at the party. It was certainly going to be interesting to see how things turned out. Agatha started upstairs to arrange for the packing of Aurora's clothing all the while wondering if her longtime bachelor son had finally met his match.

Chance wasn't sure how he felt about Rori's new-found family ties. He figured none of it would matter, though, because once he told her that he loved her, everything would be fine.

It seemed to Chance that he would never reach the Prescott home, but when he did, he practically sprinted up the stairs. He knocked with gusto on the door, fully confident that he would get to see Rori and have the opportunity to tell her how he felt.

Rori had been in the front sitting room with her great-aunt Charlotte when she saw Chance coming up the walk toward the house. Just the sight of him set her blood racing through her veins, but she fought down her excitement with the memory of his torrid embrace with Bethany.

Rori went pale as the pain of losing him flooded through her. Her hands began to shake at the thought of trying to act coolly around him, and she was forced to set the tea cup she'd been holding aside. She might be able to pretend to be a lady when she was out in society, and she might even eventually come to believe it herself, but she wasn't a good enough actress to carry off an air of nonchalance around Chance so soon. Knowing that she'd never have his love hurt her too badly. Tears swam in her eyes, and she stood up, meaning to flee the room and the house if she had to.

"Aurora . . . what's the matter? You look like you've seen a ghost," Charlotte said, her concern very real as she saw the tears.

"I . . . um . . . I just saw Chance coming up the front path, and I don't want to talk to him." She stood there nervously.

Charlotte was puzzled. Chance had supposedly been her guardian. Still, she was not about to let anything upset the newest member of their family. Aurora was too precious to them. They'd just found each other, and she wanted their time together to be happy. She would protect that fiercely.

"Don't worry, dear. If you don't want to see someone, you don't have to," she told her.

"Really?" Rori brightened.

"Really. Now, you just wait here. I'll handle everything."

"Thank you, Aunt Charlotte," Rori breathed in relief. The last thing she needed was to see Chance. The farther away from him she stayed, the easier it would be to get over him.

Charlotte left the sitting room and entered the hall just as Chance knocked on the front door. She summoned the butler, who was going to answer it.

"This is a caller for Miss Aurora, and she doesn't want to see him. Please make that plain to the gentleman."

"Yes, ma'am."

Charlotte retreated to the sitting room with Aurora and shut the door just as the servant answered Chance's knock.

"Good afternoon. I'm Chance Broderick, and I've come to see Rori. Is she here?" he asked, trying to look down the hall past the manservant hoping to catch sight of her.

"Yes, Miss Aurora is in. However, she is not taking any callers right now, sir."

"She'll see me. I'm sure of it. Just tell her I'm here, please." Chance was trying to be cordial, but he was growing slightly frustrated. Where was Rori? He needed to see her.

"I'm sorry, sir."

"What do you mean you're sorry?"

"Miss Aurora gave specific instructions. She doesn't want to see you."

"But, why?"

"I'm sure I wouldn't know, sir. If you'll excuse me? I will tell her that you stopped by."

"Yes. Thank you." Chance stepped back outside and had the door closed in his face. Confused and bewildered, he glanced at the house as if expecting it to reveal the answer, then turned to go.

Charlotte watched from the window until he was out of sight and then told Rori, "He's gone."

"Thank you, Aunt Charlotte."

"Aurora," she ventured cautiously. "Is this something you'd like to talk about? Chance has always impressed me as being such a nice young man, and yet you seemed really upset at the prospect of seeing him." Charlotte knew that they were just now getting acquainted and that she was intruding on her niece's private business. But she wanted Aurora to know that she'd be more than happy to help or advise her in any way.

"It's something personal . . . something I'm just not ready to talk about yet, that's all."

"All right," she agreed, allowing her her privacy. "I shall tell all the servants that you do not want to see him. That way you won't get any unwelcome surprises," Charlotte decreed. She was concerned about Aurora's mood, but didn't press her. Their relationship was too new, too fragile. She would do whatever was necessary to make

Aurora feel safe and protected. She was a Prescott now, and nothing would ever hurt her again as long as she lived.

Chance returned home, his mood black. He tried to figure out why Rori was refusing to see him, but could come up with no answer. The last time they'd spoken had been the night before when they were dancing at Bethany's. It had been their usual sparring, nothing out of the ordinary. He wracked his brain trying to figure out what had happened. His mother had said she was upset and they left the party early . . . Maybe his mother was the key to this. He went looking for her and found her in the parlor.

"Mother . . ."

"How did your visit with Aurora go, dear?" Agatha asked, trying not to sound too eager for news of the encounter.

"Last night you said you left the party early because Rori was upset. Do you know what was bothering her?"

She gave him a knowing look. "I take it you didn't have a very good meeting with her."

"I didn't even get to see her."

"What do you mean?"

"She told the butler that she didn't want to talk to me. Do you know why?"

"No, dear. She didn't tell me a thing. Did you two have an argument last night?"

"No. In fact, I didn't even know that you two had gone home early."

"You didn't?"

He shook his head. "I had already left."

This surprised Agatha. "Why?"

"Bethany. She fancies herself in love with me, but I'm not in love with her. I told her so last night, and then I left the party. I spent the night in a saloon down on the waterfront."

"Sounds like a pleasant evening," she remarked dryly.

Chance shot her a scowling look just as Big Jake happened to lumber into the room. His heart gave a decided leap as he realized that the dog could be the key to seeing Rori. "I don't know why she won't see me, but I'm going to find out, and Jake's going to help me. How soon will her things be packed and ready?"

"They're ready now. Why?"

"I think Jake and I will accompany them to the Prescotts'."

Chapter 33

"Well, what do you think?" Charlotte asked Rori as she showed her through the extra bedrooms on the second floor. They had been used strictly for guest rooms until now, and she was eagerly anticipating redecorating whichever room Aurora chose. "Pick whichever one you like."

"I don't know . . ." Rori wasn't sure what to say. Her room at the Brodericks' had been large and comfortable, but all these here were even bigger and more expensively furnished.

The room they were in was a nice-sized one at the front of the house, and it had large, airy windows that overlooked the street below. They added an openness to this room that the other bedrooms were lacking, and Rori decided that this one was her favorite. She liked the brightness and the feeling that she wasn't closed in.

"I think I like this one, if it's all right with you?"

"It's fine with me," Charlotte told her, and then confided with a grin. "In fact, this one is my favorite, too."

They laughed easily together. When Charlotte began to offer ideas about changes they could make in the decorating scheme, Rori stared at her in confusion.

"Change it? Why would you want to change it? It's perfect."

"I thought you might like to add a few feminine touches here and there, something that would make the room say it was yours and yours alone."

"I love it just the way it is, Aunt Charlotte, but thank you." She gave the older woman a hug. "I've never had anything so wonderful in my whole life." Rori spun around in the middle of the room, delighted at the thought that it was really hers, all hers.

"I'm glad you're pleased." Charlotte smiled as she watched her grand-niece. She was glad that Aurora was happy, and she hoped she stayed that way. She still wondered what had caused her to be upset earlier that afternoon when Chance had come to call. If there was a problem, she wanted to help with it, but she knew she couldn't be pushy with her.

Later, it seemed to Charlotte that it was almost as if she'd conjured him up. One minute she was thinking about Chance and the next Rori was turning away from the window, her face pale.

"Oh, no," Rori groaned, as she saw the Brodericks' carriage draw up in front of the house and saw Chance get out with Jakie.

"What is it, dear?"

"He's here *again*!"

"Who? Chance?"

"Yes. Why doesn't he just go away?"

"He must want to talk with you about something."

"I know, but there's really nothing left to say," Rori responded miserably.

Charlotte was one astute lady. The look in Rori's eyes coupled with her answer clued Charlotte in to the truth of what was happening. Aurora loved Chance Broderick, but for some reason things weren't going too smoothly. The match would be a good one, she decided immediately. She just had to find a way to help smooth out their troubles. It was obvious that Chance cared about her. Why else would he keep coming back, especially after he'd been turned away so abruptly earlier that day? Her eyes were aglow at the thought of young romance, and she remembered the terrible time she and Joseph had had before they'd finally worked things out nearly forty years before.

Charlotte moved to the window to glance out and saw Chance coming up the walk with a huge monstrosity of a dog. "Is that a dog he's got with him?" she asked in wonder.

"Yes, that's Big Jake. I know I should have told you before, but I was so excited . . ."

"Told me what?"

"Big Jake's mine," Rori confessed, hoping desperately that her aunt would not object to him living with them.

"He's yours . . ." Charlotte repeated, thinking comically of how her family was growing by leaps and bounds that day.

"Yes, and he's real well trained, so he won't give you any trouble at all, Aunt Charlotte. Honest."

"I'm sure if he's your dog, he must be. We have plenty of room here. Big Jake will be most welcome."

"Thank you," Rori breathed in relief, then realized her dilemma wasn't over. She still had to deal with Chance . . . "I guess Chance thought he had to bring Jakie to me."

"Do you want to see him or shall I send him away?"

Charlotte led the question easily. Rori's expression was so tormented that it confirmed Charlotte's belief that she did harbor deep feelings for him. She didn't know what had happened between them, but she was certainly going to do what she could to get these two together.

"No . . . no, I don't want to see him."

"I'll handle it, then. You wait here."

"Thanks."

Both Chance and Big Jake were a bit hesitant as their carriage drew to a stop in front of the Prescotts'. Chance didn't understand why Rori had sent him away earlier, but he felt certain that she wouldn't refuse to see him if he came with the dog. Jake gave Chance an uncertain look as they got out of the carriage.

"It's all right, big guy," Chance told him as he paused to pet him for a minute. "Rori's here and everything's going to be just fine. The Prescotts are going to love you, and if they don't, you can come live with me."

Jakie gave a happy wag of his tail and, led on his new leash by Chance, accompanied him up to the house. Chance knocked as he had earlier that day, but this time it was Charlotte who answered the door.

"Good evening, Mrs. Prescott," he greeted her, keeping a firm hand on Jake.

"Good evening, Chance," she returned. "Is there something I can do for you?"

"I came to see Rori. Is she here? I've brought Big Jake for her."

"Yes, she's here, Chance, but she doesn't wish to see you."

Chance couldn't believe that she was still putting him off. "Are you sure?"

"Very sure," she replied.

"Mrs. Prescott, I have to speak with her. It's important. Would you get her for me, please?" Chance's disbelief was rapidly changing to anger. *What was the matter with Rori? Why was she hiding from him?*

"I'm sorry, Chance, but I can't do that." Charlotte was firm in her refusal, although she really wished she could. She had a feeling that if these two would just talk to each other they could straighten everything out, but she wouldn't betray Rori's request.

"Why not?"

"Aurora trusts me, Chance. She told me that she doesn't want to talk to you. I have to respect her wishes in this matter."

"But I don't understand . . ." Chance was truly perplexed. He'd never wanted to declare his love to a woman before, and now that he was ready to, the woman he loved wouldn't have anything to do with him. He needed a drink, a stiff one.

"I don't understand it either, but perhaps if you just give her a little time alone to think things out . . ." Charlotte's eyes were sparkling as she dropped the hint. She only hoped Chance was smart enough to understand what she *wasn't* saying.

"Here's Jake." He handed her the leash. "Would you see that she gets him, please? Also, I have her trunks in the carriage. I'll need some help with them."

"Of course, Chance. I'll send someone right out."

"Fine."

"Thank you for stopping by and bringing the dog."

Chance was totally frustrated as he strode down the walk to his carriage. A servant came out to help him unload Rori's things. When that was done, he climbed back inside the vehicle and ordered the driver to head home. Troubled and feeling oddly alone, he settled back in his seat, completely unaware that Rori was watching him from her upstairs bedroom window and that tears she wanted to deny were coursing down her cheeks.

Much later that night, Chance sat by himself in the dimly lit study. He had pushed his chair back away from the desk and was sitting with his feet propped on the desktop, his legs crossed at the ankles. In one hand, he held a half-empty tumbler of bourbon and in the other a nearly empty bourbon bottle. It had been a long afternoon and an even longer evening.

Chance had tried to work when he'd come home, but the effort had proven pointless. He had been obsessed with thoughts of Rori, and he hadn't been able to put the memory of her from him. He kept going over in his mind what had happened at Bethany's the night before, and he kept coming back to the same thing—nothing. They had danced, and they had argued about her choice of friends. Nothing out of the ordinary there, for they always seemed to argue about something.

Certainly, Chance reasoned, *Rori would not have cut him out of her life over a simple fight about Strickland.* Feeling comfortable about that conclusion, he started to go over the events of the evening again. He had danced with Rori, then Bethany had maneuvered him outside to say good-bye to the departing guests. They'd embraced, he'd told her he didn't love her, and he'd left. Chance took a deep drink from the potent liquor and didn't even notice how strong it was. He didn't notice that his mother had knocked on the study door and then opened it.

"Chancellor?" Agatha said his name worriedly as she stepped into the room. Upon spying him sitting there drinking himself into a stupor, she spoke up. "I thought you were in here working!"

"I tried for a while," he replied vaguely, taking another drink.

"And?" she prodded. She had not spoken with him

since he'd returned from the Prescotts'. He had come back in the house and had disappeared into the study and shut the door. She was dying to know what had happened and had waited as long as she could.

"And I didn't accomplish much," he paused thoughtfully. "Tell me something."

"What?"

"At Bethany's, you said Rori got upset . . . said she didn't feel well."

"Yes. I had seen her leave the ballroom with Evan and I decided to make sure he didn't try anything untoward with her, for we both know how innocent she is about such things."

Did he ever, Chance thought. "Yes."

"Well, as I went out into the hall, she was coming out of the study, and I must say she looked just ghastly."

"The study?" he remarked sharply, and he knew then exactly what had happened. Rori had been in the study, and he had been right outside the study windows making an ass out of himself with Bethany. She'd seen everything . . . well, not everything, because if she had, she wouldn't be upset. If she had stayed there long enough, she would have heard him tell Bethany that he didn't love her.

"Yes, dear, but don't worry, Evan didn't harm her in any way. They'd hardly had time to do anything."

"I know," he told her, almost delighted. He stood up, setting the glass and bottle aside, and went to her to kiss her cheek.

"You do?" Agatha was staring at him as if he'd suddenly grown two heads.

"Yes. Thank you very much."

"You're welcome very much," she replied, mystified by this sudden change in him. "I came in here to ask you if you wanted something to eat. Since you didn't join me at dinner . . ."

"No. I'm not hungry," Chance told her as he made his way back to his desk and sat down, acting as if he was going to go back to work. "I think I'll try to work a little more."

"All right. Well, good night, then."

"Good night. I'll see you in the morning."

As soon as Agatha left from the room, Chance refilled his glass and leaned back in his chair. He knew now why Rori was mad at him, but he still didn't know how he was going to get to her to explain what she'd witnessed that night.

He downed some of the bourbon, remembering what Charlotte Prescott had said to him about giving Rori time to think things out. Maybe she had known what was troubling Rori and had been trying to tell him to leave her alone until she calmed down. He would do it, he decided. He would give her whatever time she needed, and then, when she was calm and would see him, he would tell her that he loved her.

Chance's spirits lightened, and he smiled drunkenly. He figured Rori had to love him if she got that angry over seeing him kiss Bethany. The revelation pleased him, and his grin grew wider for a moment before faltering. Rori had to love him, because if she didn't, he didn't know what he'd do.

The next few weeks passed in a whirlwind of activity for Rori as Charlotte took charge of her life. Daily instructions in the basics of education were followed by dancing lessons and lessons in the social graces. She was fitted for a more complete wardrobe, and those visits to the dressmaker alone took hours and hours. She went to a few dinner parties in the company of her aunt and uncle, but Chance was never in attendance. Evan Strickland was, though, and she enjoyed being with him. His approach was unthreatening, and his conversation was interesting and witty.

Yet, even as Rori enjoyed Evan's companionship, she found herself thinking of Chance. She realized dishearteningly that he hadn't tried very hard to see her. He had only come to the house twice and had never come back again. Rori supposed it was because he really didn't care about her and was probably spending all his time with Bethany. She wondered why she hadn't heard any announcement of an engagement between them, but never asked because she truly didn't want to know. It was difficult enough just picturing them together, but to think of them married would destroy her.

Rori decided to concentrate her attentions on Evan, and when he tried to steal a kiss from her when they were unchaperoned for a few minutes, she did not resist. His kiss stirred no great passion in her, though, and she was glad. His embrace was pleasant, and she figured that's the way the rest of her life was going to be . . . pleasant.

Charlotte was not overly enthusiastic about Rori's relationship with Evan Strickland, but she could think of no reason to disapprove when Rori invited him to dine with them. Evan came to the house for dinner on two occasions, and though he was always the perfect gentleman, Charlotte somehow sensed that he was not all that he appeared to be. She could find no particular reason to back up her opinion, she just knew she didn't trust him completely and that he bore watching.

Charlotte kept hoping for an accidental meeting between Aurora and Chance, but it hadn't happened yet, and she was beginning to despair that it ever would. Several times, she'd noticed Aurora sitting alone with Jake, looking rather sad and lonely, but she'd never been able to get her to open up to her and talk about what she was feeling. Charlotte hated to think that Rori was going to let love pass her by, but she was helpless to do anything but watch and wait and hope that Evan didn't come to mean too much to her.

Evan was smiling widely as Bethany opened the door. "I got your message."

"Obviously," Bethany answered bitterly as she led the way into the parlor.

"You said in that note that it was urgent," he complained when she didn't show any sign of being glad to see him.

"It's as urgent as it can be, I guess."

"What is?"

"My situation with Chance."

"What's happened?"

"Nothing, and that's the problem." Bethany's expression was disgusted as she sat down on the love seat and motioned for him to join her there. "I've seen him all of three times since the night of his homecoming, and each time he's been as cool as he could be to me. I had thought it was a stroke of luck when the Prescotts claimed Aurora, but it doesn't seem to have helped matters much. He still hasn't started to return my affections again. We have to find some way to get Aurora completely out of the picture. Then when she's gone, he'll be all mine."

"As in . . . ?" For a moment, Evan feared that Bethany wanted to see the other woman dead.

"As in married to somebody else," she finished.

He breathed an audible sigh of relief, and Bethany smiled coldly at him as she gave a soft, conniving laugh.

"You thought I wanted her dead?"

"It crossed my mind."

"It crossed mine, too, but the other way's better."

"I agree completely, and if she'd have me, I'd marry her tomorrow."

"You've certainly changed your tune, since you found out she was the Prescott heiress."

"I liked her when she was poor, so to speak. I love her now that she's rich," he answered calculatingly.

"So propose to her," Bethany urged.

"Not yet."

"What do you mean 'not yet'?"

"She hasn't warmed to me enough."

"You mean you haven't kissed her yet."

"Of course I've kissed her, but the passion's missing."

"For all that money, passion can be bought, Evan. Think of something. I've never known you to be without a plan when it comes to getting what you want."

"That's true enough, and I did have one idea when I first heard that she'd come into quite a fortune."

"Tell me about it. I'm willing to try anything if it will mean getting Chance back. I have to have him, Evan. I have to!"

Evan's eyes were glowing with greed as he related his plan to Bethany.

Chapter 34

Nilakla rubbed her back wearily, trying to ease the nagging ache that had been plaguing her all day. She couldn't afford to have anything wrong with her now, for there was still too much to do. The house on the newly named Lazy B Ranch was an old, three-room adobe structure, and they had been working feverishly on it to make it livable for better than a week now.

Nilakla looked around herself and smiled bitter-sweetly. Douglas kept saying that this was their home, that this was where they'd raise their children. She wanted to believe him, but she knew the truth. She had heard it herself, and she knew the truth would not be denied. As soon as the baby was born, he was going to leave her and go back to Boston.

She gave a weary sigh as she rested one hand on her rounded belly. There was so little time left. Just a few short months, and it would be over. She'd deliberately refused to think about the future lately, but now, for some reason, the feeling of impending loss was threatening to overwhelm her again. Nilakla had tried to dismiss it, telling herself that she was just tired, but it had continued to haunt her day and night.

Suddenly, as Nilakla was standing there, a vicious, breath-stealing pain unexpectedly stabbed through her midsection, and she doubled over, gasping for breath. Another one followed shortly after, and she collapsed heavily to the floor, her arms wrapped around herself. In denial, she began to cry. *It couldn't be the baby . . . it just couldn't be. It was too early . . .*

Lone Hawk had been greatly concerned about his daughter's health. When she'd refused to stay in the village until after the birth of her child, he'd sent Wild Dove, a short, heavyset, widow woman, along with them to help her through her time of childbirth. Wild Dove was returning to the house now, carrying the bucket of water she'd gone to fetch for Nilakla. As she stepped into the cool interior, a shriek of horror escaped her to see Nilakla curled up on the floor in agony.

"Nilakla!"

"Help me, Wild Dove. I think it's the baby," Nilakla gasped, crying from a combination of fear and pain.

Douglas had heard Wild Dove's shriek, so he dropped what he was doing and ran to the house. He came charging through the door to find his wife on the floor and the other woman kneeling beside her.

"What is it? What's wrong?" Doug demanded, dropping down next to Nilakla and quickly taking her hand.

"It's the baby, Douglas, I'm . . ." Nilakla bit down on her bottom lip as a wrenching pain tore through her.

"Dear God . . ." he cried hoarsely, panic leaving him immobile.

"We must get her on the bed," Wild Dove directed as calmly as she could. She knew it was too soon for the child to come, but she also knew there was nothing they could do to stop it now that it had started.

Doug needed no more prodding. He swept Nilakla up in his arms and carried her to the bed, settling her gently there.

"Wild Dove . . . this can't be happening. It's not time yet!" He turned to the older woman, his expression frantic.

"If a baby wants to be born, there will be no stopping it, Douglas," she told him seriously. "I need your help . . . Nilakla needs your help."

"What can I do?" Doug was desperate.

Wild Dove sent him to bring more water and to get some cloths, mainly to give herself a few minutes alone with Nilakla. While he was gone, she helped her undress and then covered her with a light blanket.

"Wild Dove, what am I going to do?" Nilakla asked anxiously.

"You're going to have a baby," she replied, trying to lighten the mood, but they both knew the danger involved.

"It's too soon . . ." she groaned.

"Many are born early," Wild Dove tried to reassure her. "Your son still kicks, does he not?"

"My son?" Her eyes brightened at the thought, and she reached down to touch her taut stomach. "Yes, my son he . . . moves a lot and strongly, too."

"Then he is a strong child, and he will be fine."

"I hope so, Wild Dove. He's all I've got . . ." Nilakla fell silent as another contraction gripped her.

Doug's thoughts were full of remorse as he hurried to get the water. Their baby was coming too early, and it was all his fault . . . He cursed his stupidity for bringing Nilakla to the ranch. He should have made her stay in the village until after the baby was born. As he condemned himself he failed to remember that she had refused to remain behind, that she had insisted on going with him. The guilt he was feeling was too overwhelming. If they lost the baby, the blame would rest squarely on his shoulders. He should have known that she wasn't strong enough for all the labor they'd been doing around the ranch. He should have protected her. Instead, he had allowed her to work herself to a frenzy, and now . . . now, their child might die because of it.

Lugging two buckets of water with him, Doug rushed back to the house. As he got close, Nilakla's scream rent the air. He came to a dead stop as a cold shaft of fear impaled him. "Nilakla!" He shouted her name as the buckets fell from his hands as he charged inside.

"Douglas . . ." Nilakla clutched at his hand as he dropped to his knees beside the bed. Her eyes were wild with fear. "Douglas, I'm so afraid."

"I know, love," he told her, bending to tenderly kiss her forehead. A moment later, when she appeared to be relaxing, he glanced over at Wild Dove. "Is this going to take long?" he demanded, expecting an easy answer.

The Indian woman's expression was sympathetic as she saw the tormented look on his face.

"There is no way to tell. Some babies come quickly, others . . ."

"Well, is Nilakla all right?"

"She's as well as can be."

Her answer was not what Doug wanted to hear and it only served to increase his anxiety. "What about the baby?"

Wild Dove was careful how she responded. She did not want to worry him unduly, but then again he had to know the truth so he could be prepared should anything go wrong. "We will not know until he is born."

Nilakla moaned in terror as she felt a contraction begin again. She tightened her grip on Doug's hand as pain built to a paralyzing peak. She was panting and gasping for breath as it held her in its terrible grip.

"How much longer?" Doug asked worriedly. He wanted this over and done with.

"Hours yet."

"Hours!?" He was outraged. He gritted his teeth in frustration as he watched his beloved straining to control the pain. "Easy, darling. Easy, love." He tried to comfort her, but he knew he was only mouthing words. There was no way he could ease her suffering, no way he could help her through the pain.

Wild Dove discreetly left the house, allowing them time alone. She knew they were both frightened, but she also knew there was nothing she could do or say to help the situation.

Hours passed, yet nothing changed. The heat within the building grew stifling. Doug took to fanning Nilakla, hoping that at least by doing that he could help her in some way. She drifted off to sleep once, and she looked so deathly quiet as she lay there that Doug almost was afraid she'd died. Only the steady rising and falling of her chest let him know she was still alive.

The thought that he might be losing her haunted Doug, tearing him apart with sharp claws of regret. He thought of how stupid he'd been. He admitted openly to himself now that he had been using her in the beginning of their time together, and he cursed himself for it. Even as late as a few months ago, he'd been ready to go back to Boston and leave Nilakla behind without a thought, and now she could die . . .

How could he have been so blind to the honesty of her love and to his own feelings? he berated himself. *Why had it taken a near tragedy for him to recognize the beautiful thing that they had? Their time together as man and wife had been so short,* he agonized. *It couldn't end now, not when it was just beginning!*

Fervently, Doug began to pray, telling God how sorry he was for not having appreciated Nilakla as much as he should have, promising God that he would never, ever leave her, vowing to be the best husband and father he could be if only God allowed her and their child to live.

It seemed to Doug, though, that his prayers went unanswered, for Nilakla was wracked by the hard-driving contractions again and again, but the baby refused to be born. Doug was beside himself with worry and as his concern deepened he blamed himself for the horror of their situation. Even though he knew Nilakla wouldn't have been happy living back East, he blamed himself for the fact that there was no hospital around, no doctors or nurses close by to help her. In Boston there would have been help available. Guilt weighed heavily upon him.

"Douglas . . ." Nilakla whispered his name, reaching out weakly to touch him. She was exhausted from the strain of the prolonged labor, but she needed to touch him, to make sure he was still there, to pretend for just a little while that everything would be all right. As she was about to speak, a pain wrenched at her, and sweat beaded her forehead. She bit down on her lip to keep from screaming and tasted blood. It twisted her body in its brutal grasp and then faded and was gone.

For Nilakla it was more than the agony of her body that was tormenting her. Her fear grew that her baby, born so early, would die, and her own will to live weakened. She believed that Douglas had only stayed with her this long because of the child, and if the child was lost . . . Without Douglas, Nilakla felt her life had no meaning. Without Douglas, she had no reason to go on. She closed her eyes and gave a deep sigh.

Doug was watching her intently, wondering how a woman could endure the torture she was going through and still survive. When she closed her eyes and went so still again, terror once more seized his soul. He whispered her name hoarsely, fearing she had gone from him. "Nilakla . . ."

She stirred as he said her name and drew a ragged breath before opening her eyes to look at him. "Douglas . . ."

"I'm right here. I love you, darling!" he told her fiercely, wanting to reassure her. When she smiled sadly, he wondered what was wrong. "Nilakla?"

"Don't lie, Douglas." There was a finality to her tone that scared him.

"Lie to you? About what?" he demanded, caught completely unawares by her cryptic statement.

"I know the truth."

"What truth?" Doug was lost to her reasoning.

Nilakla turned her head away so she wouldn't have to look at him.

"What truth?" he repeated.

"I know that you'll leave me just as soon as the baby is born," she said, her tone flat and lifeless.

Doug stared at her in complete surprise. *Leave her after the baby was born? Where had she ever gotten such an idea? Leaving her was the last thing he'd ever do! She was all* he cared about in life, didn't she know that? Didn't she realize that he'd given up everything for her? Nothing mattered to him but her. She was his life, his future, his only reason for existing.

"Nilakla." His voice was strangled with emotion as he moved to sit next to her on the bed. When she still didn't look at him, he reached out and gently cupped her cheek, turning her face to him. "Nilakla, I love you. I would never leave you."

Her dark eyes met his, and for one poignant moment he could see all the anguish and torment that was locked within her.

"But I heard you!"

"You heard me?" Doug frowned, unable to imagine what she was talking about.

Another pain seized her right then, and Nilakla gasped and tightened her hold on his hand. Doug wished that he could make her pain his own. He murmured soothingly to her as he smoothed her hair back from her forehead. When it had passed, and she had relaxed a little, he continued.

"What was it you thought you heard me say, love?"

"I heard you tell Chance *I'll wait until the baby's old enough and then I'll make the trip back*," Nilakla blurted it out.

Doug remembered the conversation very well. "I did tell Chance that," he affirmed in a gentle tone, wanting to comfort her. "I intended for all of us to make the trip together once you and our son were well enough."

Nilakla searched his face for some sign that he was lying, but saw none. "You did?" she whispered, stunned.

"I did, and I still do. I love you, darling," he said earnestly as he bent over her and kissed her softly. "You are my world. I love you, and I'll never leave you . . . never!" he finished devotedly, his voice breaking.

Tears sparkled in Nilakla's eyes as she listened to his

declaration of love and devotion. "Do you mean that, Douglas?"

"I love you, Nilakla," he vowed, his own eyes filling with tears as he lifted her hand to his lips and pressed a cherishing kiss to her palm.

Her heart swelled to near bursting with the joy of her discovery. Happiness filled her, and she lifted her arms to draw him down for a tender, emotion-filled kiss.

"I love you, my husband," she told him.

Doug held her close for a moment, and then as another contraction took her, he lay her back on the bed. He stayed with her, never leaving, never wavering in his vigil. Still, the hours stretched on, but now Nilakla was fighting. She was tired, but she was determined that her son would be born and live. Wild Dove came in often to check her progress, but there seemed to be little change.

As the shadows of dusk lengthened, Nilakla's contractions grew closer and closer together. Wild Dove tried to get Douglas to leave the room, but he refused. He was determined to stay by his wife's side through the entire birth.

Near midnight the pains folded one on top of the other until in a moment of taut silence, Nilakla's and Doug's son was born. Nilakla collapsed back on the bed as Wild Dove took the tiny baby. Douglas kissed his wife joyfully in celebration of the birth of their son, but then they both noticed that it was quiet in the room, too quiet.

"Wild Dove . . . my baby . . ." Nilakla pleaded with the other woman who was standing with her back to them, the babe shielded from their view.

"How is he?" Douglas had unconsciously come to his feet and taken a step toward her when she faced them.

Wild Dove was smiling widely as she held out the tiny,

blanket-wrapped infant to him. "Your son is small but fine," she told them happily.

Douglas was in awe as he took him from her. The baby barely seemed to weigh anything in his big, powerful hands, and Doug stared down at him, enthralled. When he looked up at his wife, his eyes were glistening with unshed tears.

"We have a son, Nilakla. We have a son."

He sat down carefully beside her on the bed and put their child into her arms. The baby nestled against his mother, recognizing her instinctively. Nilakla looked up at her husband, her love for him shining in her eyes. They were a family now, and they would be together forever.

Chance was bored. There was no other way to phrase it. He let his gaze drift around the ballroom crowded with people and wondered what he was doing there.

In the weeks since Rori had gone to live with the Prescotts, he'd lived the life of a hermit, staying home, working all the time and never going out though invitations were constantly pouring in. Tonight, he'd allowed his mother to talk him into escorting her, but now he was rather sorry he had. Without Rori by his side, life had become unbearable.

Chance wondered how much longer he could restrain himself from going over to the Prescotts' and forcing his way inside to confront her. He knew the very thought of him barging into someone's house would outrage his mother's delicate sensibilities, but he still liked to entertain the idea—especially since the note he'd sent to Rori that morning had been returned within the hour, unopened.

"Chance . . . it's so good to see you," Bethany purred, thrilled to find that he'd finally showed up at a party.

He'd been absent from the social scene for so long that she was ready to go directly to his home just to see him.

Chance smiled coolly in greeting the lovely blonde. "Good evening, Bethany. How are you tonight?"

"I'm just fine, but how are you? I haven't seen you at any of the soirées lately, and I was worried that you might be ill or something."

"No," he replied drolly, "I haven't been ill, just busy."

"I see." She gave him her most flirtatious look. "Well, it's just wonderful to see you again."

"Would you like to dance?" he offered, ever the gentleman.

"I'd love to, thank you."

Chance took her in his arms and guided her expertly out onto the dance floor. Bethany was lovely to look at, and she certainly was an excellent dancer, but still he found himself wishing it was Rori in his arms. The one dance he'd shared with her so long ago had spoiled him for other women. There could never be anyone else for him but Rori. He just had to figure out a way to get her, that was all.

Had Bethany been aware of Chance's thoughts, she would have been furious. She knew from Evan that Chance had not seen Aurora since the day she'd moved in with her aunt and uncle. She was hoping that, by now, whatever attachment he had felt to her was fading. She didn't know that she couldn't have been more wrong.

They began to chat as they danced. Since Chance had been closeted away from everyone, Bethany filled him in on all that was going on with their mutual friends. He was paying little real attention to the gossip, just making the right responses at the right times, until she touched on Rori.

"You'll probably be interested to know that Evan has become quite extraordinarily fond of your former

protége." Bethany had deliberately brought up Aurora.
She'd noticed that she didn't have Chance's full attention, and she knew she'd be able to judge how he felt
about the other girl by the strength of his reaction to
her news.

"Rori?" he asked sharply, intent on her every word.

"Why, yes. They've been seeing each other regularly
since my party for you. Didn't you know?" she asked innocently enough.

"No, I hadn't heard."

"Yes, well, it's getting quite serious. I know he's very
serious about her."

Chance tensed at the news. Evan was serious about
Rori? She was as innocent as a lamb going to the slaugh-
ter with him! He knew Strickland like the back of his
hand, and he knew he was a no-good, fortune-hunting
blackguard. He wanted to go to her and tell her, but he
knew there was no point to it. He'd tried once before,
and she hadn't listened. What made him think she'd
listen now? Still . . .

Bethany noticed that he had suddenly seemed to
withdraw from her, and she asked, "Is something wrong?
Have I said something to upset you?"

"No," Chance denied quickly as the music came to an
end. "No, not at all. If you'll excuse me?"

Chance strode off leaving Bethany standing there
fuming as she watched him go. It was time to put their
plan into action. She and Evan had hesitated until now,
allowing nature to take its course, but they could no
longer afford to let things ride. Chance was not changing. He still cared far too much for Aurora, and she had
to get her out of the picture.

Chance realized he was probably being idiotic as he
climbed into his carriage and ordered the driver to the

Prescotts' house. He knew he would probably be turned away again, just as all his previous attempts had been, but he knew he had to try this one last time. It was late, but he didn't care. He was determined to warn Rori about the dangers of getting involved with Strickland. When the carriage pulled to a halt, he got out and moved purposefully up the walk to knock at the front door.

"Why, Chance . . . what a delightful surprise," Charlotte greeted him warmly. She had feared that he'd given up on Aurora completely.

"Good evening, Mrs. Prescott," he replied, surprised by her warmth.

"Won't you come in?" she invited, surprising him even more.

Chance moved into the foyer, puzzled by the change in her attitude. "I was wondering if I could possibly speak with Rori for a few minutes?"

"I'm sorry, Chance, but she's gone out for the evening. Is there anything I can help you with?"

He considered this for a moment and then decided to speak his mind openly. Charlotte Prescott was, after all, Rori's guardian now, and she might not know the truth about Evan Strickland.

"There is something I'd like to talk with you about if you have a moment?"

"Of course. Come into the parlor with me. Joseph has gone out, so I've been here reading all night. It will be pleasant to have some company." She ushered him into the sitting room. "Would you care for a drink? A bourbon, perhaps?"

"No, thank you. I'll just say what I have to say and be on my way."

"All right. Well, sit down and tell me what's troubling you. You look worried about something."

"I am, Mrs. Prescott. I'm worried about Evan Strickland."

"Evan? Why should you be worried about him?"

"I've heard that he's been seeing Rori, and I thought you should know what kind of a man he is."

"Go on," she encouraged. Charlotte wondered if he was going to confirm the suspicions she'd harbored about the far-too-nice Evan.

"I've known him for years. He's nothing but an opportunist, a fortune-hunter, and I don't want to see Rori hurt," Chance told her earnestly.

"What happens to Aurora matters to you, doesn't it?" she asked pointedly.

"It matters very much," he answered, their gazes meeting and locking in complete understanding.

"I'll see what I can do, Chance."

"Thanks. That's all I can ask."

Chapter 35

"Evan!"

The hushed call of his name shocked Evan as he descended from his own carriage and started inside his house late that evening after seeing Aurora. He looked around cautiously, finding it difficult to believe that anyone would be outside his house at this time of night calling him.

"Evan!"

He realized then that the voice was coming from a carriage parked across the street, and he recognized the vehicle as Bethany's.

"Bethany?"

"Yes! Come here, I have to talk to you."

She sounded so distraught, he went to her immediately. "What is it?"

"Get in here so we can speak privately." When he was seated opposite her inside the plush conveyance, she went on. "We have to do something and we have to do it now!"

"Are you talking about Chance?"

"Yes. I swear the man is maddening. You and I both know he hasn't been out socially for weeks now. Tonight, he finally shows up, and he's still as hard to reach as ever. We were dancing and . . ."

"That's something." He tried to sound encouraging.

"Ha!" she scoffed. "The minute I brought up Aurora's name he changed."

"Why did you mention her?"

"Because I had to know the truth, and now I do. He still cares about her."

"So? I'm the only man she's seeing. We've become quite a couple, don't you think?"

"I think we'd better implement our little plan if you want to remain a couple."

"Your worries have no bearing on my relationship with Aurora," he began slowly, and at her sharp intake of breath, he smiled. "But I have no objection to speeding up my 'courtship.' If a compromising situation will lead to a quicker marriage between us, then why not?"

"How soon can we do it?"

"As a matter of fact, we've made plans to go on a picnic tomorrow."

"How about taking her out to your family's hunting lodge?" she suggested, knowing it would be the perfect place for an illicit tryst. "If she's . . . accidentally discovered there with you, alone and in a state of . . . dishabille. Well." Bethany shrugged expressively, her eyes sparkling with malicious venom.

Evan smiled. "It just might work."

"Might?" Bethany scoffed. "It's perfect! Here's what we'll do . . ."

They plotted their actions in detail so each would know exactly what to do and at what time.

"Then I'll show up with several good friends, and we'll 'accidentally' witness everything!"

"And I'll have a rich, beautiful bride within the week," Evan concluded with a smug smile. "It sounds as if it could work."

"It *will* work, my friend," Bethany told him fiercely. "Then, with Aurora *really* out of my way, Chance will be mine."

Evan wondered if Bethany honestly believed Chance would automatically fall into her arms, but he didn't argue the point. This little scenario they'd come up with would give him exactly what he wanted from life—wealth and a gorgeous wife, in that order. He certainly wasn't about to say anything to upset the plan, not when he was going to come out the winner.

Morning couldn't come quickly enough for Evan, and he headed for the Prescott mansion, eagerly anticipating the coming day. The butler admitted him to the house, and he found Aurora dressed and ready for her day in the country with him.

"We're going up to my family's hunting lodge, but I'll have Aurora home long before dark, Mrs. Prescott," Evan assured her.

"You do that, Evan," Charlotte remarked.

Evan glanced at her curiously because her tone was unusually stern. "There are others going along, if that concerns you. Robert Hamlett is going with his fiancée Midge. Diane will be there with Peter. Nancy and Sandra are supposed to come, and I think even Regina and

Bethany may show up. It should be a fine outing. The weather certainly promises to be nice."

"We'll have a good time, and we'll see you later then." Charlotte kissed Rori good-bye as they started from the house. Ever since her conversation with Chance, she'd been having second thoughts about this picnic. She didn't like the idea, but Aurora had been so excited at the prospect of a day out-of-doors, she hadn't had the heart to revoke her consent. Charlotte watched them ride off now, ignoring the instincts that were screaming at her that she was wrong to let Aurora go.

Rori was excited at the thought of spending a day outside. As much as she was enjoying being pampered and spoiled by her aunt and uncle, she missed the life she and Burr had led and the open wildness of the desert. Sometimes, it seemed to her that there were too many people in too small a space here in Boston. She longed for the vastness of the territory where they could ride for miles and never see anyone. Rori doubted that this picnic was going to be anything like a day riding in Arizona, but at least she would be outside in the sunshine, enjoying herself.

Rori gave Evan a sidelong glance as they rode from the city, and she smiled to herself. He had turned out to be the entertaining companion she'd hoped he'd be, and she was glad that they spent a lot of time together. He had kissed her several times, but his embrace held none of the torrid, soul-shattering excitement Chance's had. He was just a nice friend, and the thought of making love to him had never entered her mind.

Evan was beside himself with excitement. He'd been wanting to make love to Aurora for some time now, and he could hardly wait to set his and Bethany's plan into action. He knew that Aurora trusted him completely and that pleased him. When they got to the lodge, things would go perfectly. She might be a little put

out to find that there was no one else there, but he felt
certain he would be able to change her mind. The
thought sent a shaft of desire racing through him. Soon,
very soon, all his wishes would be fulfilled.

Charlotte left the house to go shopping a short time
after Rori and Evan departed. She was in her carriage
heading for the shopping area when she happened to
look out the window to see Midge and Diane strolling
leisurely into one of the dress shops. Charlotte went still
as she eavesdropped on what they were saying before
they disappeared inside the store.

"Let's look here, Diane, and then we'll meet Nancy
and have lunch," Midge said.

*What were they doing here, if they were supposed to be meet-
ing Evan and Aurora in the country?* Charlotte worried.
Suddenly, everything Chance had told her echoed
through her mind, and she knew her niece was headed
for trouble. She rapped on the top of the carriage to get
her driver's attention.

"Take me to the Broderick house at once!" she ordered, and he hurried to do as he was told.

When they arrived, Charlotte climbed quickly out of
the carriage and hurried up to knock on the front door.
When Agatha answered it herself, she was relieved.

"Agatha, dear, I must speak with Chance at once."

"Of course, Charlotte, come in. What is it? Has something happened to Aurora?" she worried.

"Not yet, and with Chance's help, it won't."

"Chancellor!" his mother called.

Chance heard the commotion in the hall and came
out of the study where he'd been working. "Yes, Mother,
what is—Mrs. Prescott, is something wrong?"

"I'm not sure, dear boy, but you're the only one who
can find out."

"What do you mean?"

"Aurora went on a picnic today with Evan Strickland." She paused as she saw Chance's expression grow grim. "Yes, well, he had assured me when they left about an hour ago that there would be a group of others meeting them at the lodge."

"Lodge? What lodge?"

"Strickland's family lodge."

Chance gave a terse nod, for he knew exactly where the secluded cabin was located. "Go on."

"Well, he clearly told me that Diane and Midge would be there, but I just saw them shopping. Now, they could hardly be meeting Aurora and Evan in the country if they're in the shopping district, planning to have lunch out. And, if Diane and Midge aren't at the lodge, how many of the others he told me would be in attendance actually are?" She gave Chance an imploring look as she touched his arm. "Chance, I need your help. If you love Aurora, you must save her now."

"Mother, have one of the servants saddle a horse for me," he ordered tersely as he strode back into the study to get a gun. He didn't know what Strickland was up to, but if he'd hurt Rori in any way . . .

Charlotte and Agatha exchanged relieved looks.

"Wait for me in the parlor. I won't be long," Agatha said before hurrying off to see that a horse was saddled and brought around front for Chance. When Chance had ridden off to find Rori just a few minutes later, Agatha and Charlotte faced each other in the sitting room.

"In a way, I'm glad this happened," Charlotte told Agatha, her eyes twinkling with good humor.

"Why?"

"Because those two young people are in love with

each other, and they're just too stubborn to admit it," she declared firmly.

"I've always suspected as much, but I couldn't understand what happened."

"Evidently they had some kind of misunderstanding, but hopefully, today will clear it all up. I know she's refused to see Chance ever since she came to live with us. It's almost as if she was hiding from him."

"Well, I hope you're right, Charlotte. There's nothing that would make me happier than a match between them. Aurora's the only woman who's ever stood up to Chance, and I'm quite proud of her."

"She is one special young lady . . . stubborn, but special. If she'd just taken the time to talk to him sooner, I'll wager none of this would have happened."

"You're probably right," Agatha agreed with a soft laugh. "But since when do lovers ever do anything the easy way."

The two matrons exchanged delighted, knowing glances as they settled in to await Chance's return.

At that particular moment, that special young lady was facing Evan across the main room of the lodge, her hands on her hips, her temper flaring dangerously.

"What do you mean 'no one is meeting us here'?" Rori demanded, wanting to know why he'd felt the necessity to lie to her aunt.

"Don't be angry, darling," Evan told her, moving to take her in his arms in spite of her initial resistance. "I just wanted to be alone with you. We never have the opportunity to really be by ourselves."

"I don't like it, Evan."

"Why not?" he asked innocently, still not trying to seduce her, only trying to calm her.

"Because you lied to my aunt Charlotte . . . and to me."

"I had to. Do you think for one minute that she would have let you come here with me unchaperoned? I had to convince her that there would be others around or she would have kept you at home."

"That might not have been such a bad idea," Rori responded a bit stubbornly, trying to get away from his hold.

Evan held her fast, though. "Ah, Aurora, you're so lovely. Don't fight me, darling," he murmured, lowering his head to kiss her.

Rori did not refuse him at first. She accepted his kiss as she had all his others—with a remarkable lack of enthusiasm. It annoyed Evan that the romantic country setting and the fact that they were alone did not arouse any passion in her, and he boldly stroked the side of her breast, hoping to stir her emotions a little.

"Evan! Don't!" Rori suddenly began to push against his chest in an effort to break free. No man but Chance had touched her intimately, and she wanted to keep it that way. Evan's caress had felt alien—uncomfortable— and she didn't want him near her.

"Aurora, come on," Evan coaxed, still not letting her go. "Relax. This can be beautiful for the both of us." He bent to try to kiss her again, but she turned her head.

"No, Evan. I don't want you to do this."

"Aurora . . ." He was beginning to lose patience with her. He hadn't expected her to resist him. "We've kissed before. What are you afraid of? It's just you and me, all alone . . ."

"I'm not afraid of anything," Rori said confidently. "I just don't like liars."

That stung, and Evan reacted angrily, pulling her more

tightly to him and capturing her lips in a dominating kiss. "I love you, Aurora. I want you."

But Rori was not about to be forced into anything. She gave a fierce shove just as she bit down on his lip. With a yelp of pain he let her go, but in the effort, her blouse was torn, baring one shoulder.

"I don't care if you do want me. I don't like being manhandled, Evan. Take me home."

Evan wiped at his bottom lip with the back of his hand and was startled to find that it was bleeding. He was furious, but he knew he had only a short time left to get her in what appeared to be a willingly engaged in, compromising position.

"I'm sorry," he apologized abjectly. "I shouldn't have been so forward with you, but I've loved you and desired you for so long now that I just lost control for a minute. Forgive me?"

He sounded earnest, and she eyed him cautiously, no longer fully trusting him. "If you'll take me home."

"As soon as we do something about your blouse." Evan came toward her, looking to all intents and purposes to be sorry for what he did. But the moment he got close enough, he tried once again to take her in his arms. "Aurora . . . just one last kiss before we have to leave."

Rori hoped one more kiss would satisfy him, and she allowed him that. To her dismay, he grew more amorous, deepening the exchange as he pressed himself erotically against her, and she had had enough. She tried to turn her head, but he tangled one hand in her hair to hold her still, murmuring her name seductively.

Rori remembered another time, another place, and another man and knew that she wanted absolutely nothing to do with Evan. Chance was the man she loved, and if she couldn't have him, she didn't want anybody.

"No!" Rori was almost shouting.

Evan paid no heed to her command, touching her boldly in hopes that he could make her feel some desire for him. Rori couldn't stand the feel of his hands upon her. She remembered her encounter with the outlaws all too vividly. She continued to try to elude his pawing.

"Let yourself enjoy this," he urged.

At that, Rori exploded in rage at his refusal to leave her alone. With all the power she could muster, she brought her knee up between his legs. Though she was hampered by her skirts, she still managed to make contact. Evan was shocked as jarring pain jolted through him, and in that moment of surprise, Rori managed to pull free.

"Why you little . . ." Evan's anger was out in the open now, and he came at her, meaning to force her to his will.

His first attempt to grab her failed as she danced out of his reach. When he tried to lunge at her again, the real Rori was ready. She drew back her fist and punched him with all the force she could muster.

"I warned you to keep away from me!" she told him, panting.

Evan stood back for a moment nursing his aching eye. His rage soon consumed him, though, and he made a fierce grab for Rori, yanking her to him.

Chance had made the ride cross-country to make better time. Now, he reined in before the cabin, his gaze narrowing suspiciously as he looked around the quiet setting. He wondered, almost fearfully, what he would find if he went inside. The thought of Rori making love to Strickland drove him from his horse, and he dismounted quickly, charging up the path to the house.

"Rori!" he thundered, pounding on the door. "Rori! Are you in there?!"

"Chance . . ." Rori managed to call out his name in a frightened voice as Evan struggled to control her.

Chance heard her cry, and in a fit of fury kicked the door in. He stood there staring in outrage at the scene before him. Rori was pinned in Strickland's arms, her hair in disarray and her blouse torn. He reacted instantly, launching himself across the room at the other man.

Evan released Rori and turned to defend himself, but he was no match for Chance. Chance pummeled him ferociously, landing blow after punishing blow. Evan tried to block his assault, but met with little success. There was a wild primitiveness about Chance's attack that sent the cowardly Evan scurrying for the door at the first opportunity. In desperation, he fled the lodge.

Chance started to go after him, but Rori's breathless, nervous call stopped him.

"Chance . . . no. . ."

He shuddered as he brought his raging temper under control, and he turned slowly to Rori. "Are you all right?" he asked, his gaze hot upon her.

"Yes. I'm fine."

"Thank God," Chance breathed.

Rori was so completely startled by his unexpected appearance here and the resulting fight that she could only stand and stare at him.

"Rori, did he hurt you?"

"No," she finally managed to say, finding it difficult to believe the fierceness of his actions. Why was he so concerned with what she was doing? He'd made it perfectly clear that he didn't care about her. After all, he was the one who'd kissed up a storm on the porch with good old Bethany and then stayed out all night!

He gave her a scathing look. "Why did you trust him? Did you want this? Did you want to be up here alone with him at this secluded lover's hideaway?"

"Not that it's any of your business, but I didn't believe

he'd get so . . . violent." Rori bristled at his insinuation. "You don't need to protect me if it's so much bother and makes you so mad. I got even with him on my own."

Chance stopped, finally beginning to listen to her. "You did?"

"Yep. Evan's sore in a real delicate, very male place, and I think he'll be sporting a nice shiner tomorrow," Rori related proudly, still mystified that Chance even cared. "I guess you could say it's a good thing I didn't bring my knife with me." Rori grinned at him.

Chance's breath caught in his throat as he stared down at her. Dear God, how he loved her . . . and then she smiled like that, so impishly, so openly and freely, she looked exactly like she had all those months ago when he'd first discovered the sweet truth of her identity. *Rori,* his heart cried out. He wanted to tell her that he loved her. He wanted to tell her the hell he'd been through these last weeks at having to stay away from her. He wanted to tell her that he never wanted to be away from her again. A bolt of lightning desire sizzled through Chance, and he could not stop himself from reaching for her.

Rori knew she shouldn't let him touch her. She knew she should tell him to go away and leave her alone, but somehow logic wasn't dictating this moment. There was nothing logical about what she was feeling, about how she'd longed for him while Evan had been kissing and caressing her. What she was feeling was love, and love was not rational.

Neither spoke as they came together in a cataclysmic embrace. They wrapped their arms around each other, drawing each other as close as possible, as their lips met in a cherishing exchange that erupted into full-fledged passion. It had been so long since they'd touched, since

they'd kissed. It was as if they'd been starved for each
other's nearness and could now feast on that joy.

. Chance's tongue sought and found hers in a deep
caress that sent shivers of awareness shuddering through
Rori. She opened to him, meeting him freely in that
exciting kiss. She wanted him—there could be no
denying it. She wanted him with all her heart and soul.

Chance lifted his head to stare down at her. He could
see the desire in her heavy-lidded, emerald gaze and the
redness of her kiss-swollen lips, and the need he had for
her became a driving madness. He couldn't stop. He
didn't care about anything but making love to her.

"Rori . . ." he murmured her name hoarsely as he
bent to capture her mouth with his once again.

They were lost in the splendor of their embrace, totally caught up in the joy of their closeness. They did not
hear the carriage coming up the drive, and they did not
hear the subdued voices of Bethany, Regina, and Sandra
as they descended from the vehicle to come inside the
house. They knew nothing of the scandal that was about
to erupt. They only knew that they had found each
other and that for this brief instant in time, they could
be together.

Bethany was excited, and it was a fierce excitement.
After today, everything was going to work out just fine.
She was smiling brightly as she led her friends up the
walk to the house.

"I'm sure Evan's here already. He told me that he was
coming out early and that we should meet him right
about now . . ."

Bethany didn't pause as she reached the door, but
opened it and walked on in. She had expected to find
Evan and Aurora in a very compromising position. She
had expected Regina and Sandra to be so taken aback
by it that the news would be all over town by sundown

that day. She had expected Evan and Aurora to be married within the week and the field to be open to Chance's heart.

"Evan?" she called out as they stepped inside, hoping she could fake her surprise.

Bethany and her companions stopped and stood gaping just inside the door. She had no trouble acting stunned. Evan wasn't there. Evan wasn't the one holding Rori. It was Chance!

Chapter 36

Chance stiffened as he heard someone enter the house calling Evan's name.

"Chance?!" Bethany croaked.

Still caught up in the wonder of Chance's embrace, Rori didn't quite understand what was going on. She twisted around in his arms to see Bethany and her friends standing there.

"Bethany?" she whispered, confused.

"Bethany . . ." Chance's voice was strained as he said her name. He realized all too clearly just what the women were thinking, and he let his arms drop away from Rori.

Rori heard the tense emotion in Chance's tone, and when he released her as he did, she thought it was because he was upset over Bethany's having seen them kissing. She stepped away from him to face the three women who were staring at them in wide-eyed curious wonder.

"Hello, Bethany," Rori greeted her with cool composure. She read clearly the surprise and outrage on Bethany's pale face and knew that she was shocked beyond belief by what she'd just seen.

Bethany looked from Rori's torn blouse, messed up hair, and love-flushed features to Chance's rigid posture. "You . . . you slut! You Jezebel!" She didn't wait to see the effect of her words, she just turned and ran from the house.

"Bethany!" Chance called out angrily, wanting to explain things before the rumors started, but she did not turn around. "Damn!" he swore in frustration. He didn't go after her, though, but took a step closer to Rori. Protecting her from whatever the other two might say was more important.

"We . . . ah . . . Evan invited us out for the day, but we had no idea . . ." Regina began stiltedly, glancing after her rapidly retreating friend.

"Evan had to leave unexpectedly." Chance spoke up, shielding Rori's shattered reputation as much as he could, yet knowing that it was already too late. The damage had been done. Rori's disheveled appearance was the silent testimony. He had no doubt that wild gossip about them would be all over Boston by sundown.

"Yes, well, I suppose we'd better go . . ." Sandra added uncomfortably. It was obvious to her that they had interrupted what had been meant to be a *very* private moment. She could hardly wait to get back home so she could tell her mother what they'd seen. Oh, what fun they were going to have with this one! The niece of the mighty Prescotts caught in an illicit rendezvous with Chance! It was just too delicious!

"Yes, let's . . ." Regina agreed, backing from the room with her and quietly closing the door behind them.

Rori was feeling terrible as she stood there with Chance. How had everything turned out so wrong? How had she and Chance ended up kissing? She knew

Bethany was the woman he loved. But now . . . Rori
sighed. She had never wanted to hurt Chance. She knew
he cared for Bethany, not her, and yet their momentary
indiscretion had ruined everything.

"I'm sorry," she told him miserably.

"You're sorry? Evan's the one who should be sorry,"
Chance stated fiercely. "He set this whole thing up,
knowing you were young and gullible enough to fall
for it."

"Fall for what?"

He was patient as he explained, "Our society dictates
that if a young, unmarried woman is found in a compromising situation with an unmarried man, her reputation
will be ruined unless they marry."

Rori looked relieved. "Well, then everything is fine.
Evan was gone when they got here."

Chance smiled softly at her obvious naïveté. "Strickland may have been gone, but I was here."

Rori blanched as she stared up at him. "They think
you and I . . . We'll have to . . ."

Chance nodded his response. He loved her, and he
wanted to protect her. They would be married just as
soon as it could be arranged. He was delighted with the
way things were working out, but the stricken look Rori
was giving him caused his heart to sink.

Rori was beside herself with guilt. She didn't want to
force Chance into a marriage. She knew he had only
come after her today out of a sense of duty, nothing
more. Now, because he had saved her from Evan, he was
going to be stuck marrying her, even though he didn't
love her.

"We'd better go back, Chance," she spoke softly, dishearteningly.

"Rori, I . . ." Chance was ready to tell her everything, but her next words temporarily silenced him.

"Please, just don't say anything. Everything's so mixed up. Just take me home. Please."

Suddenly, seeing how really distressed Rori was, doubts crept into Chance's thoughts. What if she didn't want to marry him? What if she didn't love him? He forced the thought away. If she didn't love him, he would make her love him. He had to, because marriage between them was now a necessity. There was no way around it. Once the gossips got hold of what had gone on here, her reputation would be in shreds.

Chance still wanted to tell her everything, but she was already walking out the door. As upset as she was, he decided to wait until later to declare himself. He would take her home now and talk to her later after she'd had time to calm down a bit.

Bethany sat silently in the carriage on the ride back to Boston. Everything she had ever hoped and dreamed for was ruined. Her perfectly concocted scheme had failed and in the most awful way imaginable. She had expected Aurora to be marrying Evan, but now her own worst fears were coming to pass. Aurora and Chance were going to be married. Bethany knew that for a certainty for Chance was, above all, a man of honor. He would do the right thing by the other woman, and it broke her heart to think of it.

The iciness that had encased her shattered before the violent fury that swept through her. Damn Evan! Damn him! Where had he gone? Why hadn't he been there! And what, oh what, had Chance been doing there?

Chance . . . despair drained her anger from her.

There was no point in going on. There was no point in fighting any longer. It was over. The man she'd loved above all others was now lost to her forever.

Rori knew people were staring at them as they rode double on Chance's mount back into Boston, but she didn't care. All she wanted to do was get home. They didn't speak during the entire trip, and when Chance finally reined in before her house, she didn't wait for him to help her down, but slid unaided from the horse's back.

"Rori." Chance dismounted and went after her as she started inside. "Wait. I want to speak with your aunt."

"Don't worry about it," Rori told him, trying to let him know that he was free to go to Bethany. "I'll handle it. I'll make up something to explain all this. You don't have to get involved at all."

"Rori, I am involved."

"But you don't have to be! Don't you see?"

"No, you're the one who doesn't understand. How do you think I found out that you were at that lodge with Strickland?" At her blank look, he went on, "Your aunt told me. She asked me to go after you. There's no way you can pretend that I wasn't there, Rori. Besides, Bethany, Regina, and Sandra saw us." He was disgusted as he said the last, because he knew what kind of gossip was probably already making its way through the rumor mill.

Rori heard the disgust in his tone and assumed he was upset because Bethany had seen them kissing.

"Then I'm sorry. I didn't mean for any of this to happen." She opened the door and came face-to-face with the butler.

"Miss Aurora! What happened to you?"

"Nothing. It's not important," she answered wearily. "Is Aunt Charlotte here?"

"No, Miss Aurora, she's out."

"See, Chance," she threw back at him as she crossed the foyer and started up the staircase, "she's not even here. You can go on and leave."

For a moment, Chance watched her mounting the steps slowly, almost as if she was defeated. His spirits sank because he thought she understood that they would have to be married right away, and she didn't want to marry him. "All right, Rori, but I'll be back."

Depressed, Chance let himself out and headed home to tell his mother and Charlotte what had happened.

"Oh, my," Agatha said after listening to Chance's explanation.

"Oh, my, is right, Agatha dear," Charlotte added. She was fighting down an urge to smile, for in her opinion things couldn't have worked out any better. "How is Rori taking it?"

"She wasn't happy, that's for sure," Chance remarked. "And she kept apologizing, although I don't know why. None of this was her fault. If I just hadn't kissed her . . ."

"It still would have looked equally as compromising, Chancellor," his mother pointed out. "Judging from what you've told me about the state of Aurora's clothing and hair, she looked rather unkempt. Is that true?"

"Yes."

"So even if you hadn't been kissing her, just the fact of your presence there with her would have ruined her."

"I know," he admitted reluctantly. "How soon do you think we can arrange a marriage?"

"Reverend Bailey is a dear family friend," Charlotte said. "I'm sure we can work something out for tomorrow—late afternoon, shall we say? I'd love to hold the ceremony at the house, if the reverend approves."

"That'll be fine," Agatha pronounced pleasantly, "and I'll plan to have the wedding feast here afterward."

"Sounds delightful. Shall we see about making our plans?" Charlotte was eager to begin.

"By all means. Just think, by this time tomorrow, we'll be family." The two older women shared a secret smile and then bustled from the room to begin their tasks of love.

When they had gone, Chance remained alone in the parlor, thinking about the events of the day. When Strickland's deception came to mind, Chance's anger returned. He hated the man. He had for a long time, and this whole ordeal just served to convince him that he'd been right. The man was a no-good opportunist. He had lured Rori to the country on false pretenses, and now her reputation was in ruins. None of this would have happened if it hadn't been for him. Yet, as Chance thought about it, he realized that he really should thank Strickland. Tomorrow, because of him, Rori would become Mrs. Chancellor Broderick.

Chance thought about his future . . . and the woman who would be his wife. He thought of the first time they'd met when he'd rescued her from the fight in the street, and a tender smile curved his lips. He'd been in love with her from the first time they'd touched. She was all fire and passion and everything he'd ever wanted in a woman. He had to admit that he was really glad that the whole thing had happened. He wanted this marriage. He loved Rori, and he wanted to spend the rest of his life with her. What bothered him was that he wasn't sure she wanted that, too. Somehow he had to convince Rori that he loved her.

Rori was lying on the bed in her room with Big Jake, trying to figure out what to do next. She was considering going to see Bethany to tell her that there was nothing between her and Chance, that the embrace she'd witnessed had just been an accident and that she was the woman he really loved. She wanted Chance to be happy, and she thought that clearing things up with Bethany would make him happy. Rori had almost decided to do it, when the knock came at her door.

"Yes?"

"It's me, darling," Charlotte responded. "May I come in?"

"Sure, Aunt Charlotte." Rori was a bit nervous about what her aunt was going to have to say.

Charlotte entered to find Rori sitting in the middle of her bed with her dog. Rori had changed into a plain blouse and skirt and had pulled her ebony hair back away from her face before letting it tumble freely down her back. She looked very young and vulnerable, despite the slight wariness reflected in her eyes.

"Aurora . . ." Charlotte regretted deeply that their carefree days together here were ending. Tomorrow, a whole new life would be opening up for her. Tomorrow, Rori would marry Chance.

"Yes?"

"Do you think we could talk for a while?" she ventured as she closed the door behind her and came to sit beside her on the bed. "There are a few things we need to discuss."

"I know," Rori replied with a heavy sigh.

Charlotte slipped a supportive arm about her shoulders and gave her a warm, loving squeeze. "Come now, it's not as bad as all that."

"Have you talked to Chance? Do you know what happened?"

"Yes. I know everything."

"You do?" The news surprised her. "Oh, well, would you care if I went over to Bethany's house then, and try to get this whole thing straightened out with her? I figured if I just told her the truth, everything would be all right. She wouldn't be so mad at Chance, and everything would be fine between them again."

"I know honesty seems like the simplest approach, but I'm afraid it won't work in this situation," Charlotte told her gently.

"Why not?"

"It's too late. The wedding arrangements have already been made for tomorrow afternoon, sweetheart." Her heart ached for Rori as she read the misery in her face.

"But Chance doesn't want to marry me!"

"You may rest assured that Chance wouldn't marry you unless he wanted to," Charlotte said confidently.

"Why is he doing this?" Rori cried miserably.

"He doesn't want to see you hurt, dear."

"But this is all Evan's fault! He shouldn't have to pay the price for Evan's deceit."

"It doesn't matter whose fault it was. The point is Bethany, Regina, and Sandra walked in on you and Chance in what is regarded as a compromising situation. Your blouse was torn and your hair . . . ?"

"Yes. Evan and I had a little run-in before Chance showed up, but he didn't hurt me. If Evan had just brought me home when I asked him to, then none of this would have happened!"

"But you must understand that Evan had no intention of bringing you home until after you were discovered by the others. Now, tell me." Charlotte paused as she gently turned Rori to face her. "Would you rather be marrying Evan tomorrow?"

"Well . . . no," Rori admitted reluctantly, her green eyes dark and clouded with worry.

"Then let's not talk about what might have been. There's no point in going over it anymore." Her tone lightened as she continued. "Right now, we have your wedding to plan."

"My wedding . . ." Rori repeated, still stunned by all that was happening so quickly.

"Aurora," Charlotte said her name more solemnly as she held her hand in hers, "I'd be honored if you'd wear my wedding dress."

"But why?" she asked, not understanding the tradition.

"Because I love you very much. You're the daughter I always wanted but never had."

Rori gave her aunt a pleading look. "Aunt Charlotte, I don't want to marry Chance. He's not in love with me. Bethany's the one he loves."

"You're wrong, Aurora," she said firmly, her steady, assured gaze holding Rori's.

"I wish I was," Rori began, almost opening up and telling her everything, but she stopped, knowing there was no point in discussing it, "but I know I'm not."

"Time will tell, my dear," Charlotte said calmly as she patted her hand. "Now, about the ceremony . . . it will be held here at midafternoon, and . . ."

Some time later, Rori lay upon her bed, tossing and turning and unable to sleep. So much had happened and in such a short period of time that she felt dazed and confused. How could a day that had promised to be so much fun have turned into a disaster? She had started out that morning thinking she was going to have a day in the country and had ended up a ruined woman.

It would have been almost laughable if it wasn't so tragic. Now, here she was about to be married to a man who didn't love her. He was being forced by this Eastern society's stupid rule to do something she believed he didn't want to do, and it broke her heart to think about it.

Rori had always longed to have Chance for her own, but she didn't want him this way. Surely, being forced went against his grain. He would come to resent her with time and maybe even eventually hate her.

Rori couldn't bear the thought of his scorn, and that terrible prospect forced her to make a decision. She would not go through with the wedding. They certainly couldn't force her to marry him if she absolutely refused to. She would tell her aunt and uncle that she wanted to take Jakie and go home to the cabin she and Burr had shared back in Arizona. Life was certainly simpler in the territory, and she thought she might be able to find happiness there.

"What do you think, big guy? Do you want to go home?" she whispered to him as she hugged him close.

Jake lifted his big head and gave her a curious look.

"I know you like it here, but we can't stay."

He gave a low-throated whine, and Rori scowled at him. "No back talk, dog. We gotta go home, just the two of us. We'll be all right. You'll see." Rori was talking to Jakie, but in truth she was talking to herself. She knew it would be lonely. She knew she would miss her aunt and uncle, but it didn't matter. Anything would be better than being trapped in a loveless marriage. "I'm going down and tell them now. You wait here, and when I come back up, we'll start packing."

Chance was restlessly pacing the study. He stopped in the middle of the room to rub the back of his neck in a weary gesture. With a grimace, he forced himself to make the decision he'd been trying to avoid for hours. He was going to go to Rori and tell her that he loved her, and he was going to go now.

Chance knew that he'd delayed long enough. The thing that was holding him back, though, was that he didn't know quite what to say to her. He'd never told a woman that he loved her. He had always expected it would be a simple matter when the time finally came, but there was nothing simple about facing Rori tonight. Girding himself to face her, he strode from the room on his way to the Prescotts'.

"Aunt Charlotte . . . Uncle Joseph . . ." Rori paused, waiting until she had their full attention as she stood in the doorway of the parlor.

"Yes, dear, what is it?" Charlotte asked as she looked up from where she sat by her husband on the love seat.

"I . . . uh, I've decided something." Rori found herself hesitating because she knew her decision was going to hurt them.

"Yes?"

"I want to go home," she blurted out, much as a small child would.

Her aunt and uncle frowned, not understanding.

"But, Aurora," Joseph remarked, "you are home."

"No . . . I mean, it's nice here, and I love you both very much, but I want to go home to Arizona. Grampa and I had a small cabin. Jakie and I could live there . . ."

"I'm sorry, Aurora, but the answer is no. You're our niece. We love you, and we want what's best for you," he attempted to explain.

"Please, please don't force me into a loveless marriage!" Tears welled up in her eyes, and her voice was strangled. Not wanting to break down in front of them, she turned and ran back up the stairs.

Joseph gave Charlotte a troubled look, but she just smiled serenely.

"Pre-wedding jitters, darling. I recall I had them myself."

"You did?" Joseph's eyes rounded in surprise at her confession.

"Every young girl does, my darling. Wait here. I'll handle it."

Someone knocked on the door as Charlotte started out into the foyer, and she answered it herself. She was surprised and pleased to find Chance there.

"You're just the young man I wanted to see," she declared, her eyes aglow with delight over his perfect timing.

"I am?"

"Yes, you are. You love Aurora, don't you?"

"Yes."

"Have you told her yet?"

"Well, no," he admitted a little sheepishly, intending to explain the situation to Charlotte, but she gave him no opportunity.

"And why not? You had all afternoon, for heaven's sake!"

"I didn't have the chance to explain things to her . . ."

"What is this younger generation coming to?" she scolded in exasperation. "Get up those stairs, young man. Take her in your arms and kiss her. Tell her the truth right now. Aurora thinks that you're in love with Bethany and only marrying her out of a sense of duty."

"She does?"

"Yes. Now, hurry. She's all set to go home to Arizona."

Chance hurried up the staircase as Charlotte called out from below, "Get the right room! It's the third bedroom on the left."

Rori was crying, and her tears were nearly blinding her as she threw open the small suitcase. She started rummaging through her closet in search of the few things she needed for the trip back. She pulled out two of her plainest gowns and tossed them on the bed, then started digging through the vast array of clothes again. When she found her old buckskins tied in a bundle at the back of the closet, she clutched them to her breast and sobbed brokenheartedly. Sitting down in the middle of the closet floor, she gave up fighting her misery. She buried her face in her hands and began to cry.

Chance knocked on the door, and when no one answered, he opened it slowly.

"Rori?" He said her name softly as he stepped inside. He heard her crying, and the sound of her ragged, desolate weeping drove him across the room to the closet. "Rori?"

Rori couldn't believe it. Chance was here? Why? Her gaze was tormented as she stared up at him. He appeared so tall and strong and handsome as he loomed over her. She remembered the heaven of being in his arms, resting against the powerful width of his chest. She longed for the safety of that haven now, but she knew it could never be. Trying to pull herself together, she got to her feet, her motions jerky and awkward.

"Chance, go away and leave me alone!" she demanded as she grabbed up a dress and stomped out of the closet, trying to wipe the tears from her cheeks as she went.

"I can't. We have to talk." Chance was stunned by the depth of her misery.

"There's nothing left to talk about," she snapped as she threw her buckskins into the suitcase and started folding up the other things in abrupt, hurried motions. She deliberately avoided meeting his gaze as she worked at packing her clothes.

"Why? What's the rush?"

"The rush is I'm leaving," she told him over her shoulder.

"Oh, no, you're not."

"Oh, yes, I am!" Rori was so upset that she started just tossing items into the suitcase.

"You're not leaving Boston. You're not going anywhere." Chance came to stand beside her. As quickly as she was throwing things into the suitcase, he was yanking them out again.

"I'll go anywhere I like, Chance. You're not my guardian anymore," she said hotly, glaring up at him mutinously as her tears continued to fall. She snatched up the garment he'd just pulled out of the suitcase and stuffed it back in again.

"I'm not your guardian anymore, but by this time tomorrow, I'm going to be your husband."

"No!" she cried, trying to hide her misery with false bravado. "Go away and leave me alone."

"I won't go away, not until we've talked. If you still want me to go, once you've listened to me and heard what I've got to say, I will."

"Chance, you don't have to tell me anything. I don't want to force you into a marriage. I know you love Bethany, so marry her. I won't stand in your way." She almost broke down completely as she spoke. "There. See? Now there's nothing left for you to say. Just leave, so I can finish my packing."

"Rori . . ." he said her name gently. "There most certainly is something left for me to say."

"What?" She turned away so she wouldn't have to look at him and started putting things in the suitcase again.

"Rori . . ." He inhaled deeply, then said his next words with deep passion, "Rori, I love you."

Chapter 37

Rori's heart skipped a beat at his declaration, and she went completely still. *He'd said it* . . . the words she'd always longed for him to say . . . and he'd said it with such a depth of feeling that she was shaken to her very soul. Did he really love her or was this just a ploy to make her go through with the wedding?

"Rori? Did you hear me?" Chance had expected some response from her, and her unusual silence worried him. He'd never known Rori to be at a loss for words. "Rori?" Chance's expression was infinitely tender as he reached out to take her by the shoulders and turn her around to face him. He took the dress she was clutching from her and tossed it carelessly aside while his eyes held hers. "Rori. I love you."

Rori stared up at him almost afraid to speak. "You don't have to say these things just to make everything seem better."

"I'm not just saying these things, Rori. I really mean them." He lifted one hand to gently wipe the tears from her face.

His touch sent a thrill through her, but she fought against it. "I want a husband who loves me," she whispered, not yet daring to believe that it could be true.

"That's what you're going to have," Chance vowed. "A husband who loves you and only you . . ." He wanted to drag her into his arms and kiss her until she cried out with desire for him, but he held himself back. He wanted to share more than passion with Rori. When they came together again, he wanted it to be a joining of two people in love, a joining of man and wife.

"But . . ." she started to protest, still believing that he truly cared for Bethany.

"I've been trying to tell you for weeks how I felt," Chance interrupted, smiling tenderly, "but you wouldn't let me get near you. I love you, Rori Prescott."

Rori wanted to believe, but she had to know the truth about Bethany. "What about Bethany?!" Rori voiced her reason for not trusting him. "I was in the study that night of her party, and I saw you with her out on the porch."

"I thought you might have. It's just a shame that you didn't stay around longer."

"I couldn't stay there. It hurt me too much to see you with her! You were kissing her!"

"I did kiss her. I admit it. But the kiss was more one of good-bye than anything. There's a dark-haired woman with eyes like sparkling emeralds who holds my heart, Rori. A woman whose kiss is more potent than the finest liquor."

Her expression was slowly losing its guarded edge.

"It's true. If you'd stayed there in the study another few minutes you would have heard me tell Bethany that I didn't love her."

"You say you don't love Bethany, but ever since I met you, she's the only woman you've talked about," Rori challenged.

Chance frowned, trying to remember any references he'd made to the other woman. "When?"

"That night you were attacked in your room and I saved you, all you could talk about was Bethany and how nice it would have been to spend the night in her bed."

"You were jealous even then?" Chance teased, thrilled to hear it.

Rori flushed, but ignored his remark as she continued. "You even told Grampa that you were thinking about marrying her!"

"The most important word in that sentence is 'thinking,' Rori. I can't deny that Bethany and I have been . . . er . . ." He paused, trying to phrase it delicately. "More than friends. But that was all before you, Rori. I haven't wanted any woman but you since the first time I touched you . . . Hell, almost since the first time I saw you." He took her by the shoulders and drew her closer.

"You haven't?" The heat of his nearness was searing her senses, and she trembled before the power of her attraction for him.

"No, and these weeks apart have been hell for me. You may have been jealous of Bethany, but I was livid over your seeing Strickland. Every time I heard that you were out with him, I wanted to go after you and drag you back here with me. Only your aunt's advice to give you some time, kept me from making a damned fool of myself." He grinned bemusedly.

Rori gave a small, warm laugh of real delight to know that he'd been as miserable as she. "I thought you were out with Bethany having a wonderful time."

"I haven't seen Bethany or anyone, Rori. You're the only woman I want or need. I've missed you," Chance told her, his voice lowering seductively.

"I've missed you, too, desperately."

"Then why wouldn't you see me? I came to see you that day after the party because I wanted to tell you that I loved you. I was going to ask you to marry me. You mean everything to me, Rori." His voice deepened with profound emotion. He lifted both hands to frame her face, his eyes meeting and locking ardently with hers in a mesmerizing exchange. "I love you, Rori, with all my heart and soul."

Rori stood motionless, totally enchanted. Chance loved her . . . If it was true, then . . .

"But Chance, I . . ."

"Hush, Rori. I'm tired of words . . . of talking . . . Let me show you how much I love you," he groaned as he bent to her. His lips touched her forehead reverently, then her eyelids and the corners of her mouth, then the sensitive area of her neck.

Tumultuous emotions swept through her . . . love, joy, hope. She had waited so long, had wanted this for so long . . . Was this really happening? Did Chance really love her?

One of Chance's hands slipped to the nape of her neck in a warm caress as the other slid down to the curve of her waist to draw her to him. "Ah, Rori, I love you so . . ."

His mouth finally moved over hers, claiming it in a possessive, yet cherishing kiss, and she had the answer to all her questions. Her doubts were erased in an explosion of sweet ecstasy. *Chance loved her . . . Chance loved her!*

Chance was so desperate to convince Rori of his devotion that he put everything he was feeling into that embrace. With exquisite tenderness and carefully restrained ardor, he revealed just how much he adored her. She was his life and his future. With her by his side, he could do anything; without her, life had no meaning and he just existed.

When the kiss ended, Chance lifted his head to gaze down at her. His eyes were glowing darkly with an inner fervor, but there was also a shadow of apprehension reflected there as he waited for her to speak.

Rori stared up at him, her green eyes wide and sparkling. "Oh, Chance . . . I love you, too! I always have!"

"God, Rori. I was beginning to think that I'd never hear you say those words." He crushed her to him, holding her to his heart. "Will you marry me, Rori Prescott? Will you be my wife?"

"Yes, Chance. Oh, yes!" She looped her arms about his neck and pulled him down to her for a flaming, wildly passionate kiss.

They were so engrossed in the heat of their embrace that neither one of them heard the knock at the door or heard it open. Charlotte entered and was not at all surprised to find them locked in a heated embrace. She stood there in the doorway, a smile of pure joy upon her face. She had been right! They did love each other. She waited, giving them a moment before clearing her throat loudly.

"I think it's safe to assume everything's fine between the two of you?" she asked archly.

Chance and Rori looked up, startled. Still stung by her earlier experience with "compromising" positions, Rori nervously tried to move out of the circle of his arms, but he held her fast, refusing to let her go.

"Rori's agreed to become my wife," he announced proudly.

"That's wonderful!"

"I love him, Aunt Charlotte," Rori confessed, glowing with happiness.

"I'm so thrilled for both of you. Let's go downstairs and tell your uncle the news. I'm sure he'll be pleased to know that everything's worked out as we'd hoped it would."

"All right."

"We can go over the plans for the ceremony, too, while you're here, Chance. We've got less than twenty-four hours left, you know, and I want to make sure everything goes perfectly."

"So do we," they both agreed as they followed Charlotte from the bedroom, their gazes fixed raptly on each other.

Chance stood before the mirror in his bedroom, looking appraisingly at himself. He straightened his white silk tie one last time, then moved to don his coat. The knock at the door surprised him.

"Come in," he called out, settling the dress coat across his shoulders and adjusting his cuffs.

"Chancellor, darling . . ." Agatha came sweeping into the room, resplendent in her gown for the wedding. "I need to speak with you for a moment . . ."

"Well." He turned toward his mother, spreading his arms out and grinning boyishly. "What do you think? Do I look all right?"

Agatha had never seen Chance look any handsomer. In his dress clothes and white tie, he looked wonderful. She smiled brightly, but the tears in her eyes were very real as she went to hug him. "You look magnificent, my handsome son. Your father would be very proud of you today."

"I hope so," Chance responded, his voice a bit gruff as he gave her a tender kiss on the cheek.

"He would be. You've grown into a fine man. You're everything he ever hoped you'd be, and you've chosen a wonderful young woman for your bride. Be happy, Chance," she said lovingly as she lifted a hand to touch his cheek.

"I will be. I love her, Mother."

"I know, and she loves you." Agatha smiled.

"Are you about ready to go?" Chance asked, ready for the wedding, eager to make Rori his.

"Yes, but first I have a little surprise for you."

"A surprise?"

Agatha handed him a key. "I've sent several of the servants on ahead to our house at the shore, dear. It will be ready for you and your bride by the time you arrive there this evening. Enjoy your honeymoon."

"Thank you, Mother." Chance was pleased.

"Your father and I spent our honeymoon on the coast . . ." she told him, remembering those wonderful, love-filled days so long ago.

"Well, I hope our marriage will be as happy as yours was."

"It will be," Agatha said with a soft smile as she gazed up at him adoringly. "I love you, darling." She hugged her oldest son, remembering him as a boy, marveling at how big he'd grown and how he'd turned into such a fine man. *Had the years really gone by that quickly?* she asked herself, trying not to let her tears fall, but failing. At Chance's concerned look, she hastened to reassure him as she dabbed at her eyes with her lace handkerchief. "They're happy tears, dear, just happy tears."

"I love you, Mother." He hugged her tightly one more time and kissed her cheek gently, with deep affection.

"Shall we go to your wedding?"

"I can't believe it's almost time," Rori said as she started upstairs with Charlotte to get ready for the ceremony.

"I know. Isn't it thrilling?"

"Yes. I thought I was going to be nervous, but I'm not. I'm excited," Rori confided as they entered her bedroom to find that Mildred, Aunt Charlotte's maid, had already drawn a bath for her and laid out her clothing.

"That's the way it should be, dear."

"You know, I miss Chance already," she told Charlotte.

"Well, after today, you'll never have to be apart again."

"I know." Rori smiled. "Isn't it wonderful?"

"It most certainly is," she replied. "Do you have everything you need here?"

"I think so, Aunt Charlotte."

"Fine. If you need anything else, just call. I'm going to go get dressed myself, and I'll send Mildred to you as soon as she's finished with my hair."

When Charlotte had gone, Rori quickly shed her clothes and stepped into the heated bath. The water was a relaxing balm, and Rori leaned back in the tub to enjoy its soothing warmth. Thoughts of the upcoming nuptials blended with distant memories of her mother and father and the warmth of their love that she could still remember after all this time. She was determined to make her marriage to Chance as special as theirs had been. She thought of Burr, too, and regretted deeply that he wasn't there to share in her happiness.

A single tear traced a tender path down her cheek as she whispered out loud, "I love you, Grampa."

Chance reentered her thoughts then, and she realized that she couldn't relax in the bath any longer, for he would be arriving at any moment. She had to hurry! She couldn't be late for her own wedding!

As Rori picked up the perfumed soap, the memory of the bath Chance had given her came to mind. She smiled in appreciation of that night and hoped with all her heart that the night to come would be even more exciting. She gave a shiver of excitement at the thought and hurried to finish washing.

A short time later Rori was seated at the dressing table wearing only her chemise, watching her reflection as the very talented Mildred worked on her hair. The maid fashioned her raven tresses up on top of her head in a style that gave Rori a regal look, emphasizing her fine bone structure and making her eyes seem even bigger than they were.

It was time to put on her dress then, and with Mildred's help she slipped into Charlotte's keepsake wedding gown. Only slight alterations had been needed, and it fit her perfectly now, the long-sleeved, high-necked, white-satin and-lace gown clinging to her every curve with demure sensuality. Rori stared at herself breathlessly in the full-length mirror as Mildred busily straightened the skirts.

"It's beautiful . . ." Rori breathed.

"Yes, *you're beautiful*," Mildred told her with a smile, admiring how the modest style complemented her.

Charlotte knocked and came into the room, saying, "The guests are starting to arrive, Aurora, and . . ." Her gaze fell upon Rori, and she paused in wonder. "Darling, you are absolutely enchanting."

"Thank you, Aunt Charlotte."

Charlotte came to her and kissed her. "If you were my own daughter, I couldn't be more proud or happy for you. I have it from a reliable source that your intended is downstairs already and that he's anxiously awaiting your appearance."

"Chance is here? He's waiting downstairs?" Rori repeated excitedly.

"He certainly is, and looking quite handsome, too, I might add."

A tingle of anticipation shot through her. *Chance was here . . . Chance was waiting.*

"But before we get your veil and start downstairs, I have something for you."

"You do?"

Charlotte quickly stepped back out into the hallway and came back into the room carrying a good-sized dress box.

"What is it?"

"Open it and see," she encouraged her niece.

Charlotte was smiling as she watched Rori tear the ribbon off the gift and part the tissue that was wrapped carefully around the garment within.

"Oh . . ." Rori picked up the delicate gossamer white negligee with great care. "Oh, it's lovely. It's the most lovely nightgown I've ever seen." She lifted her wide-eyed gaze to her aunt's.

"You like it?"

"I love it!" Rori told her earnestly as she went to embrace her. "Thank you."

"I thought you needed something special for tonight."

"You've given me so much," Rori said in a choked, emotional voice. "How can I ever repay you and Uncle Joseph for all you've done for me?"

"My darling, you've already repaid us, more than you'll ever know. You've brought love and laughter into our lives and given us so much happiness. We love you."

"And I love you," Rori sniffed.

"Now, now, don't you start. I'll have no crying brides at this wedding!" Charlotte scolded lovingly. "Are you ready to put on your veil?"

"Is it time?"

The faint sound of music drifted upstairs from the parlor below where the guests and Reverend Bailey were waiting with the anxious bridegroom.

"It's time," Charlotte answered as she got the veil and helped Rori put it on. "You're lovely, darling. Every bride should be so stunning."

"Do you think Chance will think so?"

"Without a doubt," she promised, and they left the room on their way to meet Joseph at the top of the staircase.

* * *

The furniture in the parlor had been rearranged to make room for everyone, and the profusion of fresh-cut flowers Charlotte had insisted upon for the occasion lent their delicate fragrance to the room. The Reverend Bailey stood with Chance before the intimate group of family and friends gathered there, waiting for the bride to make her entrance on the arm of her uncle. When the organist changed his tempo to announce her coming, Chance looked toward the door and saw his love.

Chance's breath caught in his throat at the sight of Rori. She was exquisite. He stared in fascination at the dark-haired beauty walking toward him, vaguely remembering a young Indian boy who'd pulled a knife on him and cussed him out thoroughly.

Rori's gaze was focused only on Chance. He looked so handsome, standing there before the minister, so tall and broad-shouldered, that her heart swelled with the love she felt for him. It seemed as if she was walking on air as she approached him on her uncle's arm. She could hardly believe that this was really happening. If this was a dream she was caught up in, then she never wanted it to end.

Chance smiled down at her as Joseph stopped before him.

"Who gives this woman in marriage?" the reverend asked.

"I do," Joseph replied, and he handed her over into Chance's safekeeping and then stepped back to join Charlotte and Agatha.

Chance and Rori exchanged special looks as the minister started the ceremony.

"We are gathered here today to witness the joining in holy matrimony of Chancellor Mason Broderick and Aurora Prescott . . ." he intoned.

Rori and Chance were held spellbound by his words, taking to heart everything the man of God said. They recited their vows with love and joy, pledging themselves to each other without question, and when Reverend Bailey instructed Chance to put the wedding ring on Rori's finger, he was ready.

"With this ring, I thee wed," he repeated the minister's words slowly.

Rori's hand was trembling as Chance slipped the slim gold band on her finger. She gazed up at him, filled with wonder at the beauty of their love.

"By the power invested in me, I now pronounce you man and wife. What God had joined together, let no man put asunder," Reverend Bailey declared. "You may kiss your bride, Mr. Broderick."

Chance and Rori stared at each other in rapturous delight before he gathered her close and kissed her with sweet abandon.

"I love you, Mrs. Broderick," he whispered as the embrace ended and they moved slightly apart.

Rori's eyes misted with tears of happiness, and she couldn't resist pulling him down to her for one more quick kiss before turning to greet their well-wishers. The day had been perfect except for Burr's absence, but Rori knew he had to be watching from heaven.

Chapter 38

The wedding feast Agatha gave in Chance and Rori's honor was impressively elegant. Each course was a sumptuous gourmet's delight, but Chance and Rori paid little attention to the dishes placed before them. They were too caught up in rapturous wonder of their love for each other. Each time their gazes met, their pulses would quicken in anticipation of the night to come, and when their hands accidentally touched, the excitement was electrifying.

It was only with a superhuman effort that Chance managed to control his desire for her. He wanted her desperately, but knew he could not sweep her up into his arms and carry her off like some knight of old during the middle of the wedding banquet.

Rori, too, was feeling the strain. Being so close to Chance and not being able to touch him or kiss him was driving her wild. She wanted to escape the gathering of loving well-wishers. Rori wanted to throw herself into his arms and spend the night making passionate love to him. It had been so long since they'd been together, and she was on fire with the need to know the fullness of his possession once again.

By the time the carriage was brought around to whisk them off to their honeymoon destination, it was dusk, and they were desperate for a moment alone. They were both more than ready, in fact, almost eager, to be spirited away.

After changing to simpler garb to make the trip, they bid their families and friends good-bye and climbed into the waiting conveyance. As soon as they started to pull out of the driveway, Chance wasted no time in reaching for the shades.

"What *are* you doing?" Rori asked in an amused tone as she settled back in her seat.

"I'm arranging a little privacy for us, my love," Chance told her huskily as he drew down the last window covering. Enclosed in their own heavily shadowed haven, he dictated, lustily, "Come here, wife. I've waited as long as I can."

Rori gave a light laugh as she moved easily into his arms. "You've restrained yourself admirably."

"I thought so," Chance said smugly, quite pleased with

himself, "considering I was ready to throw you over my shoulder and make a great escape at least a dozen times during dinner." He stared down at Rori in the dimness of the carriage, studying her loveliness. He knew that she held him in the palm of her hand and that he was hers forever. "God, you're beautiful," he declared as he kissed her.

It was a sweet, adoring exchange, their lips touching lightly, tentatively. When it ended, Chance gave a slightly frustrated sigh. He had thought that he would be able to hold Rori, share a few kisses, and just enjoy her closeness on the trek to the cottage, but now he knew he'd been crazy to even consider it. She was like a fire in his blood, and just one taste of her was not enough.

"It's going to be a very long drive to the beach house," he complained.

"I kind of thought it was going to be a long, wonderful drive," Rori teased sensually as she ran one hand over his chest, toying with the buttons on his shirt, but not unfastening them. "I mean, we're all alone here in this fancy carriage . . ." She had been aching for his touch all day and she didn't want to wait any longer.

Chance gave a choked groan as he grabbed her hand to stop her. Her play sorely tempted his passions. It would take very little to encourage him to lay her down right there and make love to her in the confines of the carriage. He wanted their wedding night to be perfect, though, not just a quick, hurried joining on their way to the cottage.

"Don't, love," Chance ordered weakly.

"Don't?" Rori lifted one eyebrow expressively in mock disbelief. "I don't take well to bein' ordered around, Broderick," she drawled, sounding like her old self. "You, of all people, should know that."

"You promised to 'obey,'" he quickly pointed out with a grin.

"So did you," she returned as she pressed herself against him and looped her arms around his neck.

"I did, didn't I?" Chance pretended surprise, and as Rori kissed his throat, he gave up trying to control himself. "I suppose I'd better not break any of my vows . . ." He surrendered to her seductive ploys with gusto, capturing her mouth for an intoxicating exchange.

Their lips met and parted as Chance pulled Rori across his lap. He wrapped his arms around her in a fiercely protective embrace as his mouth plundered hers. His tongue sought out her tongue in a love-duel, and she willingly met him in that intimate, erotic caress.

"Oh, Chance . . . I love you," she whispered, gazing up at him adoringly when the kiss had ended.

His expression was completely serious as he stared down at her in the semidarkness. "There was a time there when I thought I'd never hear you say those words, love."

"You'll never have to worry about that again. I'll tell you every minute of every day if you want me to," Rori offered giddily.

"That means we'll just be talking all the time, doesn't it? I don't think I like that idea at all."

"You don't?"

"No. There are other things I'd rather be doing with you than talking . . ."

"Oh? Such as?"

"Such as showing you, instead of telling you," he answered, kissing her again, and this time there was no doubt about what he wanted and needed.

Chance put all the love he was feeling into that embrace. What little restraint he'd managed to retain over his raging desire was lost when Rori matched him in his eagerness. Fiery passion exploded between them, and they strained together as they kissed and then kissed again, each exchange growing more and more heated.

"Love me, Chance," Rori begged.

Chance knew he could not deny her or himself any longer. With trembling hands Chance began to work at the buttons on her bodice. When they were undone, he parted the material and shifted her chemise aside, freeing her sensuous flesh to his questing touch. He caressed the pale, sensitive mounds with ardor, glorying in the way the crests tautened against his palms. Wanting to be nearer, needing more than just these maddeningly arousing caresses, Chance laid Rori back on the seat. Though it was cramped, neither seemed to notice as he began to press hot, devouring kisses to her breasts.

Rori moaned in pure ecstasy at the touch of his mouth upon her bosom, and she held his head to her as she instinctively arched against the hardness of his male form. It felt so good to be in Chance's arms, so right. She had wanted this for so long, and now he was hers. With a lightly erotic touch, she returned his touch, restlessly exploring the broad width of his muscular shoulders before slipping her hands between them to unbutton his shirt.

Chance drew slightly away to help her with the buttons. He wanted to feel her bared flesh on his, to know that exquisite intimacy. When he moved back over her, the heat of his hair-roughened chest seemed to sear her tender breasts, and she gasped at the sensation.

"Oh, Rori . . . I want you. I want you now," he admitted feverishly.

"Yes . . . oh, yes, Chance. Love me. Please love me," she urged, pulling him down for a flaming kiss.

There was no stopping for either of them. With passionate abandon, Chance went to Rori, brushing aside the barrier of her skirts and undergarments. His hands were gentle as he readied her for him, and then, freeing himself from his pants, he moved between her thighs.

They came together in a blaze of desire. The passion

they had for each other that they had so long denied erupted quickly. Their loving was brief, but thrillingly intense. The ultimate fulfillment swept over them in a crescendo of ecstasy. Their breathing was labored as they rested in each other's arms.

The carriage hit a bump in the road, and the tenuousness of their position finally occurred to them. They moved apart reluctantly, neither wanting the moment to end. After straightening their clothing, they clung together, sharing tender kisses and soft words of love and breathlessly anticipating their arrival at the cottage.

The carriage finally turned up the drive and pulled to a halt before the small summer house on the rise that overlooked the ocean. When the driver opened the door for them, Chance climbed out first, then turned to help Rori down. She started to step down to the ground and was startled when Chance picked her up.

"Chance! What . . ."

"Tradition, love. A bridegroom always carries his bride across the threshold on their wedding night," he explained.

"But why?"

"I have no idea, but anything that gets you into my arms is fine with me," Chance said with a wide grin.

"Me, too," she agreed, nestling happily against the rock-solid strength of his chest.

Chance strode purposefully up to the few steps to the door, and Dora, the maid his mother had sent on ahead to ready the small four-room cottage for their coming, was there waiting to open it for him.

"Good evening, Mr. and Mrs. Broderick," she greeted them pleasantly.

"Good evening, Dora." Chance returned her greeting and then kissed Rori soundly before setting her to her feet in the midst of the sitting room. "Has everything been taken care of?"

"Yes, sir. Everything is just as your mother instructed. As soon as I unpack what you brought with you tonight, I'll be finished."

"Thank you."

Dora hurried off to see to her duties, directing the driver to take their trunks into the master bedroom while Chance pulled Rori back into his embrace.

"In just a few more minutes, Mrs. Broderick," he said, punctuating his words with quick kisses, "we are going to be all alone."

"I know," Rori replied in a sultry voice, "and I hope she hurries." Rori slipped her arms around Chance's lean waist and rested her head against his chest. The steady beat of his heart sent a soothing blanket of peaceful contentment through her. She closed her eyes savoring the moment. He loved her.

Chance cradled Rori to him, cherishing the feel of her so soft and loving. He smiled tenderly as he wondered how they had ever come to this. Rori had hated him, pulled a knife on him, fought him at every turn, and now . . . now, he couldn't live without her.

"What are you smiling about?" Rori asked as she lifted her head to gaze up at him.

"You," he murmured throatily.

"Me?" She was pleased. "I'm glad I make you smile."

"You do more to me than make me smile, Rori," Chance admitted with a lusty laugh. "But until Dora finishes up and leaves, I can't do anything about it."

Rori was filled with a great sense of feminine satisfaction. "Pity . . ." she teased, her eyes alight with mischief.

"Rori . . ." Chance said her name threateningly, but she only grinned at him and moved out of his arms.

Dora came bustling back into the room then and interrupted what else he might have said. "I'm done now, but if you should need anything I'll be in the servants' quarters."

"Good night, Dora, and thank you."

"Good night." She hastened from the cottage, quietly closing the door behind her, leaving the newlywed couple alone at last.

Rori and Chance both eyed the master bedroom door. They were eager, yet suddenly a bit tentative.

"Would you like a few minutes alone?" Chance asked.

Rori thought of Aunt Charlotte's gift packed carefully away among her things, and she knew she needed a few minutes to prepare for the glory of the night to come. "Please," she asked softly and then disappeared into the bedroom, closing the door quietly behind her.

Rori stared at the wide comfort of the bed and a thrill tingled through her. Soon she would be sharing that intimacy with her husband . . . with Chance. Dora had spread the negligee out on the bed, and Rori hurried across the room to pick it up with trembling hands. She caressed the filmy fabric for a moment and then laid it gently back down. Shedding her traveling clothes, she quickly washed up and then brushed out her hair so it fell about her shoulders in a tumble of gleaming, ebony silk. Feeling ready at last for Chance, she slipped on the delicate nightgown and moved to open the door and invite him to join her.

Chance poured himself a brandy after Rori disappeared into the bedroom and then settled in to savor the potent drink as he awaited her return. He barely tasted the heady liquor, though, for he was completely preoccupied with thoughts of his lovely wife. Their joining in the carriage had only served to increase his desire for her. He needed more of Rori . . . much, much more.

"Chance . . ."

The sound of her voice, so low and inviting, drew his attention, and he turned to see her standing in the bedroom doorway. She was wearing the most beautiful negligee he'd ever seen. The white, semi-transparent garment clung to her body, revealing just enough of her slender curves to entice him to action. His throat tightened, and heat surged through his veins like molten lava.

Chance was mesmerized as he set the tumbler aside and came to his feet. Never taking his eyes off of her, he crossed the room to where she waited for him. Without speaking, he extended his hand to her. They entered the bedroom and shut the door behind them. Chance drew her near for a deep kiss and then moved away from her to quickly divest himself of his own clothing. Kneeling on the edge of the bed, Chance lowered both Rori and himself onto its softness.

They came together eagerly, embracing passionately as their mouths met and lingered. Chance sculpted her body with his hands, stroking her through the gossamer gown. Rori stirred wantonly beneath his exciting touch as flames of desire threatened to consume her. She reached out to him, holding him near, caressing him incessantly, letting him know with her body that she loved him and wanted him. When Rori daringly touched that most manly part of him, Chance inhaled sharply.

"Do you like that or should I stop?" she asked, wondering if she'd hurt him or pleased him.

"Don't stop," he groaned his pleasure at her sweet boldness.

"I want to please you," Rori whispered, trailing kisses down his throat to his chest.

"You do, my temptress wife," he declared, reaching down to draw her back up to him for another kiss. Chance loved it when Rori wore her hair down around her shoulders, and he gently combed his fingers through the soft tangle of curls.

With utmost care, they embraced again. It was a tender moment. A moment of beauty and of devotion. They had both wanted this for so long and now it was truly happening.

They took their time as they came together, savoring every moment. Each touch, each kiss became a reflection of the depth of their devotion. There was no need to rush to sate their passions. There was no guilt or fear in their coming together—only deep abiding love and a wonderful sense of rightness.

With trembling need, they clung to each other, their limbs entwined. Chance traced fiery patterns of arousal upon her satiny skin as he brought her to the peak of urgency again and again. When the waves of pleasure finally pulsed through her releasing her from his sensual bondage, Rori shuddered and called out his name in rapturous fervor. Though she felt weak from the excitement of it all, she was still aching to give Chance the same gift of joy he'd given her.

"Let me love you now," Rori told him huskily. She moved over him to take him deep within her.

Chance guided her hips as she began to move, savoring the hot, tight wetness of her body sheathing his. Ecstasy filled him as he realized that Rori was his wife now. He pulled her down to him and then rolled to bring her beneath him. Chance kissed her wildly as he continued his steady, rocking rhythm, driving deep into the womanly heart of her.

Chance strained toward the pinnacle and Rori, too, was caught up in the force of his need. They were enraptured by the power of their love. Soaring to excitement's peak together, perfect splendor burst upon them both, and they gloried in the triumph as they lay sated on their bed of love. They were one. They loved.

As the night passed, Chance and Rori came together again. It seemed they could not get enough of each other, that every minute, every second was important to them. They cherished what they had very nearly lost.

It was much later when the first blush of morning stained the eastern horizon that Chance rose from the bed and drew Rori with him. "I want you to see something," he told her as he moved to the window facing the water.

Because they'd arrived at night and had had other, more important things on their minds, Rori had paid little real attention to their surroundings. Now, however, in the first light of the morning sun the view from the bedroom window that faced to the east was incomparable.

Stretched out before her was the Atlantic Ocean in all its beauty. It was deep blue in color and crowned here and there with white-capped waves. The sky overhead was peach and gold tinted with no hint of clouds or bad weather. Sea birds drifted by, coasting on the fresh morning breeze, calling out their greeting to the new day.

"Chance . . . it's beautiful here." Rori was awestruck.

"I'm glad you like it."

"I love it. Can we bring Jakie up here some time soon?"

"Of course, any time you like. We can even build a home here if you want to."

"I'd like that. The ocean reminds me of the desert, so wild and free that no one will ever tame it completely."

Chance smiled. "Your description sounds more like you several months back."

Rori lifted sparkling, emerald eyes to meet her husband's. "You've tamed me, Chance."

"I never wanted to tame you, Rori. I only wanted to love you," he told her huskily.

She gave him an inviting smile as she moved away from the window and back to the bed, settling upon its softness in an alluring pose.

"Then love me, darling." She lifted her hand to him, and he took it, joining her there.

Once more they were lost in the wonder of their passion as they came together in rapture's delight, sharing the joyful ecstasy that only true love can bring.

Epilogue

Arizona Territory, Two Years Later

"Grumma . . ." two-year-old Daniel repeated in a husky voice.

Agatha smiled brightly at the sturdy little toddler who clutched at her skirts with chubby little fists. "That's right, Daniel darling. I'm Grandma," she cooed as she reached out to scoop him up in her arms and hold him on her lap.

"He's quite taken with you, Mother," Doug said proudly as he watched his son gaze up at her with great interest. He was thrilled that his family had decided to make the trip to Arizona for a visit. It had been nearly a year since he and Nilakla had made their trip to Boston, and he found that he'd missed his mother and brother a great deal during the separation.

"He's obviously a very discriminating judge of character," Agatha replied with delighted dignity as she kissed her grandson. She glanced back up to where Doug stood with Nilakla. "He's grown so much in the past year," she said in amazement. "I hate to think that I'm missing so much by living so far away."

"You know you're welcome to stay with us for as long as you want," Nilakla told her mother-in-law. She had been very intimidated by Agatha when they'd first met, but the older woman had sensed her discomfort and had immediately put her at ease. Since then, they'd come to love each other deeply and share an abiding mutual respect.

"It's a tempting offer," Agatha began, thinking of the cold winters she suffered through back East, and how much she missed Doug and his family.

"But it's an offer she's going to refuse," Chance put in as he came into the room with Rori, carrying Rebecca, their year-old daughter, in his arms.

"I am?" Agatha arched a brow at her oldest son.

"Of course," Rori agreed quickly. "What would we do without you? We need you at home."

"It's wonderful to be in such demand." Agatha was beaming. It did her heart good to know that she was so loved by her children.

As if on cue, Rebecca called happily, "G'ma, G'ma . . ." She held out her arms to Agatha, who promptly took her from her father and cuddled her on her lap beside her cousin.

Agatha was proud of her grandchildren and, in the way of all grandparents, thought them the most magnificent youngsters around. She was certain Daniel, with his dark hair and dark eyes, would grow up to be a real charmer, for he greatly resembled his own father at the same age. Rebecca, though still so young, already bore the promise of great beauty with her big green eyes and raven hair, and Agatha knew they would do the Broderick family proud.

It was much later that Rori managed to slip away with Rebecca from the house and all the celebrating for a few minutes alone under the starry sky. She walked a short distance away to a small rise that overlooked the desert and rugged mountains beyond, and it was there that memories of her life with Burr overwhelmed her. In the quietude of the Arizona night, she could almost feel her grampa's presence, and she smiled in sweet understanding. Though Burr's grave was many miles away, his spirit was not contained there. Burr had loved the vast openness of the territory, and now his spirit was as free as the desert wind.

"Your great-grampa lives here, Rebecca," Rori told her daughter in a confiding tone. "Someday, when you're older and can understand, I'm going to tell you all about what a brave, wonderful man he was." Even after all this time, the thought of Burr could still bring tears to her eyes, and she lifted her tearful gaze to the heavens as she snuggled her daughter close to her breast. "See, Grampa, everything worked out fine. Chance loves me, and we have a beautiful daughter . . ." Rori struggled not to cry from sadness, but to realize the joy of her life now.

Jakie had followed her from the house with another golden-haired, long-legged dog at his heels. He had sat a little bit away from Rori, but when she seemed upset about something he immediately went to her side and nudged her leg. His companion followed suit, but being years younger, he was a little more rambunctious in his attentions.

Rori gave a light laugh at their antics. "Grampa . . . even Jakie settled down," she said as she petted the two. "He and his Boston bride had offspring just like me and Chance, and most of them even looked like their daddy." She was chuckling at the comparison.

"Who looks like their daddy? And who were you talking to?" Chance's deep voice came to her out of the darkness, and Rori turned to find her husband striding toward her.

"I was telling Grampa how Joshua looks just like Jakie when he was little more than a pup," Rori answered with a grin.

"Think he heard you?" Chance asked as he came to stand beside her, slipping an arm about her waist and drawing her to him.

"I know he did," Rori replied without a trace of doubt.

"I know he did, too," Chance agreed as he bent to press a gentle kiss first to her cheek and then to his daughter's.

Rori gazed up at her husband, cherishing his devotion and knowing that she would spend the rest of her days loving Chance.

Chapter Note to Readers

Dear Readers,

I hope you enjoyed *Arizona Caress* as much as I enjoyed writing it. I'd love to hear from you. For an autographed bookmark, send a self-addressed stamped envelope to:

Bobbi Smith
c/o ZEBRA BOOKS
119 West 40th Street
21st Floor
New York, NY 10018

If you love rugged Western heroes,
don't miss Elaine Levine's
LEAH AND THE BOUNTY HUNTER,
coming in August.

Dakota Territory, June 1868

Jace Gage rode slowly down the main street in Defiance, the leather of his saddle loud in the quiet stillness of predawn. Expecting a sharpshooter, he scanned the street, rooftops, and alleys. No shadows moved furtively. No sentries kept watch. His absence over the last few weeks had lulled the sheriff's men into complacency. Maybe ghosts were all that remained in Defiance.

The morning wind whistled around the empty buildings, disturbing the tumbleweed skeletons piled here and there. A couple of saloons were boarded up. A billboard sign hung askew over a bank's gaping front entrance. Several businesses had broken windows or missing doors. The few houses he could see fared no better; their weathered, wooden siding looked dingy in the faint morning light. A swaybacked porch on one house leaned over a collapsing stoop, its intricate fretwork forgotten.

He didn't like the feel of this town. He didn't like the looks of it, or the smell of it, or the sound of it either. Even Mother Nature wanted to forget this place, wipe it off the face of the Earth like the infected rat's nest that it was.

And Jace was happy to oblige.

He had two thousand dollars in his pocket for riding into town. The U.S. marshal in Cheyenne had a like sum waiting for him once Sheriff Kemp and his cohorts were gone.

Dead or gone, to be exact.

A commotion broke into his thoughts as he approached the general store. Two men and a boy were scuffling. A black timber wolf crouched nearby, a massive, growling shadow braced to join the fray. Jace dismounted and tied his horse to the hitching post. The men laughed low in their throats, their attention focused on the boy they shoved back and forth between them. The sexual overtones in the play turned Jace's stomach. The boy, trying to get away, pleaded with them. He had to be young—his voice hadn't changed yet.

Jace pushed the edges of his jacket back behind his holsters and flexed his hands beside his Colts. He'd never cleared a place as foul as this, where the outlaws had turned to the town's boys for their pleasure. He'd enjoy killing these two.

The sun crested the horizon just then, washing everything in its brilliant pink glow. As if sensing their time for play was ending, one of the men ripped the boy's shirt and vest open, revealing the sweetest pair of tits Jace had seen in a month of Sundays.

Maybe a whole year of Sundays.

And then all hell broke loose. The kid shouted for the wolf to attack. Instantly complying, the beast jumped at one of the men, clamping his powerful jaws down on a meaty forearm, yanking and twisting as if to separate limb from man.

Taking advantage of the second man's shock, the girl dug her fingers into the notch at the base of his throat and used it as a handle to yank him to his knees. Before he'd even hit the ground, she'd palmed her knife and pressed it to the soft flesh beneath one of his eyes.

"Take a long look, mister, 'cause it's the last thing you're gonna see," the girl warned softly.

The hairs rose on Jace's neck at the sweet sound of her voice, the harmony of it jarringly discordant with her actions. Whether his response was in warning or desire, he couldn't distinguish. She was fierce, lethal even. And she made no attempt to hide what she was—a killer.

"While you're on your knees, friend," Jace spoke up, "best ask the kid's forgiveness." The man's gaze shot to Jace, though he didn't move his head. The girl showed no reaction to his presence. "You see, this is my town now, and we don't treat women—or kids—like that here."

"Goddamn, Johnny! Listen to his voice! That's the Avenger!" the second man hissed. He was on his back, his bloodied arms thrown up to protect his face. The wolf's powerful jaws hovered near his neck, long fangs bared in warning as he awaited a single word from the girl.

Johnny swallowed hard. Careful of the knife, he glanced up at his captor. "Our apologies, Miss Morgan. Don't know what came over us."

Miss Morgan? Jace cursed and gave the girl another look, watching while she considered her next move. After a tense few seconds, she released the man's hair and sheathed her knife.

"Wolf! Come!" she called the black beast to her side. He lowered his jowls over his teeth with a cough, giving his victim a last, one-eyed glare before trotting over to sit at her heels. The two men scrambled to their feet, eyeing Jace warily before scurrying away.

Leah finally felt her heart hammering against her ribs, in her throat, in her ears. She'd been afraid the third gunfighter had come to join the other two and had no choice but to make a move to keep them all at bay. Until that moment, she'd tried to keep the scuffle quiet, worried that Jim, the shopkeeper, would come out of the store to defend her.

She was shocked to discover the third man was the famed "Avenger."

The gunfighter walked toward her, his spurs making a chink-chinking sound with each step of his long stride. He was fortified like a one-man army with a rifle over one shoulder, two bandoliers loaded with rifle cartridges crossing his chest over his loose jacket. A gunbelt was strung across his hips with twin Colts strapped to his thighs. A Bowie knife the length of her forearm hung next to the buckle of his gunbelt. Her eyes traveled the long distance down his thighs to the boots that came almost to his knees. She wondered what other weapons he held concealed within them.

Folding her arms to close her shirt as best she could—and to hide her shaking—she studied his hardened visage—and disliked what she saw. A few days' growth of beard covered his square jaw. His lips were hard slashes between lines that bracketed his mouth. High cheekbones made hollows above his jaw. His eyes were by far the worst of his features. As blue as chicory flowers, they were windows into the blackest soul Leah had ever seen.

She remembered the rumor that this man had survived a hanging. Unable to curb her curiosity, she let her eyes dip to his Adam's apple and the scar that circled what she could see of his neck. He hadn't even attempted to hide the livid white twists burned into her skin. A frisson of warning rippled through her.

What kind of man could survive a hanging? She met his gaze again. His blue eyes held hers before sweeping over her hair and down the column of skin that her ripped clothing exposed, examining her as she had him. Her breathing quickened, but she resisted the urge to pull the torn edges of her shirt and camisole closer together. She did not back away.

He arched a brow at her. She lifted her chin. Wolf began growling.

"Nice pet, kid," he said in that desert-parched voice of his that made her thirst for an endless drink of water. He moved around her and headed to the steps leading up to the boardwalk in front of the store.

For two weeks, she'd hidden in her house, frightened of the monster the Avenger was rumored to be. It was said he had more kills than Cullen Baker, that no man could outdraw him. And his skill with a knife was legendary. The sheriff's men had bandied stories about town of the Avenger throwing a knife with such swift accuracy that he buried it deep in his opponent before the other could even cock his gun. Seeing him now, she felt foolish for her fear; he was just another gunfighter, like all of those in town.

Yet even as she thought it, she knew it was a lie. He was unlike any who had come for the sheriff. Jace Gage was a man who had already cheated death once. Perhaps he could do it again. Perhaps he would succeed here.

"Some avenger you are," she challenged him with a bravado she didn't entirely feel. "You might have stepped in sooner."

"Didn't look like you needed help," he rasped without breaking stride or looking back. Outside the entrance to the general store, he did pause and sent her a look over his shoulder. "A word of advice, kid. The next time you draw a knife on a man, you'd best use it. A dead enemy's a whole lot less trouble than a living one."

"I have no enemies in this town, mister."

The man nodded, contemplating her words. His eyes narrowed as he looked from her to the two men running for the sheriff's office. He let his gaze swing back her way as he answered, "I'm guessin' you do now." He entered the store.

Leah drew a long, calming breath. Wolf stopped growling, but a lip was still snaggled up over one of his fangs. He watched her patiently through one golden eye and the milky one long ago ruined by an angry porcupine. He was a sorry sight, she had to admit. He'd been losing his winter coat for a month, and now the tufts of downy gray underfur pushing free of his black hair made him look like a half sheared lamb. She adjusted her clothes to cover their torn state as best she could, and then went inside Jim's store.

Everyone was standing around stiffly, staring at each other. "Leah, come with me," Sally, the storekeeper's wife, ordered with a wave from the storeroom. Sally always hid there when trouble came to the store. Leah ignored the invitation. She was done hiding.

Jim broke the silence. "Good day, stranger. What brings you to Defiance?"

"I have business with the sheriff," the Avenger answered in his gravelly voice.

"You a friend of his?" Jim asked.

"I don't count outlaws among my friends. I've come to take Kemp to Cheyenne."

"You with the law?"

"Nope."

"You the one they call the 'Avenger'?" Jim asked.

The Avenger winced and shook his head. "I'm just a man trying to earn his keep. Name's Jace Gage."

"I'm Jim Kessler, and this is my wife, Sally. Seems you met Leah Morgan already."

Gage tipped his hat to Sally but completely ignored Leah. "Is there a hotel or a room still to be had in this town?" he asked Jim.

"Maddie, down the street, runs a boardinghouse. ⌐ah's heading that way. She can show you."

"Jim! No!" Sally complained in a whisper loud enough for all to hear.

"He ain't gonna hurt her, Sal. Besides, between Wolf and her knife, she can take care of herself," he said meaningfully.

Leah shot a glare at the Avenger, then headed for the door. He could follow or not; it was up to him. Wolf fell into step with her as she walked down the boardwalk and into the street. A bend in the road, then two short blocks separated Jim's from Maddie's. Leah lived across the street from Maddie, so Jim had been right—she was headed that way. She hadn't gone far when she heard the jingle of Gage's spurs as he caught up to her. She didn't slow her stride. He drew even with her, leading his horse. Wolf moved to walk between him and Leah.

"Friendly critter, aren't you?" he said.

Struck by his rudeness, Leah stopped to gape at him. She set her hands on her hips. Too late she remembered her torn clothes. She quickly gripped the ragged edges and gave a little huff of air before answering him. "No one invited you to this town, mister. In fact, Defiance needs another gunfighter like a hole in the head. You've got no call to be rude."

A grin whispered across his hard mouth. "I was talking about your wolf. He's very protective of you."

Leah blushed, something she'd done about as many times as she could count on the fingers of one hand. She had grown up in Defiance with four-fifths of its population male. There was little men could say or do that shocked her, but for some reason, this stranger easily got her riled.

As if he was aware of her confusion, his smile deepened. Leah resumed walking in stony silence, turning down Maddie's drive a few minutes later. It led around the boardinghouse to a small stable and carriage house. Right past the main building, she caught sight of a movement over by the stable. She stopped abruptly and dragged the Avenger back against the house—no small feat in itself, for he was much larger than she was.

"Wait! Don't move!" she hissed, caring little that he landed with his back against the house or that she now stood with one of his legs wedged between hers. She pressed a hand on his chest to hold him in place as she peeked around the corner.

"You got a shortage of men in this town, kid? Or do you wrangle all the newcomers this way?"

His words made Leah aware of several things—how tall he was, how close to him she was standing, and exactly where his leg was. His glance razed the pale skin of her chest. Her cheeks heated up again. She hastily took a step away from him and crossed her arms over her torn clothes. "I saw someone near the stable. You can't go over there. They'll kill you."

"They're likely to kill you, too, if you stay so near me. I think I can manage to get a room without your help."

"You know, I should let them blow your fool head off. You can't win against the sheriff and his gang. There's too many of them. Others have tried, and not a one of them left with the bounty he came for, if he was lucky enough to leave."

She looked up at the Avenger's granite face and crystalline blue eyes. "You should leave town, Mr. Gage, 'cause you're as good as dead if you don't." She slipped the reins of his horse from him and moved as if to head toward the stable.

"Whoa, what do you think you're doing?" He pulled her back. Wolf stepped on his boot, his one good eye glaring up at the man.

Leah frowned as she pushed against him. "I'm gonna buy you five more minutes of living by putting your horse up for you."

"No, you're not," he said with a lopsided grin. "You've

come far enough. Just run along now. I'll take it from here." He eased the reins from her.

Leah peered into his eyes, studying him even as he watched her. He was so alive now, and he wasn't very old, late-twenties to mid-thirties, she guessed. It would be a shame to see him killed. But she'd learned how easily death came to anyone, in this town especially.

"Well, good luck to you, then." She moved away, walking backwards so she could give him one last warning. "If you're partial to being buried, I suggest you leave some money with Maddie to buy you a pine box and a hole in the cemetery. Otherwise, they'll dump your body a ways out of town for the scavengers to pick clean." She pivoted and walked down the drive, toward the street. She didn't look back—there was no point—they'd be burying him in the morning.

She wondered which of the sheriff's men would get his horse.

Books by Bestselling Author
Fern Michaels

___The Jury	0-8217-7878-1	$6.99US/$9.99CAN
___Sweet Revenge	0-8217-7879-X	$6.99US/$9.99CAN
___Lethal Justice	0-8217-7880-3	$6.99US/$9.99CAN
___Free Fall	0-8217-7881-1	$6.99US/$9.99CAN
___Fool Me Once	0-8217-8071-9	$7.99US/$10.99CAN
___Vegas Rich	0-8217-8112-X	$7.99US/$10.99CAN
___Hide and Seek	1-4201-0184-6	$6.99US/$9.99CAN
___Hokus Pokus	1-4201-0185-4	$6.99US/$9.99CAN
___Fast Track	1-4201-0186-2	$6.99US/$9.99CAN
___Collateral Damage	1-4201-0187-0	$6.99US/$9.99CAN
___Final Justice	1-4201-0188-9	$6.99US/$9.99CAN
___Up Close and Personal	0-8217-7956-7	$7.99US/$9.99CAN
___Under the Radar	1-4201-0683-X	$6.99US/$9.99CAN
___Razor Sharp	1-4201-0684-8	$7.99US/$10.99CAN
___Yesterday	1-4201-1494-8	$5.99US/$6.99CAN
___Vanishing Act	1-4201-0685-6	$7.99US/$10.99CAN
___Sara's Song	1-4201-1493-X	$5.99US/$6.99CAN
___Deadly Deals	1-4201-0686-4	$7.99US/$10.99CAN
___Game Over	1-4201-0687-2	$7.99US/$10.99CAN
___Sins of Omission	1-4201-1153-1	$7.99US/$10.99CAN
___Sins of the Flesh	1-4201-1154-X	$7.99US/$10.99CAN
___Cross Roads	1-4201-1192-2	$7.99US/$10.99CAN

Available Wherever Books Are Sold!
Check out our website at **www.kensingtonbooks.com**